PRAISE FOR JEREMY ROBINSON

"Reading Jeremy Robinson is dangerous for your sleep pattern. He spins monster yarns so well that you cannot stop turning pages. Giant monsters, creepy islands and writing that is both smart and furious in intensity and pace."

— Famous Monsters of Filmland

"Project Nemesis turned out to be the first book in years where I read it from cover to cover in just under a day. I kept my eyes peeled on those 250 or so pages as if it was crack! It was that good! Nemesis is a true American Kaiju by every definition. This is a definite must for any fan of the Kaiju genre. It gets a full fledged 5/5 rating."

— Kaiju Planet

"A brisk thriller with neatly timed action sequences, snappy dialogue and the ultimate sympathetic figure in a badly burned little girl with a fighting spirit... The Nazis are determined to have the last gruesome laugh in this efficient doomsday thriller."

— Kirkus Reviews

"Relentless pacing and numerous plot twists drive this compelling stand-alone [SecondWorld] from Robinson... Thriller fans and apocalyptic fiction aficionados alike will find this audaciously plotted novel enormously satisfying."

— Publisher's Weekly

"Robinson blends myth, science and terminal velocity action like no one else."

— Scott Sigler, NY Times Bestselling author of NOCTURNAL

"Just when you think that 21st-century authors have come up with every possible way of destroying the world, along comes Jeremy Robinson."

— New Hampshire Magazine

ALSO BY JEREMY ROBINSON

Kaiju Novels
Island 731
Project Nemesis
Project Maigo
Project 731

SecondWorld Novels
SecondWorld
Nazi Hunter: Atlantis
(aka: *I Am Cowboy*)

Standalone Novels
The Didymus Contingency
Raising The Past
Beneath
Antarktos Rising
Kronos
Uprising (aka: *Xom-B*)
Flood Rising
MirrorWorld (2015)

The Jack Sigler Thrillers
Prime
Pulse
Instinct
Threshold
Ragnarok
Omega
Savage
Cannibal (2015)

The Continuum Series
Guardian

The Chesspocalypse Novellas
Callsign: King
Callsign: Queen
Callsign: Rook
Callsign: King – Underworld
Callsign: Bishop
Callsign: Knight
Callsign: Deep Blue
Callsign: King – Blackout

The Antarktos Saga
The Last Hunter – Descent
The Last Hunter – Pursuit
The Last Hunter – Ascent
The Last Hunter – Lament
The Last Hunter – Onslaught
The Last Hunter – Collected Edition

Writing as Jeremy Bishop
Torment
The Sentinel
The Raven
Refuge:
    Night of the Blood Sky
    Darkness Falls
    Lost in the Echo
    Ashes and Dust
    Bonfires Burning Bright
    Refuge Omnibus

PROJECT MAIGO

JEREMY ROBINSON

BREAKNECK MEDIA

ISBN 978-0-9886725-6-7

Cover design copyright ©2013 by Jeremy Robinson.
Cover art by Cheung Chung Tat. Used by permission.

Printed in the United States of America

Visit Jeremy Robinson on the World Wide Web at:
www.jeremyrobinsononline.com

For all you crazy Kaiju fans who made Project Nemesis a hit, and helped make Project Maigo a reality. Thank you for your support, and for all the art!

ACKNOWLEDGMENTS

I must first thank the awesome Matt Frank for his amazing creature designs. He has helped shape the look and feel of Nemesis, and without him, I'm not sure the series would have gotten the traction that it did. With *Project Maigo* there is even more art from Matt and five brand new creature designs.

For supreme editing, big thanks to Kane Gilmour, who also prodded me into writing my dream Kaiju project. This book is not only better for your edits, but might not exist without your nudging. Thanks to Roger Brodeur for cleaning up the text and hiding my many typos.

Thank you to Simon Strange at Sunstone Games for making Nemesis the boss character in the Colossal Kaiju Combat video game and for lending your support to the book. I very much look forward to kicking some Kaiju butt with Nemesis!

At the end of *Project Maigo*, you will find a fan art gallery including more than twenty-five pieces of art. Thanks to everyone who submitted their work. None of my other novels have inspired such a creative, talented response, and being an artist who grew up drawing Kaiju, I'm extremely grateful for it.

And as always, thanks to my amazing family. My wife, Hilaree, is my biggest supporter, and my three Kaiju...err, children...you continue to inspire me and keep my imagination rooted in my monster-loving childhood. I love you all.

—Jeremy Robinson
New Hampshire
November, 2013

PROJECT
MAIGO

PROLOGUE

Hong Kong

"Somebody shut that bitch up." The sound of flesh striking flesh followed the command, stifling the chained woman's whimpers and reminding the others why they shouldn't speak, cry or even breathe loudly.

Satisfied with the silence, the man known simply as Tinman crouched down to inspect the woman. He reached out a dirty hand, held her chin and yanked her face back and forth. She was hard to see in the dim multicolored light provided by the distant towers of Hong Kong. He snapped his fingers. "Flashlight."

A light was flicked on and placed in his hand. The inside of the blue, 40-foot-long, steel shipping container lit up, revealing two rows of young women. Thirty-three in all. They were prisoners. Slaves. And yet, not one of them was bound. Not physically, at least.

The light shone into the eyes of the slapped woman. She didn't blink. Her pupils remained dilated. She simply stared straight ahead, no longer afraid. No longer...anything. Tinman noted the red hand print emerging on the woman's face. Dingle had struck her hard, but he had remembered not to use a closed fist, at least. Damaged goods fetched a lower price. And this one—a Japanese girl—would get good money from their Western patrons. "How long will they be...pliable?

The auction starts in thirty minutes. Most of our guests are already here."

"They're pretty doped," Dingle replied. He was a skinny man with greasy blond hair, shiny black leather garb and purple sunglasses—despite the late hour. He shook his hand, still recovering from the open-palm blow he'd given the woman. "But they'll be able to walk, among other things."

"Nothing happens on the premises," Tinman reminded him. "We're not a brothel. We're an outlet. What they do with the product is their own business and on their own time."

Dingle nodded. "I know the drill."

Tinman knew Dingle was capable. They'd bought and sold more than two thousand women during their last three years together, and they had become the number one import/export outfit in the Asian flesh trade. Business had slowed after that mess in Boston, though. People had grown afraid. Some of his clients even attempted to return their merchandise. But the monster—Nemesis—hadn't returned. And business was booming, or as Dingle liked to say, their 'business was banging.'

Tinman sometimes told himself that some of the women were being used for more noble pursuits, like house cleaning or manual labor, but if he was honest, he knew the lucky ones found themselves locked inside a plush hideaway for a few years before being used up and discarded. The unlucky ones wouldn't make it a week. Some might not even survive the night.

Not my problem, he told himself.

He looked down the row of women, casting the bright white light along their faces. Most were Asian—Korean, Japanese, Vietnamese and Chinese. Most of them Chinese, on account of Chinese parents not putting up too much of a stink when the girls disappeared. Mom and dad might not appreciate them for being born female, but Tinman's clients would. *At least*, Tinman thought, *some of them will feel desired before dying.* A few of the slaves were Western girls. A couple of sluts from California who practically volunteered. Two Germans. A French girl. And two Spanish—Mexican Spanish. While the Asian girls attracted Western clients, these Western girls would fetch top dollar with his Eastern clientele. Everyone always wanted what they perceived as exotic.

He crouched to the left, shining his light in the next girl's eyes, seeing the same vacant look. Like this, mindless and oblivious to what was going to come, Tinman didn't find the girls attractive. He thought the kind of men who did were...off. But they paid well enough for him not to care.

The girl had a bit of an overbite. He pulled a black marker from his pocket and placed a single dot on the back of her right hand, signifying that the bidding on her should start at a lower price. She'd be one of the unlucky ones. No one spent good money on a temp.

"Hey, Tin," a man called from the container's opening. Tinman turned to find his two guards silhouetted against the city lights. A stiff breeze brought the scent of smog and ocean decay to his nose. He hated Hong Kong. This was as close as he ever got. The docks. The auction and the exchange of money and girls would all happen on his freighter, which also conducted more legitimate, but less profitable business. When they were done, he'd sail away richer than when he arrived.

Tinman blew Hong Kong's stink from his nose. "What is it?"

"They're all here," the guard reported.

Early, Tinman thought with a grin. Early meant eager. Eager meant high bidding. He clapped his hands together and glanced up at Dingle. "I'll inspect each girl before she's made available."

Dingle nodded. "Going to be a good night."

"*Very* good," Tinman shuffled to the left one more time, out of habit. He raised the flashlight to the girl's face. One of the Americans. A blonde. Fit and slender, which was a hard sell in Asia, since they were accustomed to slender builds, but at least she wasn't slender in the places that mattered, and her face... She was stunning.

She squinted at the light.

Her pupils constricted.

Brows furrowed.

Tinman's distracted mind registered all this too late to stop the foot rising for his crotch. The woman's boot found the soft flesh between his legs and crushed it upwards, while the rest of him crumpled down. He was in a full fetal position by the time he hit the steel floor.

Through clenched eyes, Tinman looked up to see the woman standing, her fists clenched, her eyes set on Dingle, who had drawn his beloved knife. It was usually more than enough to keep the women in line. But this one? Not only had she clearly not been drugged with the rest, but she had a fire in her eyes. *She's a cop*, he thought. The American's slutty ignorance had been a ruse. But there had been two of them. Where was the—

The sound of fighting at the far end of the crate answered his question. He tried to shout an order, but he hadn't yet taken a breath.

Suddenly, the container tipped forward, then back, as a large wave passed beneath the ship. It didn't feel big enough to worry about, but it was the kind of wave encountered on the high seas, not in port.

The descending crate knocked Dingle off balance. It was the opening the woman needed. She lunged forward, and with a speed and precision Tinman had never seen, she knocked the knife from Dingle's hand. Before the blade struck the metal floor, she broke his wrist and punched his throat, dropping him hard.

A second wave struck. He could hear the dock's moorings creaking under the strain.

Tinman took his first gasped breath. The woman looked down at him, sweat melting away makeup from her forehead, revealing a red scar...or was it something else? She paid him little attention and shouted to her partner. "All clear?"

"Affirmative," the other woman replied, her accent Russian. "We are good."

"Let's wake 'em up," the blonde said, pulling a cylinder from her pocket. She mashed down the top of it. White gas hissed out, quickly filling the container.

Tinman tried to hold his breath. He didn't know what kind of gas the woman had deployed. But his need to breathe after being kicked overrode his caution, and he sucked in a lungful. His body felt instantly revived. Energized. Though the intense pain of his injury remained.

He heard the women around him wake from their stupors, their confusion melting away with a din of rising voices. The blonde was now a ghost in the mist, but he could hear her shouting commands in a variety of languages. *More than a cop*, he realized.

The ship beneath them shifted again, canting backwards at a sharp angle. For a moment, Tinman thought he was feeling another wave, but he quickly realized the ship was tilting in the wrong direction. And they weren't dropping back down. It was as though some immense weight were pulling the aft down.

He wracked his mind to come up with a theory of what could cause the massive ship to tip back so quickly. Only one theory made sense. The realization helped him to his feet, but the shipping container was struck hard from above. The jolt swept his feet out from under him. He hit the floor again hard, leading with his face this time.

The woman's shouting grew more fervent, and the sounds of running feet echoed all around him. Then her boots clanged on the floor. Despite the danger, she was leaving last. Well, not exactly last. For a moment, he hoped the sudden flood of women fleeing across the deck of his ship would buy him time, but then he remembered what motivated the monster.

Nemesis.

Poems called her the winged tilter of scales.

She's here for me, he realized.

A shriek of metal turned his eyes upward. Huge claws hooked into the container's ceiling and pulled. The top came off like the lid of a can of soup. The white gas the blonde had deployed was sucked up by the lifting ceiling. The breeze carried it away. The container was empty now, save for him and Dingle. The two guards lay at the end, dead or immobilized. The women, all thirty-three of them, were gone.

Tinman got back to his feet, stepped over Dingle, who sounded like he was gagging, maybe even dying, and ran for the shipping container's end. Before he made it five steps, he noticed his shadow, long and framed by bright orange light from above.

He was right. She was here.

For justice.

For vengeance.

For him.

Tinman turned around to confirm his fate. He turned his eyes upward and screamed more loudly than any of the women he'd bought, sold and tortured ever had.

SCYLLA

1

Colorado

You would think that being deep in the woods of Southern Colorado with a smoking hot redhead, with no one else around for miles, would give me nothing to complain about. Under other circumstances, that would be true, but it turns out I don't know what poison ivy looks like. Also good to know, if you get the oil on your hands and then proceed to scratch your arms, stomach and balls? Your world pretty much goes to hell.

Seriously.

My arms and stomach are bearable, but it's the middle of summer. It's hot and humid here on the Ute reservation. So I decided to go commando. Didn't even pack underwear. My boxer-briefs would have at least held everything in place. But now, every movement instigates a wicked stinging itch. My loins are literally burning. What should have been another useless, but otherwise memorable, investigation of a strange-creature sighting has become an itchy wet blanket the likes of which I doubt any man has ever before experienced in the history of the world.

To make matters worse, we're leaving. Again, doesn't sound too bad, but we're ten miles from our car and another twenty from the nearest pharmacy, where I will single-handedly boost the stock of calamine lotion.

I'm walking like I just spent the past month riding bareback, and the toe of my boot strikes a rock funny. I stumble forward just a little bit, but it's enough for things to move around like some kid with ADHD is ringing the bells of St. Mary's.

I stagger to a stop, wincing. Legs splayed like the St. Louis Gateway Arch. "Fuuuck."

Ashley Collins, my investigative partner at the Department of Homeland Security's one and only Fusion Center dedicated to protecting the United States from paranormal threats, stops in her tracks. She turns around with that adorable smirk of hers, and I already want to slap it off her face. Of course, she'd kick my ass if I tried. "Man up, Hudson."

"I will only accept criticism from someone with testicles," I say, hands on knees.

"I've got an elastic band in my pocket," she says, still wearing the smirk. "My uncle showed me how to castrate a goat once. Just put the elastic on tight, stop the flow of blood and—"

"C'mon," I say, unable to keep myself from chuckling. "Seriously, this hurts."

She digs into her pocket, pulls out the elastic, stretches it a few times and in a sing-song voice, says, "We could be gal-pals."

I find myself unable to reply. Not because I don't have a comeback. We tease each other like this frequently. We could ping-pong creative insults back and forth for hours. It's the hair on the back of my neck, standing straight up that stops me. And I have no idea why. I didn't hear anything. Or smell anything. It's just an instinct. Some part of my mind shouting at me to run, or fight.

When Collins slowly moves her hand to her sidearm, I know she feels it too.

We're being stalked.

"What is it?" she whispers.

I shake my head, but I know it's one of two things: a brown bear or a mountain lion. Both are common enough in this part of the country, and both occasionally take a whack at people. My preference would be the bear. Not only do I have experience fending off bears, but we'd hear it coming. A cougar...their hunting and fighting abilities are nearly supernatural. So much so, that they're revered by the local Ute population. We wouldn't know it was here until it attacked, which is exactly what's happening. I give my answer without fully processing the potential ramifications. "Mountain lion."

Collins's hand moves from the holstered handgun on her hip and shifts toward the tranquilizer rifle slung over her back. Dressed in camouflage, carrying a backpack and armed like a guerrilla, she looks like she should be in a Red Dawn reboot. I'm dressed the same, but right now, with me all hunched over and uncomfortable, she's the only one who really looks the part. "Or maybe another big cat," she says.

The realization causes me to stand up straight and ignore the molten lava between my legs. Like Collins, I reach for my rifle. But while hers contains a tranquilizer dart, mine contains a tracking device. We're not exterminators. We're only here to find out what people are seeing. In this case, the creature of choice is a black, cat-woman. Over the past year, Collins and I have investigated scads of creature reports, including chupacabra, the Jersey Devil, a handful of ghost sightings, poltergeists, UFO sightings, alien abductions and natural phenomena. If you don't count the 300-foot tall monster that laid waste to Boston—and Bigfoot, which we found and tagged a few months later—the FC-P department of the DHS has once again become a black hole of wasted time. That's if you're only looking at our investigations into the strange.

We've also been busy building cases against several people involved in the debacle that led to thousands of deaths at the hands, and feet—that's awful—of an ancient vengeance goddess genetically merged with a murdered little girl named Maigo. I shake my head at the thought. *Nemesis.* That a laboratory could take the DNA of a girl and merge it with something probably long dead, and horrible, to create a gigantic, city-destroying monster, still sounds impossible. Yet, that's what happened. And she stomped her way south, from Maine to Boston, eating people, whales and everything else with a heartbeat. With each meal, she grew, every pound of flesh eaten transferred to her own mass. But she wasn't just eating. She decimated everything in her path—homes, ships, entire cities and everything the military threw at her—until her thirst for vengeance was sated by the dramatic slaying of Maigo's father.

But whatever is hunting us now, it isn't Nemesis. She's hard to miss. Whatever this is...it's good at hiding. I spin around, taking in every tree, searching every shadow.

Very good at hiding.

Rustling brush spins me and Collins around, rifles raised. We won't kill whatever is there, but if Collins's aim is true—and it usually is—her target shouldn't make it more than a couple of steps.

The brush shifts again. Low to the ground. Something small and black flits in and out of view.

I lower my rifle. "Was that a skunk?"

Collins sighs and lowers her weapon. "Looked more like a house cat to me."

"Was walking kind of funny for a house cat." The hair on my arms springs up as I speak, and my subconscious tightens my grip on the rifle. Before I fully comprehend the small creature I saw, or respond to the fresh wave of panic coursing through my body, a breeze blows past.

Moving with the breeze is a shadow that smells like roses.

I react on instinct, raising the rifle as I spin toward the shadow. The rifle, armed with a tracking device, will do little. My attacker doesn't know that, though, and reacts to the pointed weapon with violence and intelligence. The barrel is thrust into the air. The fired dart is sent sailing into the forest.

I don't care. My gaze is held by a pair of yellow eyes, both feline and human at the same time. They're framed by a feminine face, again human, but with a small nose and whiskers. The cat-woman. She's real.

And pissed.

The rifle barrel bends in her hands. An amazing feat of strength that I would applaud, if I wasn't concerned about the same technique being used on my arms.

Collins takes aim with the tranq rifle, but never gets to fire. The cat-woman spins and kicks out a clawed foot, knocking the rifle to the tall grass around us. Continuing her fluid spin, the cat-woman slams her foot into my chest, knocking me back against a tree and knocking every molecule of oxygen from my lungs.

Collins goes for her sidearm. She's a quick draw, but the cat-woman has leapt into the air—*twenty feet* into the air—flipping up and over Collins. The creature lands behind her. Collins spins around to fire, but her weapon is yanked up. A single shot tears into the air, garnering several small squeaks of fright from the nearby brush. Collins shouts in pain as she's forcefully disarmed. But she's a warrior. She gives up the weapon so she can use another. Her fists.

The cat-woman doesn't see the first blow coming. Collins's fist connects solidly with the side of the furry head. I recognize the strike. She was aiming for a knockout blow, to end the fight without having to kill the creature. But the cat-woman doesn't go down. The creature staggers for two steps, shakes it off and lunges, tackling Collins to the ground.

I try to run to Collins's aid, but I can't complete a single step before falling to my knees. I have yet to catch my breath. The best I can do is plead with the animal. I suck in a loud breath and manage a whisper. "Stop."

The creature rains down blow after blow, using fists. She has fingers, I realize, not paws, though I'm fairly certain she has claws, and I'm glad she's not using them. Collins is doing a decent job fending off the punches, but she'd be shredded by claws. The cat-woman is tempering her attack. Given her strength, I'd say she's pulling her punches, too. Still, too much more of this and Collins will be in real trouble.

Remembering I'm carrying an actual gun with real bullets, I reach to my hip and draw the weapon. My arm shakes as I take another deep breath. Not wanting to kill the creature, or Collins by accident, I speak again, this time finding enough strength to shout. "Stop!"

I don't really expect the cat-woman to respond. But she does. She stops—and glances back at me, her eyes full of anger, distrust...and understanding.

My aim falters. "Oh, my God, you know what I'm saying?"

The woman's feline eyes squint at me. "You shouldn't have come here."

2

In that moment of distraction, when the creature's eyes lock on mine, Collins pistons her knees up into the cat-woman's backside—which, I might add, is also quite human and feminine. She'd be attractive, if not for the long tail. Sure, she's also covered in black hair, but the shiny coat clings to her like spandex. Caught off guard, the cat-woman is pushed forward. Collins uses the momentum, heaving her arms up against her attacker's chest. The creature is flipped off over Collins's head, but like a true cat, the cat-woman lands on her feet and is ready for action before Collins can even get up fully.

The cat-woman's legs coil. She's about to pounce on Collins's back. And this time she's got her claws out.

"I'll shoot," I say loudly, aiming at the fully exposed creature. I won't miss, no matter how fast she moves. Not at this range. "I know you can understand me."

The cat-woman turns her yellow eyes from Collins to me, squinting like a miffed teenager. In fact, now that I'm looking at her face again, she looks fairly young in human terms. Maybe twenty. But I have no real way of evaluating her age. "I don't want to kill you," I add. "But if you attack her again, I won't hesitate."

The cat-woman's face scrunches with frustration. "Yyyyou attacked us first!"

God, she sounds young, too.

"We didn't attack anyone." My defense sounds childish as I say it, but it's the truth.

"Yes, you did!" she shouts, our conversation devolving toward 'Uh-uh!' and 'Ya-huh!' But then she clarifies. "You pointed your rifle at my girls."

Girls?

Her girls.

"Holy shit." I glance toward the brush where we saw the small black creature. "They're your children?"

She snarls, bearing white, pointed teeth.

"I didn't know," I say.

She looks ready to pounce. "Too late."

"For what?"

"You've seen them," she says. "I can't let you leave."

The threat makes me realize I've lowered my aim some. I bring the barrel back up, sighting her chest. I really don't want to kill this creature. She's amazing. I just need her to—

The growl building in the cat-woman's chest focuses me. I slide my index finger over the trigger.

"Wait!" a distant voice shouts from behind me. It's masculine and very human. I watch Collins's eyes for signs of surprise or danger, but she just looks confused. Whoever is approaching is human and unarmed. "Don't shoot!"

I can hear the crunch of running feet on the ground, crushing twigs, leaves and pebbles with each hurried step.

The cat-woman seems to relax as the newcomer gets closer. The growl fades. Her muscles loosen. She's no longer about to pounce. But I don't lower my aim. Can't take the chance. In part because I know the woman is still dangerous, despite her changed body language. And I have no idea who this guy is.

The man rushes past, heading straight for the cat-woman. He carries himself in a comfortable, fearless way, how a father might approach a child. "Lilly," he says, his tone harsh, but concerned, "What are you doing?"

Lilly? Seriously? The cat-woman's name is Lilly?

"They were going to shoot the girls."

The man stiffens. I don't see a weapon, but he now has an air of danger about him.

"First," I say, still hoping to avoid a confrontation, "one rifle is a tranq gun. The other fires a tracking dart. Our job is not to kill...people...or whatever. Second, we never really saw your children. We thought they were skunks. And if you must know the truth, *you* got too close. If you hadn't been stalking us, we'd have never drawn our weapons."

The newcomer sighs and gives a shake of his head.

"I was just watching them," Lilly grumbles.

"You know that's against the rules," the man says.

"I just—"

"If something had happened to the girls today, it would have been your fault," the man says. "Do you understand that? And now you've put all of us at risk."

Lilly's feline body deflates under the verbal smackdown. "I'm sorry."

"Why are you here?" the man asks, and it takes me a second to realize he's speaking to me.

I'm about to answer, when I remember that I'm the one in charge. "Actually," I say, "you can answer that question for me. I am the one with the gun."

The man hesitates, but then answers. "We live here."

I look around. "In the woods?"

"A few miles to the north."

Reservation land. "You don't look like one of the Ute."

"Grandfather is Ute," Lilly says, but she's quickly shushed by the man.

"Where did she come from?" I ask.

"Can't tell you that."

"I'm afraid you're going to have to," I say, adjusting my aim toward the man, as I now suspect he's got a gun tucked into the small of his back.

"Not going to happen." The man's defiance is infuriating.

"Then I'll just have to arrest you both," I say.

The man starts to spin toward me, but stops when I shout, "Move and you die!" When the man complies, I add, "Hands in the air."

"Who are you?" the man asks again, his hands rising slowly. "Are you from DARPA?"

"DARPA?" I ask.

"Defense Advanced Research Projects Agency," Collins says, picking up her handgun. She steps around the man, looking at his face, and adding her weapon to the threat of violence.

"I know what it stands for," I say. "And no, we're not with DARPA. We're here because of several recent reports of a cat-woman."

The man's head snaps toward Lilly.

I add some details so he gets a better idea that we're here for a good reason. "She's been peeking in people's windows, sneaking through yards and scaring kids. Fifteen sightings in the past two months."

The man's head lowers. "Son-of-a-bitch."

"I—I just wanted to see other people," Lilly says. "I'm stuck here in the woods all the—"

"It's not safe," the man says. "You know that."

Lilly stomps her foot on the ground, crushing a pinecone. "The only people I ever see are you, Grandpa Goodtracks, Joliet and Uncle Bray!"

The man cranes his neck to the sky, totally exasperated, like I remember my parents being with me.

"Look," I say. "I don't *need* to arrest you. That's not really our job."

"What *is* your job?" the man asks.

"To identify and monitor potential threats. As long as everyone plays nice, nothing bad happens."

The man slowly turns his head toward me. I can just see the side of his face. Something about him is familiar, but a beard conceals most of his features. "Who are you?"

This time I answer. "Department of Homeland Security."

The man grins. "Fusion Center-P?"

That he knows which department we're from isn't too surprising. After Nemesis tore through Boston and we played a critical role in saving the day, most people on the planet have heard of us. It's the man's reaction when I say, "Yes," that catches me off guard.

He raises his hands higher and turns around slowly. "I was wondering when you might show up, Jon."

Again, I'm a fairly recognizable person now. But the casual way he says my name clears some of the cobwebs from my mind. I *know* this guy. But I don't recognize him until I see his brown eyes. "Mark?"

My weapon lowers in time with his raised arms. Mark Hawkins was an adventuring buddy. During our younger years, we trekked the woods together, went hang gliding, went base jumping and white water rafting. Then we became adults. I joined the DHS. He became a park ranger.

"I should have recognized the beanie," he says with a smile, pointing at the red cap affixed to my head, cloaking my receding hairline. "How's Betty?"

In my stunned state, I answer without thinking. "Dead. Took a bullet for me."

Hawkins's jaw goes slack. "Holy... I'm sorry."

His stunned look and sorrow-filled eyes confuse me, until I realize that Hawkins never met the truck I named Betty. "You think I'm talking about girlfriend Betty!" I say with a laugh. "We broke up."

"Who were you talking about then?" he asks.

"Truck Betty," I say, like it's all the explanation he needs. "She's dead. But Helicopter Betty is fine."

"You *know* them?" Collins asks, her weapon still partially aimed at Hawkins.

"I know *him*," I say, looking at Hawkins. "Not his friend."

"It's okay," Hawkins says to Lilly. "He's safe."

"I would never harm you or your girls," I say, holstering my weapon. Sensing the girl's unease, I step forward and extend my hand. She stares at it for a moment, and I think she might bite it off, but then she takes hold and shakes. Her fur is soft, but her grip is killer. "My name is Jon. Nice to meet you, Lilly." I motion to Collins. "This is Ashley. She's my partner."

"She's more than that," Lilly says with a sly grin. The kid has been watching us for a while, since before I got my poison ivy. Speaking of which, I turn my attention back to Hawkins. "I don't suppose you have any calamine lotion, do you?"

"Back at the house," he says.

"Thank God."

"But first," Hawkins motions behind me. I turn to find a small blonde holding a handgun and an old Ute man with a rifle. "This is Howie Goodtracks and Avril Joliet."

"AKA, backup," I say with a grin. I take a step toward them, hand extended, when my sat-phone begins playing the Imperial March from *Star Wars*. This will be my colleague, Anne Cooper. We follow a strict radio-silence rule during investigations. What's the point of searching for elusive creatures if a ringing phone might scare them off? But we also have to remain available, hence the sat-phone. And if Cooper is calling, that means something bad is going down.

I answer the phone. "What's happening?"

As I listen to the voice on the other end, my face falls flat. Collins steps closer, a look of concern on her face. Hawkins, Joliet, Goodtracks and Lilly join her, all waiting to hear what I'm being told.

"I need an address," I say to Hawkins. When he hesitates, I clarify. "For a helicopter pick-up."

He gives me an address, and I relay it to Cooper before hanging up.

"Is it Nemesis?" Collins asks.

"Where?" Hawkins asks. He looks ready for action, and I wonder what his life has been like and how Lilly came to be a part of it. We'll have to catch up on all that later. Right now, we have a helicopter to catch—and that bottle of calamine lotion.

I turn north and strike out, answering, "Hong Kong."

3

Katsu Endo, formerly of the Japanese Self-Defense Force, had done things he wasn't proud of to survive. First, was the shooting of Master Sergeant Lenny Wilson. But the act had saved his life and ingratiated him with General Lance Gordon. But his allegiance was never to Gordon. It was to the dead monster they had found buried in the wilds of Alaska. He'd spent his childhood admiring Japanese *Kaiju*, or 'strange beasts,' the way other kids admired superheroes. So, where the monster's corpse went, his allegiance followed. And right now, his loyalty belonged to Zoomb, an Internet search engine turned technology behemoth.

At first, his duties involved protecting Zoomb's CEO, Paul Stanton, but over the past year, fear of reprisal from Gordon had faded. Endo's unique skill set, combining high intelligence, lethal fighting skills and special ops training, made him the ideal candidate for the R&D unit's 'field research team.' In less politically correct terms, they were a corporate-espionage strike team, capable of stealing the competition's technology and prototypes, ferreting out leaks or simply handling competition the old fashioned way—with bribery, extortion and threats of violence. In the corporate world, motivated primarily by money, these techniques worked better than actually killing people, which pleased Endo, because he was not fond of taking lives. He was driven but not coldhearted.

Thankfully, his passion and the goals of Zoomb's R&D department were aligned. There was no higher priority for them than the original monster, Nemesis-Prime. They wanted to understand the creature. Where it came from. What motivated it. They wanted to extract technologies. They not only saw massive profit potential, but a way to change the entire world.

They had the original Kaiju creature's carcass hidden away, but its petrified form kept most of its secrets well guarded. Although they had managed to extract a viable sample of the creature's DNA, it had been lost with the destruction of the laboratory that gave birth to the new Nemesis. They had nearly succeeded in advancing medicine to a point where lives could be saved and extended, but instead they had succeeded only in creating a new monster—a successor to the original. But the monster's creation also provided opportunity. For science. For medicine. And for war.

Zoomb didn't just want to study the new beast, they wanted to *control* it.

So when reports of the attack on Hong Kong came in, Endo and his team were on board a Cessna Citation X—the world's fastest private jet, clocking in at 717 miles per hour—cruising across the Pacific, covering a mile every five seconds.

Endo crossed his legs, settled back into the plush leather seat and glanced out the window at the blue sky and bluer ocean below. Somewhere down there was a 300-foot tall monster capable of destroying entire cities. Perhaps the world. A smile came to his face.

"Sir," a woman said.

He turned to Maggie Alessi, his second in command. Like him, she was dressed in black slacks and a black jacket. The attire served to conceal their weapons, but also made them look like government officials. FBI, CIA, even the DHS. Whatever they needed to be. Zoomb had the resources to create any ID they needed, and the R&D department had a higher budget than most government agencies.

"What is it?" he asked.

"We just got confirmation. The FC-P is in the air."

"Hudson?" he asked.

"And Collins."

He nodded. He had nothing against Jon Hudson. In fact, he admired the man for standing unshaken before Nemesis and offering Maigo's father, Alexander Tilly, to the monster as a sacrificial lamb. The man was guilty of murder, but at the time had not yet been convicted. Hudson had been scrutinized for the act at first, but no one could deny that he'd saved what remained of Boston, and countless more lives. When evidence proving that Tilly had murdered his wife and daughter emerged, the matter was dropped. Despite Endo's admiration for Hudson, he knew the feeling was not mutual. Hudson would arrest him just as soon as he had evidence linking Endo to one of the many crimes Gordon had had him commit.

He looked at his watch.

"We land in an hour," Alessi said, tucking her straight black hair behind her ears. Like Endo, her heritage was Japanese. Unlike Endo, she was born in the U.S. and had no love for Kaiju, fictional or real.

"Plenty of time," Endo said.

"Not exactly."

Endo raised a single eyebrow, a habit he had picked up from General Gordon.

"They were seen boarding some kind of stealth transport. Our military sources say it was already headed to Hong Kong to pick up other assets. If it's as fast as they believe..."

"How long will we have?" Endo asked.

"Thirty minutes."

"It's enough."

"Enough for what?" Alessi asked. "The attack is over. Authorities haven't found any physical remains. And the few witnesses still alive aren't talking, because they're afraid they'll be next. What do you expect to find?"

"Evidence," he said.

"For what?"

"That the creature responsible..." He turned his eyes back out the window, seeing a world filled with amazing and horrible secrets. "...was *not* Nemesis."

4

"This is all wrong," I say, staring over the wreckage of Hong Kong's port. I've never been to the city before. Honestly, I'm not much of a city guy. And Hong Kong is *all* city. Even the mountains struggling to rise up taller than the myriad skyscrapers are marred by crisscrossing lines of homes, businesses and cell towers. It's like everyone in the city is trying to get higher than everyone else. If they were trying to get out of reach of Nemesis, I'd understand, but like everywhere else on the planet, height is somehow associated with success. Sure, you can see for miles, but here that means gazing out your window at buildings, smog, a congested port and an ocean cluttered with cargo ships.

Most of which are now half sunk.

The port is in ruins.

Thousands of massive shipping containers are strewn about like torn open Christmas presents, except that each of these gifts weighs several tons. And they've been tossed about so casually, there is no doubt, something of stunning strength put a whooping on this port.

"I know," Collins says. "Early estimates put the dead and missing at three hundred twenty."

I wipe my arm across my sweat-slicked forehead. It's hotter and far more humid than it had been on the Ute reservation. To make matters worse, I can practically feel the smog clinging to the wet air, caking me in filth. And since I didn't get to take a bath before our flight... Well, let's just say that I'm riper than a peach left too long in the sun. At least Hawkins came through with the calamine lotion. He let me keep it and a bottle of anti-itch spray. "That's not what I meant."

She glances at me. Doesn't need to ask. She knows I'll fill her in.

"If this were Nemesis, it would be worse."

"Worse? But—"

"Boston worse. Or Beverly. Or even Portland." Nemesis very nearly wiped Boston off the map. She decimated Beverly harbor. And when she hit Portland, she was only half grown, yet she still left a path of destruction in her wake that dwarfed what I'm looking at. A ruined container catches my eyes. "Look. See the gouges?"

The wounds in the thick metal are ominous. Powerful. Three claws have peeled through the metal like it was little more than paper.

Collins sees it. "Shit. You're right."

"Maigo's—Nemesis's claws wouldn't just slice through one of those containers, they'd obliterate it. The destruction here is just too small in scale."

"But what about the human trafficking ring that was hit?" Collins asked. "All of the clients were killed, not to mention the ringleader. That's a lot of very bad guys. It fits Nemesis's M.O. of doling out justice."

I nod. She's right about that. And other than Nemesis, nothing else I'm aware of is capable of this. *Aware of* is the key phrase. "There's something more going on here. What if we were *supposed* to blame Nemesis for this mess."

"Please don't tell me you think someone is setting up Nemesis." Her voice oozes with doubt.

"You saw the news on our way here. There isn't any doubt in the world's eyes that this was Nemesis."

Collins purses her lips. I can see she wants to believe me, but she's struggling. In part, because the evidence is damning, but also because my belief that Nemesis isn't entirely bad irks her. Not enough to create a divide between us, but certainly enough for her to cast doubt on my judgment of the beast. Which I appreciate. People who aren't held accountable tend to make really poor choices. But this time, I have support.

"He's right," a voice says from behind.

We both turn to find the silhouette of a woman. The day is overcast and a brown-tinged haze fills the air, but it's by no means dark. Yet this woman has found the perfect spot between two shipping containers to cloak herself in shadow. I squint, trying to see through the gloom, but she's dressed in black. The only color I can see is her blonde hair, which hangs over her face. She doesn't want to be seen.

"Who are you?" I ask.

"Can't tell you that," she says. Her voice is confident. American. "But you hitched a ride on my plane."

That's all I needed to know. The plane that brought us here—some kind of classified stealth transport—is unlike anything I've ever seen before. The special-ops group it belongs to has got to be the best of the best. And apparently, this woman is one of them.

"How is he right?" Collins asks, all business.

"This wasn't *your* monster," she says.

I'm not sure I'm comfortable with her emphasis on the word *your*, like Nemesis belongs to me...or is somehow my fault. Though she is certainly my problem, as I'm in charge of preventing a repeat of Boston.

"Then what was it?" Collins asks.

The woman shrugs. "Something else. Smaller. I didn't get a good look at it."

"Why not?" Collins's tone suggests she doesn't trust this woman.

"Because I was running for my life with thirty doped-out sex slaves, that's why." The woman pauses, composes herself and continues. "Look, all I know is that it was big, but not three-hundred-feet tall big. It cast a bright orange light and it was hungry."

"Hungry?" I ask.

"You won't be finding the missing," she says. "They were eaten. All of them."

"How do you know they were eaten," Collins says, "if you were running away?"

The woman twists her neck to the side, and I hear her vertebrae pop.

I had a friend that did that too much. Neck got all screwed up. "That's not good for—"

"Shut the fuck up and listen," she says. "I've dealt with my fair share of monsters before. I understand that you two are new to this, but let me assure you, I know what someone being eaten sounds like. Fuck, you two are way more bitchy than your partners."

"Partners?" I ask.

"Two DHS-P agents. Man and a woman. North side of the port."

Shit. Right now, Collins and I are the only field investigators at DHS-P. I've been given the green light to hire more, but haven't. And not because I'm lazy. The low-key, don't-give-a-shit Jon Hudson is on vacation. Collins and I have just been so swamped with calls since Nemesis, that I haven't had a chance to even look at applications. Cooper has been trudging through them with Watson back at the office, but they can't conduct the interviews or hire people. So, I know without a doubt, that the two people this woman has just described are imposters.

And I'm pretty sure I know who one of them is. I pull out my phone and open the photo app. "Hold on a second," I say, scrolling through the images like I'm trying to show her a photo of my kids, which I don't have. When I find the image I'm looking for, I hold it up to the gap between the crates.

The glowing screen illuminates the woman. She's not dressed like a soldier. In fact, she's dressed kind of slutty, in a tight black skirt. Lots of cleavage. Her blonde hair is dirty and hangs over her face, though I can see one of her piercing blue eyes. Perhaps this is why she wanted to remain in the dark. Who would take her seriously?

She must see all this in my eyes, because she glances down at herself and explains. "I was undercover." Then she looks up at the phone and adds, "That's the guy."

"He give a name?" I ask.

"Collins," she says. "Jon Collins."

I grunt in annoyance. "Son-of-a-bitch."

That asshole. Endo is mocking us.

"There a problem?" she asks.

"I'm Collins," Collins says.

"And I'm Jon."

The woman actually laughs. "Sounds like you two have your hands full. I'll let you get to it."

"We could use your help bringing him in," I say, motioning to Endo's photo.

"Sorry," the mystery woman says. "Got a plane to catch before the world goes to hell again."

I turn to Collins. "Let's go find him." When I turn back to thank the woman for the information, she's gone. Like Batman. Silent and mysterious. Maybe she's just lying on top of one of the containers, but I don't want to know where she went, because it was pretty cool. I turn to Collins. "Ready for a run?"

She just turns and starts running north. I follow, moving fast, leaping debris and dodging fallen containers. *Endo.* For the first time since Boston, he's within reach, and I intend to put that bastard over my knee and spank the shit out of him, like I'm a card-carrying member of the Pat Robertson fan club.

5

"What the—" I manage to say, before slamming into the steel wall of a bright red container. I grunt and take a deep breath, replenishing the air knocked from my lungs and catching a strong whiff of oil and fishy ocean. "It's not fair that my girlfriend can manhandle me."

"On mission, we're partners," she reminds me. "Remember? Also, you like it."

She's right. My girl is buff and can fight. Not many guys would admit it, but that's pretty hot.

"And if you're not too busy whining like a sissy," she says, "maybe you'd like to help me catch Endo?"

"You saw him?"

"About 200 feet ahead. Walking away with a woman. Straight black hair."

I inch closer to the side of the container and peek around it. When I was running behind Collins, I couldn't see much of what was ahead. But I quickly spot the pair, walking away casually like they were supposed to be there. Endo nods to a few of the Hong Kong police searching the area for evidence, and they give curt waves back. Not quite friendly. More like tolerant respect. The FC-P is known throughout the world. Although other agencies wouldn't have been granted immediate access to a catastrophe in China, the FC-P is welcome, mostly because the images of Boston laid to waste are impossible to forget. No one wants that to happen to their city. That Endo is using our credentials to gain access to sites like this, no doubt on behalf of Zoomb, feels like a frontal wedgie from Hulk Hogan.

I manage to control my ire and focus. "We can follow the rows of containers on either side. Flank them. Catch them in the middle."

Collins nods and heads off, moving quickly down the left side of a container row, which was undisturbed by the previous night's attack.

A quick peek around the other side reveals that Endo and his friend haven't changed course or pace. They're unaware of us. Moving casually, like I belong, I look south and walk across the open space between containers. Even if they had been looking, they wouldn't have been able to I.D. me.

Safely hidden by the containers on the other side of the alley, I continue to the far side, but the path isn't nearly as clear as the one Collins took. Several containers have been knocked over and crushed, their contents disgorged. Toilet seats, clock radios and what appear to be massagers or maybe sex toys, litter the concrete.

I do my best to hurry through the mess, but there isn't much room to place my feet. After thirty seconds of stumbling, my foot rolls atop a massager, which shoots out from under me. My unceremonious fall is stopped by a toilet seat—the squishy kind, so that's something. But my knees take the brunt of the fall, and I quickly come to the conclusion that Endo will be long gone by the time I pick my way through this mess. As the massager buzzes at me, I get back to my feet, find the nearest ladder and then throw myself onto the rungs.

Move, you idiot, my internal monologue shouts at me. I climb the ladder, reaching the container's top quickly. I now have a clear shot down the row. I can see Endo, now much further ahead. In a minute, he'll be outside the port, no doubt whisked away by a waiting vehicle. I take two steps and stop. Not only are the metal containers slick with morning dew, but my boots sound like thunder as I move.

A menagerie of cuss words flow from my lips as I quickly remove my boots. I'm probably going to cut my foot on the metal and die from some kind of exotic strain of tetanus, but at least my bare feet have better traction, and I'll be able to move in relative silence.

I sprint down the string of containers, sticking to the right side where the metal doesn't flex as much and where I'm less likely to be spotted. Half way to Endo, I'm caught off guard by a five-foot gap, but I manage to jump the distance and continue on. Feeling like a real action hero, I turn on the speed, knowing I'll catch up to Endo before he can escape.

Collins must have seen my approach and realized our flanking plan wasn't going to work, because she steps out in front of Endo and the woman, reaching into her coat, like she's got a gun.

Endo and the woman stop in place. They don't raise their hands, but they don't make a move for weapons, either. Knowing that they'll soon call Collins's bluff, I shift my aim to the left and leap, aiming for Endo. Yeah, it's kind of a far fall, but Endo is going to break it for me.

As I sail through the air, Collins doesn't reveal a thing. Her eyes stay on Endo. Her expression doesn't change. Nothing about her gives away my attack, and my approach is all but silent.

Yet, Endo somehow senses my aerial approach. He doesn't turn to attack me or dive out of the way. I could have lived with some kind of dramatic conclusion. He just takes a single step to the side, moving out of the way just enough, so I fly past and land hard on the ground.

I'm able to curl in on myself, rolling as I hit, but holy hell, concrete is an unforgiving surface. I'm going to be in serious pain tomorrow. And since I'm not a ninja, or Endo, my sprawling roll doesn't end until

I slam into the side of a metal container. The empty container bongs from the impact, like a symbol at the end of a joke.

To my surprise, when I right myself and turn around, Endo and the woman are still standing there. "Don't move," I say, sounding very un-authoritative. I climb to my feet. "You're under arrest."

Endo smiles. "We're in China."

"I don't give a fuck."

He turns to the woman, his confidence never wavering. "I'll see you at the plane."

She nods.

Then they split like an atom, exploding into two different directions. Despite having already sprinted the length of a football field and dropping from the sky like Evel Knievel at Snake River, I throw myself after Endo and shout, "Get the woman!" I don't look back to see if Collins is giving chase. I know she is.

Endo is a blur. He's not a big guy. Maybe 5'5", and he's skinny. Maneuvering through the maze of containers, both upright and spilled, is far easier for him, than it is for me. Where he moves with finesse, I—well, I just do my best. And somehow, I manage to stick with him.

Until I don't.

He ducks into an alley between two bright yellow containers, and when I follow, he's gone. Fifty feet separate the corner from the next turn. No way he could have made it all the way. Unless he's been running slow on purpose, pulling some kind of pursuit rope-a-dope.

"Ahem." The cleared throat comes from behind me. I try to hide my surprise as I turn around, but Endo knows I'm flabbergasted. The smile on his face mocks me like a childhood bully.

He leans back casually against a container. Glances up at the sky, like he's got nothing better to do than wonder whether or not it's going to rain. Then he says, "We don't have to be enemies."

"We're not," I say. "You're a criminal. I'm in law enforcement. I'm just doing my job."

"You've been trying to find evidence against me all year," he says. "Sounds like a vendetta to me."

I nearly deny it, but it's clear he knows better. I suppose when you work for the most high-tech company in the world, even government secrets can't stay hidden for long. Which makes me wonder what else he knows. Man, I've really got to get this guy in an interrogation room.

"You're a murderer," I say, stepping closer.

"When I killed, it was under the orders of a United States general." Endo stands up straight, taking his weight off the container. "When you brought Tilly to the edge of that roof and offered his life to Maigo, you weren't under orders. He hadn't been convicted or sentenced. According to the law, you took an innocent man and had him executed."

Two things stop me in place. First, I agree with him. Technically, I killed Tilly, or was, at least, an accessory to his murder. I just don't feel bad about it, because he murdered his wife and daughter, and my taking the law into my own hands spared the city from further destruction. Second, Endo is the only other person I've ever heard call the monster by the name *Maigo*.

His grin returns. "We want the same thing: to protect the world from further destruction. We're just going about it differently."

"How's that?" I ask, stepping forward again, closing to within striking distance.

"You think brute force will stop her," he says, and he's wrong about that. I'm not sure anything short of a nuke could stop her, and I'm entirely against that option, though some in Washington disagree. "I believe in a more subtle approach," he says.

Going for the unsubtle approach, I take a swing, hoping to catch him off guard. No matter how experienced a fighter he is, one good clock to the head will drop him. If only the man didn't have the reflexes of a mantis shrimp, it might have worked.

Ducking my punch, which overextends my body and leaves me open for a painful counter-attack, Endo simply leaps up and slaps me across the side of my head, striking my temple with his open palm.

He jumps back out of reach, standing casually once again, a smile on his face.

I groan, exasperated by his cocky attitude and the realization that he's just screwing around. "Seriously?"

"Like I said, you're going about it all wrong," he says. "It's not about brute force. It's about intelligence. Knowledge. Technology."

"Shut up, Steve Jobs," I grumble, clenching my fists. "Sometimes a little brute force goes a long way." I take a step toward him, trying to visualize my attack. My fist is about half the size of his head. Just one punch. *One* punch.

He takes a step away, and I think I've got him. He sees how pissed I am.

Nope.

He just wants to get in the last word.

"It's about control," he says, before tapping what looks like a small Bluetooth phone attached to his right ear. "Stop."

The world goes wonky. I'm still aiming for his head, but my mind is telling me he's floating away, hovering smoothly over the ground, a fixed distance from me. But that's not the case. The truth is worse. He's not gliding away, *I'm* no longer moving.

"Sit," he says. "Don't talk."

I plop down onto the damp concrete, sitting in a rainbow swirled oily puddle.

I can move my eyes, but otherwise, I have no control over my own body.

He steps up in front of me, my life in his hands. With a broad smile he taps my head with his finger. "Control the beast. Save the world." He steps back. "I hope the next time we meet, it will be under different circumstances. Our goals are aligned. Maigo is important. To both of us."

I want to hurl four letter words at him, but I'm a statue.

He glances to the side, like he's just heard something. He steps between a pair of containers and slips away. Ten seconds later, Collins appears. She looks unharmed, but pissed.

"What are you doing?" she asks, clearly annoyed.

When I don't respond in any way except to stare at her, her mood shifts from anger to concern. She slows her approach. "Are you booby trapped or something?"

I move my eyes back and forth, doing my best to communicate a 'no,' and I turn my eyes toward my left temple, where Endo slapped me.

She looks at the side of my head and squints. "The hell?" Leaning in close, she reaches out, takes hold of something and tugs. A stinging pain lances through my head and I shout, "Oww!" Then I'm immediately relieved, because I can talk again.

I rub the side of my head, and my hand comes away with just a little bit of blood. Collins holds out a dime-sized device. Its surface is smooth black, but three golden prongs, tinged with my blood, extend from its side.

I'm about to ask what it is, when the thing starts to smoke. Collins flinches in pain and yanks her hand away. A jet of flame shoots from the side of it, but extinguishes as the device lands in a puddle. I quickly pick it up, hoping the fire and water haven't completely destroyed the technology inside.

"What did it do to you?" Collins asks, helping me to my feet.

"Controlled me," I tell her. "I would have done whatever he asked."

"You're okay?"

I nod. "He...just wanted to talk."

"Be glad he didn't leave you doing the running man dance."

I smile, but the attempt at humor doesn't really lift my spirits. "I know what Zoomb is after."

She waits.

"Control..." I tell her with a frown, "of Nemesis."

6

"We are now live outside the Sydney Opera House, standing atop the Forecourt stairs, which we're told creates a natural amphitheater. This allows each and every one of the nearly one thousand audience members to clearly hear the Sydney Orchestra's every note." Olivia Jones gave the camera a smile and dipped her head to the right, letting her straight blonde hair swing out over one eye. The movement wasn't intentional, but the newsroom knew it meant she was done talking.

The voice of Chuck Wilson, the studio reporter that only she and the TV audience could hear, spoke in her ear. "Very good, Olivia. I'm sure we'd all like to be there with you."

Olivia nodded, like she agreed, but she wasn't a fan of orchestral music. Had the concert been the B-52s or R.E.M. she would have been pleased, but when was the last time either of those bands played in Australia—or anywhere for that matter? "Absolutely. It's going to be a fantastic night, full of magical music followed by fireworks and an exclusive after-party, where we're sure to spot a few celebs and some of Sydney's—"

"Olivia," Chuck said, cutting her off.

She nearly lost her cool on live TV. If there was one thing she hated more than anything else, it was being interrupted. She had a boyfriend once. Stunningly handsome. Smart. Wealthy. But he interrupted her constantly, even if they weren't fighting. The man had ears only for his internal monologue, and he would express whatever fresh insight he'd just delighted himself with, regardless of what she was saying. He almost didn't hear her breaking up with him.

Now, she forced a professional smile, and said, "Yes, Chuck, what is it?"

Chuck was a prick, but he was dashing and attracted a younger, more female demographic, which the advertisers loved. He would be untouchable at the network until he started to wrinkle. There was a time when she was the nightly news' sex appeal, but two children and time had conspired against her. She'd be lucky to have two more years on the air. Then they'd move her to the news room, or if she was lucky, to a morning show where the audience was primarily more geriatric.

"It looks like some kind of light show might be starting before the concert."

Olivia glanced at her camera man, squinting in confusion. He pointed behind her. "Over the water."

Olivia spun around. The giant white 'sails' of the Opera House filled most of her view. Next to Uluru, it was the most recognizable site in all of Australia. The giant arching sails reminded her more of a pod of whales, rising to the surface while feeding on schools of small fish, but like most people, she thought the design was stunning.

The Opera House was surrounded by ocean harbor on three sides. From where she stood, Olivia could see the water leading inland beneath the massive steel arch of the Sydney Harbor Bridge. It was a view she'd seen on a number of occasions as the city's nightlife correspondent, but this time, it was different.

A pulsing orange light, just above the water, glided toward the Opera House. The wavering glow was beautiful. Mesmerizing. *If this is part of the show*, she thought, *I might actually be impressed.*

The orchestra began tuning up—a melodic mix of instruments, rising and falling as the musicians tightened strings and loosened lungs. The show was about to begin.

Olivia felt her attention tugged back toward the orchestra—she'd spent too much time not talking already—but the orange glow was just fifty feet from shore now, illuminating the audience with a calming radiance. *Like one of those orange salt crystals*, she thought.

The camera man was the first to question the light's beauty, primarily because he turned his lens away from Olivia and zoomed in on the light. The triangular swatch of color no longer appeared as a solid light source. It was liquid. Molten.

Alive.

"Oh bloody hell," Jim whispered, pulling the shot back to reveal a massive, black form sliding out of the night.

Chuck, who could see the shot on a monitor in the studio, reacted next. His gasp was loud enough to make Olivia wince. On camera. Then he shouted, actually shouted, in her ear. "Olivia!"

She responded by taking a deep breath and rolling her neck. She didn't want to lose her cool on television, but Chuck was—

"Olivia!" his voice was shrill this time. Full of fear.

Olivia didn't hear the tone of his voice until after she'd shouted, "Get stuffed, ya fuck-wit!"

And just like that, all of Olivia's childhood in bush country with four older brothers seeped through her defenses and ruined her career. But the strange part was, no one noticed. Not Chuck. Not Jim.

The producers would have normally cut the live feed and started chewing her out already.

When something stepped into the light of the Opera House, providing Olivia, the orchestra and the seated guests a clear view, she understood that her language and demeanor would be forgotten or later considered justified. The next word out of her mouth was all the excuse she'd ever need.

"Nemesis."

But it wasn't Nemesis.

Although she hadn't ever seen the creature in person, she had studied photos of it, just like nearly every other living soul on the planet. This...thing...shared some of the same features as Nemesis— thick and dark gray flesh, obsidian claws, bony protuberances and the orange, glowing membranes, but its body shape was all wrong. Nemesis stood three-hundred-feet tall. This creature stood no more than a hundred feet—nearly fifty of which must have been still underwater. It had no tail. None of the giant spikes on its back, nor the wing-hiding carapace. It was a smaller, sleeker model, but the look in its luminous yellow eyes was somehow worse than the brown-eyed glare of Nemesis. She didn't see vengeance in these eyes.

Only hunger.

Presented with the journalistic opportunity of a lifetime, Olivia composed herself and stepped into the picture's frame, aligning herself to the right so the monster could still be seen, rising out of the ocean, to her left.

The monster's head vaguely resembled a hunched-forward hammerhead shark, in that its eyes were set to the sides of its horizontally elongated skull. Its lower jaw dropped open, revealing long, curved teeth that looked both fragile and deadly. A thick right arm reached up out of the water and dropped down on the marble walkway, sending a shockwave through the crowd.

The impact jarred everyone from their stunned immobility, and a collective scream of horror filled the night like an orchestra of the damned, voices booming off the granite stairway.

Olivia cringed at the noise, which drowned out her voice. But she kept reporting, commenting on the scene like no one watching through the TV could decipher what was happening.

The crowd's scream, as harsh as it was, sounded like the gentle chirp of a cricket compared to the fog-horn roar that blasted from the monster's open maw. Tendrils of saliva stretched out of the thing's mouth, clinging to its teeth before losing their grip and spraying the fleeing crowd.

Warm air and the scent of rotting flesh washed over Olivia. She gagged, but maintained her composure. She faced the camera again, speaking unheard words, while the monster in the background reached into the crowd, swept its giant clawed hand to the side and lifted twenty well-dressed people into the air. Its hand gave a mighty squeeze, squelching out the few people still screaming in horror, and filling the air with the sound of snapping bones. It then scraped the victims over its lower jaw, depositing most of them into its mouth and impaling a few on its teeth. As the bodies slid down the long, smooth teeth, the creature reached out again, this time leaning forward.

Olivia knew that all hell was breaking loose behind her. She didn't bother looking, but she could hear the monster feasting on the crowd. While safety in numbers normally didn't apply, she felt the monster wouldn't pay attention to a single person standing still. At least not while the chaos of a fleeing audience held its attention. She would be hailed as the world's bravest reporter, her job secured for all eternity.

She stayed at her post, even when Jim glanced up, eyes wide, and ran away from his tripod-mounted camera. This is how she wanted the audience to remember her. Stalwart. Brave. Wrinkles be damned.

Then a two-ton, black hand slammed down atop her, smearing her into the granite, unnoticed by the monster above and quickly forgotten by the audience, as they watched the feast continue for ten more horrific minutes through the undamaged camera.

7

The view from the Crow's Nest, the FC-P headquarters, is bleak, even after a year of clean-up. Located atop the tallest hill in Beverly, Massachusetts, we're provided with a view of the surrounding city to the north, south and west. To the east is the blue ocean, as pristine as ever. But between us and the harbor is a mile of charred destruction. The far side of the harbor, in Salem, looks just as bad. The bridge between the two cities is still in ruins, but a temporary structure has been erected. The blackened remains were left in the wake of what I've come to call Nemesis's 'self-immolation.' That orange blood, or whatever it is, ignites upon contact with the air. Expose enough of it, and you've got yourself something just short of a small nuclear blast, minus the radiation.

At first, I believed the explosive fluid was some kind of defense mechanism—wound the monster in the wrong place, and you pay the price. But later on, she purposely gouged out the membranes over her chest, using the resulting explosion to punch a hole through downtown Boston. If that wasn't bad enough, her final stage, the bright white, winged goddess of vengeance, allowed her to focus sunlight into a powerful beam that incinerated Maigo's murderous father, the building I stood on and the Hancock building, which nearly fell on my head. I call that particular attack her 'divine retribution.'

Corny, I know, but I was a comic-book kid. Attacks need names. And oddly enough, the military asked for attack codenames, to more quickly communicate Nemesis's tactics in the future. Of course, other than self-immolation and divine retribution, 'smashing the living shit out of everything' covers the rest of her attacks adequately.

I've looked at this slowly changing view of the devastation for the past year, not because it's pretty, but because it reminds me that despite being part Maigo, Nemesis is also a monster. She destroyed my city. She attacked my country. She murdered thousands of innocents. And it's my job to make sure that doesn't ever happen again.

So in addition to investigating new sightings of the strange and otherworldly, my office—Cooper and Watson mostly—has been coordinating military strategies and deployments around the country, primarily on the coasts, since Nemesis can't head inland without being noticed. While the military works on developing weapons capable of piercing Nemesis's super-thick skin, we're making sure that every mile of coast is protected. There are fighter jets in most small airports now, including Beverly airport. Harbors are protected by lines of howitzers or tanks. Our country's coasts haven't been this well protected since World War II.

We're not under any delusions that we could actually stop her, though. The goal would be to simply slow her down, so people could evacuate. We've laid down wider highways leading away from all the highly populated coastal areas, built underground bunkers for those that can't get away and deployed a growing fleet of buses, helicopters and jets, whose sole purpose in life is to assist in evacuations. Someone suggested building a massive wall around the country, but that's obviously a horrible idea. And while the expense has been vast, the value of human life cannot be quantified in dollars.

"How long has he been standing there?" Rich Woodall, aka 'Woodstock,' is our fearless helicopter pilot. He's an old vet. Fought in three wars. Flew birds for the U.S. Marine Corp for twenty-five years. At first glance, he's not the kind of guy you'd want flying for you—messy gray hair and mustache, wild blue eyes and a surly personality, but he can fly like a bastard, and he's willing to get up close and personal with a 300-foot tall behemoth. He's whispering, but I can hear him just fine.

"Thirty minutes," Watson replies. He's not so good at whispering, and Woodstock shushes him even more loudly. Watson's also the last person you'd expect to find in an elite government agency. Picture Chunk from *The Goonies*, all grown up, but how you imagined him, not how he actually turned out. Watson's a good guy. The kind of friend everyone should have. And I owe him for setting me up with Collins. He's a little OCD and can't stop himself from timing people. Sometimes I stand here, just thinking about stuff, to see who will break for the bathroom first.

"Leave him alone," Cooper says from the far side of the room. Her voice is muffled by whatever book, diagram or directory she's got her nose buried in. "He's thinking."

"About what?" Woodstock asks.

I actually hear Watson shrug. He's a bit...portly, and the shrug manages to push some air from his lungs. Poor guy. If we ever had to evacuate, he'd be the snack that slowed the monster down long enough for us to escape. "Ashley said he didn't talk much on the way home. Called him a brood, which is actually an alien race in the X-Men comics, but I don't think that's what she meant."

I hear the high-heeled clack of Cooper's approach. Without seeing her, I can visualize her dark power suit, tightly tied-back raven hair and her thick-rimmed glasses. I'm dressed in my usual summer-time uniform of brown outdoorsy sneakers, cargo shorts, an orange t-shirt and my red beanie cap. My winter uniform includes the addition of a red hoodie sweatshirt. But let's be honest, sixty percent of men under forty-five in New England wear the same uniform—minus the beanie—like we're all part of some secret club that has little fashion sense and really warm legs. Or maybe we're all just lazy douche bags.

Cooper is still kind of a stick in the mud and a scrooge with regulations, but she's transformed herself over the past year. She nearly died when Nemesis self-immolated in Beverly harbor. Although we were far enough away to avoid being burned, the shockwave shattered the windows—which are now two-inch-thick tactical glass—impaling Cooper. After physical therapy, she kept the same workout schedule, and she now has a sexy librarian look about her. If only Watson could get moving, he might have a chance. The affection is there. The attraction...well, he's a grown-up Chunk. "Leave him be," she says, shooing the duo away. "You know he's—"

"Don't worry about it," I say, lifting my hand in a backwards wave. "I'm done thinking. Anyone catch the Sox game last night?" When I turn around, my team is looking at me like I've got Nemesis drool on my face. "What?"

"You haven't said a word since arriving," Cooper says.

"Allow me to translate," Woodstock says, wandering back to his station, which is basically a lounge chair when he's not flying. He kicks back and crosses his legs. "She expected you to have come to some kind of conclusion or insight while staring off into the blue."

"How poetic," Cooper says. She's not entertained, by either of us.

Watson comes through for me. "Five to three. Sox over the Yankees."

"See, that wasn't so hard. On to the—" I search the room—a 1000-square-foot space on the fourth floor of the brick mansion that serves as our home and headquarters. There are ten work stations, most of them unused, and a large, ornate staircase at the back of the space. What once was a highly organized office of mostly nothing, has become a partially organized (thanks to Cooper) mess of case files, sent to us from every conceivable law enforcement agency, local and federal, going back fifty years, long before the inception of digital storage. But there's one thing missing. "Where's Collins?"

At the mention of Collins's name, Buddy, aka Bud or Buddy-Boy, depending on who is talking to the dog, runs up to me, an excited look in his brown Australian shepherd eyes. He looks for Collins, his favorite, despite the fact that he belongs to Watson, and settles for me when he can't find her. His head appears beneath my right hand, and I dutifully pet him.

"Went to get coffee," Cooper says. "Said you hadn't slept much on the flight home."

That was an understatement. I'm not sure I slept at all. The one time I got close I was woken by a nightmare. Not of Nemesis. It was a clown riding a panda bear, chasing me through a house while smacking my back with a broken car antenna. I've had nightmares about bears since my close encounter a year before. And everyone hates clowns. Not sure about the car antenna. Maybe I'm being haunted by the ghost of Truck Betty. It's more plausible than most of the cases stacked around the office.

"Sleep is overrated," I say. "Coffee, on the other hand, is delightful." I walk to my station and sink into my office chair, staring at the black screen for a moment. "Hong Kong..."

I turn to the others and find them waiting expectantly. Even Woodstock sits up and leans forward, hands on knees.

"It wasn't Nemesis," I tell them.

"Then what was it?" Watson asks, already typing at his computer, bringing up images of the ruined Hong Kong port. "What else could have done this?"

"Not sure," I say. "Something we haven't seen."

Cooper crosses her arms. "How do you know? There weren't any witnesses."

"There was one," I say, thinking of the mysterious blonde. "Whatever struck the port glowed orange like Nemesis, but was much smaller."

"What about the prostitution ring?" Woodstock asks.

"Slave traders," Cooper says, clarifying the crime.

Woodstock nods. "Right. What 'bout them? Don't they fit Nemesis's M.O.?"

"They do," I say. "But there weren't any bodies."

"What's your point?" Cooper asks, brows furrowed.

"Nemesis stopped eating people once she was fully grown. We'd hardly make a snack for her now. So why would Nemesis raid the port, eat nearly three hundred people and then leave?"

Watson scratches his head. "She's...growing again?"

"Not her." I say.

"Oh," Watson says, pausing mid-scratch. His hand slowly falls to his lap. "Ohhh."

I nod. He's figured it out. "Whatever this thing is, it's growing, too."

A blaring sound from Cooper's station makes us all jump. After I calm myself, I recognize the klaxon for what it is. "Is that Homer Simpson screaming?"

While Cooper runs for her desk, Watson says, "I set it up for her. She likes *The Simpsons*."

First, Cooper doesn't let anyone play with her computer. Second, I didn't know she had a sense of humor. I've clearly spent too much time out of the office. "What's the alarm for?"

"Nemesis sightings," Watson says, and I feel my face pale, as the blood leaches away.

I head for Cooper. "Where?"

"Australia," she says. "Sydney. At the Opera House."

"How did it get from Hong Kong to Sydney in a day?"

No one has an answer, because its impossible.

"There's photos this time. Lots of them." She clicks away with her mouse, and the large view screen on the side wall of the room lights up, displaying several pictures of what appears to be a 100-foot-tall, part hammer-head, part gorilla creature with a familiar glowing triangle of membranes at the center of its chest.

"Could Nemesis have shrunk?" Woodstock asks.

"That's *not* Maigo," I say, letting slip my alternate name for the creature who nearly killed Cooper.

She shoots me an annoyed glance, but says nothing about it. "Then what?"

I step up to the large screen, looking at photos and watching short video clips. The monster is eating people. Devouring them whole, like a kid reaching into a bucket of Halloween candy. Ravenous. Starving. I've seen this before, when Nemesis was still pounding her way through Maine. But this...this isn't her. "I'm not sure. It's something else. Something...new."

That's when another alarm sounds, once again making us all jump. But this time, we're all looking around, trying to understand from which station the dull air-raid klaxon has come. That's when I realize it's not coming from inside the Crow's Nest. It's coming from *outside*, but it's muffled by our brick walls and armored windows.

I step over to the wall of windows and look out toward the ocean, where a vast dark shape is sliding through the water, heading straight for shore. Homer starts screaming again, beating me to the punch.

Nemesis has come back.

8

The ocean grew warmer as she rose from the depths, moving steadily toward shore, toward the life-force drawing her attention. She had lurked in the deep for a year, healing, until the tug of mankind's wrong-doing became impossible to ignore. But her strength had not fully returned. Struggling to ignore the ever present urge to lay waste to mankind, she fed on whales, giant squid, schools of fish, sharks or anything else she could find.

With her strength returned, she felt herself pulled in all directions. Evil was everywhere, calling to her, beckoning her wrath. As she swam toward a city she knew was called Rome, she felt pulled in the opposite direction, back toward the site of her birth.

Vengeance for a legacy of wrong-doing was so close, she fought against the desire to return home. But in the end, the mighty Nemesis lost the battle. She turned around, just twenty miles from the coastline of Italy. With every beat of her tail, a sense of urgency blossomed at her core, mixed with a strange new feeling she didn't understand.

She had struggled over the past year, trying to understand what she had become. Her thoughts were primal. Driven by emotion. She knew who and what she was—*Nemesis*. Her place in the world went without question, and in her absence, a darkness had consumed mankind. It was her place to purify the world. But her thoughts and feelings were muddled. Confused. There was a time when she sensed only the energy emitted by vile acts. Now, she felt so much more—sensations for which she had words: love, forgiveness, mercy—but which she did not fully understand or enjoy. If anything, she longed to unleash her wrath more than ever before.

The long ocean crossing gave her rage time to fester and build. But it also gave her time to think...something she'd rarely done before.

Her identity was called into question, dual sets of memories coming and going. Separate goals, desires and morals had been fused.

I am Nemesis, she thought, but the very idea of thinking so specifically called her identity into question. Nemesis felt. She didn't think.

As she neared the coast of her home, her emotions rose, drowning out the smaller voice tucked away inside her mind. She wasn't drawn to any particular source of wrong-doing. This time, it was a person calling to her.

Visions of destruction filled her thoughts. Of fire. Explosions. A battle with humanity. Her massive heart beat faster, surging hot blood through veins big enough for a person to swim through. Her thirst grew as the new continent's population and all their dirty secrets reached her. Beckoning retribution.

But it was the man who held her attention.

Her...target.

Why him? she wondered, and then she sneered at the wondering. Why, didn't matter.

As she slid through the familiar waters, her belly hovering just feet above the bottom, a surge of confusing emotions made her flinch. She'd felt intense pain here. Both of her halves had. The memories stung, but they were being smothered by something darker. An intense evil drowned out her small voice, sending her into the purest of rages.

Her tail beat harder against the water, kicking up billows of silt and clouding the ocean water above her. The closer she got to shore, the more intense her feelings became. But there was something else there, mixed in with the rage. She had no word for it, but it somehow intensified her anger. She hadn't felt so driven and focused since Boston, when she'd...

The images were squelched.

Her thirst for justice surged once again, powered by a second source of evil.

Something familiar.

Something confusing.

With a roar heard by every submarine monitoring the Atlantic Ocean, Nemesis rushed toward the coast, the energy and force of her body generating a wave above her. All thought vanished. All that remained was the unceasing desire for vengeance—for what, she couldn't recall or detect. But her thirst would soon be quenched.

9

In the silence that follows my discovery of the approaching shadow, I head to the white board, grab a dry erase pen and head back to the window. The shadow is moving in a straight line, its trajectory predictable.

"What are you doing?" Cooper asks. "We need to coordinate—"

"She's been spotted," I say, placing a black dot on the glass, at the front of the distant shadow. "All of our protocols are going into effect right now. What we need, is information. Why is she here? Who is she after? What's her target? The quicker we figure all that out, the sooner we can redirect her."

Several of the President's military advisors suggested that we simply offer criminals up to Nemesis, that she be allowed to exact her scorching justice. After all, it worked for me, and it saved Boston. But that was a decision made out of desperation, after thousands of people had already been killed. After pointing out that such a plan was illegal and unconstitutional, which was hard to do without incriminating myself, we opted for an alternative—find the target and move them. Far away. From there it would be a waiting game to see whether Nemesis would give chase and how far she would go.

Would she circumvent entire continents to track someone? Would she cross continents on land? Or would the distance take that person off her retribution radar? This will be our first chance to attempt answering those questions.

But avoidance can take us only so far. Eventually, we'll have to find a permanent solution to our Nemesis problem. It's not my favorite subject, but I understand the need. Maigo doesn't just threaten individuals, her compunction for leveling everything and everyone in her path makes her a threat to the entire planet.

I draw a second dot and measure the distance between them with a ruler. After a quick mental calculation, I say, "She'll reach the coast in three minutes." With the pen and ruler, I draw a straight line between the dots and step back.

The line is perfectly vertical.

"The big gal's coming for *us*," Woodstock says, voicing my thoughts with one exception.

She's coming for me.

"Cooper, Watson, implement evacuation plan alpha," I say. This removes them from the site and initiates an offsite backup of our data, which would not include the stacks of old cases still waiting to be scanned. "Get the hell out of town."

The pair springs into action, Watson moving far quicker than I would have ever thought him capable. He lands in his chair, rolls to his terminal and taps a few keys. "Backup in progress."

"I've updated the DHS," Cooper says, stepping away from her computer, keys in hand. "I'll start the car, babe."

Babe? I'm about to ask when Watson replies. "Be down in a second."

Holy shit, I think, and I look at Woodstock. He gives me a sideways grin that raises one side of his mustache. "Might need to brush up on your investigative skills, boss."

While this revelation is almost more shocking than the arrival of Nemesis, I file it away for later and say, "Get Betty warmed up."

"You think buzzing her again is a good idea?" Woodstock asks. "She's gonna swat us good, eventually."

"We don't need to get close," I say. "We need to see if she follows us."

"I'm not sure *I* follow you."

I glance at Watson. He's busy backing up a laptop that will allow him to continue his job off site. In a low voice, I say, "I think she's here for me."

Woodstock's squinting eyes tell me he's still not following.

"I'm the only one here who had any kind of direct contact with her. Maybe I shouldn't have offered Tilly up? Maybe I made it too easy? We have no idea how she thinks. But if she's coming here, it's for me. Has to be."

"And if you're right and she follows us?"

"We'll rendezvous with the Theodore Roosevelt strike group. They're stationed off the Cape." The strike group holds enough firepower to single handedly conquer most countries on the planet. In addition to the aircraft carrier, referred to as 'Big Stick' by its crew, and its ninety attack jets and helicopters, the strike group has eight destroyers, two nuclear submarines and a host of support ships. Basically, the collection of vessels and their firepower are the human equivalent of a Nemesis monster, only bigger and with a wider reach. If we bring Nemesis to them, they'll have a go at her, but I'm fairly certain conventional weapons will just make her angry.

"And from there?" Woodstock asks.

"You come home."

"And you?"

I smile at his concern. "Protocol says Siberia, if the Russians are still willing. You want to come?"

"Home sounds good," Woodstock says, heading for a side door that leads to the roof stairwell. "We can be airborne in one minute."

"I'll catch up," I say, as he charges up the stairs. When he's gone, I turn to Watson, still packing his bag. "Watson."

He glances up. "What?"

"Leave."

"But I need—"

"She's going to make landfall in the next sixty seconds. When that happens, she's only a hop, skip and a jump from our doorstep. This hill is two-hundred-feet tall. We're at the top, on the fourth floor of the hill's tallest structure. You don't want to be the filling in this brick tart if she decides to take a bite."

"You don't think..."

"I don't intend to be here when she arrives."

He nods quickly and stands, cords dangling from his bag like dreadlocks.

"Do me a favor and contact Collins. Tell her not to come home."

He hasn't stopped nodding yet. He heads for the stairs down, whistling for Buddy, who is quick to follow, while I make for the roof.

Before I reach the stairs, the air-raid siren skips a beat and then pulses three times before continuing. I recognize the protocol. I wrote it. Something has changed.

I haul myself up the stairs, but I don't run for Helicopter Betty's open door. Instead, I run beneath the wash of the chopping rotor and stand at the edge of the eastern facing roof, hands planted firmly on the short brick wall.

A mile away, ocean water parts. A face emerges.

Not Nemesis.

It's another creature, like the one in Australia, and I'm assuming Hong Kong. Unlike the Australian creature, though, this one has a pug face, squished inward, lips permanently stretched up in a sneer, revealing large triangle-shaped teeth. Its eyes are wide and frantic, brown like Nemesis's. As it hops through the shallows on all fours, moving like a short dog, I see it has the same thick black skin as Nemesis, as well as plated armor over its back, sides and limbs, mixed with rows of black spikes. As the thing emerges, it looks like some kind of canine-turtle-Nemesis hybrid.

Free of the ocean's slowing grasp, the thing reaches the shore and breaks into a colossal sprint. I stand transfixed as the monster reaches the remains of what was once an ocean-side mansion and smashes through it, black dust billowing into the air. I note an orange glow beneath its body, but don't linger long enough to discern its source. The monster is very definitely heading our way, and I don't want to be here when it arrives.

This thing might not be Nemesis, but it's at least a hundred feet long, and it'll make short work of the FC-P headquarters.

As I leap into Helicopter Betty's passenger seat and slam the door closed, I barely notice us lift off. I dig into my pocket for my phone, start the FC-P emergency app, designed by Watson, which allows me to communicate with local law enforcement, emergency response crews and every branch of the military. With the tap of a button I can speak privately with Woodstock, or with *all* response forces. Any conversation held through the application's network will be known to every branch involved in a threat response. After quickly popping on the helicopter's headset, which has been modified to work with my phone via Bluetooth, I start the conversation.

"Target is *not* Nemesis, but should be considered an equal threat." I glance out the windshield as we rise up into the air. The creature is pounding its way through the charred remains of East Beverly. "Target is in the black zone. Risk of civilian casualties is low. Engage now. Weapons free. Let's see if we can stop this thing before it reaches civilization."

"Copy that," says a voice, and my phone's screen reveals the speaker as an Air Force representative. "Helicopter support is two minutes out. The heavy hitters are three minutes out. Over."

"We're moving into position." This comes from the National Guard, who are now armed with tanks, among other things typically reserved for foreign theaters of war. "ETA, two minutes. Over."

The way the app is set up, we could all talk at once. Saying 'over' isn't really required, but it does keep everyone from talking over each other.

"Copy that," I say. "Two minutes. Don't hold anything back."

After a series of confirmations, I turn to Woodstock.

"What's the plan?" he asks.

"We need to keep it busy for two minutes," I say.

I expect him to frown at this, perhaps unleash a string of curses, but instead, he grins. "Time to see how Betty's upgrades work." He activates the chopper's new weapons system. The windshield fills with digital information, providing data about the outside world, possible targets and ammo. Although Woodstock has trained on operating Betty's weapons while flying, the best performance was while he flew and I worked the weapons.

I wrap my hand around the second joystick, which has two triggers and four red buttons that allow me to switch between armaments. Feeling very much like I'm playing a videogame, I grip the joystick and fight to suppress a smile of my own.

The helicopter pitches forward and accelerates rapidly. Woodstock's war-whoop is loud in my headset. My voice chimes in, but I'm not sure if I'm joining the cheer or just screaming. Feels like both. And maybe it is. After a year of failed cases, part of me is glad to be back in the thick of it. The rest of me is just trying hard not to crap my pants.

SCRION

10

The destruction below us is a stark reminder of Nemesis's power. The remains of charred homes look disturbingly like skeletons rising out of the earth. Where tall oaks and maples stood undisturbed since the English settled Beverly in 1626, there are now blackened, leafless limbs pushing through the soil, like giant hands, reaching for us. The homes that were more solidly built have west-facing façades that look almost normal. Some even have lawns and shrubs where the building sheltered the earth from the flames. But the east-facing sides are burned out and gutted. Nothing was spared her fury, not a single home or person who was still inside the circle of carnage. They're still picking remains out of the debris.

All of this is fresh in my thoughts as we close in on the...whatever this is. "Needs a name," I say to myself, but Woodstock can hear me.

"We could call it Fucktard," he offers, with a twitch of his mustache. He's enjoying himself entirely too much.

I looked at the shelled monster, plowing through the city's remains, still headed straight for us. "Scrion."

"The hell is a Scrion?"

I've been brushing up on my ancient mythology, hoping to turn up more information about Nemesis's origins. If we can understand where she came from, we might be able to figure out a way to stop her, or kill her. "Scrion was the son of Poseidon. A bandit."

Woodstock glances at me. "You know it's Sciron, not Scrion, right? You're not the only one who's been catching up on their Greek myths."

I frown and wave him off. "Scrion sounds better. Who's going to know?"

Woodstock shrugs, indifferent. "And this ugly prick reminds you of him, why?"

"He was eaten by a giant sea turtle."

"Makes sense, I s'pose," he says. "But I still prefer Fucktard."

So do I, I think, but the codenames I come up with will be used by local law enforcement and the military. The powers that be, and the media, not to mention the vast number of people in the world without a sense of humor, wouldn't appreciate it.

I lift my phone, which is actually more of a hand-held super-computer that looks like a phone. We call it 'Devine,' which sounds like a transgender stripper, but is really just a cute way of saying DVIN (Digital Vanguard Intelligence Network). Granted, that's the name of the network and not the phone itself, but we got a kick out of effeminately saying, "That's just Devine," when calls came in. It does everything modern smartphones are capable of, just a lot better, much faster and with a few bonus options the public will never see on their devices, like the ability to pilot a drone or paint an airstrike target.

I switch the communication app so everyone can hear me. "Attention all response units, target Kaiju designation is now Scrion. Images are incoming."

Yeah, *Kaiju*. The word that came to define the giant monster genre that includes city-stompers like Godzilla and Gamera has become our official term for any creature that is...well, not natural, with the under-standing that it be reserved for things capable of mass destruction. A snail with tentacles wouldn't qualify—unless it was ten stories tall. Scrion? It's a Kaiju for sure.

I aim the camera's 75-megapixel camera through the front wind-shield and snap a photo, which is instantly sent to everyone with access to Devine. I switch the phone back to its private mode so not everyone can hear me talking to Woodstock. "Take us around. I want to get this thing from every angle."

We bank left, low to the ground, the g-forces pushing me into the side window, allowing me to keep an eye on Scrion. It's still moving forward, but tracking us with his round eyes and squished-up face. When its head can't turn any further, the body follows.

My eyes widen.

It's following us.

It *is* after me!

"Faster," I say.

"Faster, why?" Woodstock asks and then banks the chopper the other way, intending to circumvent the monster. He understands when we level out and he's still looking at Scrion head on, through the side window. "Shee-it. The son-of-a-bitch is chasin' us!"

Betty's front end dips forward as Woodstock pours on the speed, but Scrion is fast.

Very fast.

Its wild eyes look frenzied, like it's lost in some kind of drug-induced craze. Its jaw drops open. This thing is no Nemesis, but it could still make a quick snack out of us.

"Hard left on my mark!" I shout. Woodstock could hear me through the headset if I whispered, but the volume of my voice does a good job of communicating my urgency. "Then head for the ceiling."

I crane my head back, face squashed against the window. The monster leaps, shoving off the ground with its powerful hind legs. As it lifts into the air, I get a look at its armored underside, which is covered in dark gray plates, split horizontally by three stripes of bright orange membranes.

"Now!"

Betty cants hard to the left. I couldn't pull myself away from the window if I tried, and given the proximity of Scrion's closing jaws, I would really, *really* like to lean back. But then I'm seeing blue sky above. The sound of a thunderous impact reaches my ears. It's followed by a jolt of turbulence. Scrion is back on the ground, no doubt once again giving chase.

A curse from Woodstock reaches my ears. I'm about to ask what the problem is, when I see for myself. The streets in the ruined part of town have all been cleared of debris. Only a few of them are open to the public, to ease traffic in other parts of town. Travel through the rest of the ruins is restricted, because the streets are rife with sink holes and every structure is ready to collapse. It's not a safe place to be. And yet, the Kaiju fanatics and sightseers can't seem to keep themselves away.

Like the people below us. They're driving some kind of small boxy car, and the driver is doing an okay job avoiding the potholes, but they're not moving nearly fast enough. I can see the people inside moving back and forth quickly. They can see the monster coming. I wonder if they're still having fun? Probably. Kaiju nerds are like that. They'd probably die with smiles on their faces. But it's my job to keep that from happening.

"We can't be sure Scrion will follow us if we turn away," I say to Woodstock.

"What's the plan?"

I look ahead. The road below heads straight toward the ocean before banking to the left and running straight out to Beverly Farms, which wasn't affected by Nemesis's self-immolation.

I nod at the joystick in my hand. "We'll run interference. Head out to sea. Hope it follows."

"If it doesn't?"

"The cavalry shouldn't be too far behind."

His only response is to quickly spin the chopper around, while still moving in the same direction, so that we're flying backwards. He performs the maneuver expertly, but it's still disorienting. My head spins for a moment, but it's quickly cleared by a surge of adrenaline brought on by Woodstock's voice.

"Holy hell!"

I catch a glimpse of what's coming. Black teeth. The mottled roof of a massive mouth. Two, beach-ball sized brown eyes with big black pupils, reflecting the red hull of Betty and my own dopy looking surprised face.

The image is erased by a stream of orange tracers. It looks like a laser beam, but the stream of hot rounds is meant to show me where the rest of my unseen bullets are traveling. In this case, they're headed right where I want them to—down Scrion's throat.

The bulldog-like Kaiju snaps its jaws closed, just missing the chopper and absorbing the rest of my chain-gun rounds with its thick skin, which like Nemesis's, seems fairly impervious to conventional ammunition.

When Scrion doesn't fall away, I realize how close to the deck we are. Just thirty feet off the ground. If not for the swath of destruction around us, we'd be plowing through trees and power lines. I hit the second button on my joystick, switching from the chain gun to one of our two rocket pods, which carry a payload of thirty-eight Hydra 70 unguided rockets, meaning you have to be up close and personal to make them effective. Which isn't going to be a problem.

Scrion lets out a bellow. It's a deep resounding warble that shakes my insides and the helicopter. I definitely hurt the monster, but I'm pretty sure I mostly just made it angry. In fact, I think it's thundering after us even faster than before.

I toggle my phone to transmit via Devine. "All forces, ETA? We have civilians in the danger zone."

"Hawk-One. ETA, thirty seconds," the chopper team leader replies. "We can see you now."

I came up with the code names. They're not very creative, but they're easy to remember, and each mobile combat unit has its own animal kingdom designation. Me? I'm still just Hudson, but if they're directing their comment to the chopper, it's Betty. For real. They hate it, but it makes me and Woodstock smile.

"Eagle-eye One. We're forty-five seconds out," says the lead fighter pilot, his voice distorted by the roar of his plane.

"Hawk-One, once the car is clear, hit Scrion with everything you have. Eagle-eye, follow up with everything you got. Let's see if we can turn this thing around." I'd like to say, 'Let's see if we can kill this bastard,' but I don't want to get anyone's hopes up.

"Understood, sir."

"Copy that."

It's nice to be listened to. Our first time around responding to the Nemesis crisis, there were a lot of toes being stepped on and even more wrong calls made. Granted, until you see it with your own eyes, a giant monster is hard to take seriously. And no one really understood it. I'm not sure anyone really does now. But we're organized, at least. Whether that matters has yet to be seen.

I change modes on Devine so my conversation with Woodstock won't be filling up the network. "Can you take us lower?"

"And you think *I'm* the crazy one." Woodstock shakes his head. "Hold on."

We slowly descend. The car is somewhere below us. Since we don't land atop its roof and I can't see it, I'm assuming they're ahead of us.

"Betty, stop!" It's Hawk-One's voice, and if he didn't sound so worried, I would laugh at the ridiculousness of his statement. Even though I'm not currently transmitting, I can still receive transmissions directed to me. "You're tail is just a few feet above the civvies. Looks like you're going to reach a turn in about fifteen seconds."

"Copy that," I say. Woodstock has heard them, too. Our descent stops short of the street and the fleeing car, which turns a sharp left and peels away, quickly accelerating like a miniature Millennium Falcon.

"You got something spiffy in mind?" Woodstock asks. "Cause now's the time."

"Ever set off a cherry bomb under a bucket?"

"A cherry bomb under a—wait, what in all shit are you...?"

I don't hear the rest of his protest. I'm focused on Scrion. Every loping leap forward not only brings the Kaiju closer to us, but it also exposes the giant's underside and the three volatile orange membranes. I normally wouldn't consider such a move, but seeing as how the membranes are much smaller than Nemesis's, the surrounding area has already been obliterated and all the force will be transmitted straight down into the ground, I don't see the harm.

Scrion hits the ground on the downside of a leap forward, bringing its bulky mass to within fifty feet. Two more of those strides, and it will have us.

It's only going to get one more.

Scrion's muscles bulge beneath its mat of rubber-like flesh, and the body comes up again. At the first sign of orange light, I pull the trigger.

11

Pitiful, he thought, observing how predictable his enemy was. Since the events in Boston, Fusion Center-P had become one of the most prominent divisions of the Department of Homeland Security, with access to all levels of government and military. And yet, their headquarters remained entirely undefended. They believed the threats they faced came in the form of giants, easily spotted from a distance.

They were wrong.

General Lance Gordon hunched down between a stand of bushes and a lush rhododendron. The space between the plants had been hollowed out. The remains of a plastic bucket and rotting popsicle sticks littered the dirt. A childhood hideout, long forgotten.

The space was barely big enough to contain Gordon's new body. He had grown taller, standing nearly eight feet in height. His bulk had nearly doubled. Thick muscles pushed against his thick skin, which negated the damage from both bullets and impacts. In Boston, he'd survived a thirty-story fall.

But he had been wounded.

Gordon had watched from the ground as Jon Hudson offered Alexander Tilly up to Nemesis. That had been *his* place. *His* mission. Before Maigo became Nemesis, Gordon had received a heart transplant from the girl. In essence, he had Nemesis's heart beating in his chest. While it didn't grow to Nemesis's size, it *did* change him. In addition to the physical changes, Gordon had become connected to Nemesis, feeling her desires. Her rage. Her targets. And he set out to help her. But when Hudson offered Tilly up, that connection had been broken. It left Gordon feeling directionless and confused.

He fled west and north, back to where the original Kaiju carcass had been discovered. Lost and alone, he wandered the wilderness, feeding on whatever animal crossed his path: mouse, elk, even Grizzly bears. They were all easy prey. But his sense of purpose never returned...until he felt the connection return. But not to Nemesis. To the others. To the unborn children.

The kids.

He had gone back to Alaska and found the eggs, still whole, buried in the back of the cave their mother had died in. He suspected that when Nemesis-Prime had died so long ago, the site had been buried by a landslide, and that the eggs had gone into some kind of hibernation. When he removed them from the cave and the light of day struck their shells, the young had quickly emerged.

He wasn't really sure how it worked, but he believed the original creature they'd found in Alaska, what Zoomb now called *Nemesis-Prime*, was like many species of plants and animals. It only reproduced when death was near, helping to ensure the survival of the species. Under natural circumstances, the five young might have fought amongst each other until the last one remaining took up its mother's mantle as judge, jury and executioner. But under Gordon's direction—with his genetic duplicate of their mother's heart, albeit human sized—all five had survived. They'd been connected to him since, but rather than him following their desires, they followed his.

And right now, that was vengeance. Against Jon Hudson. And against Nemesis for turning away from him.

His dark skin kept him concealed in the shadows, as he watched the woman in the car. She looked to be waiting for someone. A moment later, a red helicopter lifted away from the roof and headed toward his child.

His distraction.

He couldn't see who was inside the chopper, but he had little doubt Jon Hudson would be one of them. Hudson would either die in that chopper or upon his return. Either way, he was going to die. Like all people, Hudson was frail, but his real weakness was the people he cared about.

When the helicopter disappeared from view, Gordon slipped from the brush and moved for the car. His instincts told him to charge forward, to roar and beat his fists. But he still had the mind of a military man. Stealth was the superior tactic. Even for a monster. An enemy taken by surprise is an enemy defeated.

The black-haired woman didn't detect his approach until he was two steps away. Before she could scream, he'd punched through the driver's side window of the small car with his sledgehammer fist, taken hold of the door and yanked it off. She fought to escape, but the seatbelt already around her chest held her in place. He took hold of the belt with both hands and tugged. It came apart like old yarn.

She fought against him, kicking and screaming, but when his large, thick-fingered hand compressed her forearm, the fight went out of her. Just a little more pressure and the bones would break. Gordon lifted the woman from the car and turned toward the large brick building's side entrance, just as a pudgy man with curly brown hair exited. A dog jumped out after him, but took just one look at him and bolted.

The man jiggled as he stopped in his tracks. A ridiculous man.

Gordon lifted the woman by her arm, her toes dangling a foot above the gravel driveway. "Back inside." His voice was deep and rumbling, unrecognizable to anyone who'd known him before—

"General Gordon..." the man whispered.

—except, apparently, this man.

"Inside, now," Gordon said. "Or I'll remove her arm."

The man nodded and turned to the door. He struggled to get through it thanks to his bulk, nervousness and the several bags he carried. Gordon watched the man through squinted eyes, wondering how such a person could work for any government agency, and how he would taste. Nothing sated a hunger like fat.

Later, he told himself. He needed them alive until Hudson returned, or died in battle.

After squeezing through the door, Gordon let go of the woman's arm. Pudgy wasn't going anywhere fast, and the way the woman ran into his arms meant she wasn't going anywhere without him.

"Upstairs," he said. He knew they operated out of the fourth story, which would also provide a view of the battle below. He took the stairs four at a time, the old wood creaking, but not breaking beneath his sizable mass. "Solid construction." He spoke the words like he was considering buying the place. Really, he just liked seeing the pair squirm when he spoke. *So frail.*

The top of the fourth flight of steps opened up into a large space with enough computer terminals for a decent-sized intelligence team. "You're the only ones here?" Despite Gordon's gruff voice, he couldn't hide his surprise. He'd seen only one person come and go that morning, but he had assumed a large crew was working inside.

"Just the two of us," the woman said. "Everyone else is evacuating."

"The woman," Gordon said. "The redhead."

The fat man nodded.

"There are only *five* of you here?" He didn't wait for an answer. He just chuckled like Jabba the Hut. This was going to be so easy, it was almost disappointing.

"Hey!" the shout was so loud and forceful that Gordon nearly jumped. Instead he turned toward the voice. The redhead had returned. She was a tall woman. Curvy too. Dressed in tight jeans and a not quite too tight blouse. Gordon glanced at her feet. Boots. Real shitkickers. This woman was a looker, but she was more than that. She held a large revolver in two hands. Probably held .50 caliber rounds. A good weapon. And it was aimed between his eyes. Gordon liked this one. Too bad he had to kill her.

"Ashley," the fat man said. "You weren't supposed to—"

The thunderous crack of the gun firing drowned out the man's voice. The bullet covered the distance between the gun and Gordon's head before the sound reached their ears. The impact knocked him back, throwing him into the room's back wall, which cracked from the strain.

Gordon's head lolled forward.

The bullet fell away, clattering to the floor.

"Get out of here!" the woman named Ashley shouted.

Gordon raised his head, glowering at the woman with his yellow eyes. A sneer formed on his lips. "I like a woman who can fight."

He shoved himself away from the wall and charged across the room.

The gun fired six more times before he reached her. He felt the impacts as little more than punches from an old lady. He reached for the woman, not intending to kill her. The other two were no doubt already running, so he'd need this one alive.

Before his hand reached her face, she ducked down and tightened into a ball. Gordon's foot struck her, eliciting a cry of pain, but he hadn't kicked her, he'd simply tripped over her. He sprawled forward, off balance, headed for the large windows.

He glanced through the glass and caught sight of the battle outside. Hudson was still on the run. Still hopelessly outmatched. But then five Apache attack helicopters roared past overhead. They would only aggravate his child. The fools hadn't learned anything.

Gordon's eyes returned to the glass. Like all good soldiers, he thought several steps ahead. He knew he was going to break through the window and fall four stories. But he also knew he'd survive the fall, recover quickly and have no problem cutting off the three fleeing FC-P agents. The first thing he'd do was rip the fat man's spine out. That would take the fight out of the other two.

His face struck the glass first.

It didn't break.

Instead, his flesh folded inwards, compressing the thick bones of his face. As momentum carried the rest of his body forward, the pressure on his face grew. Something popped and then crunched, and for the first time in a year, Gordon felt pain.

He put his hand up to his nose. The flesh felt looser. Warm fluid covered his fingertips. He couldn't make out the color against his charcoal flesh. But he knew what it was. Blood. The bitch had actually hurt him.

He thrashed out an arm, obliterating a workstation with one strike. He turned toward the woman, who he expected to find on the floor, clutching her side in pain. She was gone. As were the other two. His plan was falling apart.

"No!" he screamed and charged toward the stairwell. When he reached the top, he leapt out over the stairs, compressed his body into a ball and struck the wall. Unlike the windows, this part of the house had not been reinforced. He broke through wood and plaster like a wrecking ball.

His fall was broken by the crunch of a car roof folding in. His body struck hard, face down. The car compressed loudly, and then all at once, it exploded into flames. The searing heat surprised Gordon, but it didn't harm him. When he stood in the flames and stepped through the curtain of smoke, he was very glad to see three sets of stunned eyes staring at him.

Ignoring the flames flickering over his chest, Gordon grinned and said. "Let's try that again."

12

I hold my finger down, launching all thirty-eight rockets. It might be a little excessive, but the rockets aren't smart. They can't lock on to targets. They just fly straight until they hit something and explode. And sometimes they don't even fly straight. Considering the amount of firepower I've just launched, the rockets don't make much noise. They just kind of whoosh away, swirling trails of smoke. There's so many of them twisting through the air, the sight reminds me of those *Robotech* cartoons I used to watch when I was a kid...and a few years ago. The twisting streaks of white are almost beautiful.

"Holy shit," the whispered curse comes through my headset. One of the helicopter pilots commenting on what I've just done, which serves to remind *me* about what I've just done.

"Where is the car?" I ask, shouting into my headset.

"They're away!" someone replies.

"Up!" I shout to Woodstock, even as he pulls us higher into the air and to the side. It's like a backwards rollercoaster ride, but I hardly notice. All of my attention is on the now-small streaks of white, headed for Scrion's underside.

The Kaiju has just leapt up, exposing the three orange membranes.

The first rocket strikes with an orange explosion that sounds like a distant firework. But nothing happens. The rocket struck high, between Scrion's neck and armor planting. I don't think it even noticed the impact.

But it's sure as hell going to. It's easy to see now, as Scrion rises and the rockets continue to strike—

It happens.

A rocket punches through the top membrane and detonates. But even as that explosion begins, at least eight more rockets pierce the other two slices of orange flesh. I don't even have time to cringe at what I've done.

The way people experience explosions is basically a race. The light, traveling at 186,282 miles per second, comes first. The bright white forces my eyes shut for a moment before it fades to luminous shades of yellow and orange. Next, comes the shockwave, which contrary to popular belief, travels faster than sound. The science of it is gobbledygook to me. Something about the compression of wave fronts or some such thing. What's important to know is that you're going to get punched first and then yelled at.

And the punch is hard. Kaiju Mike Tyson hard. The helicopter is slammed back, and for a moment I'm looking through the windshield at nothing but blue sky. Warning lights flash. Woodstock utters a string of unintelligible curses like it's the Pentecost. Before all the shaking is done, the sound hits. If not for the sound-canceling headphones on our ears, I'm positive Woodstock and I would be deaf. The pulse of sound knocks the air from my lungs and pitches me forward as my insides quiver. Woodstock somehow manages to fight this effect and not only keeps his hands on the controls, but regains control of Betty. He brings us level again, about a mile from the explosion—over the harbor—but just a couple hundred feet up.

Not that I'm concerned about height. I don't think Scrion would be able to reach us at this height while swimming. And then there is the fact that the monster is gone.

Totally.

A crater the size of a football stadium is all that remains.

"Did you vaporize the dang thing?" Woodstock asks, leaning forward in his seat like the extra foot of nearness will help him see more. "Ain't nothin' left!"

I have a hard time believing it. Whenever one of Nemesis's membranes were punctured, the resulting explosion would lay waste to the surrounding area, but it would also cauterize the wound, healing her. But Scrion appears to have been obliterated.

Then I remember my analogy. *A cherry bomb beneath a trash can.* The energy, directed down toward the Earth, would reflect back and slam into Scrion. While it might not scorch the monster, it would no doubt propel it...upwards.

I lean forward as far as I can, searching the blue sky for an aberration. I toggle Devine. "Any eyes on the target?"

"No, sir," says the lead Apache pilot. "It's g—"

"Eagle-Eye Three," calls out a pilot. "I have eyes on target."

"Where?" I ask.

"About five thousand feet."

I can't help but smile. Woodstock actually lets out a chuckle.

"Forty-five hundred," adds the pilot.

The new information wipes the shit eating grin from my face. It's coming down fast, though I still can't see it.

"Is the target alive?" I ask.

"And pissed," the pilot says. "Target is above the water. Are we clear to engage?"

"Engage!" I shout. "Engage!"

Looking through a pair of binoculars, I see the planes—three F-22 Raptors, just small triangles in the sky high above—the moment they let loose a barrage of missiles. And these aren't like the rockets I shot off. Not only are the AIM-7 Sparrow missiles guided and guaranteed to hit a target without countermeasures, they're real heavy hitters. And they should be since each missile costs more than my yearly take-home pay. Six years of working for the DHS and my collective taxes aren't enough to pay for just one of those missiles. So when the first missile strikes, the explosion is satisfyingly large, though still dwarfed by the conflagration I caused on the ground. But it's joined by another, and another. The string of orange flame allows me to track Scrion's descent.

It's headed for the harbor, behind us. Woodstock swings us around slowly so we can follow its fall.

"Gonna make one hell of a splash," Woodstock says.

I barely hear him. I'm too busy trying to control the missiles through sheer willpower. If one of them can sneak inside those now open membranes, there's a small chance we might actually kill the monster. If not, I have little doubt it will survive the fall and swim away—if not press the attack once more. If that happened, there would be little we could do about it. The only silver lining is that the evacuation is well underway.

Of course, it's not interested in wreaking havoc. It's after me. "If Scrion survives, and still has eyes for me, we need to lead it away."

"Right," Woodstock says with a nod. "The aircraft carrier."

The ninth and final missile detonation fills the sky with an orange plume of light. Man-made thunder rolls past. Scrion descends. I find it in the sky, now just fifteen hundred feet up. I have trouble tracking the beast at first, until I bring the lenses into focus. It's like a giant flying turtle-dog, which is just ridiculous. When I see its flailing limbs splayed wide, Scrion looks borderline silly. But it's not really funny, because it's still alive, even after a severe beating. But is it hurt? I shift my view to the side, finding its head.

The still crazed eyes are staring straight back at me like some obsessed ex-girlfriend who doesn't know when to stop wearing a guy's jersey, or whatever it is women do these days. "Shit!" I pull the binoculars from my eyes.

"Aircraft carrier?" Woodstock asks.

"Hell ye—"

A mash of voices fills my ears. Shouting. I can't make out a word of it, but the tone is unmistakable. Shock. Panic. Urgency. Somewhere in the mix, I hear the words "Behind Betty."

As the words register, a dark shadow falls over us, like a cloud has just blocked the sun. Some days just start out shitty. Like today. No coffee. Then Scrion. And now... I don't even need to look. The blocked sun and the fear in the voices of military professionals tells me everything I need to know.

It's like the cliché moment in a TV show or movie, when Jack (or whoever) is bitching about Steve, who just happens to be standing behind him. He stops and say, "He's behind me, isn't he?"

That's where my mind is as I come to grips with what I suspect will be my last few seconds on the planet.

She's behind me, isn't she?

But it's not a grumpy boss or an over-emotional wife.

It's Nemesis.

And this time, it's for real.

Woodstock must be having the same realization I am, because he acts without being told what to do. Our slow spin becomes rapid as we snap around.

Fifty feet from Betty's windshield are Nemesis's brown eyes. Like with Scrion, her massive brown eyes seem to be locked on me. *It's the helicopter*, I think. *She must remember the helicopter.* We should have painted Betty blue instead of matching her truck's namesake.

But I see no anger in those eyes. Instead, I see...

"Maigo."

The name comes from my lips as a whisper, though Woodstock can hear me.

Water pours from her head as she rises from the ocean. Her jaws open wide, revealing sharp white teeth bigger than me. Her skin, gleaming white the last time I saw her, is thick and gray once more. She's whole again.

She rises in time with the chopper, her head—*her jaws*—remaining level with us as we ascend. *She's taller*, I think, glancing at our altimeter as we pass three hundred feet. While we haven't flown above her yet, we are moving back. As the distance increases, more of her massive body comes into view. The orange membranes lining the sides of her neck glow bright orange, reminding us of her deadly potential. The thick folds of skin on her neck shift and stretch, as she lifts her gaze away from the helicopter.

"What the hell is she doin'?" Woodstock asks.

I'm pretty sure he wasn't expecting an answer, but I have one. "Playing fetch." I toggle Devine. "All units, hold your fire. I repeat, hold your fire!" I ignore the litany of doubt-filled complaints that enter my ears, but when no missiles streak past, I know my orders have been followed. They'll understand it in 3...

Nemesis's height tops out at three-hundred-fifty feet. Her giant arms rise up, trailing waterfalls. A shredded fishing net clings to the sharp spikes on her left elbow. Clumps of seaweed slip from her chest and fall away. The pulse of her orange membranes is bright. The explosive liquid within swirls, as though eager to get out.

2...

Her long tail snaps up, twisting back and forth like an agitated cat—if cat's tails had a trident of spikes the size of 747 wings. I note that the color of her claws and spikes has changed from black to beige. The armor plating on her shoulders looks thicker. She's ready for battle, radiating power. I catch just a glimpse of her back as we twist away. The massive spikes have moved back to the middle, the thick armored carapace once again protecting delicate reflective wings capable of great destruction.

And then it happens.

1...

13

Former small-town sheriff turned FC-P special agent, Ashley Collins struggled against her fight-or-flight instinct, which was cheering wholeheartedly for her to make like a freshly baked gingerbread man and run. But she couldn't. Not while Cooper and Watson were still in harm's way.

"Get out of here," she told them, but the pair stood their ground.

"We're not leaving you, Ash," Watson said, his voice quivering. The man was fighting his fear, just like Collins. She appreciated his loyalty, but if they all stayed, they all died. If they ran, she might be able to slow him down long enough for them to get away. This was a fight they couldn't win, so a strategic retreat was not only their best option, it was also their only option.

Gordon, still smoldering, grinned, his sharp teeth gleaming white. A low, rumbling chuckle rolled from deep inside him. He was enjoying this little drama, taking pleasure in it. He knew the eventual outcome as well as Collins did.

"Leave, dammit!" she shouted, trying to reload her revolver. She used speed-loaders, which allowed her to reload all six rounds at once, but it was still hard to do with shaking hands. "Now!"

When they still didn't budge, she tried logic. "You're not field agents. This isn't your job."

Before they could respond, Gordon started toward them, hands open, ready to grab and crush.

As the trio backed away, Collins said, "How about we at least don't make it easy on him then. Scatter!" As she shouted, Collins twisted the back of the speed-loader off, snapped the cylinder back in place, took aim and squeezed off a single shot.

Gordon's head jolted back, halting his approach, only for a moment, but long enough for Watson and Cooper to head in opposite directions. Watson disappeared around the side of the large brick house. Cooper ran back inside.

Now facing Gordon on her own, Collins didn't like her plan.

"And here I thought they were going to stay with you until the end." He started toward her again. "Cowards."

She pulled the trigger again, the noise of the gunshot rolling over the hillside. Gordon flinched as the round struck his cheek and bounced away. "Aiming for my eyes," he said. He stopped, opened one eye widely, propping it open further with his thick finger. "There. Go ahead. See if it helps."

Shit, she thought, *Gordon would never expose himself to injury so willingly, unless it really didn't matter.* She fired anyway, hoping it would at least cause him some pain.

It did.

He howled as his head rocketed back. One of his armored hands clutched the wounded eye. When his head came back down, his remaining horrible eye glared at Collins. But he was still smiling. He took his hand away from his face. White, fluid gore oozed from his punctured eye. It was followed by something black and viscous. When it hit the ground, it made a ticking sound—metal on pavement. The bullet. When she looked back up, Gordon's ruined eye was whole once again. And he was charging straight for her.

Collins fired her remaining bullets, none of them effective. She lunged to the side, hoping Gordon's momentum would carry him into the brick wall at her back, but his reach was too wide. He caught her around the waist, clutching her with one hand. Her feet scraped against the pavement as she was pushed back. The scraping stopped when she was lifted up and slammed against the brick wall.

The air in her lungs coughed out. Her head struck the red brick, leaving a darker red stain. Her vision blacked for a moment before returning with spinning points of light. *He could kill me,* she thought, *so easily. Why is he holding back?*

Gordon leaned in close, his jaw dropping open. Impossibly wide. Sharp teeth just inches from her skin. The smell of rotting fish, carried by his warm breath, flowed over her.

Before his mouth reached her, a brick slammed into the side of Gordon's head. The only effect it had was to gain his attention.

Watson stood twenty feet away, a brick clutched in each hand. "Leave her alone!"

Gordon released his grip on Collins. She slid down to the pavement, leaning against the wall. Somewhere deep in her mind, she shouted at her body to move, but there was a disconnect. Watson was on his own, armed only with bricks.

His patience gone, Gordon stomped toward Watson with deadly intent. Watson lobbed the bricks. One bounced off Gordon's armor-plated shoulder. The next missed entirely.

Watson put his hands up in a defensive posture. Gordon raised his fists. He wasn't holding back this time. As the fists came down, a loud boom filled the air. Gordon stumbled to the side as Cooper, holding a shotgun, ran to Watson's side.

As Gordon recovered, Cooper pumped the shotgun and fired again. Gordon absorbed the shot, but took a step back. Cooper fired again, and again.

Collins tried to stand. Cooper would be out of ammunition in two more pulls of the trigger.

Boom.

One more.

Collins fought her shaking legs. She lifted herself a foot off the ground, but began sliding back down.

A hand caught her, holding her weight.

She looked up into the eyes of Katsu Endo.

The thunderous roar of Cooper's shotgun filled the air once more. Not knowing the weapon held only six shells, the woman gave it another pump, raised the weapon and pulled the trigger.

The explosion that followed was unlike anything Collins had heard before. Light blossomed all around them. Trees cracked, as a mighty wind blew past. They were protected by the brick house, but she could feel the heat. The sound that followed shook her insides and sent her head spinning anew. She knew the explosion had come from the distant battle with the Kaiju, but she watched as Gordon reacted as though he'd been shot.

He fell to the side, stumbling until his head collided with the burning car. He dropped to the driveway, clutching his chest. But the effect was short lived. His eyes snapped open and turned skyward. She couldn't see what he was looking at, but he wasn't pleased.

As Gordon got back to his feet, Collins looked for Endo, but the man was gone. "What the...?" Had she hallucinated him? Was he a side-effect of a concussion?

Doesn't matter, she decided. He was gone. And Gordon wasn't. She dug into her pocket, searching for her last speed loader. As her fingers slid over the bullets, her mind cleared, and she realized she no longer held her gun. With blurred vision, she searched until movement caught her eye.

Gordon stood, one hand resting on the smoldering car. Whatever that explosion was, it had hurt him somehow. A series of nine more explosions reached her ears, though none compared to the first. But with each distant concussion, Gordon twitched.

It's the Kaiju. He's feeling what it feels.

The information, while interesting and pertinent, did nothing to help her current situation, and it would likely die with her.

A grinding sound turned her eyes to the driveway. Her revolver slid across the pavement and stopped against her boot. *The hell?* She bent, snatched up the weapon and nearly passed out. Fighting the wave of darkness that filled her vision, she leaned against the wall, fumbling with the speed loader.

When her vision cleared, Gordon was lumbering for Cooper, all of the anger still in his face, but some of the energy missing from his movements. Watson joined Cooper, standing guard, the pair now inseparable.

Run, Collins thought. *Run, you idiots.*

A blur of motion kept her from expressing her thoughts. A black-clad man leapt from the hood of the burning car, landing on Gordon's back. *Endo.* In the flesh. The man drove both hands to the sides of Gordon's head. The *snap, snap, snap,* of an electric taser joined the sound of Gordon's pain-filled scream. The whir of a drill came next. Collins squinted, trying to see better. Was Endo drilling a hole in the side of Gordon's head?

If he was, he never got to finish. Gordon reached up, caught hold of Endo's clothing and hauled him off, throwing him twenty feet through the air. Endo landed on the estate's green grass, rolling back to his feet like the whole move had been choreographed.

Gordon's hand went to the side of his head, feeling the freshly drilled hole. He seemed as confused by it as Collins was. Fearlessly, Endo charged Gordon, shouting at Collins. "Keep him busy!"

She was about to ask how, when she noticed she had finished loading her revolver. The idea of working with Endo, a killer they couldn't convict, irked her. The man had an ulterior motive for being there. Collins had no doubt about that. But Watson's and Cooper's lives were at risk. She would take any help she could get.

Walking unsteadily, Collins raised her gun and fired. The shot missed, and she nearly dropped the high caliber weapon, but each step forward increased the blood flow to her head, clearing her thoughts and her vision. Gripping the weapon with two hands, she adjusted her aim and fired again, striking Gordon in the side of the head, which whipped toward her in response.

Distraction achieved.

Endo leapt into the air, moving fast. He extended a leg and delivered a brutal kick with his heel, just as Gordon faced him again. The big man's already squashed nose bent further inward with a crunch, but nothing more happened. Endo simply bounced off and fell to the ground. Gordon roared—really roared—and swept downward with both arms.

Endo was too quick. He dove forward and rolled between Gordon's legs. Then he was up and leaping onto Gordon's back again. There was no zap of a taser this time, but he thrust a small drill against the side of Gordon's head again.

Gordon thrashed about, but Endo held on, grunting as he shoved the drill deeper.

Then things changed.

Gordon grew weak. He yelped in pain. Shrunk in on himself. Fell to his knees and pitched forward, gritting his teeth against some unseen pain. Endo never let up. He kept pushing that strange drill into the side of Gordon's head. And then it happened.

Gordon shot up and let loose a violent, wailing scream. The suddenness and force of this movement knocked Endo loose. The pain and anguish expressed by Gordon's scream sent goose-bumps up Collins's arms. She almost felt bad for him. But not quite bad enough. She took aim, tightened her grip and—

Gordon leapt to his feet, barked at Collins, and part ran, part stumbled away.

Whatever sent him running, Collins didn't think he'd be coming back. Which left just one problem remaining. She hobbled over to Katsu Endo, who was still lying on the pavement. She reached out a hand. When he took it, she hefted him up, and then cracked him in the side of his head with the butt of her gun. Public enemy number two had gotten away, but number three wasn't going anywhere.

14

Jaws wide, head turned to the sky above, Nemesis jumps up and catches Scrion in her mouth like a dog playing Frisbee. The smaller Kaiju kicks and flails, wiggling its helpless head back and forth. I can't hear it, but I envision a kind of mewling cry coming from its wide-open mouth. I watch, unable to think or care about anything else, as Scrion's body compresses. I half expect the thing to just burst in half, but Nemesis goes full-on dog again, shaking her head back and forth.

Seawater sprays with each shake. Scrion's extended limbs are now jutting straight out, locked in panic. Then the water turns tan, then brown, and I realize it's no longer water at all.

It's blood.

Scrion's blood.

Unlike Nemesis, who bleeds red, this thing bleeds brown, which is both gross and fitting.

"Whoa," Woodstock says, pulling us further back as Scrion is suddenly spinning through the air, spraying circles of blood. Nemesis has flung the smaller creature.

Scrion lands on the blackened shore, tumbling through a ruined neighborhood. When it comes to a stop and regains its footing, I expect it to do what any other creature in its situation would do: run like hell. And yeah, it runs, but in the wrong direction. After a long arcing sprint to build up speed, Scrion turns straight for Nemesis, charging the monster that's nearly four times its size, the crazed look back in its eyes. When it reaches the shoreline, it leaps, soaring up and over the water.

Nemesis doesn't react. She simply stands her ground, waiting.

The giants collide, but for Scrion, it's like hitting a wall. The smaller Kaiju would have bounced off if it hadn't bitten down hard on Nemesis's chest, just missing one of those deadly orange membranes. The creature is fearless and savage, but clearly not very intelligent. It reminds me of a bully from second grade. Ricky Denali. *Rick the dick.* He was a runt, but made up for his stature through savagery. He terrorized kids twice his size, because of his in-your-face violent nature, his sharp tongue and the quickness with which he shifted between the two. That all changed when he decided to try the same tactic on Larry Studebaker, the new kid. Although Larry was a kind guy, he was also three times Ricky's size, and he could take only so much abuse before he struck back. And when he did...man, one punch. A glancing blow. Didn't take much.

One punch. *C'mon...*

When it happens, it's not so much a punch as a bitch-slap. Reaching up one of her mammoth, clawed hands, Nemesis swipes down hard and knocks Scrion away. Scrion falls ungracefully, twitching madly, trying to turn itself over before landing. It fails miserably, landing on its side in fifty feet of water.

After thrashing about pitifully, Scrion rights itself. Still moving quickly, the monster breaks for the shore again, but makes it only two leaps. Nemesis takes a lunging step forward and thrusts out her clawed hand. Her index and middle fingers are the longest—the ring being small and the pinkie not much more than a spiked nub—and the claws extending from them are unnecessarily huge.

They're also sharp.

Scrion falls flat as Nemesis's middle claw pierces its hind leg, pinning it in place. But the monster isn't done. Its madness compels it forward. Nemesis's claw tears through the leg as the smaller monster pulls away. Brown blood gushes into the blackened earth.

And then Scrion's free. For nearly two seconds. Then Nemesis is upon it again.

I almost feel bad for the pug-nosed Kaiju. Nemesis is clearly toying with it. Or perhaps testing it. Either way, it's an unfair fight that could have ended the moment it began, which starts me thinking: *Is this what she'll do to me?*

While pinning Scrion to the ground with her giant left hand, Nemesis catches hold of the wounded leg with her right, grips down tightly and yanks. Scrion's head turns upward, eyes dazed, as the leg comes free, dangling tendrils of flesh and pouring muddy blood.

Then Nemesis lets go.

And damn, Scrion takes off running. It's not quite as fast as before with its less coordinated, three-legged hop, but it's still hauling ass. Not only that, it's coming around again for another strike. For a moment, I'm impressed with the thing. It's going to fight to the end. Then its arc becomes a circle. The dazed and wounded creature is playing 'duck, duck, goose' all by itself, sprinting around an imaginary ring.

Even Nemesis seems confused by this behavior. She stands still, watching. And then, as though she's seen enough, she reaches down, catches Scrion by the protective plates of its back and lifts the pitiful thing into the air. Holding the smaller Kaiju aloft, she wraps her big hand around Scrion's head and neck, and then squeezes. For a moment, there's some resistance. Scrion is built similarly to Nemesis, and is no doubt powerful. But it's no match for the original. Nemesis's hand twitches and collapses inward, crushing Scrion's head. A smear of brown and white fluid oozes out from between her fingers.

She relinquishes her grip, dropping Scrion's body into the ocean. A wall of water rushes up and over the beaches, flooding the husks of empty homes.

And then—*shit*—she turns toward me.

And stares.

"Umm," Woodstock says. He has us hovering a half mile away, which suddenly feels not nearly far enough. "So I'm officially starting to get freaked out by all the giant monsters looking at us the way Michael Jackson looked at kids."

He's right. Nemesis's glare is decidedly unsettling. Unlike Scrion, who's eyes—despite their focus on us—had beamed with mindless chaos, Nemesis's eyes, which are brown and quite human looking, reveal something deeper.

Thought? Meaning? I have no idea, though part of me really wants to know.

Her furrowed eyebrows come up. The rage and tension gripping her body melts away. And suddenly, in my mind, she's no longer Nemesis.

Woodstock sees it, too. "There she is," he says, his voice something between awe and surprise. "Maigo."

Knowing Woodstock has seen what I have felt all along sets my resolve, and when I hear the words, "Target locked! Clear to engage?" in my ears, I react quickly, toggling Devine to transmit openly. "Negative! Do not engage! I repeat, do not engage! Scrion is down. Maigo is *not* the target!"

As those few words replay in my mind, I inwardly cringe, knowing that just one of them is going to land me in hot water. I called her 'Maigo.' And while Woodstock might agree with me now, the opinion of a sixty-two year old retired Marine Corp pilot re-hired for the FC-P against the advisement of my superiors, is probably not going to help my case.

"I repeat, Nemesis is not the target." My order lacks its previous conviction, and I hope using her true designation will help people miss my foible, but I know it won't. I've just put the express shit-train on full speed and sent it toward my doorstep.

The jets fly past overhead. There are nine of them now, converging from the airbases to the north and south. In another ten minutes, there would have been thirty. A line of ten Apache helicopters takes up position along the shore, three hundred feet up, boldly hovering close enough to unleash their payloads.

Nemesis pays them no attention.

"Take us closer," I say.

Woodstock lowers his head at me to peer over his aviator glasses. "You're shittin' me, right?"

"I need to test a theory."

"I can save you the trouble and just say you have the biggest balls in the world, how 'bout that?"

"Any sign of trouble, we can bug out, and I'll give the order to fire."

Woodstock twitches his mustache back and forth for a moment and then throttles us forward.

"Bring us up to eye level," I say.

"Roger that, Cap'n Ahab."

As we rise up, growing closer to Nemesis, her brown eyes track us, still oblivious to the helicopters and jets swirling around her like black flies in the summer.

"That's as close as I get," Woodstock says, when we're a hundred feet away. Just out of arms reach. Unless she decides to step forward when she swats us down. They we're just screwed. But I don't think she's going to do that.

Betty rises up until we're at eye level. The chopper is about the size of Nemesis's eye, but at a hundred feet away, her face is about the size of someone standing a few feet away. And there is no doubt she's looking straight at me.

"I'll be damned," Woodstock says. He sees it, too.

Then I do something stupid. I reach out a hand and wave, saying, "I'm okay," quickly adding, "We're okay," mostly so I don't feel so weird.

And then, I'll be damned, she turns away and starts trudging out to sea.

I go to toggle Devine and find the system still set to broadcast.

Damnit. I hate myself. Everyone heard our little Kodak moment.

"All units, stand down," I say, trying to sound more authoritative than embarrassed. "Begin tracking protocols. Follow her for as long as you can."

I switch off Devine and lean back, watching Nemesis retreat peacefully back into the depths, leaving a trail of Scrion's brown blood in her wake.

"Sooo," Woodstock says, turning to me. "Wanna tell me what just happened?"

I really don't want to, but seeing as how I'm going to be asked the same question by just about every damned person on the planet, I decide to answer truthfully, or at least what I believe is the truth. "Nemesis wasn't here to kill me. Or anyone."

"But Scrion was," he says, starting to understand. "It was after us. After *you*."

I nod. "But Nemesis...she was here to protect me."

15

The flight back to the Crow's Nest is made in silence, both Woodstock and I processing the things we just experienced. I feel shaky, mentally and physically, thanks to a now dissipating adrenaline rush. Were I on the ground, I'd take my mother's frequent advice to me as a child and run around the house a few times. Stuck in a chopper, all this nervous energy has nowhere to go, so I'm bouncing my legs like I'm Lars Ulrich playing *Enter Sandman* double time.

As we descend toward the landing pad atop the FC-P headquarters roof, Woodstock speaks up. "You gotta plan?"

"For what?" I ask, knowing exactly for what, but trying to downplay the whole thing.

"Maigo," he says, using the name freely.

I shrug.

"You know..." His voice is uncommonly unsure, like he's going to say something he shouldn't. His body language belies nothing, but that's probably because we're coming in for a landing and one wrong move could send us plummeting to the lawn or smashing into the Crow's Nest's thick windows, which actually look a little dirty from the outside. "I always sort of rooted for her. For Nemesis."

I forget all about the dirty windows. Before he can continue, I double-check to make sure Devine's transmit function is disabled.

"Not for killing all those people, mind you. But...who she was... once. All she wanted was justice. You helped make that possible. And you saved a lot of people because of it. And I think she knows that. She owes you. I know you feel the same. We all do. You don't hide it as well as you think."

I smile. "Not like you?"

"Boy, I was in the Marines for thirty God dang years, and I was never once written up for anything unsavory. You know why? Ain't cause I was a goody two-shoes. It's cause I can hide shit from a turd-burglar. But you? You transmit your feelings to the world like a billboard. I swear if you weren't an FC-P agent you'd be some kind of crunchy artist type, thrusting your inner self all over everyone."

He's got me laughing now, despite the shit-storm no doubt descending on the FC-P. "You realize how gross that sounds, right?"

"Other people's emotions usually are," he says. "Point is, you gotta work on keeping that shit to yourself. Cause your job isn't about paintin' happy trees or retarded looking faces. It's leading the damn world against a monster who also happens to be a little girl. Now git out of my chopper and go face the music. I'll be down in a few."

I was so intent on listening to Woodstock that I hadn't even noticed we'd landed. After removing my headset, I give him a pat on the shoulder. "Thanks."

"Ayuh," he says, and that's the end of it. Everything he just told me amounts to a few weeks worth of talking to an old Mainer like Woodstock. Means he cares. And 'Ayuh,' means it's time to shut the hell up about it.

I find myself running toward the roof exit. I'm not sure why. There shouldn't be anyone here. The rest of the area will stay evacuated for 24 hours, but Cooper, Watson and Collins will come back sooner, along with other emergency services. The evacuation alone probably caused more than a few accidents, heart attacks and violence. The police, fire department and hospital are going to have their hands full for a few days at least.

As I drop down the stairs three at a time, the dirty window returns to my thoughts. I'd stared out that window this morning. There wasn't a spot of dust or a smudge anywhere on it—well, except the line I drew. So what had smeared all over it while the Crow's Nest and everyone else for ten square miles was busy evacuating?

For some reason I'm not consciously aware of, I draw my sidearm upon reaching the bottom of the stairs. When I shove through the door to the Crow's Nest, I have the gun up, sweeping back and forth, looking for trouble. The first thing I notice is that there's no one here. That's a good thing, because they're supposed to be gone. The second thing I notice is that it looks like someone rolled a giant bowling ball down the middle of the space. Chairs are overturned. Two workstations have been obliterated. And the water cooler is slowly bleeding to death through a crack in the blue plastic. But it's the third thing I notice that holds my gaze. The smear on the window is fluid—and brown. It's either a chocolate milkshake or Kaiju blood.

My gut says it's the latter.

Seeing no one inside, I head for the main stairwell and slide to a stop. There's a big, round hole in the wall directly across from where I'm standing, ten feet up from the first landing. My first thought is *rocket-propelled grenade*, but there is very little debris on the stairs, meaning that whatever punched the hole in the wall, came from *inside.*

I descend the stairs like a peregrine falcon, shrieking out names, "Ashley! Watson! Coop!" Part of me is relieved when I get no reply, but silence often means one of two things: they're gone or they're dead. Detecting no signs of life or trouble on the second and first floors, I sprint over the dark hardwood floor and make for the home's rear exit. The wooden door is open.

While we don't have a ton of security here, we still follow the basic rules of a mansion living on the fringe of an urban city. The door should be closed and locked. Whatever happened here, it led outside. Of course, the rhinoceros-sized hole in the wall told me that, too.

I hit the screen door at a run, smashing the handle down as I barrel outside onto the driveway and a scene of destruction.

The first thing I see is a body laid out on the pavement, by the husk of what used to be Cooper's car, ironically, a coupe. Even the clothing I can see—black pants and slick black shoes—is all wrong. My first thought was that this was Collins. But then *she* stands up on the other side of the wall that is Watson and looks my way.

My relief is short-lived. Collins is alive, but her eyes look a little hazy and her blouse is stained with blood. As is her hair. I rush toward her, lowering my weapon. Then I see the body's face. Endo.

Something about Endo being unconscious doesn't make sense. Collins couldn't take him by herself, and I don't think Watson or Cooper would be much help in a fight. But I really don't give a shit. It's clear that he attacked the Crow's Nest, but they somehow got the upper hand.

Despite my growing anger, I pause beside Collins. "You okay?"

"Probably a concussion," she says, sounding more lucid than she looks.

Endo groans.

Without a thought, I reach down, grab his shirt and pull him up roughly. "You don't get to wake up yet!" I move to knock him out again, breaking all sorts of rules, but no one's going to care if he assaulted a government facility.

My arm is caught mid-swing. I turn to question Collins and find the face of the Asian woman from the port of Hong Kong glaring at me. "Let. Him. Go."

"Go. Fuck. Yourself." I say. Collins is going to pop her any second now, and then we'll have both of them in custody.

But my partner doesn't move. Instead, she sits down on the pavement, looking tired.

I look from Collins to the stranger and then to Watson and Cooper. "Could someone please explain why you haven't pig-piled Lucy Liu over here?"

"That's racist," the woman says.

For some reason, this totally flabbergasts me. Not only is she kind of right, but I'm really not in the mood to have a conversation with an associate of Katsu Endo, who freaking paralyzed me the last time I saw him.

"Look, if it makes you feel better, Lucy Liu is a hottie."

"It does," the woman says, "but she's also Chinese. I'm Japanese."

"Actually," Watson says, raising a finger. "She's American. Born in—"

"You know what I meant—"

"I can see you're going to fit right in." All eyes turn down to Endo. He's awake and looking at his partner, who is still holding my hand back.

Fit in?

"Give me one good reason I shouldn't club you," I say.

"She could kick your ass," he says, smiling, motioning to the woman.

"Two good reasons."

"I saved them."

"Saved who?"

"Us," Collins says. "If it makes you feel better, I already knocked him out once."

The tension goes out of my clubbing arm, and the woman's grip relaxes. Saved them? From who?

The hole in the wall.

The destroyed car.

The brown blood.

"Gordon was here," I conclude, yanking my hand away. If what I'm being told is true, I won't knock Endo senseless, but I will arrest him. Standing clear of the woman's reach, I aim my weapon at Endo. "Why didn't you let us know?"

Endo sits up, feeling the goose egg on his forehead where Collins must have clocked him.

"About what?"

"Gordon."

"I didn't know he was here."

I turn to my team. "Did he try to put something on Gordon's head?"

Collins's shifting expression answers the question. "He had a drill. He was..." She was with me in Hong Kong. She saw what happened to me. Even knocked silly, the pieces aren't hard to put together. She turns to Endo. "You were trying to control him."

"Empty your pockets," I say, shaking my handgun at him.

He complies. There's a folding knife, a pack of Juicy Fruit, a wallet and the same device he slapped on the side of my head. He must have been trying to drill through Gordon's thick flesh so the device could work.

"I was following orders," he says.

"Zoomb is *not* the United States government," I reply. "You don't have to do what they say, and their orders do not put you beyond the reach of the law, no matter how much money they have."

Endo stretches, working out the kinks. "My employer didn't send me here. I was requested."

I make a show of aiming my gun more carefully, leveling the sights at his wang. I nearly say so, but I quickly realize Lucy Liu will just accuse me of being racist again. "*By who?*"

My phone rings. The ring tone—Marylyn Monroe singing *Happy Birthday, Mr. President*—tells me who's calling. It the boss. Not my boss. *The* boss. I dig the phone out of my pocket, accept the call and place it against my ear. "Mr. President, the situation is—"

The man cuts me off with a very curt explanation of my situation, which feels like an enema while he's talking, and something a little rougher when he hangs up before I can argue. I manage to maintain my composure, say "goodbye" to cellular silence, and lower my weapon. "Well, looks like we're pals now."

"*What?*" Collins, at least, shows an appropriate amount of disgust at this announcement.

But I can't talk about it now. I head for the door.

"Where are you going?" Collins shouts after me.

"To squeeze the shit out of my stress doll!" I didn't need to shout, but after everything I just experienced, everything I just *survived*, the last thing I needed was to be told to play nice with a guy whose nuts I'd like to use for a punching bag. I step inside, slam the door behind me and head to my room on the second floor.

After recovering my stress doll—I think his name is Bob—I head for the bathroom, yank down my pants and sit down on the toilet. If I lay down on my bed, someone would be in to get me inside of five minutes. Here, I can have some quality me-time. Here, I can—

A familiar-shaped white and pink plastic device is poking out of the top of the small trash can beside the toilet. I share this bathroom with Collins. Our rooms are joined by it. With a shaking hand, I reach down to the trash can and move aside the unused toilet paper that had been placed to partially cover the device.

My throat feels like Gordon's got his hands wrapped around it.

I lift the pregnancy test, looking at the two windows. For a moment, I can't make any sense out of it. One line, not pregnant. Two lines, pregnant. I look back and forth three times, because the test must be wrong. Two lines means pregnant. And there are two lines.

Two lines means pregnant.

Two...lines...

Bob's head cracks open.

16

I'm ten years old. Lying in bed. Another sleepless night seeing monsters in the shadows and skulls in my discarded tighty whities on the floor. To say I had an active imagination is an understatement. But that's not what kept me awake. Not really. To this day, I don't know why, but some nights my arms and legs would feel heavy. Really heavy. Like they were moving through swamp muck. This unnatural and strange feeling drove me to my parent's bedside. More than the monsters. Or the noises. Or whatever else kids fear in the dark. It pushed me past my fear of violent repercussions. To seek comfort from the unwilling.

The heaviness in my limbs faded as I grew older. I haven't thought about it in years. But as I climb the stairs toward the Crow's Nest, pregnancy test in hand, I finally understand the heaviness that plagued my childhood nights. It was fear. Primal, unfiltered fear. As a person grows, barriers are erected. Mental defenses are fortified. Pride becomes the dominant emotion, keeping fear from being fully expressed or perhaps even realized. It's how Woodstock and I can look into Nemesis's eyes and not scream like frightened goats.

But now, my legs have never felt heavier. As my bare feet pad across the cool, hardwood floor of the Crow's Nest, heading for Collins, who is sitting at her work station talking to Cooper, I feel like I'm ten again. I can feel the hallway floor beneath my feet. The humidifier hums behind me. The orange glow of the bathroom night-light guides my path. I expect no real comfort on the other side of my parent's door, just the knowledge that the world as I know it still exists. An assurance that reality hasn't fundamentally changed.

My hand reaches for the knob and turns. But the knob is Collins's shoulder. She spins around, tired eyes like my mother's. But then she smiles and looks concerned. She asks, "What is it? What's wrong?" Then, I realize why I love this woman so much, and why I shouldn't be terrified right now.

Not that this knowledge lightens my arms any. Lifting the pregnancy test feels like I'm bench-pressing Watson. My lips stay firmly shut, pinched white. The visual aid and my mortified expression will say everything that needs saying.

Collins's eyes widen as the pregnancy test rises.

She reaches for it, but my leaden arms pull it away.

"No one is supposed to know!" she hisses.

I'm instantly offended.

The weight lifts from my limbs like I've been touched by Jesus himself. A quick cure for fear is anger. "Not supposed to—how the hell do you keep something like this from me?"

"Jon, I—"

"You're a field agent!" I'm shouting now. I'm not sure who else is in the Crow's Nest now, but I've just included them in my drama. "You could have been injured on the reservation. You *were* injured today!" My eyes look her up and down. "You need to go to a hospital."

I take hold of her wrist, but Collin's yanks away. "Jon!"

"We're not even married yet!" I shout.

"Jon!" Collins now has a hand on my wrist. Her crushing grip is made more painful by the skillful thrust of her middle finger into a pressure point. My head clears instantly. A quick cure for anger is pain. "Shut-the-fuck-up."

I lower my voice. "Tell me why I shouldn't be angry at you for hiding this. Give me one good reason."

"It's not mine."

"It was in our bathroom."

"Because *no one was supposed to know yet.*" The words come out as a low growl. My anger is in full retreat now, pursued by Collins's. Mercifully, she releases my wrist.

"But...then who..." I glance at Cooper. She's white as a sheet. Eyes locked across the room. I turn to follow her gaze. Endo is there, sitting with Lucy Liu and Watson. Endo and the woman are smiling. Enjoying my faux pas. Watson...poor Watson. He's now in the position I was just ten seconds ago. I'm not sure how I missed their relationship. They did a better job hiding it than Cooper did this test. But I've also been in the field a lot.

"Two things," I say, all of the childhood trauma and fresh anger gone from my system. I turn to Cooper with a grin. "First, congratulations. Second, the wetness on this test is from *your* pee. Gross." I drop the test into the empty waste can besides Collins's station.

To Watson's credit, he handles the news far better than I did. He strolls across the room, calm as can be. Before reaching Cooper, who is still frozen in place, he bends down and takes the pregnancy test from the trash. He lifts it gently, like it's a baby. The gentleness with which he holds the urine-covered device makes me feel like an asshole. He glances at Cooper. "This is yours?"

She nods.

"Ours?" he asks. His hand is shaking now.

Cooper nods again, and before I understand what has happened, they're in each other's arms, rocking back and forth.

"Thank God," Watson says, and I'm not sure if he's expressing happiness over the baby or the fact that Cooper wasn't injured today. Maybe both. Doesn't matter. What matters is that the man is joyful. Not terrified.

Dammit, I *am* an asshole.

"I was going to tell you at the end of the day," Cooper tells him.

Watson shakes his head, messing up her perfect bun. "Doesn't matter."

Feeling like an asshole and a peeping Tom, I say, "Why don't you two take some time. Collins and I will help our...visitors get settled."

After the briefest of nods from Cooper, the pair head for the stairs. An odd couple, no doubt, but their affection for each other fills the room like warm taffy, gooey and sweet. I'm happy for them, really, but I'm glad when they're gone, because gooey and sweet is not the mood I want lingering when I speak to Endo.

I turn toward my own personal nemesis, or one of them. What's that make him? One of my nemesi? Nemesises? Or can you only have one nemesis by definition? Endo is still grinning at me. So is...*fuck.*

"What's your name?"

I can't keep thinking of her as Lucy Liu. It's totally racist.

"Maggie Alessi," she answers, not a trace of an accent.

So is Maggie.

I take a step toward them but am stopped when Collins takes hold of my wrist. No pressure point this time. She grins up at me. "Not married, *yet?*"

I try to hide my grin, but fail. "Shut-up."

When I head for Endo again, I'm feeling far too happy. Not only are Watson and Cooper an item with a baby on the way, but Collins caught me with my guard down. Found out what was on my mind before I wanted her to. Looong before. So when I pull a chair around, sit down on it backwards and says, "Let me catch you up to speed," it tastes bad coming out.

I clear my throat and stand. "Let me try that again." I sit back down and point to each of them as I speak. "Fuck you. And fuck you."

Alessi raises her eyebrows, her lips turning in the opposite direction like I've impressed her somehow. "He's more articulate than you said."

Collins clears her throat. She's standing behind me, arms crossed, face grim. Alessi's smirk goes into full retreat. Collins is so much more badass than me, it's not fair.

"Why are you here?" I ask. "And please, no bullshit. I've been ordered to work with you, but if you're not 100% honest with me, I'll feed you to Nemesis."

"You mean, Maigo," Endo says. I'm about to rip him a new one, when I realize that he's not taunting me. He thinks of her the same way I do: part monster, part victimized child. "And I'm sure she would oblige you. After today, I mean."

"What's that supposed to mean?" Collins asks.

She didn't hear, I realize. But somehow, Endo did. He knows exactly what happened and what was said. I lean to the side, looking at Endo's ear. There's a small device inside.

He confirms my suspicion, saying, "Your emergency network isn't as secure as the DHS would like to believe. If you'd had Zoomb—"

"I know why you're here, Endo," I say, hoping to change the course of this conversation. "And I'm telling you right now, you're never going to control Nemesis. She will never be your weapon. Or Zoomb's. Orders from the President be damned, I won't allow it."

"I'm afraid you misunderstand our intentions," Endo says. His voice is annoyingly calm and confident. "While I share your...infatuation with the monster, Maigo, I lack your...connection."

I feel Collins shift behind me. She's still not on the same page, but she remains silent.

"If the technology works, the U.S. Government will be paying Zoomb untold billions of dollars. It won't be me controlling her, nor will any other Zoomb employee. The technology will be owned and used by your employers, a fact that will be kept secret from the rest of the world."

"I don't believe this!" Collins walks away for a moment, rolling her head from side to side. She returns, fists on hips. "You're going to *weaponize* her?"

"She will be under the full control of a responsible government agent. Her actions will—"

"Who?" Collins asks. "What kind of an idiot would control—"

"Shit." The word comes out as a whisper, but stops Collins in her tracks. She's heard the whispered expression enough to know I've figured something out. "Shiiiit."

"You know who it is?" Collins asks.

I look up at her, the weight returning to my limbs. "Me."

17

My legs burn as I trudge up the hillside. Collins and I are out for a walk, while the blissful Watson and Cooper babysit Endo and Alessi. I figured a few minutes alone with the two lovebirds would be enough to wipe the self-righteous smirks off their faces. Also, I needed some time with Collins. Working together as a couple isn't always easy. We spend a lot of time together. If things get tense between us, we suck at our jobs. So we try to work things out before they become things at all.

As usual, the first few minutes of our stroll around the streets atop Powder Hill—named for the civil war gunpowder house that still stands just up the street—are spent in silence. A year ago, the homes here were full of families. Kids roamed the hilltop in packs, playing hide and seek, playing dingdong ditch and breaking windows with balls of every shape and size. Now, there isn't a child, man, woman or car in sight. Although the hill was cleared for residents six months ago, no one returned. 'For Sale' signs line the streets, and no one ever comes to look. Some people incorrectly worry about radiation or some other kind of poisoning leaking from the destruction that begins at the bottom of the hill to the east. Others worry, more accurately, as seen today, about a repeat. The suckiest part about those people being right is that I think it's my fault we had a repeat at all. *If I'd been somewhere else...*

"So," Collins says.

I shake out of my thoughts. I'm standing at a tall oak tree in front of a white house. A family used to live here. I remember them. Three boys. Two golden retrievers. Lots of noise. The home was a focal point for other kids. Always busy. Now the place is empty. The windows, blown out a year ago, have been boarded up. Shards of broken glass glitter in the tall, un-mowed grass. I place my hand against the old tree and peel off a shard of bark. I flip it over in my hands. The rough, diamond shape reminds me of the reflective scale-like 'feathers' that fell from Nemesis's wings.

"What happened today?" It's been nearly twenty seconds since her "So." She's afraid to ask. I suppose she should be. Being in a relationship with a man who attracts Kaiju is probably not the best choice. *Mom, Dad, I'd like you to meet Jon and his 350-foot-tall baggage.*

"How's the head?" I ask.

"Fine," she says.

And that's all she'll give me. It was a weak attempt at best. Paramedics already saw to the wound and declared her fit for ass kicking. Nothing a few painkillers couldn't manage, though they asked her to avoid any further impacts to the head for a week, as if she threw herself into the brick wall on purpose.

Seeing no other way to delay or derail the conversation, I say, "They were here for me."

"Endo was ordered to be here. We have no choice."

"Not Endo." I shake my head. If it were only Endo, this would still be a salvageable day. "The Kaiju. Scrion. Nemesis. They were here for me."

"Don't be—"

"Ask Woodstock. Scrion came to kill me. Nemesis came to protect me."

"You can call her Maigo around me," Collins says.

"I'm not sure that thinking of her that way is a good thing," I say. "She's a monster. She killed thousands of people and destroyed Boston."

"But she was driven by the memories of a murdered little girl," Collins says. This perspective is new for her. She's either been doing some thinking or she's just trying to be supportive. "I think the people we really need to blame are the ones who made her, accidentally or not."

"Gordon," I say.

She nods. "And Zoomb."

"And Endo."

"We just need to play nice, okay?" She grabs my shoulders and digs her thumbs into my back, loosening the tension. "You can't go all 'fuck you' to everyone and expect to gain their trust—"

"Or gain any useful information." I toss the chunk of bark into the grass. "I get it. But I'm not happy about this. The idea of controlling Nemesis...it's just...no."

"It's dangerous," she says.

"It's a break of trust," I say. "If I do have some kind of connection with Nemesis now, if she's somehow locked on to protecting me, then maybe the best thing for the world is for me to move to Antarctica or something?"

"That's not going to happen," Collins says, but I'm not so sure. If it kept Nemesis from making paste out of people, I'd gladly spend my life in the frozen South. Well, maybe not gladly, but I can't put my personal happiness above the rest of the world.

Speaking of which... "I can't stay here."

She stops rubbing my back. The silence that follows is a big question mark.

"Gordon was here for me. Scrion was here for me. Scrion is dead, but if Gordon comes back, we might not be able to stop him. You all got lucky the first time. And there are probably two more Kaiju roaming the planet right now. If he's controlling them, too..."

I don't have to finish the thought. My presence here puts the team in danger. It makes the whole city a target. And I'm not about to let Beverly become my own personal Tokyo, to be stomped on over and over.

"Wherever you go," Collins says. "I'm coming with you."

I'd like to be the brave and noble hero and say, 'Never! You must live your life, fully and gloriously and blah, blah, blah,' but I don't. Instead, I wrap my arm around her waist, my fingers finding her hip bone, and I pull her close. "I wouldn't have it any other way."

My phone rings, playing *Gangnam Style* by Psy.

"Who's that?" Collins asks.

"Endo," I say. "I programmed him in before we left."

She smiles. "You are so totally racist."

"What? Endo is Japanese! Psy is—"

"Korean."

Dammit!

I answer the phone. "What?"

I listen to Endo speaking, his voice calm as usual, with a trace of arrogance or superiority. As he talks, I hear Betty's rotor chopping through the air in the distance as Woodstock warms her up. When I hang up, I have a mix of feelings. First is anger. Endo is highjacking the FC-P. Second is anger. Yeah, that's the same as the first, but they're directed at different people for different reasons. Apparently, when Endo was trying to control Gordon's mind, he was also embedding a tracking device.

On the plus side, I dodged the matrimony bullet that was no doubt coming next. That conversation scares me for two reasons. First, I haven't fully thought it through yet. I don't even really know how I feel about it. Second, and this is what really scares me, I haven't the foggiest clue about what she thinks. Her first husband turned out to be an abusive prick. I'm not sure that's a path she wants to walk down again, and if we could avoid the topic, that would be dandy. Of course, with a little Cooper-Watson on the way, that might be hard. Pheromones are in the air.

"What's going on?" Collins asks, when I lower the phone without saying goodbye.

"Gordon," I say. "We know where he is."

18

By the time Collins and I reach the helicopter, its rotor spins madly. Gravity struggles to hold it down. It took us only a minute-thirty to get back, but we then took the time to prepare for an encounter with hulk-Gordon. We're both wearing black tactical gear. While the armor we're wearing isn't designed to stop bullets, it helps absorbs impacts and is designed specifically to stop knife attacks, or in this case claw attacks, which in our line of work, is the more common danger. But that doesn't stop us from arming up like Schwarzenegger in *Commando*. Beyond our usual high caliber sidearms, Collins and I are packing M4 assault rifles with M320 grenade-launcher attachments and laser sights. That's more *Mission Impossible* than *Commando*, but I prefer muscles and cigars over missile-launching wrist watches. Mostly because the latter isn't real. If I could have a missile-launching wrist watch, too, I would. The point is, we're carrying enough firepower and ammo to make a Mexican drug cartel jealous.

Which is why I'm surprised to find Endo and Alessi, sitting in the chopper's rear cabin, still dressed in their black business attire. Their only new accessories are the headphones covering their ears. I just shake my head and let it go. Maybe Gordon will take care of Endo for me.

Collins gets in the back with Endo while I take my seat up front.

"Already got the coordinates plugged in," Woodstock says, after I've donned my headphones. "Just waitin' on you."

I plug in my phone and swipe a finger across it to open up Devine's menu. I'm going to treat Gordon like a Kaiju and bring in everything I have. A hand on my arm keeps me from activating the transmit feature. I turn to find Endo's fingers on my arm. I nearly punch him in the nose, but he'd probably dodge it and make me look like an idiot, so I refrain. "What?"

"We need to go alone," he says.

"You need to see a psychiatrist." I turn back to my phone.

"If we show up in force, he'll be gone before we get there. He's still on land, but if he enters the ocean..."

Not wanting to waste any more time, I nod to Woodstock and point to the sky. We're airborne a moment later, heading northeast toward Halibut Point State Park, in Rockport. The old, fresh-water filled quarry, which is separated from the ocean by a 50-foot-thick band of solid rock, should be devoid of civilians. Most towns to the north and south of Beverly should have evacuated their coastal areas, too, which is probably how Gordon made it there without being spotted, unless he's driving a really big truck with tinted windows.

"...we'll never find him again," Endo finishes.

My thumb hovers over the transmit button. "What's your plan?"

"If we can control Gordon, we might be able to diffuse the situation with the children."

I simulate the sound of a tire screeching. "Back up. Children?"

Endo looks annoyed, like this is something I should already know or have figured out, which pisses me off, because it means that maybe I haven't been doing a good job this past year. "The Nemesis-Prime carcass, which, before you ask, is in a secure location, was discovered beneath a mountain in Alaska. Removal of the body completed around the same time that Maigo-Nemesis emerged in Maine. Those in charge of the excavation decided to close up shop before they were noticed."

"You mean Zoomb," I say.

Endo shrugs. "But the excavation was incomplete. On the final day of digging, a clutch of five large eggs was discovered. Lacking the time and resources to safely and securely remove the eggs, they were left behind with the intention of removing them at a later date, when the fallout from the incident in Boston subsided. But when they returned—"

"The eggs were gone," I say.

"The eggs had *hatched*," Endo says. "The bones of several people, as well as moose, deer, elk and bears were all that remained. Analysis of the footprints revealed all five of the young were alive and well. But they weren't alone."

"Gordon was with them," Collins says.

"Gordon *raised* them," Endo says. "Do you know why Gordon is the way he is? A heart transplant. From the Maigo clone before she grew into Nemesis. He has the girl's heart—the *monster's* DNA—in his chest. It is likely Prime's young bonded to him at birth. Before the events in Boston, Gordon developed a strong bond with Nemesis, feeling her desires and acting to help fulfill them. I suspect that bond was broken when you fulfilled Nemesis's goal, but I believe that same bond might exist now between Gordon and the children."

"They're carrying out his desires," I say. "His new soldiers."

"Exactly," Endo says. "And for the most part, those desires are compelling the young to eat and grow. If they grow at the same rate Maigo did, we will have four 300-foot Kaiju to deal with, inside of a few days. And with Gordon here...it is likely the young will follow. Scrion was just the first."

"The question is, why is Gordon here?" I say.

"Isn't it obvious?" Endo says.

I hate this man.

He doesn't wait to hear my theory. "Gordon is here for you."

"I know that," I say, "but why?"

"Gordon is a military man. He is responding to a threat." Endo leans forward, like it will help me hear him, but he could lean back and I'd hear him the same. "Imagine that Gordon is part of a special ops team. He is in hostile territory, but he can't act until he gets orders. Now imagine that the enemy has put up a tower that blocks communications. What do you suppose becomes his primary target?"

"I'm the tower," I say.

"I wasn't sure until Maigo saved you today. While you lack the deeper connection that Gordon had, I believe the potential for that connection exists."

"With your mind-control doohickey."

"It is a neural implant," Endo says. "It allows us basic, thoughtless, control of the target through electrical impulses to various parts of the brain. We can render the target immobile, as you experienced, or we can put them in a rampage. But there is a second option. A pathway into the target's mind that allows for a deeper connection, which would facilitate complete control and transmission of detailed instructions."

"Like telling someone to sit," I say. I'm facing forward, watching Beverly Farms pass by beneath us in a blur. Endo can't see my face. My clenched jaw. But the anger in my voice is impossible to disguise. "Devine's security isn't flawed, you stole the access codes from my fucking mind."

I can't look at the man. If I see even a hint of a smile, I'm going to jump back there and throttle him.

"Isn't that kind of dangerous?" Collins asks. "What if the target's mind is more powerful?"

It's a good question, but I wish she wouldn't have asked it. Because if the answer is that Endo's mind is more powerful, my ego is going to be flushed down the toilet.

"The electrical impulses guarantee that the conversation is one way. The target won't even be aware of the intrusion."

He's right about that. I had no idea he was in my head, which begs the question, what else did he learn about me? I draw my pistol, lean around the seat and level it at his head. "If you ever use that thing on me again, I will kill you, without warning, without mercy. Understood?"

For the first time I've ever seen, Endo looks a little unsettled. He's a smart guy. He sees my finger around the trigger. The safety off. The look in my eyes. I'm one smart remark from putting a hole in his head. He does the only thing he can. He nods. Lucky bastard.

I face forward again, holstering my weapon. "You took a peek inside my head. Should have seen that coming."

It takes a lot to get me angry. But man, Endo gets under my skin. And the fact that he violated the privacy of my mind... If I'm ever able to control Nemesis, that guy is getting an atomic wedgie the likes of which has never been seen in the history of the universe.

"We're over Rockport, now," Woodstock reports quietly after a few minutes spent in silence. "ETA, two minutes."

I close my eyes for thirty seconds of those two minutes, focusing my thoughts, erasing all trace of my feelings for Endo. He's working with us for now, and having an antagonistic relationship with the man is going to end up getting someone killed. Besides, I don't think he'll be pushing me again anytime soon. When I open my eyes again, I can see the quarry ahead. "Endo, how sure are you that your neural implant is going to work?"

"Gordon, at the core, is human," he says. "It will work on him the same way it worked on y—our test subjects. The challenge is punching through his thick skin. If the hole I began hasn't healed yet, it will take just a second."

"Going to be one hell of a bronco ride," I say.

He laughs lightly "Second one today."

"Any chance Zoomb is working on a projectile alternative?"

"For the Kaiju," he says. "The prototype is nearly complete."

"So Gordon is kind of a beta test then?"

"How do you mean?"

"Cause you and I both know that he's not at all human anymore."

Endo grunts. Maybe it's something he hasn't considered.

Woodstock sets Betty down on the stone barrier between the dark blue ocean and the light blue quarry pond.

"Only one way to find out, I suppose." I open the door and hop out onto the light brown stone. Ocean air fills my nose, lacking the stench of ash that I've become familiar with in Beverly. Endo exits beside me as Collins and Alessi hop down from the other side. Once we're clear, I give Woodstock a thumbs up, and he heads for the sky. He'll circle the area, keeping an eye out for trouble. He can provide some heavy hitting backup if we need it, sans the thirty-eight rockets that have yet to be replenished.

I place an earbud in one ear, toggle Devine to communicate with Woodstock and say, "You read me?"

"Ayuh," he says. "Be careful."

As the dust kicked up by Betty's rotorwash settles, I scan the area. The park is basically a big circle of land surrounding the old quarry. Tall grasses, small trees and large stones cover the area. Came here with a girlfriend once. Almost got to second base. Good times. Not the worst place in the world to die. Nice view anyway. If the quarry weren't captivating enough, the view of the ocean stretches out three miles to the horizon. The few boats on the water are streaking steadily north, evacuating like everyone on land.

A loud seagull perched on top of a dark rock catches my attention. It's holding a crab, panicked legs spread wide. The bird lets loose a white stream of crap before smashing the crab down. For a moment, I sympathize with the smaller creature. I've felt just like it.

I nearly miss what happens next. A shifting darkness behind the stone pinches the bird's neck, eliciting a high pitched shriek that's suddenly cut off. The bird tumbles to the side. The crab scurries free.

I take aim with my M4 and say, "Gordon's behind the rock."

Endo steps up next to me, a taser in one hand, his drill-tipped neural implant in the other. "No," he says. "Gordon *is* the rock."

The used-to-be man must hear us, because the dark rock shifts and stands. I haven't seen Gordon since Boston. The man is a giant. Far larger than I remember. While he's covered in thick, black skin like Nemesis's, his facial features are still distinct enough to recognize him as the former general-turned-traitor, turned monster. When he sees me, a grin slowly spreads across his face. I'm beginning to think that not bringing a squadron of Apache helicopters was a big mistake.

19

A violent blossom of orange fire erases Gordon's face. The explosion makes Endo, Collins and Alessi jump.

"A little warning next time," Alessi grumbles.

I move my finger away from the grenade launcher's trigger. "If I had warned you, I'd have warned him." The under-barrel launcher is typically a one shot deal when the stinky, brown fan is spinning. It's not like bullets. There's no magazine full of grenades. Seasoned warriors can reload in two seconds flat—under fire. But I'm still getting used to the heavy hitting gear. Still, I manage to use the ten seconds it takes for the swirling smoke to drift away from Gordon's face to eject the spent round, pull a fresh grenade from my mole pouch, slide it in and slap the breech closed. Locked, loaded and ready to rock 'n' roll.

I'm going to need it.

Gordon is still smiling.

This is going to suck.

"Keep him occupied," Endo says. "I need to get on his back."

Really suck.

"You heard the man," I say, stepping toward Gordon, M4 aimed and pressed against my shoulder. "Time to make a sacrifice play."

Before I can engage Gordon, Alessi runs past me, headed for Gordon. Endo runs out diagonally, ducking behind some tall rocks, no doubt looking to come up behind the monster of a man, while Alessi distracts him. He wasn't even speaking to me.

I lower my weapon and glance at Collins. She looks as mystified as I feel.

"Should we help?" I ask.

"Probably should," she says, not moving. "In a minute. I want to see what they can do."

So we watch the show.

Alessi lets out a banshee wail that instantly attracts Gordon's attention. He no doubt knows that Endo is the true threat, but the fearless woman charging him, no weapon in sight, is hard to look away from. She's got guts, that's for damn sure. But if she's not careful, they're going to be spilled all over the rocks for the gulls to snack on.

Gordon's fists clench. He doesn't wind up for a punch, but I doubt he has to. When he strikes, it's a blur, but he strikes nothing. Alessi slides between his legs. As Gordon spins in pursuit of the small woman, Endo emerges from behind the tall rocks, coming back around. The whole move was choreographed to make Gordon believe Endo would be coming up behind him. When he turned around after Alessi, he might have expected to also find Endo. Instead, he became an unwitting participant in a practiced maneuver.

Alessi ducks two close punches, and just when I think she's run out of fancy moves, Endo leaps from a two-foot-tall boulder and lands on Gordon's back like he's a Velcro wall. Gordon flails, but Endo clings on tightly with his legs. Unshakable. With his left hand, Endo stabs the taser into Gordon's left temple. With the right, he jams the drill-tipped neural whatsamabob into Gordon's right temple.

Gordon shouts in frustration, but not pain.

Then some part of Gordon's mind remembers that he, like Endo, is a highly trained soldier who knows how to fight. And when someone is on your back, you don't reach for them or shake around.

Gordon flings himself backwards toward a tall, brown stone rising up from the beach rocks like a long-lost Easter Island bust. Despite my distaste for Endo, I flinch. The man's about to die.

As the pair falls back, Endo punches his fist into Gordon's temple and then leaps away. He falls clear of the rock as Gordon slams into it, but this part of the dance hasn't been choreographed. Endo hits hard, landing in a field of slippery seaweed-covered boulders. Despite his best effort, there's no way to slow his fall. He takes a hard hit to the ribs and then rolls away, disappearing into a tide pool with a splash.

To hell with this, I think, and toggle Devine to transmit. "Hawk-one, this is Hudson. I need three birds to my coordinates, ASAP."

"Our target, sir?" Hawk-One's voice fills my ear.

"Lance Gordon," I say. "This is a priority one target. Lethal force authorized. Be aware, there are four friendlies on site. Pick your target carefully, but be quick about it."

"Copy that," Hawk-One says. "ETA, ten minutes."

Shit. This will be done in ten minutes. The only friendlies they're going to find are smears. I should have never listened to Endo. At least we still have Betty.

"Woodstock, come around for a flyby," I say. "If we're clear, light him up."

While Betty's rocket pods are empty, she still has a high powered chain gun. It's nothing compared to the heavy hitting armaments of an Apache attack helicopter, but it should do more than tickle.

"Let's go," I say to Collins, raising my weapon again and heading for Gordon. While Endo and Alessi have clearly been training for an up close and personal confrontation with Gordon, Collins and I have been working on coordinated weapons assaults. Granted, we generally have about twenty more men supporting us, but we're both competent.

"Aim for the eyes," Collins says. "Won't do any permanent damage, but if he can't see, it will slow him down."

Gordon shoves himself off the rock and looks for Endo. Not seeing him, the traitorous general throws himself at Alessi, who looks a lot less sure of herself, now that the plan has fallen apart. She manages to duck his sweeping arms, but he recovers quickly and reaches out to grab her head. One good squeeze and she's done.

She stands in between Gordon and me. His hunched body is just a little taller than hers. And they're both moving. It's an impossible shot. The odds of my hitting her are—

Crack!

Collins squeezes off a single round. It doesn't hit Gordon's eye, but the impact on his cheek is enough to get his attention. Alessi uses the distraction to duck away, running into the maze of rocks lining the ocean. And now Collins and I are Gordon's only remaining targets.

He lumbers toward us, yellow eyes blazing. "You're making this too easy for me. You should have stayed away."

As I depress the trigger and hold it down, emptying my magazine at Gordon, I realize he's right. The attack in Beverly was all about me. If I really am what's keeping Gordon and Nemesis from having a mental pow-wow, the results could be catastrophic, especially if he's able to influence her the way he is these other Kaiju.

As Collins and I both run out of ammo and move to reload, Gordon breaks into a run. I quickly move my hand to the weapon's second trigger and pop off a grenade. It hits Gordon head on, stumbling him, but nothing more. While I unload another magazine at his head, Collins fires her grenade. The fragmentation device strikes Gordon's forehead, exploding with enough concussive force to knock the wind out of me. The shards of metal sprayed by the grenade have no effect on his thick skin, but there's enough of the stuff flying around that his eyes both take hits. His approach grinds to a halt as he rubs at his face, growling in frustration.

It's just a momentary delay. But it's enough.

When Gordon opens his eyes again, fully healed, Collins and I are gone, hiding behind a granite block inscribed with information about the park. In our place is Betty, chain gun already spinning.

A look of unadulterated annoyance wipes across Gordon's face a second before Woodstock pummels it with a stream of bullets. The weapon sounds like a giant, angry bee, firing ten rounds per second. Just a fraction of a second is enough to reduce the average person into a hunk of unrecognizable meat. Nasty stuff. But Gordon takes it like it's a fire-hose blast of water. He just leans forward, arms raised to protect his face, and keeps on coming.

For me.

But then there is hope. Flecks of black start shooting away from the flesh on Gordon's arms and chest. The high caliber bullets are punching through his skin!

And that's when Betty runs out of bullets.

Gordon straightens up and flexes his chest. The black flesh is all torn up. As his broad chest widens, its cracks open up, revealing lines of bright orange.

Then he's running again, his big feet pulverizing the earth with each step. At least it won't be hard for a forensics team to put together the story of my death. Realizing that wasting more ammo on Gordon isn't going to do anything but put us in harm's way, I shout, "Run!" and turn to follow my own command.

I'm a pretty observant guy, so as I spin 180 degrees and move my legs, I notice the tall, green grass ahead, the way it glows yellow in the sunlight and waves in the cool ocean breeze. I also notice the grasshopper, clinging to a thick blade, perhaps watching the unfolding scene with detached curiosity. But all of this flashes in and out of my mind in a fraction of a second, overwhelmed by the appearance of a moving shadow. It slides across the grass, shrinking just above the grasshopper, until Gordon lands. He jumped clear over me.

The grasshopper is a goner.

So am I.

Before I can fully stop, Gordon reaches out and catches me around the waist with his left hand. He lifts me from the ground, and I feel like a kid again, lifted off my feet by that horrible Gravitron carnival ride, helpless and ill. He quickly drives his right fist into my stomach. The armor I'm wearing helps absorb and redirect some of the force, but I still feel like I've been hit by a car. And I'm promptly hit by it two more times, each impact getting closer to liquefying my insides.

A gun fires, close and fully loaded. Six shots. Collins. She manages to pause his barrage, but only long enough for him to spin around and use me like a club. When my body strikes Collins, Gordon lets go, and the two of us topple to the ground. I'm not sure if I black out or not, but before I can even think about getting up, he's above me, blocking out the sun, the grin still on his face.

He has no quipy final words for me. He just raises his meaty fist, eyes on mine, ready to squash my head. Bruised, battered and out of breath, I don't have the energy or ability to move anything more than my hand, which I use to find Collins's hand, and squeeze. A silent goodbye.

The fist descends like a blunt guillotine.

DRAKON

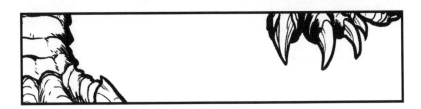

20

"Stop!" The voice is distant and weak, but the effect is impressive.

Gordon's fist freezes, cocked back, still ready to mash my face, but unmoving. That's not entirely true. The limb shakes against the invisible force holding it. Gordon, his face scrunched tightly in anger, teeth bared, is still trying to kill me. He just can't.

Still unable to move and save myself, I let my head loll to the side. Endo limps toward us, his weight supported by Alessi. He's clutching his ribs and he's soaked through, dripping tide-pool water.

Why is Gordon—the neural implant! It's attached to his temple. And it *works*.

"Step away," Endo says. It's almost a request, but Gordon obeys. Not without some resistance though. His body shakes with agitation, revolting at the idea of obeying his former subordinate.

A deep growl builds in Gordon's chest, escaping through his grinding teeth as a muffled roar. His yellow eyes blaze with fury. I suspect the growl is an outward sign of his mental resistance, because Endo grunts and falls to his knees, holding his head.

I push myself up, despite the pain. If Endo loses his grasp on Gordon, I don't want to be laying down waiting for him like a loose floozy.

Alessi helps keep Endo upright. "Are you okay?" She turns to Collins. "Help me."

Collins seems torn between helping me up and assisting Endo. It's nice that she cares, but we kind of need Endo to stay conscious.

"Go," I tell her, pushing myself up like I'm tough shit and quickly regretting it. My whole body hurts. Going to for days. Despite me being Gordon's punching bag, Endo looks worse off than me.

"What's wrong with him?" Collins asks Alessi, helping hold Endo up.

"It's Gordon," Endo says between gasps. His eyes are clenched shut. "He's fighting it. He's—"

"Get out of my head!" Gordon screams, clutching the sides of his skull. I don't think he knows the neural implant is there, but he could still break it by accident. However this ends, it seems clear that Endo's control of Gordon is only temporary.

Endo spasms and falls back, hanging limp in the women's arms. "I...know...what...he—argh!" Endo's back arches. Blood pours from his nose.

This connection with Gordon's brain is killing him. I reach for Endo's ear piece and yank it away. Nothing changes. I'd assumed the headset was what allowed Endo to connect with the target mind. I was wrong. "How can I break the connection?"

"You can't," Alessi says.

"It's going to kill him," I counter, and part of me asks, *why do I care?*

She looks down at Endo. "Only he can break the connection."

Endo's eyes open wide. He reaches out and clutches my arm. "I was right. It's you. He's going to kill you. But it...has to be...*him*. Ahh!"

Gordon is seething. He stumbles about, grunting and groaning, thrashing back and forth like Endo is still clinging to his shoulders. As I watch the twisting giant, his chest flexes. The ruined skin splits, revealing bands of orange light.

Like Nemesis and the other Kaiju, Gordon now has an explosive defense system, which I now know from experience, also makes for a useful propellant. As strong as Gordon is, I suspect he lacks the mass to stand against the force of that kind of explosion.

"Endo," I shout. "Move him away. Get out of his thoughts, and move him toward the ocean!"

Endo and Gordon gasp in unison. Their thoughts in sync for just a moment as they both turn toward the ocean and speak, "She's coming."

Since the events of the previous year, there is pretty much only one reason why someone might look to the ocean in fear and speak those words. Nemesis. My unwanted protector. Racing to the rescue. And she's hard to miss. Two miles out, a 50-foot-tall mound of water rushes toward the shore, cut through by the 30-foot-tall spikes that line the carapace of her back.

While the monster's intentions are noble, or instinctual as the case may be, she's going to get us all killed. When she stops—*if* she stops—that massive wave is going to keep right on coming. I think it's safe to say that Nemesis has no understanding of Newton's first law of motion.

But before we can head for higher ground, we need to deal with Gordon.

"Endo," I say. "Focus, you son-of-a-bitch. Push him toward the water."

Gordon, eyes still on Nemesis, takes a furtive step. Then another. He must realize that he's being controlled again, because his movements become shaky and unbalanced. Endo's body quivers. His eyes roll back. But Gordon keeps on moving.

I point to the large cube of inscribed granite. "Take cover!"

Collins and Alessi drag Endo behind the five-foot-thick marker while I drag myself. All of my limbs are working, but the pain I feel with each step slows me down. When I reach the others, I look back to Gordon. He's a good two-hundred feet away. *Far enough*, I decide, and I draw my pistol.

"Endo, if you can hear me, turn him around."

Gordon slowly faces us, his eyes locked on me. *I am so getting sick of being on the receiving end of a Kaiju glare.*

"Open his arms," I say. "Flex his chest."

My unwanted teammate shakes. Drool slides down his cheek.

Gordon shakes, fighting the movement, not because he knows what I'm going to do, but just because he's a stubborn prick who doesn't like to be controlled. Which is understandable. I've been in his position.

With a pain-filled shout, Endo arches his back and falls unconscious.

My head snaps back to Gordon. He roars with victory, raising his fists. He turns his head skyward and lets out a howl, doing exactly what I wanted him to.

Looking over the barrel of my handgun, I notice that my vision is a little blurry. No time to let it clear. I squeeze off a shot. Then another. And another. They have no effect. Because I'm missing.

A louder gunshot rings out to my left.

Collins.

Oh crap. Collins won't—

The world turns orange as a hand shoves down on my shoulder and pushes me behind the large stone. Heat and flames rocket past. My face stings. My armor heats up. And then it's gone. While the explosive force from those orange membranes is impressive, the blast begins and ends very quickly, as the wound gets cauterized.

The grass on either side of us is charred and smoldering. I stand to find Gordon still on the rocky coastline, the area around him blackened by the blast. He's on his knees, clutching his chest. *He didn't know*, I realize. The explosion must have come as a shock, and probably hurt like hell. For the first time, he looks weak. Wounded. Perhaps vulnerable.

I'm not sure *we* could kill him, but having seen how Nemesis handled Scrion, there is no doubt she could make a snack of him.

Speaking of which... "Woodstock, we need immediate evac!"

Betty circles around overhead, dropping toward the stone between us and Gordon—and the giant wave, which is now just a half mile and thirty seconds away.

"Jeesum Crow!" Woodstock's shout punctuates Betty's sudden maneuver. The chopper pitches back and shoots away. Behind the thunderous rotor chops, I hear a splash, like a vast, wet, sucking noise.

A shadow covers the area.

Then it rains.

I turn my gaze upward and see the strangest looking, low hanging rain cloud ever. My misinterpretation of the shape is quickly undone by three orange circles.

Dammit. It's another Kaiju.

The monster has leapt out of the fresh-water quarry and is soaring over our heads like some demented version of Free Willy. The creature is smaller than Scrion, seventy-five feet from snout to tail tip, and faster. I can't see its face or back, but it's got four long, spike covered limbs jutting from its sides, like a lizard. And its long tail is flattened vertically at the end, perfect for swimming. This thing isn't here to fight, it's Gordon's getaway vehicle.

The monster pays us no attention as it lands between us and Gordon. It simply runs forward on its wide-spread legs and opens its triangle-shaped jaws. It scoops Gordon inside, almost delicately, and then the thing is in motion again. It dives into the ocean, and with two hard swipes of its tail, it disappears into the water.

The mountain that is Nemesis quickly alters course, giving chase, but it's clear the larger Kaiju will never catch the sleeker model now racing out to sea.

Propelled faster by Nemesis's sudden turn, the tidal wave races toward the shore.

"Let's go!" Collins shouts. Her voice pulls me out of spectator mode. Woodstock is already landing again. Collins hefts Endo over her shoulder and runs for Betty. Alessi is right behind her. And me... I'm hobbling after them like the Hunchback of Notre Dame with a leg cramp.

Collins throws open the side door and tosses Endo onto the floor. Alessi doesn't complain about the rough treatment. She just dives inside.

Looking through the open door and the window on the opposite side, I see nothing but water, racing up the shore.

My lungs feel like they're not working. I can't catch a breath, drowning in the open air. I know something is really wrong when my vision starts to fade. But I don't stop. I *can't* stop.

Collins reaches for me. "C'mon!"

I jump.

And collide with the outside edge of the chopper's floor. Pain shoots through my body, so intense that I can't feel anything save for the sick twisting sensation in my gut. Darkness blocks my sight. I try to fight it, but in the end, I decide I might not like to be awake when I drown, so I let myself slide into oblivion.

21

She felt...chaos.

Everywhere.

Her mind was torn. Her body burned with energy, but she was pulled in separate directions. Even as her holy rage compelled her to lash out and silence the corrupt voices in the world—*everyone* in the world—that still small voice that was also *her*, whispered for her to stop. To have mercy. To protect. There was a time when the voices sang in unison, for blood and retribution, but now, they were at odds.

And yet, they were each other. The same.

Nemesis and Maigo.

Monster and girl.

Every situation she encountered and each set of decisions, while tearing the pair apart, unified them in the end, as confusion became action, and action felt...good.

She knew the dark man. Felt her heart in him, as she had once before. But while she had changed, he had not. His thirst for vengeance, for destruction, grew. While those feelings were still a part of her, and were a thirst she would quench, she had found balance. She sensed the dark man's desperate longing and ignored it. Their hearts, once the same, were no longer aligned.

But there was another. She sensed his heart only vaguely, but she knew it well. She felt it the day retribution had been brought upon the man who... As powerful as she felt, the memories—the pain and loss of that day—were still too disturbing to think about. She had been helpless then.

He understood that.

He...sympathized with her pain.

And he had helped deliver her from it.

While the world around her cried out for punishment, his weakness drew her attention. Because the dark man still lived. And his dark heart wanted to consume the other. The...light man.

So the world and its evil would wait until the dark man tasted vengeance for his crimes against the light. The most recent of which nearly claimed his life. He was alive, she knew. Though she could sense the billions of souls on the planet, his stood out as a beacon and a reminder of who she had been.

Who she still was.

The dark man slid away into the darkness, her tether to him growing more faint. Like the light man, the dark man's heart had grown weak. But he was protected, too. Swept away by a creature like her...but not. It saw the world as she did, in shades of light and dark, good and evil, but it judged the world more harshly, as she had once done, when she was separate. When she was alone.

But was that other self, so long ago, the same being she was now?

Questions like this, malformed and jumbled, entered her mind on occasion, but she was not of the mind to find answers. She was a creature of instinct. Of purity in all its forms. She could feel only the answers.

And she felt the light man.

So faint.

And weak.

So she waited in the deep, at the base of a steep shoal, where her bulk would go unnoticed by the enemies still seeking her out.

When the light man woke and the dark man returned, she would rise to exact her justice, first on the dark man, and then...then, she didn't know.

22

I wake to the sound of wheezing mixed with a chorus of beeps. With my eyes still shut, I know where I am. The antiseptic scent and background voices of a busy hospital are easy to identify.

My eyes flutter and open. I have a spectacular view of the speckled white, dropped ceiling above me. I dwell on the night sky in reverse image, my mind slowly returning to me.

I remember Gordon, the new Kaiju, Nemesis and the wave. And the pain, which regrettably hasn't really faded. Movement to the left draws my attention. A wall-mounted television. *The Golden Girls.* An involuntary groan escapes my lips. My mother watched *The Golden Girls* religiously, starting in 1985 and ending on the day of her death, twenty three years later, when I found her in front of the television, a smile on her face, Betty White playing dumb to some kind of accusation.

That had been a hard day. My father had died five years previous. But it wasn't until mom went that I felt...free. When her soul left, she mercifully pulled away a burden that I had buried long ago. But she'd forgotten to take my loathing for the Golden Girls.

Estelle is talking. Loudly. Something about spaghetti sauce.

"Fuck you, Estelle," I say to the TV, hoping my mother is somehow able to hear how I feel about the show, which I could never express while she lived.

"Ehh?" says a too loud voice that hurts my head. "What's that?"

My neighbor looks old enough to be Estelle's father. He's gotten to the ripe, old age where liver spots cover more of his skin than not, no hair remains on his head and the size of his nose is dwarfed only by the girth of his ears. If we were in a jungle rather than a hospital, I might mistake him for a proboscis monkey.

"Nothing," I say, waving him off. My voice is raspy and deep. I feel like someone took a cheese grater to my throat. *Tubes*, I think. They had tubes down my throat. I look at my hand. An IV line runs up to a clear bag hanging nearby. A heart monitor—the beeping—is attached to my index finger.

"Suit yourself," the old man says, but he knows. He's clutching the TV's remote. Golem's precious. No one with any good taste or sense of decency watches *The Golden Girls*, especially the spaghetti episode. He knows, all right. He catches me looking and hugs the remote tighter.

"Hey," says a sleepy voice.

It's Collins, sitting on the other side of me. Looks like she just woke up, but she's otherwise just as smoking hot as usual. A couple of details leap out at me, though. Her tactical gear is gone, replaced by jeans and a t-shirt. And her red hair has some bounce to it. She's had time to shower and change. Assuming Woodstock flew straight here, during the middle of the day, and Collins stayed by my side through the night—like she would—until someone sent her home to change out of her stink, all that and the now missing throat tubes tell me a few things. First, I was in bad shape. Second, I've been here for at least a day.

"Two days?" I guess.

"Three," she says.

"Nemesis?"

"Gone," she says. "Gordon, too. It's been all quiet."

"Too quiet?" I ask with a chuckle that makes me pay in pain.

"Try not to laugh," she says.

"Is that why *The Golden Girls* is on?"

"What?" she asks, glancing at the TV. I've never told her about my loathing for the show. She'd probably think I just hate old people. I glance at my neighbor. Right now, I kind of do. He catches me looking and makes a face which communicates an unmistakable 'fuck off.'

I raise my middle finger at him and he turns away.

"Hey!" Collins says, smacking my shoulder, which actually hurts a lot.

I sigh, slowly and carefully, managing the intensity of the pain. "So, what's the damage?"

"Two broken ribs. A scratched lung. They said it was very nearly punctured. And a lot of internal bruising, but no bleeding. You hit your head pretty good when you fell in the chopper."

"I thought I jumped."

"If you jumped, it was the most pitiful jump I've ever seen. Like this guy—" she nods to my neighbor, "—doing hurdles."

The image of the old guy tumbling through a line of hurdles brings a smile to my face. I nearly laugh, but tamp it down with the memory of pain. Collins smirks at my struggle. "Jerk," I say.

"So, have you picked out a ring yet?" she asks.

I involuntarily convulse with surprise, which sends lightning bolts of anguish through my body.

Collins covers her mouth, laughing at my pain.

"Asshole!" I say, smiling despite the pain. When the pain subsides, my thoughts turn back to my last memories. "What happened to Endo?"

She motions to the wall behind me. "Next room over. He's...in a coma."

This sobers me up quickly. I still loathe the man, but I clearly recall him saving my life.

"They haven't figured out why yet, but I think—"

I know where she's going. "The neural implant."

She nods. "Lessi thinks it overloaded his mind. That with time he'll be fine."

"'Lessi?'"

"We've had time to get to know each other." Collins looks at the wall like she can see through it. "She cares about him. Though I don't think their relationship is anything but professional. She's still here, though. Says a lot."

I reach out and take Collins's hand. "Yeah, it does. Should I give you the ring now?"

Collins gasps and leans back, eyes wide, hand to her mouth. When I laugh, it hurts like hell, but it's worth it. Vengeance is mine. I'm Nemesis with a sense of humor. When I've recovered once more, I set my mind to more serious things. "Cooper and Watson?"

"Fine," she says. "Monitoring the coast and overseeing the evacuation's end."

"I meant the baby."

Collins smiles like it's the sweetest thing in the whole wide world. "Yes, all three of them are okay."

"What about Zoomb?" I ask. "Any word on their prototype?"

"I haven't asked," she says. "The small version on Gordon nearly killed Endo. I can't imagine what would happen if—"

"But it worked," I say. "He controlled Gordon."

Any good humor she had a moment ago, melts away. "And *almost died.*"

"Gordon was resisting," I point out. "Maigo—"

"Is a monster!" Collins stands, hands on hips. "She destroys cities. Kills mercilessly. If you go inside that mind, you might *never* come back."

"She also saved my life. Twice."

"And nearly killed you in the process."

"If me being in a coma for a while is the price I pay for saving thousands or even millions of people, so be it."

Collins stares at me. She knows I'm right. It sucks, but I'm right.

"I hate you," she finally says, and sits back down. "But not until you're better."

"Or until she makes another appearance. Speaking of which, maintain evacuation protocols. If I'm still here..."

"Right. Shit." She takes out her phone and stands. "I'll be right back."

As she leaves the room, phony laughter pulls my eyes back to the TV. Estelle is in her nightgown. I roll my eyes toward my aged neighbor. "Hey buddy, just so you know, Nemesis eats people who aren't nice to me."

He stays calm, leaning back in his bed. "Yeah, well, you haven't met my wife."

We share a smile. Peace made.

If Nemesis is anything like the old guy, this mind-meld thing will be a snap.

I take a breath and let it out slowly. Yep, I'm screwed.

23

Gordon woke slowly, a lingering dream about his childhood home fading, as he became aware of his surroundings. He was in bed. A heavy blanket covered him. Protected him. Nightmares couldn't reach him here. Since the operation that gave him a new, more powerful heart, Gordon's body had undergone significant changes, but so had his mind. Powerful nightmares filled his sleep. That's what he believed them to be at first. But he knew better. They were glimpses into the past. Into her past...and his. Millennia of strife. Of war. Hate. All of it calling to him in his dreams. Fueling his bloodlust.

But here, warm and safe, he...

Gordon remembered he no longer had a bed.

Or a home.

He opened his eyes slowly. The subtle movement exhausted him. He hadn't felt this weak in a long time. The darkness of slumber was unchanged by the opening of his eyes. So he focused on his other senses. He could feel the bed and blanket. The weight of it felt good, but it was warm...and damp. As was the air, which smelled of rotting meat. Whale meat. He'd come to know the scent well, as his children swam the oceans, consuming everything they could catch to keep up with their rapidly expanding size. Lacking the growth hormones given to Maigo, they couldn't match Nemesis's growth factor, but they were catching up. And while three of them were smaller, the other two...

Gordon grinned.

He knew where he was.

The blanket was a tongue.

Rise, he thought, and he felt the bed beneath him shift. When it leveled out again, he thought, *open*. Wide jaws opened slowly and carefully, like the cargo door of a C-130 Hercules transport plane, if you ignored the three-foot-tall teeth.

The tongue lifted, and Gordon stood. He walked to the edge of the mouth on shaky legs and held on to a tooth for balance. It was night, but he could see the ocean before him, lit by the moon.

He'd been afraid of the ocean as a young man. Mostly because of *Jaws*. Being eaten alive, while drowning, had been the most prevalent nightmare of his youth. Now, there wasn't a creature alive that he feared. Save one. Part of him wanted to run the other way. He had the children. In time, their strength would match Nemesis's. Combined, they already did. But while he had the children, he also had her heart, and it was impossible to ignore. He needed her back, or...

His mind, still in the gap between sleep and wakefulness, considered new options. He'd been driven to strengthen his tether with Nemesis, to make himself whole again. But what if that tether could be fully broken? Painful, perhaps, but he would be free from this constant nagging desire.

No, he thought, the idea of losing that part of him felt revolting.

But... *If there's no other recourse...*

"I'll kill her," he said, speaking to the ocean. Saying the words aloud made him cringe. Could she hear his thoughts? Could she feel his desires? There were times he felt the connection between them growing stronger, but it always faded, leaving him feeling empty and lost.

His eyes dropped and his head turned down. He was weary. His chest looked different. Where there had once been thick, black skin, there was now a smooth, milky band of flesh. He placed a finger against the surface and rubbed. The white came away like wet chalk. He squinted at the gunk, confused by its presence, but he quickly forgot about it as a soft orange light glistened over the night time water. He searched the area for a boat. For a helicopter. But he was still alone, with his child.

The light is coming from me, he realized, looking down again. *From my chest!* He wiped at his chest, shucking away sheets of white until the darkness was pushed back by a warbling orange glow. Gordon grinned. His chest was full of swirling orange liquid.

Memories of his last confrontation with Jon Hudson and Katsu Endo returned. The explosion. It hadn't been a weapon. It was *him*. He'd exploded! The blast had weakened him, but he had survived. For a moment, he dared to hope that Hudson had been killed in the explosion, but his connection to Nemesis had not changed. The man still lived.

For now.

And Endo. He'd done something. Violated his mind. Controlled him. But that wasn't all. In the moments before the explosion, Gordon glimpsed Endo's thoughts. He felt Endo's desires. He saw how they would be accomplished. And he understood the enemy's plan. Endo had unknowingly supplied Gordon with the keys to victory.

As his strength returned, Gordon smirked. He reached up to the side of his head, felt the device still there, and pinched it gently. With a secure grip, he pulled it from his thick flesh and looked at it. The small device looked harmless, but Gordon understood its threat. It could turn anyone, or anything into a weapon. It could undermine his control of the children and prevent him from reconnecting with Nemesis.

Endo and his employers would need to be eliminated. Then Hudson. And if the connection to Nemesis couldn't be re-established, she would follow. It was a vague plan at best, but it was a start. And upon its completion, he and the children would carry out the deepest desires of their hearts—the judgment and execution of the human race.

Gordon closed his eyes and focused on the children, spread out around the world. At first, they had dispersed to feed, so that the disappearing wildlife would be less noticeable. When they rose to strike Hong Kong and Sydney, it was to spread confusion, to keep the enemy looking elsewhere while he closed the distance. If not for Nemesis, that plan would have worked. But now...there was no reason to hide. No reason to separate.

Gordon was still a general.

The time for war had come again.

He needed his army.

24

The roof of the FC-P headquarters has become my sanctuary while the work crews repair the damage to the stairwell wall. They're using a lot of the original bricks, knocked out by Gordon, so it won't look too funny. Not that I care about aesthetics, but seeing a lighter red circle of bricks in the wall every time I pull into the driveway would be a glaring reminder of what I had nearly lost that day. Collins, Cooper and Watson. All three of them could have been killed. Were damn lucky they weren't.

Which brings me to my next source of constant agitation. Katsu Endo. Not only had he saved my life in Rockport, but he'd saved my team, too, at great personal risk. I still don't trust his motives, or Zoomb's, but I'd be an ass to not award the man some brownie points, especially since he was still in a coma.

The view here isn't all that different from the Crow's Nest below. I can still see the ruin of what once was Beverly's coastline. Except out here, I can smell it, too. I barely notice the stink of ash. On the shore of what was once Dane Street Beach, a crew of Zoomb employees have descended like vultures. With practiced efficiency, they're disassembling Scrion's body and carrying it away by helicopter, large chunks of dark meat dripping brown all over the city.

This might even be the same crew that dismantled the Nemesis-Prime corpse—the first in a long line of people responsible for the birth of a city-destroying monster. And now they're back to work, this time with the President's stamp of approval, despite my best attempts to change his mind. In the months following the Nemesis disaster, I had the President's ear. He took my warnings, responded to my requests and increased my budget exponentially. But since Nemesis's reemergence, the man has gone silent. Since ordering me to work with Endo, he hasn't taken my calls, and requests from the White House are once again being filtered through the mustache brigade that is the DHS.

I'm not out of the loop. Not entirely. And I'm still in charge of the FC-P, but there is an election coming up, and Zoomb's support can help fill ballot boxes. Strangely, the security I feel about my job comes from Endo. Sure, he's a threat, but he needs me.

After what happened to Endo, Collins would have me strung up and lashed with a barbed cat o' nine tails before letting me mind-meld with Nemesis, but I'm convinced it's our best option. Not only is Nemesis still a threat, but now there's Gordon and three other Kaiju that are still growing. Something has to be done. Something drastic. And if I know the powers that be, and I do, they're going to start dropping nukes. Call me crazy, but I'd rather risk a coma if it meant not dropping nukes on American soil. Or *any* soil for that matter.

"What do you think?" I ask. "Am I crazy?"

"Craziest son of a bitch, I know," Woodstock says.

I spin around in surprise. Hadn't heard the man's arrival.

"You okay?" he asked.

"Didn't know you were there."

He looks back and forth. "Who the hell were you talkin' to then?"

I hitch a thumb toward Betty, resting silently on her landing pad. If anyone understands talking to inanimate objects, it's Woodstock. He proves it by nodding like he should have known. "She's a good listener."

"Ayuh," I say, offering some traditional Maine agreement.

He joins me at the roof's edge. Sits atop the small wall, oblivious to the height. "You thinkin' what I think you're thinkin'?"

I sit down next to him, watching a crane peel back Scrion's turtle shell-like carapace. "Probably." Woodstock and I are often in simpatico. It's why I like having him as a pilot. But it also means he knows when I'm thinking of doing something stupid or reckless. "You won't tell Collins?"

"This one of them 'bros before hoes' situations?"

I nearly fall four stories from laughing. Collins would kick his balls into his brains if she heard him, and he knows it, which makes it all the more funny.

He shakes his head. "Can't say as I'd blame her for stopping you, though. Heard 'bout Cooper and Watson. Having a kid. Good news. It's not yours, but it could have been. And before you tell me you use protection, I fought my way past a condom and a diaphragm. If the kid wants to be born bad enough, it will happen. And if it doesn't... well, you still have your lady to think about."

I'm not sure what to say. Woodstock has never held me back before.

Then he goes and reads my mind again. "I'm not telling you *not* to do it, mind you. It's risky, but that's our job. I'm just saying that the damage you do by sneaking, by risking your life without saying goodbye, would be far worse than being up front and disagreeing. Even if she's pissed. The easier option for you, in this case, will be the harder to forgive."

"Sage relationship advice from an old, single man," I say.

"The ladies don't come to me for advice, son," Woodstock says. His grin turns wicked. "They come to me for—"

Part of me is relieved by the sound of approaching feet that interrupts Woodstock's sentence. The other part is horrified when I turn to find Collins, just a few feet away, arms crossed. She heard. I know she heard. But I don't say anything yet. She has company.

"Endo," I say, climbing off the wall and standing. "You're awake." He's more than awake. He looks good. As usual. Like he'd suffered little more than the loss of a good night's sleep. I look around his shoulder, carefully avoiding Collins's eyes. "Alessi isn't with you?"

It's a strange question, I know, but the two have been inseparable since we first encountered them in Hong Kong.

Endo squints at me. Collins's brows furrow deeper. They have both misunderstood my interest. Like I need any more help tightening the noose around my neck.

"She's coordinating with Cooper and Watson," Endo says.

The casualness with which he uses their names bothers me, like he's just part of the team and always has been. It's the familiar tone. He hasn't earned it.

Woodstock clears his throat at me.

Right. Honesty. No TV romance.

I turn to Collins. "I—"

"—have no choice," she says. "I know. Your new best friend—" she glances to Endo, "—told me all about it. To stop the monster, you have to understand the monster. Know your enemy. I get it."

"It's more than that," I say. "We won't just know her, we'll understand her. What she wants."

"Where she's from," Endo says.

"How to stop her," I add, knowing that if Endo expressed this sentiment, it would be, 'How to control her.'

But that's not my goal. If she leaves the human race be, I'm content to leave it at that. I don't see the need to pick a fight we might not win if we can avoid it. And I sure as hell don't agree with using her as a weapon. Maigo tearing apart Boston in search of her murderous father, isn't all that dissimilar from the American use of atomic bombs in World War II. Or our assaults on Iran and Afghanistan. Or Vietnam. Korea. How many innocent people have we killed to execute the villains we've targeted? I'm not opposed to just wars, I just don't think our judgment is any better than Nemesis's. The best solution is to appease her violent nature.

Or destroy her.

So as much as I'm playing along, I have no intention of trying to control her. And that's why it's going to work. Endo felt a backlash from Gordon that was strong enough to put him in a coma. But he was trying to control the man. I'm aiming for a dialogue. If that's even possible. Who knows, maybe my head will explode. I just think it's worth the risk.

"Well, then, since we're all on board," I say. "How do we get this done? It's not like we can call Nemesis on the phone and invite her for dinner."

"Actually," Endo says, a gleam in his eye that says I'm wrong. "I think we have confirmed that there is one way to draw Nemesis out of hiding."

Collins, Woodstock and I stand silent, waiting for his revelation, because we sure as shit don't know what he's talking about. But then Collins groans and turns her head to the sky. "You can't be serious."

"What?" I ask, feeling stupid for not figuring it out.

"You're the bait," she says.

"Not exactly," Endo says. "Nemesis is not interested in harming you. Her intentions seem to be the opposite, in fact. She will come if you are in danger. In *mortal* danger. To save you."

I turn away from the others. I'd rather watch Scrion's body be dissected than look into Collins's eyes. Not because she's disapproving, but because I might change my mind. "I need to be in mortal danger."

Endo nods.

"Still sounds like a worm on a hook to me," Woodstock says.

"We can't do that here." Despite the charred remains of the city coast, the area is still densely populated. "And we can't travel to a remote location without wasting a lot of time. Who knows how long it would take her to follow us, or even if she would? So there's really only one place we can do this, right?"

I know he's come to the same conclusion already, so it's no surprise when Endo steps up next to me and says, "Correct."

Looks like Boston gets to be Nemesis's Tokyo after all. "To Boston, then."

25

Fourteen hours later, I'm standing on top of a 325-foot-tall apartment building, not all that dissimilar from the one Maigo was murdered in—except that this building stands on the coast of Boston's North End. Or rather, what once was Boston's North End. While work crews have been slowly working their way toward this part of town, clearing debris, they've barely scratched the surface. I've heard estimates between five and ten years just to clear out the rubble. Needless to say, this part of town is empty. A wasteland. Although the building beneath my feet was somehow spared, the skyscrapers to my back, and the New England Aquarium to my left, look like they've weathered the apocalypse. Those buildings that are still standing are missing windows, their skeletons exposed and their insides rotting in the humid summer air. Straight down the middle is a stretch of molten destruction, where Nemesis self-immolated to clear a path.

So we've chosen this harbor-side high-rise with the hopes that Nemesis will choose the path of least resistance. She may not. She might tromp right over Logan Airport again, which has been rebuilt. But the airport has been evacuated of people and planes, so if she does take the shortcut, damage will be primarily to the runways.

Our plan was met with extreme backlash, but in matters of National Security regarding Nemesis, the FC-P pretty much has final say. And with Zoomb supporting the plan, the White House wasn't about to decline our rather large requests.

So here I am, pacing over the tacky-hot surface of the black tar roof, waiting for Nemesis to come to my rescue. There's just one problem. I'm not in danger. "We've been here for three hours now. I'm not sure Gordon's going to show up."

Endo, the only other person on the roof with me, glances back over his shoulder. He's been standing at the roof's edge, staring out to sea, waiting for Nemesis's arrival, pining for her return. "I'm not certain he will."

I groan. The last thing I expected this mission to be was boring. I toggle Devine, connecting with Woodstock, who is circling the area with Collins and Alessi. Betty has been retrofitted once again, this time with Zoomb's prototype, Kaiju neural implant. "See anything up there?"

"Not a thing," Woodstock replies.

A year ago, I wouldn't have volunteered to stand on a building, waiting for a man-thing who wants me dead, and his Kaiju pets, with the hopes that Nemesis will come to my aid, thus allowing me to enter her thoughts via a neural implant. And now that I'm thinking about it, I realize the ridiculousness of this plan.

"This isn't going to work," I say to Endo. "Gordon's not an idiot. He's not going to come after me here. Admiral Ackbar would see this coming a mile away."

Endo actually chuckles and mumbles, "It's a trap."

I sometimes forget that this cold, killing, fighting machine was once a sci-fi loving kid who became obsessed with Kaiju. I've done my research. I know his public history, and his private. Interviewed his old friends. His parents. They haven't seen or heard from him since he joined up with General Gordon, and thinking he was dead or missing, and that I was on the case, they filled me in on his geeky beginnings. That he understands my Star Wars reference shouldn't come as a surprise. The humor doesn't last long, though. "I never expected Gordon to show up."

My pacing stops. "Excuse me?"

"Gordon's not a fool."

"I thought..." Past conversations play through my mind. I try to remember the specifics of this plan, as they were presented to me by Endo. I realize that every mention of Gordon in relation to my imminent danger was presented by myself or my team. Not by him. "So we're just hoping Nemesis is going to show up, then?"

Endo shakes his head. "She will come."

He says it with such confidence, I nearly believe him. But without me being in danger, the plan won't work.

"You're life is in jeopardy," Endo says, answering my unspoken question. "It has been since the moment you and I stepped on this roof."

"How so?" I ask.

He looks at his watch. "Because in ten minutes, I'm going to kill you." The cold glare he shoots my way removes any doubt that he's bluffing. I take a step away from him, reaching for my sidearm and cursing when I find my hip empty. Endo had told me the metal weapon could interfere with the neural implant's connection to the hardware on my head. In reality, it would have interfered with the severe ass-kicking I'm about to receive.

Reaching lower, I pull my cell phone out, swipe the screen and try to connect with Woodstock again. No signal. Since Devine can use any and all cell towers, it's nearly impossible for me to not have a signal. That I'm unable to connect means Endo is blocking my signal, which also means he's got Zoomb's support in this.

Maybe the President's.

Damn, damn, damn. How did I not see this coming? As much as I loathe Endo, he must feel similarly about me. Probably worse. I see him as a dangerous criminal. A murderer. It's my job to not like him. But me? I stole his dreams, albeit, by accident. I'd really rather not have a 350-foot-tall guardian.

Endo keeps his back to me, knowing I won't try to attack him. I'm not in a rush to die. I back step toward the roof entrance. Try the green door's handle. Locked. The door feels solid. Metal. No way I'm kicking my way through in the five seconds it will take Endo to reach me. I look for Betty and find her five hundred feet up and a half mile away. Even if one of them is looking in this direction, which I doubt, they'd never see me.

I'm on my own.

"I think we've waited long enough," Endo says, turning toward me, his hawkish eyes locked on me, unblinking.

I stand my ground, fists clenched. "How can you be sure this will work?"

"I can't." He circles me slowly. "But either of the two prospective outcomes will be positive."

Two outcomes. 1) Nemesis shows up. 2) I die.

Great.

Endo breaks out of his circular route and struts toward me. His walk becomes a kick that misses my nose by inches. But this was just a diversion, because he's spinning still and airborne, his other leg coming up. I raise both arms just in time to block the kick, but his shin on my forearms is still painful as hell. And the force of the blow knocks me to the roof.

The sticky tar clings to me as I push myself up. I'm not sure if Endo is being sporting or just trying to prolong my suffering, but he gives me time to collect myself. I shake out my arms. My fingers are cramping up as the muscles in my arms try to shift back in place. I'm lucky he didn't break them.

He comes at me again, this time leading with his fists. The man's a blur, punching from every possible direction with the quickness of a striking cobra. I focus on blocking. If I attempt to strike back, I'll just leave myself open. He batters my aching arms, and despite my best efforts, he lands a few solid blows. To my cheek. My ribs. My gut. This last one pushes me back, hunched over, sucking in air. My heel hits something solid, and I start to fall.

When my body reaches a thirty degree angle, I catch a glimpse of what's beneath me. Nothing. I'm falling off the side! My only escape. I embrace it and let myself drop.

Then I stop, hovering out over a 325-foot fall. Endo has me by the shirt. When I reach out to wrench his hand away, he catches my wrist, yanks me up and flips me. After a short flight, I reach the terminus of my descent, landing square on my back. I'm wracked by coughs, as I roll to my knees and climb to my feet. Endo stalks toward me again and resumes his merciless assault, this time landing more punches than not.

A slap strikes my cheek. An *open-palm slap*. The man is fucking with me. Humiliating me! Before I can think, I lean into his punch, absorb it with my kidney and throw my hardest jab. I'm not sure whether it's a good punch or because of the sudden reversal in strategies, but the strike connects hard with Endo's chin, snapping his head back. While he stumbles back, I crumple to the roof, clutching my side, wishing I had arms like Shiva so I could clutch the rest of me.

Endo rubs his jaw. Blood drips from his mouth. "You can't win."

His arrogance is really starting to grate on me. As he closes in to resume my beating, his guard up, I lose my patience. With an angry shout I charge forward, linebacker style, arms spread wide. He makes me pay for the sloppy move by driving his foot into my crotch, but momentum and anger carry me past the pain.

I hit him hard, lifting him off the roof. I can feel his elbow driving into my back, again and again, but the pain is numb. Distant. It's like when you have a headache and someone tells you to bite your finger, one pain driving the other away. Whatever he's doing to my back can't compare to the pain in my balls.

I jump, lean forward and slam the much smaller man into the roof, allowing my shoulder to compress his belly. He shouts in pain. Satisfying pain. Before he can recover, I fling myself away from his fist and wrap his lower limbs in a vicious leg lock. When I'm done with him, his days of prancing around me will be over.

I squeeze hard, eliciting a scream of pain from Endo. His muscles tear. His ligaments stretch, ready to snap. "You can't win!" he screams again. Before I can wonder why he's still convinced of victory, I feel a burning sensation spreading through my thigh. The burn transforms into mind-numbing pain, and my brain screams at me that something is fundamentally wrong with my body. I lean up to look, my side roaring in pain, and I see what's happened.

There's a knife in my leg.

26

The part of my mind that hasn't gone numb, quickly takes stock of the injury. The blade is buried in the muscle of my leg, to the right of my femur, nowhere near my femoral artery. So I'm not going to bleed out. But that's a weak bonus when you consider the fact that I've still got a fucking knife in my leg.

And then, it's not. Endo pulls the blade free, and the pain loosens whatever grip I still had on the man. While I scream through grinding teeth, Endo rolls back to his feet. His face is flushed with pain and anger. I nearly had him.

My eyes find the knife in his hand. A small, two inch blade. The damage to my leg won't be severe. While I climb to my feet, mental gears spin, tumblers fall into place, and I come to a realization.

Endo could have killed me. Probably several times during our fight, but certainly with the knife. I checked for my femoral artery because in a fight to the death, that would get the job done. And Endo certainly has the skill to have inflicted the wound, even while leg-locked. But he didn't. He stabbed my muscle. With a small blade. The effort was enough to free himself, but not to seriously wound me. Sure, I'll be limping for a while, but I'm far from dead, or even incapacitated.

Fists clenched and head tilted to the left, I share my discovery. "You're not actually trying to kill me."

Endo is expressionless for just a moment, but then his shoulders sag in defeat, and I understand: Endo wasn't trying to kill me, but he needed *me* to believe he was. That was the plan all along, but I couldn't be told.

A vibration moves through the roof, nearly knocking me over. "The hell was that?" I ask.

Endo, eyes wide, reaches into his pocket, removes a device and pushes a button.

"...on top of you!" Woodstock's voice suddenly fills my ear. "Do you copy? She's right—"

He doesn't need to finish his sentence. The building shakes again, and we know exactly what's happening. "Copy that," I reply, trying to sound unfazed by everything. "Get into position and stand by." I turn to Endo. "I'd start running, if I were you."

He does run, but not the direction I expect. He comes at me, reaching into his black sport coat. He removes a slender box from the inner pocket, opens it and pulls out what looks like a black swim cap with white circles all over it. "Put this on."

I do what he says, but ask, "What is this?"

"It will boost the strength of your interface with Maigo."

I put my hand up to the headset in my ear, identical to the one Endo had worn when he controlled Gordon, and me. "But this..."

"Is just the transmitter." He slides the tight hat onto my head. Feels like my beanie cap.

"But you weren't—"

He taps his head. "Surgical implant." He looks back over his shoulder while the building continues to shake beneath our feet.

I've got a long list of questions, about how things work, about safety and protocol, but we're out of time. The sound of rushing water rises up over the building's roof.

Endo removes his coat, revealing the base jumping parachute that is his escape route—the very same method of egress I'd attempted to use by falling over the building's edge. "Good luck," he says, and sprints away.

I might normally watch his fall, see if the chute deploys in time to keep him from becoming a stain, but the massive form rising up on the other side of the roof has me transfixed. Water is whisked away by the wind, and the giant face, now above me, turns her brown eyes toward me. I see fury and anger, terrifying in its closeness and scope.

This...was a mistake.

I'm a dead man.

A sacrifice, like Alexander Tilly.

I can feel it with every fiber of my being.

And then I can't.

Maigo's giant eyes shift back and forth, searching for something that is no longer there. Endo. His disappearance and my relative safety has her confused. Her giant body begins tilting to the side. If she sees Endo, he's in a world of trouble, and so am I, because her rage is blind. In her pursuit of the man who would have killed me, she might plow right through this building.

"Endo," I say quickly and quietly, "Stay close to the building. She's looking for you." I don't wait for a reply. "Woodstock, are you ready?"

"Good to go," he says.

Nemesis continues to lean, her head now level with the building, and I'm sure she's going to spot Endo. I limp toward her, fighting against every one of my instincts that are screaming like terrified, high-pitched Japanese anime girls. "Maigo!"

She either doesn't hear me or she's ignoring me. I take a deep breath and catch the scent of ocean still dripping from her maw. I shout louder this time, my voice scratchy with desperation. "Maigo!"

The beast pauses.

The one eye I can still see shifts toward me. I can see my reflection in her pitch black pupil; I'm bleeding and leaning to the side, eyebrows turned up in abject fear. It's an embarrassing image. But it's erased as she stands up straight again, looking down at me. A hot breath, rank with the scent of oceanic decay washes over me. Nearly knocks me to my knees—from the stink, not the force.

"Woodstock," I whisper, trying not to move my mouth. "Now."

I hear the distant whoosh of a rocket being fired, but I try not to react. Instead, I sit down. Nemesis's eyes track me as I move, perhaps confused by my attempt at communication. Or perhaps trying to understand why she's compelled to protect me. Maybe she's just remembering the last time I stood atop an apartment building like this on the other side of the ruined North End.

"It's the hat," I say, touching the tight blue cap on my head. "Looks weird, right?"

No reaction. We're definitely not communicating in any meaningful way right now. The part of her that is Maigo seems to respond to the name, but maybe doesn't even know why.

Doesn't matter, in a few seconds I'm going to have a front row seat to the madness that is Nemesis's mind. I lie back on the scorching hot, tar roof, feeling its pliable surface give a little. If there's a chance I'm going to end up in a coma, I want to do it lying down.

The building shakes as Nemesis shifts her weight, perhaps bored or impatient, preparing to leave. But she doesn't get a chance. The rocket arrives with a roar, on target and unavoidable. It strikes the side of Nemesis's head. Her temple, if she's got one. But there's no explosion other than the outer shell shattering and flitting away. Nemesis reacts less than I would if a mosquito flew into the side of my head.

Before the device that remains can fall away, four sharp claws snap out from the sides and clutch to Nemesis's rough skin. A whirring sound pierces the air—the machine's diamond tipped drill, burrowing into Nemesis's skin. The neural implant looks tiny on the side of her massive face, but it appears to be doing its job.

Nemesis huffs in frustration, looking back and forth for the source of the irritating sound, and I realize the mosquito comparison is even more accurate. It's nothing but a—

"Ahh!"

Seizing pain lances through my body, which arches involuntarily to the point I fear my back is going to fold over on itself. Then everything goes black.

When I awake, I find myself standing.

The floor beneath my feet is tile. Hard and white.

There's a wall of windows to my right. A view of Boston, unscathed by Nemesis. But something is off. My perspective. I'm...short.

I look down. My hands are small. Tan. I'm wearing the clothing of a young girl just home from prep school. A Hello Kitty backpack rests at my feet.

Oh, shit. I know where I am.

"It's okay, Maigo," a sinister sounding male voice says.

I turn my eyes slowly up, pausing for a moment to watch the dark red fluid trace a path through the squares of grout on the floor. Then I see him. His face, pale and fat. Eyes burning like blue dwarf stars.

I hate him. For who he was and for what he's done.

"It was an accident," he says.

I know he's lying, but I can't say anything. Instead I stare at the motionless form of my mother, her manicured nails soiled with blood.

Mother...

In a blink, I'm me again.

But I'm still short.

The world has changed, but I know where I am.

I'm home. Christmas Eve. 1979.

No...No! I try to shout, but can't. I'm on autopilot, reliving a nightmare.

27

The shouting stopped ten minutes ago. But it didn't end like normal, which would have been slamming doors. It just...stopped. Suddenly. Mid-shout. I weep for several minutes, clutching my knees in the corner of my bedroom, bathed in the rainbow glow of a ceramic Christmas tree. When I stand, it's not out of bravery, but curiosity. Perhaps things are okay?

Maybe they're still wrapping my presents?

I decide to check. I move slowly across my room, pausing every time the radiator hisses or clicks. But I don't make a sound. I open my door, pushing against it with my foot to keep the tight latch from thumping open the way it does.

The stairs are covered in thick rug and don't creak, so the next part will be easy. Still, I take it slowly, lying down beside the banister at the top of the stairs, peering down into the home's foyer. The dining room to the right is lit by the warm glow of electric candles in each window. To the left, the living room blinks with light from the TV. *They're watching a show*, I think, and I start down the stairs, confident that neither of my parents will move until a commercial.

When I reach the bottom, I slowly peek around the doorway, but my view is blocked by the Christmas tree mom and I put up and decorated. The ornaments are old. 1950s stuff. The bulbs are the fat kind, not the small ones my friends have. My favorite part is the candy canes. They're real, and no matter how many I steal, my mom keeps resupplying them. I crouch and look beneath the tree. The red and green striped blanket is still draped around the base, but there are no gifts.

Maybe they're wrapping after the show? Or during and just haven't put them under the tree yet? Most of my friends still believe Santa does all that work, but I caught my parents last year. Got spanked for it, but now I know the truth. Remembering last year's spanking makes me wary. But curiosity is blind to the past. I lie down and slide behind the tree, pausing to take a deep breath of its pine scent.

When my father laughs at the television program, the last of my fear melts away. The fight is definitely over. With eager eyes, I push myself up over the side of the couch. My father sits at the far end, turned toward the TV in the corner of the room. My eyes move to the TV. *The Golden Girls*. Dad doesn't normally watch this. Certainly not alone. But I don't see—

A pair of feet on the floor catch my attention. I lift myself up a little higher and find my mother, sprawled out on the rug. There's blood on her forehead. A scream rises in my throat, but I'm shushed.

The part of me that is an adult spectator is confused by the noise. That's not how I remember it. When I look up, there is a girl standing above my mother. The me from minutes ago: plaid dress, Hello Kitty backpack, Asian. Maigo is here with me. Watching. She has an index finger pressed to her lips. "Shh! He will hear you!"

But he didn't hear me. I contained the scream, slunk back out of the room, ran upstairs and used my parents' rotary phone to call the police. I never saw my father again. My mother recovered from the attack that broke ribs and knocked her unconscious, but she was never really the same.

The memory resumes, playing out differently than I remember.

I step out from behind the tree and say to my father, "You did this."

He looks startled. Hurt. "No! I found her like this. She did it to herself."

I look back down at my mother. She's covered in blood. Shot.

"She killed herself, Jon."

"She wouldn't," I say. I've never believed anything so firmly in all my life.

"She *did*." My father stands to his feet, his shoes squeaking on the white tile floor.

I shake my fists. "You killed her!"

My father frowns, crouches by my mother's body and moves her hand.

"Leave her alone," I demand.

My father looks me in the eyes, a rare calm expression on his face. "Your mother killed herself, Maigo," my father says, "but she killed you first."

The gun, now in my mother's limp hand, is pointed at me.

The explosion makes me flinch. But I feel no pain. No impact. I turn to find Maigo, clutching her stomach, tears streaking down her smooth cheeks. She falls to her knees, dark almond eyes locked on me. *I've see those eyes before...* Then she pitches forward, landing hard on the cold tile floor, a pool of blood spreading from her core, mingling with her mother's.

I feel the pain of this moment acutely. The heartbreak. The rage. It was very nearly my own fate. And therein lies the heart of my connection to the monster that is Nemesis. I don't just sympathize with a murdered young girl, I understand her. That thirst for vengeance.

I've hid from it all my life, but it's there, in my dreams. I'm not sure where my father is, or if he's alive, but I've thought of finding him more than once. My position at the DHS would make it easy. But then what? Kick the shit out of an old man?

"What if he'd killed her?" Maigo asks from the floor, her dead eyes looking at me? "What if he'd killed *you*?"

"I...don't know," I tell her. But I do know. I already answered this question a year ago when I offered up Alexander Tilly for execution, and I did it without an ounce of guilt. But it's still not the same. One guilty man doesn't justify the killing of untold innocents. I attempt to say as much, but suddenly I feel strange.

My living room that is also Maigo's high rise condo, disappears. I'm surrounded by darkness and otherworldly screams. I've never heard anything so horrible. Then pain. Electric. Burning. I've never felt such searing pain. I feel my mind slipping away. And then, just as quickly, I'm pulled back to lucidity, and more pain. Never ending. I'm being driven mad, all the while a flow of information is flooding my mind, drowning whatever I had been.

A moral code.

Unshakable.

Indisputable.

And for those that break the code, death is the only recourse. No mercy.

A doubt lingers.

The pain returns, worse than before. I scream, joining the chorus of shrieking voices.

The flow of information repeats. I see images. Murders. Rapes. Unspeakable violence. I feel the difference between what is right and wrong. My anguish is slowly replaced by rage for the perpetrators. I want to stop them.

No, I want to destroy them.

I *must* destroy them!

Mercy means suffering. Relief only comes from the slaying of corruption. I am addicted to their destruction. And I will annihilate anything and anyone that stands in my way.

The cycle of pain and information continues until there is nothing else. I experience years of pain-based programming in a matter of seconds. Pain and screaming, good, evil and vengeance. This was the birth of Nemesis. The creation of the monster. Whoever...whatever, she was before, has been erased. But I know for certain that she was not the winged goddess of retribution. Someone made her this way.

Against her will.

The darkness is empty again.

I hear footsteps, small and gentle.

Maigo emerges.

"You cannot control me," she says, and I know she's right. The blind rage of Nemesis is beyond anyone's control...except Maigo's.

But... "You're not Maigo."

She stands still, staring at me.

"And you're not Nemesis," I say.

"I am new," she says. "And I am not. We are one, but...separate and different."

"Confusing," I admit.

"Very," she says, though she doesn't really say it. I feel it. This conversation isn't really happening. It's in my mind, translated into something I can understand. Whether that's me, Maigo, Nemesis or Endo's device, I have no idea.

"I—I am sorry," she says with a frown.

"I understand."

She nods. "I know. But... I..." She shakes her head. "I will always be—us. The past is inescapable."

I get it. She's not apologizing for Boston. For the deaths of countless innocents. She's apologizing for whatever happens next. The destruction. The judgment. She can't stop it. She knows we might be enemies again. That the struggle will continue. The history that made Maigo and Nemesis destroy Boston still exists. The urges, while tempered by a young girl, drive the monster, whose strange origins compel her to execute those she deems guilty, no matter who or what stands in her path.

And still, I understand.

Nemesis, like Maigo, is a victim.

Maigo walks toward me, a smile on her face. "Thank you for understanding." She reaches out, places a hand on my forehead.

"What are you doing?" I ask.

"Your gift," she says, and we're suddenly back in my living room, two kids in front of a Christmas tree. "To help stop the dark man."

A white hot heat burns my skin. I scream as that ancient, white-hot rage courses through my body.

"Hold him down!" I hear someone shout.

"I can't! He's—"

My eyes open. The rage fades like a dream. The blue sky above is blurred and fluttering. Two shapes lean over me. I recognize the red hair before my vision focuses. "Ash," I hear myself say.

Collins turns and says, "He's okay! He's back!"

My vision clears, and I see Collins above me, her long red hair tickling my cheek. Beside her is Alessi, and I'm surprised by the concern I see on her face. I grunt and turn my head to the side. Betty is on top of the apartment building roof, just a few feet away. The rotor blades chop above us, twisting hair and filling the air with bass-drum thunder.

"Where is she?" I ask.

Collins understands the question and looks out to sea.

"Help me up," I say.

Alessi moves first, more accustomed to following orders than questioning her boyfriend. But Collins helps her out, and I'm on my feet a moment later, hurting so badly I nearly ask to be put back down. But from my standing position, I can see what I need to.

Nemesis.

Maigo.

She's in the harbor, trudging back into the ocean, no sentence to carry out.

I sigh with relief, thinking about my bed. I turn to order everyone home.

That's when I hear the jets.

28

"What is that?" I ask, but Collins and Alessi have no answer. They turn toward the east along with me, confusion in their eyes. Looking over the ruins of Boston's North End, I see a squadron of jets, more than thirty of them. F-18s, F-22s and the tank-killers called A-10 Thunderbolts, whose distinctive high-pitched whine shrieks like a Valkyrie's battle cry. All heavy hitters. That I can hear them before they arrive means they're flying slow, below the speed of sound. Cautious. Deliberate.

This is no patrol. They're not here to watch or escort Nemesis back out to sea. They're here to attack. This is ridiculous for three reasons. First, it won't work. And there isn't a single person in the chain of command that doesn't know this. Second, to assemble a strike squadron this size means they've pulled jets from the north and south, leaving large portions of the country partially undefended. While ground defenses will still be in place, the jet patrols can see things coming first and react faster. Three, Nemesis might be in Boston, and an easy target at the moment, but we know that there are at least four more Kaiju roaming about, not to mention Gordon.

All of this is bad. Really bad. But none of it pisses me off more than being kept out of the loop. This was done behind my back. Again. And there is only one person who could have approved the assault, which explains why I wasn't consulted. The President knows I would have opposed this plan. But by not having my objection on record, he won't look like a complete fucking moron when this blows up in his face. And that's the rub. He knows this is going to go sideways. At best, it won't work and Nemesis will escape. At worst, he's going to piss her off. Then we're all screwed.

Despite Maigo being a very real part of Nemesis, I felt the creature's tortured past. It's not going to react well to being prodded.

With an aching hand, I lift my phone and switch Devine on so I can communicate with all emergency forces. "This is FC-P director, Hudson. Incoming Air Force personnel, please—"

"Target is acquired," a pilot says, his voice cool. "We are green across the board."

"No," I say. "Do not—"

"You are go for stall action," someone responds. "Fire when ready."

They're not hearing me. I've been cut out.

"Dammit!" I shout. I grip Collins's arm, as I turn toward Betty. "We need to go. Now!"

I shout in pain as we run to the chopper. The pain is excruciating, but I know to linger is to die. Updates continue to flood my ears. A countdown. Ten seconds.

We pile into the chopper. I throw a headset on and shout to Woodstock. "Get us the hell out of here!"

The chopper lifts away from the apartment building roof just as I hear someone say, "Missiles away."

"Down!" I shout.

We roll to the right and drop over the side of the apartment building's eastern side. Looking up, through the chopper's side window, I see missiles rip by, trailing streaks of white. We level out at two hundred feet, and I turn my gaze right in time to see the missiles—at least thirty of them—close in on their target.

Before the first missile strikes, I think, *at least they're not aiming for her chest.* All those orange membranes would be impossible to miss. The problem with aiming for her back is that the thick, spike covered carapace is her most well defended side. The missiles are little more than paintballs fired at a bulletproof vest.

The first missile strikes with a burst of orange flame. If Nemesis feels it, she doesn't show it. The rest of the missiles strike at roughly the same time, generating enough energy to shove her forward. She stumbles in the water, but stays upright. Then she cranes her head around, spotting the jets.

The roar that follows, angry and earth-shaking, confirms my fears. Despite our little bonding moment, the goddess of vengeance won't let the attack go unpunished.

"Missiles away," I hear, just seconds before another barrage streaks past. If she turns around...

"Moab ETA, two minutes," someone says. "Continue stall action."

Stall action?

"They're pinning her down for some reason," I say.

"MOAB," Woodstock says. "Mother of all bombs."

Holy shit. He's right. The MOAB acronym actually stands for Massive Ordnance Air Blast. It's a vacuum bomb equivalent to eleven tons of TNT. The largest non-nuclear weapon in the U.S. arsenal that basically melts everything inside a nearly one mile radius. Right now, that's Boston harbor and maybe a smidge of the North End, which has already been destroyed. Oh yeah, and us.

Anticipating my order—get the fuck out of here—Woodstock tilts us forward and sends Betty to the North. We don't make it far.

Alessi leans forward, poking her head into the cockpit. "Katsu is still down there!"

I think for just a moment, and I come to a conclusion. "There isn't time for a pick up."

"Jon!" Collins says. "You can't just—"

"I'm not leaving him," I say. "But you're not coming."

Before she can argue, I grip Woodstock's arm. "Get them out of here and don't come back."

He nods. A good soldier.

I glance to the back, find Collins's confused eyes and say, "Love you." Then I throw open the side door and jump.

If Collins replies, I don't hear her. The roar of rushing air, of missiles and of Nemesis, fills my ears. Vibrates my very bones. Things are about to get very loud around here.

I pull the ripcord for my base-jumping parachute after just one second of freefall. Another second longer and the chute wouldn't have time to deploy. It's a close call already. The black fabric unfurls, catches the air and arrests my fall just thirty feet from the ground. I land hard, shouting in pain, as my legs fold beneath my weight.

After pulling myself free from the chute, I hobble to my feet. I'm standing by what remains of the New England Aquarium. I strike out to the west, heading for the back of the apartment building, where Endo should have touched down. I realize he might not be there. He could have bugged out. I could be risking my life for nothing. That he didn't check in with Alessi is what concerns me, though.

The pain in my leg increases with each limping step. I press my hand against the limb, covering the wound, and I feel the warm tacky wetness of blood. A lot of blood. Moving is probably a bad idea, but at this point, I don't have a choice. As I reach the end of the wharf, upon which the aquarium was built, I shout, "Endo!"

The lack of reply doesn't slow me down. I've got just over a minute before the mother of all bombs turns me to dust. I turn left and spot a billowing black shape. "Endo!" I hurry forward. The parachute is tangled with a mass of ruined outdoor tables with blue umbrellas. "Endo!"

A groan. Movement. I yank away the chute and find him lying amid the debris. His face is covered in blood. "Came down too fast," he says and glances up. "Hit the building."

I glance up. A seven story, concrete building looms above us. He must have bounced off the building and fallen into the tables. "Can you move?"

"I'd prefer an ambulance," he says.

"Either get up or all you're going to get is dead."

"Nemesis?"

I turn my eyes skyward, find the black triangle of a stealth bomber high above and point it out. "MOAB."

"Shit," he says with uncommon surprise, pushing himself up. I pull him to his feet, but after that, he's on his own. I can barely stand as it is.

"This way!" We hobble back past the Aquarium, heading for a green railing above which is mounted a circular sign with a big T in the middle. The red brick is unforgiving beneath my feet, each impact a new kind of agony.

The sound of a continuing missile barrage, coupled with Nemesis's roar, draws my attention back to the harbor. Nemesis is aglow with explosions, writhing in pain or fury. Probably both. The fighter jet pilots have done a good job of avoiding those orange membranes.

Then the missiles stop.

The jets flying past overhead peel away, afterburners roaring as they flee the scene.

A tiny black dot falls from the sky, headed toward Nemesis.

MOAB.

I look forward, the subway station is just fifty feet ahead. If I were healthy, I could cover the distance in a few seconds. Now...it's going to be close. The problem with MOAB is that it's a fuel-air explosive, meaning it will detonate before it strikes Nemesis, creating a thermobaric wave of stunning force and heat not unlike Nemesis's self-immolation.

Ignoring the bomb and its target, I push past the pain, willing my legs forward. Endo reaches the stairwell before me and plunges into the darkness. He shouts in surprise about something, but I don't slow as I reach the steps. Instead, I throw myself downward, expecting a brutal but potentially lifesaving fall. The surprise comes quickly as I splash down into salt water. The subway is flooded. We're still too high!

"Down!" I shout, ducking beneath the water and swimming for all I'm worth, while the salt water burns my wounds. After just five strokes, a wave of pressure moves through the water and my body, drawing the air from my lungs. I instinctually head for the surface, but I bump my head. Seeing stars, I spin, pressing my hands against an invisible ceiling, unable to tell if they're moving through water or air, or even if I'm right-side up. I'd shout if I could. Scream like a madman. But there's no air left in my lungs.

And then, from the darkness, some unseen predator strikes hard, pulling me to my doom as water rushes into my lungs.

29

I have no memory of how painful my birth felt—to me, not to my mother. I imagine it wasn't comfortable, being squashed down in too tight of a space, head compressed, limbs twisted. Torn from the world I knew and thrust into a coldness without connection. Could there be anything much worse than that?

The answer to that question, I now know, is: fuck yes.

I feel several things at once. My lungs and throat tear with wet coughs. Blinding jolts of pain explode from my ribs with each heave. The surface beneath my back is hard and uneven. Stairs, I think.

And then the rest of my full body pain returns. Screw childbirth, this must beat an afternoon in an iron maiden. But it's not enough to knock me unconscious, which is both fortunate and unfortunate.

I hear breathing in the dark.

"Endo?"

"I am here."

"The fuck did you do to me?"

"You drowned."

The simple explanation is enough. I drowned. He performed CPR. Saved my life again. Damn him. Of course, I saved his, too. People are going to start thinking we're pals. Feels like a few more of my ribs are broken. "Didn't hold back, did you?"

I sit up with a grunt, clutching my ribs. The motion moves blood into my legs. The knife wound throbs. "You were pretty convincing. Up there on the roof."

"There have been times when I would have liked nothing more than to kill you." His honesty is disconcerting. If he changed his mind now, I'm not sure I could do much to stop him. "But," he says. "you have been chosen for a purpose."

He's speaking about Nemesis. About my connection to her, which I understand a little bit better now. Not how it works, but why she would choose me.

I slide up against a cool, damp wall, pushing myself higher. "You have nice parents, Endo? A good childhood?"

He's quiet for a moment. Then drops a bomb. "It's your father."

"The hell do you know about my father?"

"I know as much about you as you do about me," he says.

"I know shit about you!" I shout.

"Then, yes," he says. "I had a good childhood. And kind parents. They are *still* kind parents."

"Asshole," I say.

I hear him chuckle, and I have a strong urge to kick his face in, but I decide that will just end badly for me. "Where are we?"

"Underground," he says, and I reconsider my boot-to-the-face idea. But then he adds, "Some kind of service tunnel. There's a ladder here."

I can't see the ladder, but I can hear his voice. Turning toward him, I look up. A thin line of light shows the border of a square hatch. I struggle to my feet, leaning against the wall, and I pause to catch my breath. The air here still smells of ocean, but stings with the tinge of toxic chemicals. The burning in my throat and lungs might not be from more than drowning and being revived, though.

With a modicum of strength returned, I shuffle across the hallway like one of the undead, and catch myself on the wall, clinging to a ladder rung for support.

Endo stands next to me. "I know that we will never be...friends."

I'm suddenly feeling awkward and uncomfortable, like when I was asked to the prom by Jenny Stillwater, my childhood-friend's little sister. Not only was she four years younger than me, not only did I remember her in diapers, but she was my friend's sister. It's *just* not done. Of course, when I saw her again, three years later and all grown into herself, I wondered if turning her down was actually the best choice. But Endo isn't about to grow anything feminine.

"I just want you to know..." he says, "you have earned my respect."

"Just because Nemesis has—"

"Not because of how Nemesis—or Maigo—views you. Or even because of how you view her. But because you repeatedly put your life at risk to do what you believe is the right thing to do. Including returning for me."

In the silence that follows, I realize that compliment time is over.

"Yeah, well, thank you, fuckface. Would you mind climbing the ladder now so we can find out who ordered that strike and kick their ass?"

"Gladly," he says. He starts up the ladder, grunting with each rung ascended. As I follow, barely containing a scream with each step up, I realize that neither of us will be kicking asses anytime soon. There's a clang of metal as he reaches the top and shoves. A flash of light reveals the brick tunnel around us. But then the hatch closes and Endo lets out a little growl. For a moment, I think we're trapped down here, but Endo climbs another step, gets his shoulder under the door and shoves. Blessed sunlight pours into the tunnel. I expect Boston's cool ocean air to follow, but I get a lungful of hot, foul smelling filth. I cough for a moment, while Endo exits.

When I reach the top, he bends to help me out. We're not far from where we started, standing on a walkway in what used to be the Christopher Columbus Waterfront Park. It had been spared destruction a year ago, but it's now a smoldering ruin. The grass is gone, replaced by ash, whisked away by the wind. Most of the trees were uprooted and either tipped over or flung away. Those that remain upright look like large incense burners, smoke twisting away from the tips of still burning branches. Anything that had been untouched by Nemesis has now been destroyed. Buildings. Wharfs. Boats.

We hobble together, toward the Harborwalk, along the shore. Through columns of rising smoke, I see the harbor. Steam rolls over the ocean's surface. The remnants of a mushroom cloud billows upward. In the distance, jets circle in groups of three, wary.

Nemesis remains.

She's still in the same spot, curled in on herself, a colossal armadillo. Smoke rises from her protective carapace, but I see no real damage.

She's motionless, but not dead. While MOAB is an impressive weapon, wonderful for killing people and destroying buildings, Nemesis is designed, or has evolved, to withstand such an explosive force. Hell, she *contains* an even more powerful explosive force.

A grinding sound turns my eyes to the right. We're standing in the shadow of a long, five-story, brick building. The Marriot, if I'm not mistaken. The red bricks, now scorched black, are crumbling.

Dread grips me. I'm not sure where it comes from, but its intense. And real. There's a mountain of shit currently heading toward a very large fan, and we are still squarely downwind. The chop of a helicopter gives me a small amount of hope. I lift my aching arms and wave.

Betty comes in from the North, flying low and fast. A cloud of ash swirls into the air, whipped up by the rotor. Endo and I run for it while the Marriot caves in on itself behind us. We're met halfway by Collins and Alessi, who silently help us into the chopper. Rather than bring me to the passenger's seat—my usual station, Collins rather forcefully guides me to the back. Once I'm in, she slams the door and takes my seat in the front.

I lean forward, fighting the pain in my ribs, and pick up a headset. Once it's on, I say, "We need to leave. Now."

"No shit, Sherlock," Woodstock says, lifting Betty off the ground. "We'll be headed north in just—"

"Not north!" I shout, the fear taking hold again. "Southeast. Through the North End. Go!"

I'm glad he doesn't ask why. I have no answer. It's just a feeling. We need a barrier between us and what comes next, and the ruins of downtown is the closest thing to a wall around here.

As we swing around and speed through the still standing skyscrapers of Boston's North End, I look out the window and up. The line of jets is incoming again.

They fire.

Useless missiles trace lines across the sky above us.

The jets follow, not peeling away. They're trying to buy time again. But for another MOAB? Or something worse? Seeing our flight-path through the North End is a perfectly straight line, I nearly ask Woodstock to fly us backwards again, but then I notice a tall building, beyond the North End, at the end of the street, still has most of its reflective windows. Looking at the reflection, I can see behind us into the harbor, all the way to Nemesis. The jets close in.

They're too close...

And then it happens. Nemesis stands tall and spins around. Her chest heaves a few times, expanding. Her neck flexes like a dog about to puke.

I have no expletives to express how I feel at this moment.

So I just watch as Nemesis performs the super-sized equivalent of hocking a loogie. But the wad that comes out isn't mucus. It's a bright orange globule—her explosive fluid contained in some kind of clear viscous film. It arcs through the air, heading for the jets. For a moment I think it's actually going to strike one of the jets, but the pilots are accustomed to thinking fast, and their planes are even faster. The problem is that the glowing projectile, if left unhindered, will sail clear over the North End and land smack dab in Boston's heart, erasing all of what's left of the city.

Of the thirty-plus pilots in the sky, one of them must realize this, too, because a missile launches from an F-22 before it turns away and kicks on its afterburners.

The missile strikes home as we clear the North End and emerge over the lower buildings in Boston's downtown. "Stay low!"

The light from the resulting explosion turns my eyes away from the reflective windows. To the left, I see the green swath of grass that is the Boston Common, just beyond the Beacon Hill neighborhood. If we have to land rough, that's the place to do it.

As the initial blast of light fades, I turn back toward the reflection of the North End, already a mile away. An orange glow chases us. Gaining. It slips through the North End like the buildings were made of air. The already stressed ruins just shatter. The metal glows yellow and melts away. What was left of the North End, is reduced to dust. It's the last thing I see before the reflective windows providing my view shatter and fall to the ground, tiny twinkling lights.

The pressure wave strikes us hard, pitching us forward, while the concussive sound of the explosion pounds against our ears and cracks Betty's windshield. Then we're out of it, cruising low over the Commons and a string of swan boats.

While everyone catches their breath, I say, "Bring us up and around. I want to see."

We quickly top out at two thousand feet, high enough to see the harbor from a safe distance. The North End is gone. It's not just ruins now, it's totally obliterated. Wiped off the map. A flattened swatch of scorched earth.

I need to have a chat with President Colossal Fuck-Up.

Just as soon as I go to the hospital, have surgery and begin physical therapy. My only consolations are that Boston was empty, so no one died, and that Endo looks as shitty as I do.

"Woodstock," I say, leaning back and closing my eyes. "Hospital. Rapido."

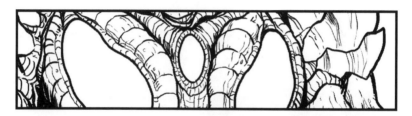

TYPHON

30

Chris Marshal's vacation had finally turned a corner. He'd traveled to Thailand from New York City, where he worked as a day trader. His life was loud and chaotic and focused on things he wasn't sure he cared about any more. Like money. Sure, he understood and appreciated what money could do for him, but the daily act of gathering and hoarding numbers like a squirrel preparing for winter had become a hollow act. At least the squirrel worked for its survival. He toiled for what? More. That's it. More. So he fled to Thailand for a week of mind clearing, and maybe the comfort of a woman. Or two. But Bangkok didn't feel very different from New York. Sure, it smelled, looked and sounded different, but the vibe was the same. All eyes turned inward, seeing only what the self desired.

So he fled again, this time taking the train south to Thailand's mountainous Pak Song region, where a carpet of green rainforest covered everything. There were no tourists and the locals spoke only Thai, which he got around using the translation app on his smart phone. Despite the communication barrier, he was greeted with smiles everywhere he went. After a week of lounging around, trying new foods and making new friends, he felt a little more human. A little less dirty in his soul. But he also felt restless.

At the suggestion of the local villagers he'd become friendly with, he set out on a bamboo rafting trip. The lazy trip down the scenic river relaxed him. Helped him forget the stress that ruled his life. As he lay on the bamboo, he listened to the wind rustle through the leaves while the water bubbled by below. He watched the clouds glide by, heavy with rain to be unleashed later in the day.

I'm going to stay, he decided. *Learn the language. Find a wife.* This was the life he'd been born to live, and with the money he already had in the bank, he could live it until the day he died without ever having to work. A permanent vacation.

Not that I'll live idly, he thought. He'd already begun helping in the village, remembering the carpentry skills taught to him by his father. Working to help people, he'd discovered, was far more gratifying than working for stacks of green paper.

The raft shook beneath him. He leaned his head up, asking, "What was that?" The three men in the raft with him, Yosakon, Gan and Tanipat, looked bewildered. They spoke rapidly among themselves. Chris reached for his smart phone, but paused. The three were talking over each other. He'd never get a translation.

Chris sat up to find the placid river transformed. Waves bounced them in every direction. He'd researched the river before leaving. There shouldn't have been rapids here. Judging by his friends' reactions, the rough water was a surprise to them too.

The next quake—he felt positive this was an earthquake—forced Chris to cling to the boat's side. The three men with him fell down, shouting.

The next booming quake shook the trees on the shore so violently that the small creatures—frogs, snakes, lizards—clinging to the branches fell into the water. A flock of bird soared past, moving away from the sound's source.

He'd never experienced an earthquake before, but he didn't think you could discern the direction from which it originated. But that last boom had definitely come from upriver. The three men with him must have realized this too, because they all turned around, speaking in worried tones. Their homes were back upriver. Their families.

Chris looked upriver, waiting for the next shake. The view behind them was mostly river and the jungle closing in on either side. But the open area above the river allowed for a spectacular view of a distant mountain. The village these men were from, where he'd been staying, was at the base of that mountain. Tiny specks appeared over the mountain, moving quickly. More birds.

But then the scene changed. It took him a moment to fully understand what he was seeing. The trees atop the mountain blurred. Then rose up. That immense unmoving mass of earth was rising! The jungle split apart, falling away. Dark earth and stone exploded into the air.

Boom!

The world shook around them, the sound drowning out his compatriots' screams. The mountain transformed, crumbling over on itself as something rose up above it from behind. *A demon*, Chris thought. Some ancient Thai god was rising from the mountain. It was Gan, one of his guides, who first understood, shouting, "Nemesis!"

The monster was known even in this backwater part of the world. While communication with the outside world wasn't common, some of the shops had televisions and phones, and a few had satellite Wi-Fi. Chris would stop at a street vendor every morning for a breakfast of two potongos, the Thai version of a donut, and some sweet custard-like sauce for dipping. The shop next door, also a post office, offered free Wi-Fi, which he used to read the news on his phone, though he'd skipped that routine this morning. So while his Thai friends knew what Nemesis was, they didn't know about the other Kaiju rampaging through the world he'd escaped. He'd never considered the possibility that the vengeful creatures would have any reason to come to this peaceful part of the world, but here it was, a monster that looked similar to Nemesis, but was not Nemesis.

It was built similarly—thick neck, horrible face, armor-plated and spike-covered arms. Thick ropey skin twisted and bundled around a pattern of orange flesh that glowed in the dim, overcast light. But it wasn't the same. Its face was actually far uglier than Nemesis's, its brow low and furrowed over a pair of radiant yellow eyes. The pictures he'd seen of Nemesis showed almost human, brown eyes. The biggest difference were the hands. Where Nemesis had five fingers, this thing had three—a thumb and two claws that looks like pincers.

A second head rose up, just behind the first, eliciting a shout of surprise and horror from Chris, but not just from its presence. It was the thing's appearance that unnerved him. It looked...human. But not. It stood tall like a person. Carried itself like a confident man. It had two arms. Two legs. Five clawed digits at the end of each appendage. Its face, while human in structure, was anything but. The mouth occasionally dropped open to reveal large triangular teeth, before snapping shut again. And like the first monster, it had angry yellow eyes, thick dark skin, spikes and a pattern of those explosive—*what are they called? Membranes.* Both creatures had thick backs, like protective shells. He knew that Nemesis hid her wings beneath a similar structure. Were these two capable of the same destructive force? Standing at least 300 feet tall, he didn't doubt it.

The pair of giants stepped over the mountain, descending the far side like two hikers out for a stroll, indifferent to the lives they were crushing beneath their feet. The mountainside collapsed, sliding down in a rush of damp earth. Chris had no doubt that the village from which they started their journey was now destroyed.

The three Thai men wailed at the sight. As one, they dug their paddles into the water and struck out—upriver.

"What are you doing?" Chris shouted. The men didn't reply, but Chris answered his own question. They were heading home. To their families. To find the dead. Maybe rescue some lucky survivors. These were brave men. But Chris did not share their commitment to the buried village. In the shadow of these two monsters, a part of his old self, which cared *only* about himself, returned with a vengeance.

After taking his phone out of his pocket, he slid to the side of the raft, looked down at the dark water and paused. He didn't know what kind of wildlife might wait for him in the river, but as the world shook again, he doubted predators would be thinking about eating. Nearly tipping the raft, he slid into the water, keeping his right hand, phone clutched tightly, lifted up. Using his legs and left arm, he kept himself above water and kept his connection to the outside world dry.

The shaking impacts came rapidly. The giants, on level ground now, moved faster. He glanced upstream and saw the raft making good time back the way they had come. Beyond them, he saw the two giants, making steady progress...downstream. He needed to reach the shore. He needed to run!

A roar cut through the air, sending ripples through the water, which continued to stir with each giant footfall. Water splashed the phone. He sucked in mouthfuls, coughing and sputtering, but never slowing his hard swim. But the choppy water fought against him, pushing him back and forth. Downstream was the only direction he could move, so he leaned on his back, kept his phone hand raised up, and kicked hard.

Despite making good time, he began to weep five minutes later. The giants were gaining on him. Each thundering step brought them closer. To make matters worse, the current seemed to be slowing down. At first he thought that the river was widening, but a look to the side revealed the truth. The banks of the river were exposed, ten feet of mud and roots. As he twisted to look, his backside struck something hard, sending jolts of pain through his body.

I've been attacked! he thought. But then his whole body ground against something rough. His journey down the river had come to a halt. Chris lifted his head to find himself lying on the smooth stoned surface of a barren riverbed. A fish flopped nearby, slapping itself to death on the stones.

He sat up, trying to make sense of this new world. *The mountain,* he thought. *It blocked the river.*

The ground shook again. Without the water buffering the blow, it felt like he'd been punched. The stones in the riverbed rattled. And then, screams. Three high pitched voices he recognized. Yosakon, Gan and Tanipat. The three men, eyes wide, clothing dripping wet, scurried over the river-bed rocks. They stumbled and fell, covered in blood, but they never stopped.

And then Chris saw why. The monster that looked like Nemesis had arrived. It towered over the jungle, eyes forward. Its massive tail swept back and forth as it walked, leveling the jungle, sending trees flying. But it never looked down. Never acknowledged their existence. It was simply passing through.

We just need to get out of the way!

Chris shouted to his friends to follow him as he ran for the shore. They could never outrun the monster, but if they could just get out of the way, they might—

BOOM!

The riverbed beneath Chris's feet lifted up and then fell away. He toppled forward, striking his head on a stone. A flash of white filled his vision for a moment and sent a wave of nausea through his body. He rolled over—and screamed.

A giant clawed foot with black and twisted skin descended toward him. He shrieked with primal fear, wondering what the end would feel like, wondering if he had a soul and wondering if he'd condemned himself to some kind of torturous afterlife. And then the giant foot struck.

Twenty feet away.

Chris bounced into the air, landing hard, but this time avoiding hitting his head. Rolling over onto his hands and knees, he managed to stay upright with each shift of the earth, which came more rapidly and more powerfully, now that he was in the gap between the two giants.

As the immense foot lifted up and away, he saw the three villagers' bodies crushed into the folds of the foot, bloody and very dead. Before he could react to this sight with relief or horror, a loud rushing sound like thunder locked him in place, his breath held.

The massive tail whipped past, sliding from one side of the barren river to the other, passing just a few feet overhead. Flattened trees landed all around Chris, lashing him with thin branches, but he remained mostly unscathed.

I'm safe here, he told himself. *As long as I don't move, I'm safe.*

Part of him knew this wasn't necessarily true, but he was a believer in luck, and this spot, for whatever reason, was lucky. So when the second set of gargantuan footfalls approached, he remained riveted to the stone beneath him.

When the giant emerged, its head turned down, like it was looking straight at him, Chris lost control of his bladder. But still, he didn't move. The colossal monster made no move for him, and Chris could see by the thing's wide gait, that he wouldn't be stepped on.

Just stay still. Don't draw attention. Don't fucking move.

The sound of a new roar turned his head skyward. It sounded different from the two Kaiju, whose roars sounded like a mix of tubas and high pitched violins gargling water through a loud-speaker. This new sound was crisp. Modern. The white streak across the sky confirmed it.

A missile.

Just one.

The military didn't have a strong presence in this part of the world. This missile must have come from far away—the ocean on the other side of the peninsula that was southern Thailand.

Chris tracked its path and then looked ahead. It was going to strike the man-monster. An easy target. Then he realized where it was going to hit.

"No," he whispered. "God, no!"

Back to his feet, Chris ran for the shore. He tripped and fell into the muddy bank, getting tangled in the roots and slippery grime. He spun around as he fought to free himself, just in time to see it happen.

The missile struck the manly Kaiju's chest. It disappeared with a *whump* and a small burst of flame. For a moment, he thought that was the end of it, that the missile had failed to inflict any damage at all. But then he saw the spray of orange liquid jet out of the monster's chest. Before he could scream, or pray or fully comprehend what he was seeing, the world turned white and disappeared.

31

The worst part about staying in a hospital for two weeks isn't the food. I've probably gained five pounds in chocolate pudding. And this time, it's not the company. My roommate is Endo, and we've been pretty content to not speak to each other much. No, what really irks me is that I'm helpless to stop the global rampage being carried out by three of Gordon's Kaiju. With nothing else to do but lay in bed, I've named them all.

There is Scylla, who first appeared in Sydney and worked its way along Australia's southern coast. It's a sharp-toothed monstrosity with a hammerhead. I named the second Kaiju to emerge from the ocean, Karkinos, one of the two monsters who attacked the port of Hong Kong. In many ways, it resembles Nemesis. The spikes. The long tail. But the eyes are all wrong, and the claws on its hands have fused together, forming two large blades, like serrated shears. It's the third Kaiju, Typhon, that really freaks me out. It stands tall on two legs. Like a man...a man dressed in Nemesis skin: spikes, carapace and all. Not only is it powerful, but in the video footage, it appears to think before acting. Considering strategies. While the others seem to be all instinct, Typhon has a brain. The fourth Kaiju, Drakon, the svelte lizard-like monster, hasn't been seen since it rescued Gordon in Rockport.

While Nemesis is nowhere in sight, Scylla made its way around Australia's southern coast and then disappeared. Typhon and Karkinos left a path of destruction along China's and Vietnam's coasts before stomping across Thailand's peninsula and disappearing into the Bay of Bengal. They made a brief stopover in Sri Lanka before showing up in Madagascar, and then again in Cape Town, South Africa. The duo sometimes attack separately. Sometimes together. But they're clearly travel-buddies.

And like Nemesis, they seem to be fairly unstoppable. The response to their journey has been global, with militaries from different regions joining to fend off the threat. Each time the Kaiju have moved on, it's been hailed as a victory. A retreat. But I don't think that's the case at all. The creatures are simply stopping in for a bite to eat while they head west.

Despite the appearance of five new Kaiju and Gordon's assault on the FC-P, my superiors refuse to believe that a traitorous general, who is supposed to be dead, is influencing or directing the monsters.

I agree that it sounds unlikely, but unlikely is pretty much the new norm. So while they've been knee-jerk reacting to the situations as they arise, I've been trying to get into Gordon's mind. Not literally. Endo demonstrated the folly of that idea.

Assuming Gordon is in control, what does he want? Vengeance. Naturally. What else would a man who received a heart transplant from the goddess of vengeance want?

But vengeance on whom?

"What was Gordon like before all this?" I ask.

Endo turns from the TV to me. He's been watching cartoons, of all things, which is far more bearable than *The Golden Girls*. After watching an episode of *Dexter's Laboratory*, we'd jokingly discussed the possibility of constructing a giant robot to fight the Kaiju. While that works for cartoons and men in rubber suits, the physics of building a suit that large, makes it impossible. Which kind of sucks, because it would be awesome.

"I didn't know him before," Endo says. "We met after I discovered the Nemesis-Prime corpse."

"Did he ever express anger at anyone?" I ask.

Endo grins. "At *everyone*."

"From his past," I say. "A wife. A bully. Co-worker? Someone he really hated."

Endo falls silent, biting his thumbnail, a habit he picked up a few days ago. It's how I know he's really thinking about something. He probably won't emerge from his mental filing cabinet for a few minutes, so I pick up the remote and change the channel.

My mind drifts as I push the button. I'm no longer seeing the TV, but am thinking about life. Specifically, my life. Endo and I are scheduled to leave in the morning. We're 'out of the woods,' according to the doctor. I'm pretty sure we were never actually in the woods, but I suspect Collins threatened the doctor to hold us here longer than normal on the grounds that we'd only exacerbate our injuries by returning to work.

And she'd have been right about that. Sitting in this bed is nearly intolerable. The one thing that has kept me obeying the doctor is the fact that there is nothing I can do about the Kaiju attacking other countries. I can't command their militaries or even advise their governments. For all I know, they've all got their own versions of the FC-P working on the problem. Had a Kaiju made landfall on U.S. soil, I'd have been up and out of bed, doctor's orders or not. Also, the pudding helps.

Something snaps me back to reality. I blink my eyes while my mind rewinds for me. The TV. A news report. Shaky video. I switch channels again, heading in the opposite direction. I stop after three pushes of the button. It's a news network. A close up of Karkinos fills the screen. There's no sound, but the upturned head and open maw tell me it's roaring. The image pulls back to reveal a packed city and a tropical coastline. The scene is dark, the sun cloaked by a tropical storm. I glance down at the news channel's image label: Rio De Janeiro, Brazil.

"Holy shit," I say, not because I'm surprised that yet another city is being attacked, but because Karkinos has made really good time crossing the Atlantic. It's only been three days since the attack on Cape Town.

The camera turns to the right. Typhon. He's bigger than I remember. Easily 300 feet tall. They both are. The orange membranes covering his chest and abs glow brightly in the gloom. His brilliant yellow eyes seem to be peering straight at the camera. At me.

Impossible, I think, which is enough beyond 'unlikely' that I believe it.

The two monsters rise from the turbulent ocean unchallenged. They've managed to cross the deep undetected, and I doubt anyone in all of South America expected a visit. They're probably wondering what they did wrong as several 'authorities' on the subject have decided that the Kaiju operate similarly to Nemesis, proclaiming judgment, carrying out death sentences. Wishful thinking.

I glance at Endo. He's paused mid-thumb nibble to watch the TV. When his eyes widen, I look back to the news feed and gasp. An orange glow moves through the ocean, sliding up behind the two Kaiju. For a moment, I think it must be some kind of weapon. A torpedo or suicidal submarine. But then a 50-foot wide, black head lifts from the ocean. Scylla. Like its siblings, the destroyer of Sydney is pushing 300 feet in height now. All three monsters are together, one big happy family. The camera operator zooms in on the new arrival. Scylla opens her mouth, roaring. Her curved needle-like teeth hold the remnants of meals past. Boat parts. Large hunks of whale meat. Human bodies. Of the three, Scylla is the smallest, but her savage appearance is unnerving.

As frightening as Nemesis is, she's never put off the kind of vile hatred these three put off. Even Scrion and Drakon were different. Scrion was a monster, but had the personality of a pug on crack. And Drakon, compared to Nemesis, wasn't very threatening; dangerous for sure, but built for speed, not sheer power. But these three... If the Earth was the prize and Nemesis the champ, Typhon, Karkinos and Scylla would be serious contenders. And the problem with that is I'm not expecting a fair fight. Three on one, the odds are not in Nemesis's favor.

Brazil's military is quick to respond. Before Scylla is even out of the water, jets streak past the camera operator, nearly knocking him over. But he rights the camera in time to see missiles streak away. He follows their course all the way to Typhon's head, where they explode. Harmlessly. I'm not sure the giant even noticed.

More missiles cruise by. Helicopters sweep in from the sides, launching rockets. The camera lurches to the side as the operator picks it up and runs. When the view stabilizes again, the camera twists to the side, as a tank rolls into place, stops and fires a round. The camera shakes, moving further back. The operator is running again. If there was sound, I'm sure he, or she, would be screaming. Who wouldn't be?

A safe distance from the action, the camera operator sets up again, pointing the lens back at the mayhem. We're higher now, viewing the city from more of an angle. Scylla is still on the beach, ravaging the string of hotels that line the shore. Karkinos is the closest. His massively thick, armored body is bent forward. His giant jaws are snapping open and closed. I'm not sure, but I think he's eating people.

And then there is Typhon.

"Jesus," I say, and it's not a swear. I avoid using the name as a cuss, out of respect for the people it deeply offends. In this case, I'm literally talking about Jesus. Typhon has tromped across the city and is scaling a mountain toward the Christ the Redeemer statue. It's not as big as the Kaiju, but standing on top of that mountain, with his arms outstretched, the giant Jesus must look like a potential threat. Or a very large meal. Typhon makes short work of the mountain, grips Jesus's arms and snaps them off. Then, with a single swipe, he knocks the top half of limbless Jesus off and sends it rolling down the mountainside, toward the city. Rio's most famous symbol of hope and forgiveness crushes through the mass of small homes at the base of the incline.

"Hey," Endo says.

Lost in the scene of destruction, I flinch at the sound of Endo's voice.

Endo turns toward me. "Jon."

Considering that this is the very first time Endo has referred to me by my first name, I'm a little disconcerted when I look at him. Not only does it reflect the somewhat friendly rapport that has developed between us while being bedridden, it also means he must have had some kind of revelation.

"I know who Gordon is after," he says.

"Please don't say me."

"Besides you," he says.

"That's still includes me," I point out.

"Just shut up," Endo says. "When Gordon first found Nemesis, he took the information—"

"To Zoomb," I say. "I know."

Endo shakes his head. "They were his *second* choice. Gordon was a good soldier. A true patriot. He brought it to the one person in the government he thought would take his wild claims seriously."

I wait for the revelation, eyebrows raised to say 'any day now.'

"At the time he was *Senator* Gary Beck."

My mouth slowly opens.

Endo nods. "Two years later he became—"

"President Dickface."

Son-of-a-bitch. "So if they're not coming for me..."

"They're headed for the Capitol," Endo says.

I hold up my hand. "Wait. Stop. Two things. First, we need to stop finishing each other's sentences. This isn't a bromance. Second, we need to warn—"

"Nobody," Endo says, face grim.

I groan in annoyance. "What did I say about finishing my sentences? And why the hell would we *not* warn the President? Besides the fact that he's a tool."

"If the President feels that he is a target, he will run. Inland. He'll try to hide, but there isn't anywhere he can go that Gordon doesn't know about. The Kaiju will pursue him across the country, destroying everything in their path. And when that happens—"

"The king of bad decisions will start dropping nukes," I say, ignoring my bromance moratorium. Endo is right. President Beck is two balls short of being a man and a few billion brain cells short of the scarecrow. He'd put the whole country in jeopardy. The question is how do we prepare to fend off three colossal Kaiju combatants without tipping our hand or evacuating the nation's Capitol? It's damn near close to treason.

Gordon is the answer. Without him, the Kaiju might become subservient to Nemesis. They might go mad. Or they might just swim around the ocean gobbling up whales. They never endured the tortures of Nemesis's past, so it's very possible the thirst for vengeance that drives her, and Gordon, won't be part of the equation.

The door opens. Collins rushes in, holding my clothes. Alessi is behind her with a bag for Endo.

"Have you seen?" Collins asks.

I point to the news channel still playing the live footage of Rio being used like a bag of snack chips.

"I brought you some clothes" she says, placing them on the bed.

While I'm pleased to see the shorts, t-shirt and red beanie cap, I ignore the change of clothes and sit up. The pain meds I'm on dull the lingering pain I feel, for the most part, but I'm still kind of a mess.

I reach my hand out to Alessi. "Phone?"

She glances at Endo and he nods. Alessi hands me her phone. "This thing is secure, right?"

"What are you doing?" Collins asks.

I dial the number. "Calling backup."

32

I toured the White House once, when I was a kid. Eighth grade. Worst few days of my young adult life. I had to sleep in the same room as my childhood bully. My wallet with $57 of birthday money I brought was stolen—I'm pretty sure by the same bully. And my girlfriend broke up with me in front of the Washington Monument. Our nation's capital has left a sour taste in my mouth since, despite the fact that my childhood bully is in jail for stealing a tank and my girlfriend blimped out, which I discovered while honing my Facebook stalker skills.

That I'm about to start my fourth White House tour of the week has me feeling a little bit of nausea. Reservations are typically made six months to twenty-one days in advance, long enough for the Secret Service to find out what they can. Using his considerable computer skills and bending a few rules, Watson managed to get us in four days in a row. And by 'us,' I mean Endo and me. As much as I prefer Collins as a partner, Endo's presence is necessary, and Collins is harder to forget. We've changed our identities each day, posing as tourists from different parts of the world, never directly communicating. Just observing. Waiting. When things go sideways, we need to have access to the President, and he's been here all week. Starting tomorrow, he'll be touring Europe, so I'm willing to bet Gordon knows this and will make his move sooner than later—and by sooner, I mean today.

This afternoon's tour guide, Mindy, is a peppy young woman with a pony tail and a bright smile. She's a real girl-next-door type, but in love with the history of her country and its Capitol, which I'm putting at great risk. *It's an acceptable risk*, I try to tell myself. Making a stand in Washington is better than letting the nation get tromped into oblivion. Of course, there's a real risk that my plan, formed without the support of our military, is going to fall apart like a roll of toilet paper strung beneath a waterfall.

"Can anyone tell me why the China room color theme is red?" Mindy asks.

A little girl raises her hand, eager. "Cause it's pretty?"

"Good guess," Mindy says.

Consumed by boredom, I open my mouth. "It matches First Lady Grace Coolidge's dress. The one in her portrait."

All heads turn toward me. Mindy looks impressed. Endo, who's disguised as an aging college professor, complete with a tweed jacket, bland slacks and streaks of gray in his hair, stares at me indifferently. He's trying not to show any kind of reaction to me at all, but his lack of outward reaction means he's *trying* to hide his true reaction, which is probably annoyance. I shouldn't have spoken at all.

"That's...right," Mindy says. "Not many people know that."

Not many people have toured the White House four times this week, I think. I'm disguised as a middle-aged man with nothing better to do than tour Washington, D.C. solo. I've got a fake pot belly beneath my God-awful sweater. A thick gray mustache that looks eerily similar to Woodstock's, matches my messy head of gray hair. I wasn't sure I could stand a wig, but it fits like my beanie cap, so I've barely noticed it.

"And do you know who else is in that portrait?" Mindy asks. She's got a slight edge to her voice, like I've challenged her historical authority and it's now time for a trivia smackdown.

I know the answer. It's Rob Roy, her dog. But getting into a mental showdown with Mindy isn't going to help my cover. We've already been in this room a minute longer than usual, and the Secret Service tends to notice things like that. "Uhh, Roy Rogers. Her cat."

Mindy snickers. "Close. It was her dog, Rob Roy."

"Riiight," I say. "I ate at Roy Rogers last night."

Satisfied with her trivial dominance, Mindy waves the tour to follow her out of the room and into the hall, where we'll turn into the Vermeil Room and learn all about the collection of silver-gilded boredom. As we enter the hallway, I notice that Endo is hanging back a bit, waiting for me, no doubt about to give me a whispered rebuke.

We come shoulder to shoulder, casually, looking in different directions. When we bump, we turn to each other, like we're apologizing.

"I know," I start, "I shouldn't have—"

"We've been made," he says.

"Because I spoke?" This is a ridiculous idea. My mustache fluffs outward as I blow between my teeth, which is how today's character laughs.

"Before that," he says. "I don't know what tipped them off, but if we don't get out now, we're going to—"

A pair of hands land on our shoulders. "You're going to what?"

We turn to find a pair of Secret Service agents staring at us. These guys look like a sense of humor was beat out of them in the womb. They're relaxed, though, and haven't drawn their weapons. Endo and I went through security. They know we're not armed. Doesn't mean we couldn't put up a fight, I guess. That's when I notice the army of black suits acting casual, but keeping an eye on the situation.

The taller of the two men, whose crow's feet and confident glare mark him as the man in charge, gives us a subtle grin. "Gentlemen, my name is Agent Dunne."

"What seems to be the problem?" Endo asks in a scholarly British accent.

"The problem," says the taller of the two agents, "is this mustache." He takes hold of my phony facial hair and yanks. It tears away from my face, bikini waxing my upper lip in the process.

My hands slap over my mouth. "Oww!"

Dunne turns to Endo. "And your gray hair is running."

I glance at Endo, and sure enough, a drip of white is sliding down his cheek.

"So, Director Hudson, I would appreciate it if you'd come with me."

I stand rooted in place. The surprise on my face must be obvious, because Dunne says, "We ID'd you on your way in today. Mr. Endo was harder because he's not a government employee, but we're aware of his presidential order to work with you."

I glance back at the tour, moving off down the hall. Mindy was never this interesting, but I very much preferred her peppy presence to the cold, knowledgeable stare of this agent.

"Look," Dunne says, a crack in his calm demeanor showing as his eyebrows descend, "I haven't tased, cuffed or kicked you shitless out of professional courtesy. But I don't care if you're the damn Speaker of the House. If you are here, in *this* house, covertly, you are my bitch. Understood? You will come without incident, right now, or your day is going to get fugly in a hurry."

I grin. I respect a man who can curse creatively. I'm also glad he didn't outright ask if we were here because of a Kaiju-related danger. I wouldn't have enjoyed lying to him. Though he's bound to ask—if he gets a chance, that is.

"Lead the way."

We're watched by a cadre of hawk-like Secret Service agents, but they stay cool, maintaining their posts. They know who we are, that the government that pays their bills pays mine, and the company that pays the President is represented by Endo. We're just not supposed to be here. Sure, maybe hacking the guest registry is a federal crime, but that was Watson, not me.

After a two minute silent stroll, we reach the West Wing, which is the business end of the White House, where the Oval Office is located. I've never been here before, though I'm familiar with the layout, and not just from watching the TV show *The West Wing*. We studied schematics of the President's home, just in case things got hairy while we were visiting. But the functions of many of the rooms on this side of the building are classified, especially those below the West Wing, which is where we're headed. We take the stairs down to the second floor. The only two rooms I even know exist down here are the Situation Room and the Navy Mess, which is actually quite proper looking. Despite the covert nature of the rooms we pass, they're all quite resplendent—all dark, stained, hard wood, polished to pristine perfection. Paintings hang on the walls. Fresh flowers here and there. The rug beneath our feet feels cushy and new. It's like a 1950s gentlemen's club, without the cigarette smoke.

Dunne stops by a door and slides his keycard through a lock. The indicator light turns green, and Dunne opens the door.

More stairs. Leading down. Now *this* is new to me. After our previous tours of the White House, you'd have thought we'd seen everything, or at least the occasional glimpse of what went on behind the scenes. But there's not even a hint that something less than regal might exist in or around the building. As I step down the concrete utilitarian stairs, I feel like I've stepped into a different world. A dark, scary cave hidden beneath the enchanted forest. The door at the bottom of the stairs is opened for us. We're expected.

"Keep going," Dunne says, when I slow down.

The hallway beyond is mostly white and devoid of decoration. We're led past several closed doors, which I suspect house the White House's security elements. This is where the Secret Service does the dirty work. Monitoring visitors. Running background checks. Detaining—perhaps interrogating—people who aren't supposed to be here. Like us.

My suspicions are confirmed when we're led into a classic interrogation room. One desk. Two chairs. A mirrored wall. I motion to the desk and raise an eyebrow at Dunne. "Really?"

"Protocol," Dunne says, reaching out his hands. "Going to need your phones."

Before handing my phone over, I say, "I have the President on speed dial. I could—"

"Last I heard," Dunne said, "President Beck had put you on the 'do not answer' list."

"He's just upset that I didn't put out last time he bought me dinner."

I'm relieved some when Dunne cracks a smile. It also makes me feel bad for what's coming next.

Dunne takes my phone, makes sure it's shut off and turns to Endo, who already has his phone held out. As Dunne begins to take the phone, Endo drops it. Dunne reaches out to catch it, reacting instinctually. As the agent dips forward, Endo slaps his wrist—and the watch that isn't a watch—against the man's head, stabbing the neural implant into Dunne's temple. The small device, once attached, takes on the color of the victim's skin, making it invisible to anyone that isn't up close and personal.

Endo holds out his hand. Dunne gives him the caught phone.

"Come inside and close the door," Endo says, the transmitter embedded in his skull allowing him to control anyone wearing the implant. Dunne dutifully obeys.

"Is there anyone in the room next door?" Endo asks, glancing at the two way mirror.

"Shouldn't be."

Endo pulls out a chair and sits down like he owns the place. He crosses one leg over the other, smiles and says, "Good. Now here's what I need you to do."

33

Water dripped from General Lance Gordon's heavy eyebrows, temporarily obscuring his vision as he slipped his head up out of the Potomac River. He could see the Washington Monument rising out of the National Mall like a beacon. It wasn't just the tallest structure in Washington, D.C.; at 555 feet it was the tallest obelisk in the world. Although he couldn't see it, he knew the White House and President Beck would be a straight shot north.

He had spent the previous two nights inside the mouth of his smallest child. Under his guidance, the pair slipped slowly upriver, until they were within striking distance. His other children waited in the deeper water of Chesapeake Bay, clinging to the bottom. The bay, at its deepest, was 208 feet down. As soon as the children stood up, they'd be revealed.

And that was the plan. Create an unavoidable threat to which all military units would respond. In the chaos that followed, he would move in quickly, before Beck could evacuate, and then...he'd kill two birds with one stone. Or one fist as the case may be.

He knew Hudson was here as well. He didn't understand how, but he knew. He could sense the man's presence. At first, he believed his plan would be undone. But neither Hudson nor Beck had left the area, a fact he'd confirmed the previous night when he'd done some recon. He found moving across the city's dark rooftops quite easy, and with his new found strength, speed and agility, he'd had no trouble avoiding detection from the local population or from the Secret Service. He could have killed Beck in his sleep, but then Hudson would have fled.

Better to let two targets become one, he had decided. And when the two men he loathed most were dead, his vengeance wouldn't be complete, it would have only just begun. He was drawn to these men on a personal level, the way Maigo's personality drew Nemesis toward Alexander Tilley. But when they were dead, he would focus his attention on the rest of the world. He could feel their corruption. It screamed at him, in his Nemesis heart. The world was begging to be purified through violence.

He would start with Washington, D.C., a city he knew to be corrupt to its core, despite the lofty promises and plastic smiles. Then he would move south. To Fort Bragg, his one-time home and the location of the only fighting force on Earth he believed posed a threat. And once they were out of the way...

Gordon smiled. He'd always wanted to see the country, state by state. But now he wasn't just going to see the country, he was going to *reshape* it. He was going to remake the world, measuring his progress in tons of ash and blood.

But first, he had to wait for darkness to return again. Then he would light up the night.

34

Our sixth tour through the White House is a little different from the previous five. The most noticeable difference is the absence of Mindy. I can't picture Agent Dunne as a jabberjaw know-it-all, but with the neural implant embedded in his temple, he's like a sedated introvert. This concerns me at first because he's just silently leading the way. But no one gives him a second look. I wouldn't be surprised if part of his job description is silently escorting visitors through the halls. The one agent that does look our way simply glances at Endo and me, and then nods at Dunne. All in all, it's a short walk back to the stairs, up one flight and down the hall toward the most famous office in the world.

"Let's avoid the secretary," Endo says, his voice quiet, but easily heard by Dunne. While he can hear Endo's voice, he's also influenced by Endo's will. I want to apologize to the man. He's just doing his job. But it's led to a violation of his freedom. I remember what if felt like to have no control, and Endo just had me sit down. Dunne is breaking every Secret Service rule, oath and precaution. For all he knows, we are here to kill Beck and he's helping.

"This way," Dunne says, motioning for us to follow through the wide corridor separating the Oval Office and the Roosevelt Room. We slip through a door and into the less formal West Wing, where several offices are located, including the Vice President's and the Chief of Staff's. Conversations leak out of open doorways. A set of fingers type too hard on a computer keyboard. Distant laughter. The West Wing is busy, though the hall is empty.

Just as I am sure we are going to be caught, Dunne opens a door to our left and motions us through. We enter a small dining room, elegantly decorated, but also functional. This is where the President eats his less prestigious meals between writing speeches, working on policy and making shitastic decisions that put me and the people I care about—not to mention millions of Americans—in danger.

But not today.

Today he'll get the chance to do the right thing.

Or not.

The outcome will be the same, either way.

I'm surprised when Dunne opens another door and motions us through, this time with a polite smile and a nod.

"Laying it on a little thick," I whisper to Endo. "When this is done, he's going to hunt you down."

"I'm no longer controlling him," Endo says.

On the inside, I'm thinking something close to, *whhhaaaaa?* But I manage to ask a slightly more intelligent question. "But...how?"

Dunne walks past us, through the study, which I've barely noticed. He pauses at a second door, listening.

"His memory of today's events are...skewed," Endo says. "He is simply doing his job."

"You didn't..." I point to my head, wiggling my finger.

He nods. "Subtle changes. In his mind, we'll always be good guys. Don't worry, it takes more time and focus to alter a mind permanently than it does to make someone sit in a puddle. You're still you."

The memory makes me frown. "That was a really dirty puddle."

"Sorry," Endo says, wearing a smile that says he's not.

I look to Dunne and decide to test Endo's claim. "What's the hold up?"

"Sorry, sir," Dunne says. "President Beck is speaking to someone. Since your meeting is private and unscheduled, I believed it best to wait."

Well holy guacamole, it worked.

"How?" I ask Endo. "You should have told me about this sooner."

Endo must know I'm right, but he's not apologetic. "Keep your thoughts simple. A key phrase that encompasses everything you want, works best. Think it over and over until it becomes their thought. Their belief."

"Their reality," I say.

"Exactly. The more complex the control, the longer it takes."

The sound of a distant door closing catches my attention. Dunne turns around, oblivious to our conversation. "Sounds like the room is clear. Let me take a look."

Without knocking, Dunne opens the door to the Oval Office.

"Agent Dunne?" It's Beck. He's confused by the sudden interruption. I detect a trace of fear as well, probably because the Secret Service would only enter the room unannounced if there was some kind of danger.

Dunne ignores the leader of the free world and waves us in, "You guys are clear."

Walking past Dunne's open arms and big smile is surreal. This is the guy who wanted to kick me shitless and fugly. Now he's like my Aunt Gertrude at Thanksgiving. These neural implants are dangerous. So much so that I'm rethinking our plan.

"What's going on?" Beck stands behind the Resolute desk. He's dressed in black slacks and a blue button-up shirt. His jacket hangs over the back of the desk chair. His red tie is loose. He wasn't expecting company. He's more angry than afraid now, glaring at Endo and then at me with his piercing light blue eyes that can look both intimidating and manic. "Hudson, I'm going to have your job for this."

I nearly smile at the way his double chin—the chubbiest part of the man's body—jiggles when he speaks. "You could probably do a lot worse than that."

"You're damn right!" He picks up the phone. "You're in the shitter too, Dunne."

Oblivious, Dunne responds, "I'll just wait outside." He steps back into the side office and closes the door.

"Before you call..." Endo starts, making himself comfortable in one of the two flower print couches positioned face-to-face in front of the large, ornately carved desk. The office itself is far gaudier than I would have imagined. The gold and white oval rug covering most of the floor is some kind of modern design that looks more like an 8-bit Mario got sick. To make it worse, red flowers cover the design like explosions, or blood. Next to Gordon and his Kaiju, it's the most horrible thing I've ever seen. The paintings around the room are equally bad, framed in gold. "...I believe you will want to hear us out. *My employer* would agree."

The phone hovers next to Beck's ear, but he doesn't dial.

"You've been ignoring your supporters," Endo says. He nods at me. "And those who have saved you in the past. That is rude, don't you think?"

"Look," Beck says, leaning forward, one hand on the desk, the other hanging up the phone. "I'm not some stooge you can just tell what to do. Irregardless of your employer's support, I need to do what is best for this country."

I raise an index finger. "First, did you really just say, 'irregardless?' And second, since when is letting giant monsters kill U.S. citizens and smash billions worth in property, what is 'best for this country?'"

"We're not going to let that happen," Beck says. "All you've supplied us with are band-aids and medical bills. Speaking of which, I thought you two were supposed to be in the hospital?"

Endo chuckles. "Thoughts can be deceiving."

"Ignore him, sir," I say. "He's an idiot, and you should have never assigned him to the FC-P." I glance at Endo. This is going to hurt my soul. "That said...I believe the technology supplied by Zoomb is our best bet at containing—"

"I don't want to *contain* this problem," Beck says. His tomato face ripens before my eyes. "I want to eradicate it. I want to bury it."

I look at the domed ceiling and sigh. "You going to nuke the Kaiju."

"You're damn right I'm going to nuke them."

"Where?" I ask. "Because in case you haven't noticed, they tend to only surface in populated areas."

Beck's anger slides away. He understands the reality of his position. "Sometimes sacrifices have to be made for the greater good."

I smile like Steve Martin just entered the room holding a banjo. Still smiling, I take my red beanie cap, which now has a neural transmitter woven into the fabric, from my pocket and slide it onto my head. It's a tight fit, but makes my head feel normal for the first time in a week of disguises.

"What?" the President asks. "You find all this amusing?"

"I'm sorry," I say. "I really shouldn't be smiling. It's just that I'm very glad to hear you say that. Because sacrifice is exactly what will be required."

Beck nods slowly, unsure whether I'm agreeing with him.

I reach out to shake his hand. He looks down at my peace offering with skeptical eyes. "This is why you entered my office unannounced?" He waggles his finger at me. "I don't think so. You're many things, but agreeable is not one of them."

I keep my hand extended. "Funny, that's how I would describe you."

"What are you really after?"

I lift my hand higher. "A hand shake."

Beck winces like King Kong just farted. My very presence offends him, most likely because I'm a stark reminder that he's a sucky president.

"Maybe you should look at what's in my hand," I say.

Beck squints at me and leans forward. "I don't see—"

I snap my arm up, twist it around and smack the face of my watch, identical to Endo's, against his temple.

The President reels back, aghast, blubbering, winding up to scream for help.

"Sit down and shut up," I say.

The man obeys. My orders—my very thoughts—are sent to his mind as though God himself were commanding the man. The connection to a human mind is insignificant compared to that of Nemesis. I feel a slight headache coming on. Nothing a few painkillers couldn't handle. I can feel his mind, like a pliable blob of clay, ready to be shaped. I'm not sure what it would feel like with a stronger minded person, but luckily, Beck is fairly weak-willed.

Endo yawns and leans back, placing his feet on the couch. "How does it feel?"

"Easy," I say.

"That's not what I meant," Endo says. "How does it feel to be the most powerful person in the world?"

I don't respond to the question. It reminds me of why I considered not going through with this. If I can control the President of the United States, what's to stop Zoomb from doing the same?

"I need you to do two things for me," I say to Beck. "Cancel your appointments and request to be undisturbed for..." I look at my watch. It's nearly 5pm. The sun won't be down for another few hours. Gordon will wait until dark like a good soldier. "...the rest of the night. And while you're at it, request a large dinner."

Beck slowly reaches for the phone, and I imagine his hand reaching for a big red button. Way too dangerous.

While Beck makes his calls, I close my eyes and focus. I've got a few hours to brainwash the President.

35

Michael Spielberger lifted the $9 bottle of wine and looked at the label. It was simple and artistic. *At least it doesn't look cheap*, he thought. He had spent a year's worth of savings on this date, which had taken three months to plan. Cheap wine wasn't originally part of the deal, but the price of renting a yacht for the night, was far higher than he'd anticipated. He'd been boating since he was a kid. Knew how to navigate the 40-foot-long yacht—it wasn't even a sailboat. But his experience didn't change the price tag. So he made due by cutting corners elsewhere.

He left the small galley where he'd cooked supper and headed for the deck, and his date, Deb Burns. She was a long time friend. His best friend. They spoke nearly daily, e-mailed and texted all the time. They had fun. Went to movies. Traded secrets. But in their fifteen years of friendship, nothing more had developed, despite Michael's desires. A year previous, his friends in the IT department where he worked, had mocked him. Declared that he'd been sent to the 'friend-zone' until Deb decided to get married to someone else and dropped him like a sack of cow patties. The thought sickened him enough to push him into action. Tonight was the result of his long-term plan to break free of the friend-zone.

He vaulted back to the main deck with a spring in his step and the wine bottle in his hand, declaring, "Vino for the voman," like he was a vampire. It was a long running joke between them. His widow's peak came to a point at his forehead, making him look like an adult Eddie Munster. Although Eddie was technically a werewolf, Michael argued that his mother was a vampire, so he was at least partly vampire, hence the accent.

Deb sat on the deck, dressed in jeans and a t-shirt. When they'd left, she believed they were going to a movie. That the dinner would be Burger King. She'd teased him for his more formal attire, joked that he was looking for love. She had been right but didn't fully understand at the time. She did now, that was for sure. She glanced in his direction as he returned, but shifted her gaze back to the setting sun, a slice of orange peeking up from the horizon behind the shoreline.

He stopped beside her to admire the view. He'd rarely seen the Chesapeake Bay waters so serene. The whole scene was perfect, straight out of a movie. The boat rental company might have ripped him off, but God had his back and was supplying the perfect backdrop.

When Deb didn't look at him, he went to work on the cork, popping it loudly with a victorious whoop. While Deb remained fixed on the view, he filled the glasses, double in his to compensate for his growing nervousness. Deb was uneasy. He knew her better than anyone, and she was distant, hardly present.

"Did you have a good day?" he asked.

She shrugged. Such a question might normally generate a half hour's worth of co-worker gossip.

Michael glanced down at the steak he'd cooked. Mushrooms and onions covered the meat. Potatoes and green beans on the side. Her favorite meal. She hadn't touched it. Had let the food go cold. He saw it as a symbol, and he knew how this was going to end.

They were right, he thought. *I'm in the friend-zone. Always have been.*

The realization came like a sucker punch. Fifteen years of strong feelings and hope for the future were crushed without Deb even speaking a word. It was like a break up. A betrayal. How could she not know? How could she not feel similarly?

He sat down, a scowl on his face, and cut into his chilled steak. He stabbed a mushroom and ate it. The food was perfection. He looked at the view again. Stars twinkled in the now dark purple sky. Wasn't this the stuff that women dreamed about?

The next piece of steak was juicy and full of resolve. "Fuck you, Deb."

The three words got the first real reaction out of her since they stepped on board the yacht. She turned slowly in his direction. "What?"

"You heard me," he said, taking another angry mouthful. "Fuck. You."

This time she whirled around on him. "No, fuck *you*! How dare you put me in this position? You knew, Michael. You knew the whole time. And now *this*? You wine and dine me, and what? You think we're going to shack up? That we're going to somehow fall in love? That I'm going to suddenly not be a lesbian?"

Michael choked, gagged and spit the wad of half-chewed steak onto his plate. "What? You're..." Michael's mind spun in circles. *A lesbian? Holy shit*, he thought, *the 'girlfriends' she told me about weren't just friends that were girls!*

His anger deflated. His shoulders sagged. "Dammit. I've wasted fifteen years of my life on you."

"Wasted?" She got angry again. "Wasted!" She raised a fist and punched the table. The loud bang rose through Michael's body like a wave of energy. When it continued well past the impact, he realized the feeling was physical, not emotional. The coastline tilted at an odd angle. His stomach lurched, reminding him of a roller-coaster ride.

The table slid into Deb, covering her in two plates of food and two glasses of wine. Her chair tipped back and spilled her to the deck. Michael fell forward, landing atop the table. He could see the ocean below him—far below—as he looked over the yacht's side. *We're tipping*, he thought, picturing a tidal wave beneath them. His scream was drowned out by the sound of rushing water, like a waterfall.

Before he could understand the source of the roaring water, the yacht reached the bay, slamming back down. Water rushed up over the side, knocking Michael back, filling his mouth. He coughed and crawled aimlessly across the deck, as the buoyant craft bobbed upright once again, throwing him down.

As water fell over him like a hard rain, Michael rolled over, expecting to see a wave crashing down toward him. The water was there, white and frothing, falling all around, but where he expected a wall of water was something else. The rough, black surface rose from the bay, shedding water like a second skin.

Skin...

His eyes moved higher, drawn by a luminous orange beacon high above. The color swirled, fluid, like a brilliant lava lamp. Recognition took root in his chest, just as Deb let out a scream.

At first, the news had simply called the giant 'one of several Kaiju,' but had recently referred to it by a name designated by the FC-P: Typhon. The monster's human-like physique was what bothered most people, but it was the malicious, glowing eyes that caused Michael to vomit into the foot of sea water sloshing around him. It wasn't just that they were pure evil, it was that they were staring down. Straight at him.

"Oh shit," Deb yelled, and he caught a glimpse of her jumping overboard.

Michael's numb mind had trouble coming up with a reason why she would jump from the boat in the middle of the bay. Unluckily, the answer was supplied for him. The ship lurched upward, the deck shoving into his backside. Giant fingers reached around both sides of the ship, claws digging into the deck below him.

He screamed louder than Deb had and ran for the stern, hoping to leap into the water. Instead, he fell into the rail and peered over the edge. He was already a hundred feet up and rising quickly. Before he could second-guess and jump, he was two hundred feet up. Three hundred. Even higher! The boat tilted back, but he clung to the rail, locking his arms around the metal.

Looking around, he could no longer see Typhon staring down at him. *I'm above it,* he realized, and then he looked to the side and down. The nausea he felt from the extreme height was dwarfed by the fright generated by two more Kaiju: Karkinos and Scylla, who had last been seen devastating Rio. They were rising out of the bay. The monsters were roaring and angry. Their glowing membranes lit up the darkness like the orange sun had returned for an encore.

Before Michael could scream again, the yacht accelerated. His arms screamed in pain as he held on tightly. The claws clinging to the deck tore away.

He was free!

Released from doom and sent...

Michael pulled himself up and found the wind in his face. At first, the view made no sense, but understanding arrived quickly. The yacht had been picked up and thrown, like it was nothing more than a kid's toy in a tub. The dark waters of the bay were invisible below, but he could see the lights of civilization growing closer.

As Michael finally screamed again, he saw a window ahead. There was a shape in the window. A man. He was looking out, to see. Then he turned his eyes up, saw the yacht and met Michael's eyes. Both men screamed right up until the end, when the 40-foot yacht plowed through the brick face of an apartment building, and in the distance, sirens began to wail.

36

"Betty, this is Bob," I say, for the benefit of anyone who might be monitoring cell phone usage in and around the White House. It would be easier to use Devine, but activating the system in D.C. would put up a red flag that would let everyone know exactly where I was. "How's that pie cooking?"

"About to put it in the oven," Woodstock replies, his deep voice now thoroughly confusing any listeners, which makes me cringe, but he turns things around by adding, "S'pose you called to talk to the missus."

"If you don't mind," I say.

"Hey, hun," Collins says, as she comes on the line. "You get in touch with your friends?"

I glance at President Beck. He's seated across from me at the dining room table, just two rooms away from the Oval Office. I just had some of the best lobster of my life, courtesy of my presidential host. So far, everyone, including the Secret Service, has given Beck the distance he requested, but I'm not sure how long that will last.

"We just finished a nice sit-down meal," I say.

Collins must be wondering if a 'sit down meal' is code for something, because she says, "For real?"

"Yes, ma'am," I say. "Lobster and all the fixings." As soon as the words come out of my mouth, I realize that if anyone is listening and knows the President's menu choice for the evening, there could be problems. I force a laugh and add, "I'm just messing with you. We had dogs and hot wings. Waiting for the game to start."

"How're you holding up?" she asks.

Something about the way her voice sounds makes me wish that it were me waiting in the chopper. They're parked somewhere, just outside the no-fly zone, waiting for things to go sour. I haven't seen Collins much in the last few weeks. I've spent most of my time with Endo, which sucks more balls than the last hole at a mini-golf course. "Impatient. Looking forward to the game's end for a change."

"I hear you, babe. You have any idea when it might start?"

A distant siren tickles my ear. I look at Endo, who is wiping melted butter from his mouth. Apparently, the lobster was good for him, too. He couldn't hear the siren, which means the sound is coming through the phone. "What's that sound?"

No answer.

"Betty," I say. "What's that sound?"

Collins's voice comes back as a whisper. "Kickoff."

It takes a moment to settle in. Kickoff. The game is starting!

"You better hurry on that pie," I say.

"I'm on it," she says. "See you soon."

I hang up the phone and turn to Endo, who is already watching me, napkin frozen over his lips. "It's time."

I dial the phone again. It's answered quickly. As per our protocol, I speak first, using our code names. "Ranger, its Bob."

"I'm here, Bob." Ranger, who was a hard sell on my quasi-crazy idea, doesn't sound enthused.

"The game is about to start."

"We're settled in and waiting for the whistle to blow."

A distant siren blares, its whine piercing the night. It's accompanied by another, and another until it's impossible to not hear them. Everyone in Washington, D.C. will be wide awake and terrified in the next five seconds.

"See you in the end zone," I say.

"We're on our way."

The line goes dead.

I place the phone back in my pocket. I can hear the rumble of approaching feet. "Here they come."

Endo stands and takes up position to the President's side. I stand on the other side, framing him in. Dunne stands half way around the table, closer to the door, looking as vacant as Beck.

The door slams open violently. No warning. No knock. Just action. At a moment like this, with the whole of Washington, D.C. under imminent attack, the President is treated like a helpless, frightened baby and whisked away to safety. Normally, I have no doubt that Beck would rush away with them. That's probably what they're expecting. But the President isn't feeling like himself.

"Sir!" one of the agents yells, stopping short of tackling the President and throwing him over his shoulder. "Three Kaiju have emerged from Chesapeake Bay! We have to leave, now!"

When Beck doesn't reply, but remains seated in front of his uneaten lobster, the man steps closer.

I get in his way.

"Step aside," the man says. His hand goes toward his gun.

Other agents crowd in, looking ready for action. Those on my side of the table get close. Those on the other side are stopped by Dunne, whom they either fear or trust. He is the agent in charge. "The President is staying here," Dunne says.

"Agent Dunne," the man in front of me says, "Protocol is that we—"

"Protocol is whatever the President of the United States says it's going to be," Dunne says, and I suspect the words are being fed to him by Endo.

I'm still connected to Beck, but I haven't tried to make him speak, I've just been...reconditioning...certain aspects of his personality.

All the agents turn toward Beck. He doesn't blink.

Shit, did I lobotomize the man?

"Sir," the closest agent says. "We need to leave. Now. It's not safe—"

"Not safe?" Beck says. He shakes his head. "Not safe. Who am I to be saved while the rest of the people are in harm's way?"

"You're the Pres—"

"I'm just a man," Beck says. "Same as the rest of you. And I'm not leaving. It's of critical importance that I stay. That the people of this nation don't see their leader as a coward. We must remain unshakable in the face of this threat, and we cannot lead effectively if our first action is the full retreat of this nation's Commander in Chief!" He punctuates this by punching the table, crushing the lobster with a spray of fishy smelling juice.

The men back down, whispering 'Yes sirs,' and nodding.

"Now go and get everyone else out! The Vice President, Chief of Staff, *my wife*. Everyone. But I'm staying until the crisis is averted. And these men—" He looks to me and then Endo. "—will be aiding in our response to this attack. You are not to hinder them in any way, and if they give you an order, I expect you to follow it."

The gaggle of agents stands still, bewildered by a President they've all known to be a man of weak character.

"Go!" Beck shouts.

The men backtrack out of the office, closing the door behind them. For a moment, there is silence, then one of them snaps out of it and starts shouting orders. Then the rumble of rushing feet moves off in a variety of directions.

"I'm impressed," Endo says, motioning to Beck. "What have you been putting in his head?"

"I kept it simple," I say. "'Be brave and do the right thing.'"

And while that sounds simple, Beck didn't act on those character traits until I really wanted him to. So he's not just going to go all George Washington on us without a little more mental prodding. That Endo and I can talk about the man, right in front of him, is proof enough. At some point, I'm going to have to free him from this neural implant and hope the reprogramming sticks. Then, maybe in a few weeks, I'll consider the moral implications of what I've done to the man. Professor X would not approve. Of course, the man *did* drop a MOAB on my position in Boston. He's lucky I don't mentally suggest he get tattoos of 'Dick' and 'Face' across his knuckles.

The sound of a distant explosion rattles the windows. I look for the orange glow, but see nothing. "Won't be long now."

Endo nods. "We should go."

I dig a piece of paper from my pocket and hand it to Agent Dunne. "Time to go shopping." He takes the list without a word and heads for the door, under Endo's control. If only everyone listened to me like that, my job would be so much easier. Dunne leaves and closes the door behind him.

"Well, Mr. President." I slap his shoulder like we're chums. "How would you like to go for a stroll in the Rose Garden? Maybe get attacked by a madman that wants us both dead?"

Beck looks momentarily confused, but I push my will on him. He slaps the table with both hands, rattling silverware, and stands up. "We'll do what needs to be done. No matter the sacrifice."

I'd feel better about it if the words were his own. But they're not. While I haven't exactly put the words in his mouth, I know they're what I need to hear, because we've just created a big-ass neon target with an arrow that says, 'Kill these guys,' and I want to run the frig away. But I can't. And won't.

The end might be nigh, but I basically invited it, so it's time to see if my plan, which feels more ridiculous now that I'm not in a hospital bed hopped up on morphine, will get the job done. I feel like I should say something inspiring too, but I'm just not feeling it. I stand and head for the side door that leads to the small office and then the Oval Office, which has an exit to the outside. I pause, hand on the knob. "In case I die tonight," I say to Endo. "Go fuck yourself."

Endo grins. He's grown accustomed to my potty mouth and my sense of humor.

"In case *I* die," he says. "Thank you for trusting me."

"I don't," I tell him. I exit the room, believing I'm walking toward my demise and wanting nothing more than to be watching a B-movie with Collins. Hell, this will probably be made into a B-movie someday.

"I wonder who will play Collins," Beck says, plucking the thought from my mind. He steps up beside me, waiting to be led to his office.

And that's how you make them speak.

As I enter the small office, I smile as Beck says, "Hey Endo, go fuck yourself." *Ahh, the guilty pleasures of a dead man.*

37

The two women, dressed head-to-toe in black, moved through the newly fallen night like living shadows. Approaching the end of their half mile sprint, the pair breathed heavily as they paused beside a chain-link fence topped with razor wire.

"Is it electrified?" Collin asked.

Alessi shook her head. "There are liability issues with an electrified fence."

"But not razor wire?"

"Not everyone can read warning signs." Alessi motioned to the razor wire. "But anyone, illiterate or not, can see that's a bad idea." She took a pair of wire cutters from her black jacket and went to work on the chain-link fence, slowly clipping a hole large enough to crawl through.

Collins waited impatiently. The warehouse was located in Harwood, Maryland, just eight miles from the coast and twenty-two from downtown D.C. The area wasn't densely populated—mostly spread-out neighborhoods, fancy golf courses and trees. No one passing by would give the warehouse's drab gray exterior a second look or guess that some of the world's most high tech discoveries were made, and kept, within. That's the way Zoomb, and the government they sold their tech to, preferred it. Congressmen, senators and a bevy of generals from the Pentagon often made the short drive, or flight, from D.C. to watch demonstrations. Even President Beck had visited the facility.

The chain-link fence rattled and fell open.

Collins shushed Alessi, but the Zoomb employee turned corporate thief was unfazed. "Security doesn't mind the rear of the building much. We saw them sweep five minutes ago. We should have five more. More if they get distracted by the news."

Collins listened to the air-raid klaxons sounding in the distance. Every TV channel, news network or not, would be airing images of the Kaiju. It had become standard operating procedure. When a

Kaiju appeared, every channel on Earth carried the story. And nearly every person with a television stopped what they were doing and tuned in. Including security guards. Which was part of the reason why they had waited until the last minute to make this errand. If they had made off with the tech at the beginning of the week, they'd have played their hand too soon.

"Isn't there more security than guards?" Collins asked.

"Some of the best security on the planet," Alessi said. "And the tech to beat it is inside."

"That doesn't sound helpful."

"Endo taught me to prepare for all contingencies," Alessi said, revealing her allegiance to the man and not to the company that employed them both. She pulled a small, phone-sized device from her pocket. "Some people steal pens from work."

Collins grinned. "You steal high tech, top secret technology."

"No one here uses pens." Alessi slipped through the hole with ease. Collins followed, but her fuller figure required a little squirming to fit through without making too much noise.

Free of the fence, the pair ran across the empty pavement. Half way to the building, Alessi stopped like there was an invisible wall. She pointed to the plain looking back door of the building. It was simple and black, like it would be easy to kick open. "Any closer, and the cameras will pick us up," Alessi said.

Collins looked the building over, left to right. "I don't see any cameras."

"That's the point." Alessi dug into her coat again. "There are three cameras monitoring the area in front of the door. There's a biometric lock and a numeric keypad hidden in the wall to the right of the door, behind a secret panel. The lock itself is a ten pound deadbolt that's retracted electronically."

"Anything else?" I ask.

"If someone tries to break in, they get gassed."

"*Gassed?*"

"Nitrous oxide. Being arrested and thrown in jail would feel like the best day of your life, until it wore off and you discovered you'd been licking the floor clean because it tasted like maple syrup." Alessi held up a black sphere with a red light. "But don't worry, that's not going to happen to us." She rolled the orb toward the door.

Collins squinted, thinking the sphere was some kind of explosive. But nothing so dramatic took place. A small red light on the ball's exterior turned green. Alessi stood. "Let's go."

Collins followed her to the door. "That's it?"

"Limited range electromagnetic pulse. Took out all of the door security. Don't worry, we were too far away for it to affect your phone."

Collins stopped in front of the door, which looked very solid up close. "Except for the ten pound dead bolt."

"That's where you come in, muscles." Alessi took one more device from her jacket: a seven-inch-wide circular disk with a solid metal handle. She held the disk up to the door and it leapt out of her hands, slapping against the metal, just above where there should have been a knob. "Heave ho."

Collins understood what she was being asked to do and took hold of the handle now secured to the door. She grunted as she pulled. She didn't think she could ever pull the magnetic disc away from the door, but she could drag it, slowly and painfully, inch by inch, until she felt the lock thump free of the side wall. She gave the door a gentle shove and it cracked open. She stepped aside and motioned to the unlocked door. "After you."

Unlike the outside of the building, the inside was like a work of modern sculpture. The walls were painted in funky colors, often sporting hip looking retro art. The lighting was soft, but bright enough that their black outfits would make them stand out like bird shit on the driver's side of a windshield—hard to miss and impossible to ignore.

"This way," Alessi whispered, leading Collins down a long straight hallway.

Collins glanced through the circular door windows as they passed. There was a mix of offices, game rooms, kitchens and labs. Zoomb wasn't segregating fun from work, which made sense. Scientists, software coders and electronic engineers who were paid to dream up ways of subjugating people probably had a lot of stress to release. *At least they're not all sociopaths*, Collins thought.

"Here," Alessi said, stopping by a keycard reader. She swiped her card, and the unit flashed a green light. The door unlocked with a loud click that felt more like a gunshot in the dark hallway.

Collins followed Alessi into a large storage room and eased the door shut behind her. Unlike the rest of the building thus far, the storage room was bland. White walls. Rows upon rows of shelves. But Collins hardly noticed the lack of décor. It was the shelves' contents that held her transfixed. "Holy hell."

The shelves were lined with hundreds of human-sized neural implants. Alessi moved past them and opened up a large, hard case the size of a kid's toy chest. Inside was a Kaiju-sized neural implant, complete with its rocket body, packed in form-fitting foam. Collins opened the next case, revealing a second device. She moved down the line, opening cases. There were twenty in all. She stopped after seven. "Why do they need so many?"

Alessi looked stunned. "I...I have no idea. I thought—*we* thought—they had only a few working prototypes."

"This looks more like mass production," Collins said. "More than what you'd need for a few redundancies."

"There isn't time to figure out why they need so many," Alessi said, picking up one of the large cases. She struggled with it, holding on to the handle with two hands, but she managed to hobble toward the door. "If someone is paying attention, they'll see that the door was opened."

Crap, Collins thought, and asked, "Will they know it was you?"

"Yeah," Alessi said, not hiding her disappointment. "They will."

She's throwing away her high paying, cushy job, Collins realized. *Risking prosecution, too.*

Collins picked up a second over-sized implant and headed for the door. It had to weigh forty pounds. They wouldn't be going anywhere quickly. She put the case back down carefully, took out her phone and speed-dialed Woodstock.

He answered with a casual, "Ayuh?"

"Going to need a speedy exit," Collins said.

"On my way."

The line went dead. Collins pocketed the phone, picked up the case and hurried to the door. They moved down the long hall as quickly and quietly as they could. Ten feet from the exit, a voice stopped them in their tracks. "Don't fucking move!"

The duo stopped in place.

"Put down the cases!"

Collins glanced over her shoulder. One security guard was fifteen feet back. Two more approached, but were still at the far end of the hall. All held non-lethal tasers, though they had guns on their belts.

"Don't fucking look at me!" the guard shouted. She could hear the nervousness in his voice. They'd probably never had a break-in before. She stole one last glance before facing forward again, confirming that the guards all wore bulletproof vests. If the guard was a little less panicked he might have seen that she wore a similar vest, and that his taser, aimed at her chest, would have no effect on it.

"Listen," Collins said, turning around casually, "I don't think you—"

The guard pulled his trigger. Two metal prongs trailing thin cables shot out and attached to Collins's chest, the *tick, tick, tick,* of electricity having nowhere to go. Collins drew her pistol and fired once, hitting the guard's chest on his right side, well away from his heart. The vest stopped the bullet, but the high caliber round knocked him off his feet.

"Go!" Collins shouted, picking up her case with one hand and aiming with the other.

Further down the hall, the other guards dropped their tasers and drew their sidearms, but neither got a chance to fire. Collins squeezed off three rounds, aiming for the ceiling above their heads. The cacophonous sound sent both men diving for cover. Collins was out the door before the men looked back up.

Outside, the chop of approaching helicopter rotor mixed with the squeal of tires from the building's front. Security and Woodstock would arrive at the same time. As bullets pinged off the metal door's interior, Collins put down her case, took hold of the magnetic disk and dragged the deadbolt back in place.

The rotor chop grew suddenly louder as Betty emerged over the fence, angling down for a hasting landing. Alessi, holding her case at her side, with both hands, was already halfway there. When Betty touched down, Woodstock flung open his door, leapt out and opened the rear door for Alessi, who slid her case inside and climbed in after it.

Not waiting for Collins, Woodstock got back inside the chopper and the rotor began spinning faster, the skids lifting off the ground.

Collins was thirty feet from the waiting chopper when a black SUV tore around the side of the building and barreled toward her. She took aim and fired her last two rounds. The first shot sparked off the pavement, but the second found its mark, punching through the vehicle's front left tire. The SUV's driver crushed the brakes and all four doors flung open.

Collins reached the chopper quickly thanks to Woodstock, who glided Betty in close, just a foot off the ground. Ducking under the rotor wash, Collins passed her case to Alessi.

A gunshot ripped through the air.

Collins shouted in pain and fell forward. Alessi caught her and hauled her inside, shouting for Woodstock to go. Betty lifted quickly into the sky, bullets ricocheting harmlessly off her metal body.

As the bullets faded and the chopper rose, Alessi quickly checked Collins over.

"I'm okay," Collins coughed.

Alessi stopped her search, finding the bullet embedded in the left side of Collins's rear body armor. "Thank God," Alessi said. Collins grinned at the woman's concern. She hadn't realize they'd become that friendly, but they'd spent a lot of down-time together while Hudson and Endo had lain in hospital beds.

Collins sat up with a groan, thinking the bullet must have bruised a few ribs. She tore off her black mask and put on a headset. "Get us someplace safe," she said to Woodstock. "We need to load these up before Jon and Endo become Kaiju snack-food."

38

Standing under the roof of the West Colonnade, we watch a bevy of cars and limos pull up and quickly whisk away some of Washington's most important people. The driveway around the South Lawn is typically reserved for foot traffic, but they're using all exits to evacuate. Not that the people in cars are going to make it very far. By now, the rest of the city is rushing to their cars, too. Within the hour, I suspect people will have given up on driving and will run on foot. The lucky ones are boarding one of five green-and-white Sikorsky SH-3 Sea King helicopters idling on the South Lawn. The choppers are normally reserved for the President, with the lead bird known as Marine One, when he boards it. But right now they're taking away key staff, including the Vice President. Had we not intervened, President Beck would have been the first one out, leaving on a chopper just for him and his mob of Secret Service agents.

I've heard a few people enter and leave the Oval Office behind us, shouting for the President. Agents, aids, maybe even generals, none of them thinking to open the closed shades and look outside. Right now, the President is AWOL and not making decisions. The people who need his approval to act are probably freaking out, but that's okay. He's exactly where he needs to be.

I hope.

If I get the man killed, I'm fairly well screwed. Worse than that, so are all the people helping me tonight. As the last of the vehicles pulls away from the South Lawn drive and the helicopters thunder into the air, Agent Dunne returns from the Oval Office. The man looks like he's going on vacation, carrying six black, hard cases of varying sizes.

I help him with the cases and open one of the three larger ones. "Is this everything?"

Dunne nods.

Inside the large case is a tactical uniform, complete with body armor. One like it came in handy against Gordon before, but we couldn't wear the gear beneath our disguises. Knowing the Secret Service would have their own on hand, we decided it would be best to borrow theirs. And there's the added bonus of looking like one of the gang. Hiding behind a row of thick bushes, Endo and I don the gear. As I cinch the last buckle, I feel much more prepared, though still fairly defenseless. To my surprise, Dunne changes into his own armor. He might be an automaton right now, but he's still doing his job.

I open the next three cases to reveal three different weapons. I take the smallest of them, an FN P90, which has a super high rate of fire and Secret Service-issue, armor-piercing rounds. It's also small and light, so my mobility won't be compromised. And that's important, because I'm probably going to be running for my life sooner than later. Endo takes the second weapon, an M4 Carbine, powerful enough to punch straight through an engine block, and hopefully through Gordon's skin. Dunne, now ready for battle, takes an MP5 and slaps on a Beta C-Mag, a dual drum magazine that holds a hundred rounds. He can hold down that trigger and spray bullets until the sun comes up.

Dunne reaches beneath his jacket and draws his FN Five-seven pistol, spins it around and holds it out to Beck. "This your idea?" I ask Endo.

"I think it's better if he can defend himself," Endo says.

"He's likely to shoot himself accidentally," I complain.

"Just tell him he's a good shot."

I shake my head. This plan is getting stupider by the minute.

A string of Harrier jets roar by above, heading east, derailing my train of thought. Missiles scream from their undersides, rocketing ahead of the jets. The mix of jets and missiles pass by quickly. For some reason, the wailing air-raid sirens fall silent. The sound of screams fills the void, rising from all over the city—police sirens, squealing tires, people. If there was a soundtrack to Hell, it would probably sound something like this. I cringe, knowing that people are already dying in the city. And it's my fault. I put them in harm's way.

Tense voices, closer by, rise up next. The remaining Secret Service are taking up positions. Activating defenses. While we call the building a house, it is actually something closer to a fortress, with reinforced walls and windows, hidden chain guns, missile defense systems and now, a nearby battalion of tanks, which I know are there, because I recommended them. In fact, all of the protocols being activated right now are, in part, my creation, put in place when I still had the President's ear.

Despite all this, it's not enough. The weaponry might slow down a single Kaiju, but we've got three stomping toward the city. And a fourth somewhere else. And it's that fourth, which we know carries Gordon around in its mouth, that is my true concern.

In the distance, missiles explode, filling the night with the sound of distant thunder. A roar follows, even louder. And it's not a wounded cry, it's just pissed. And closer than I would like.

A rumbling shakes my legs. The grinding squeal of tank treads scoring pavement. M1 Abrams tanks take up positions around the White House, on the far side of the South Lawn and along Executive Avenue, defending an empty building. Well, almost empty. They must know that Beck has decided to stay.

Proving this assumption correct, a ten-man squad of fully armored and armed Secret Service agents burst from the White House and take up defensive positions around Beck, and us. Endo and I share a grin. *Now this is more like it.*

Amid the chaos, I become aware of a pulse moving through the colonnade floor, slowly growing more intense. With the White House empty of people and the Secret Service on board, it's time to move. I focus on the sentence I want the President to say.

"Let's move to the roof," Beck says. "So we can see what we're up against."

Before any of the agents can complain about this tactic, Dunne says, "Right this way, sir," and charges back into the Oval Office. When Endo and I, dressed as agents now, quickly follow, leading Beck inside, the rest fall in line. It's like high school again, leading innocent freshman behind the gym to smoke their first doobie, except that those freshman had a good time and weren't in danger of a violent death.

We hurry through the White House in a blur. After being here day after day with halls full of tourists and employees, seeing the place empty feels surreal. We charge up a flight of stairs, and while Beck is encircled by agents, he's holding his handgun at the ready, looking fearless. The most awkward part of a roofward charge is the elevator. We hurry inside, cram in tightly and then stand still while the elevator rises. I want to ask if the elevator exits at the roof. I want to make a Muzak joke. Both would invite suspicion, though, so I keep my mouth shut. The elevator doors open and all fourteen of us are vomited into the hallway beyond. The hall is black. Red emergency lights glow from the ceiling, allowing us to see while acclimating our eyes to the night. We hurry down the long stretch to a short staircase, at the top of which is a solid-looking door with a numeric keypad and a hand print security system. I step aside and let Dunne do the deed. Cool night air washes over us, along with the sounds of a panicked populace, the din of distant battle and the sound of something approaching.

Something large.

The roof has been transformed. Chain guns line the roof walls, two to the north, two to the south. What normally look like air conditioning units have been revealed for what they really are—missile launchers—controlled from inside the security room buried several levels below us. In addition to Secret Service, there are soldiers on the roof, armed with an array of weapons, including anti-tank missiles and grenade launchers.

"The men look afraid," Beck says.

Endo shoots me a questioning glance. I shrug. I didn't put the words in his mouth. I'm barely looking at the soldiers hurrying about. My eyes are turned southward, past the South Lawn and the Ellipse, all the way to the Washington Monument.

"Men!" Beck shouts, raising his hands in the air.

Someone says, "Oh my God, is that the President?"

"Our darkest hour is upon us, but we must stand together, as brothers, as equals! I will fight with you, and if I must, I will die with you!"

The number of cheers equals the number of confused faces.

"Now let's send these Kaiju sons-a-bi—"

A roar interrupts Beck's speech. It comes from the south. All heads turn.

Drakon, now 200 feet long from snout to tail comes flailing out of the reflecting pool at a dead run. The monster still has a low to the ground body, like a lizard, but like all the other Kaiju, it's wearing a Nemesis skin, with coils of dark flesh, a jagged spike-covered back and glowing membranes, which are thankfully on its underside, illuminating its approach like a punk-ass teenager's undercar lighting.

As its wide limbs scramble and claw at the grass, the thing tumbles and rolls, slamming into the Washington Monument. The sound of stone cracking is like a cannon blast. I swear I see the obelisk waver, but it doesn't fall. Then Drakon is back up and charging straight toward the White House. It will cover the half-mile distance in seconds.

Beck steps forward, hands on the south wall of the White House's roof. "Fire!"

KARKINOS

39

The thunder that follows the President's order drowns out the sounds of the wailing city. The sirens. The screaming. Even Drakon's roar. The amount of firepower launched from the White House is mind numbing. Missiles cruise over the South Lawn. I can feel the heat from their fiery rockets on my face. A wall of bright orange tracer rounds follows the missiles, showing the paths of thousands of bullets, all headed for Drakon. And then there's the ordinance we can't see: grenades launched above it all, tumbling through the air toward the monster's back.

While the modern and primal destructive forces race toward each other, I turn to Dunne and grab his arm and point to Beck. "Get him to the PEOC!" The Presidential Emergency Operations Center is a bunker beneath the East Wing, and it was built to withstand a nuclear blast. It won't stop four Kaiju from digging him out like colossal dogs going after a buried bone, but it will protect him if one of these sons-a-bitches self-immolates. And while I'm not a fan of Beck—at least before I gave him a bravery boost and a moral adjustment—he's still the President, and my boss.

Dunne looks confused for a moment, but then Endo turns to him and says, "Go. Now." The agent nods and takes Beck's arm. The President resists for a moment, but I give him a mental shove, and the pair runs for the roof exit.

A series of explosions nearly knocks me over. I turn back to the south and see Drakon emerge from a billowing mass of fire. Tracer rounds greet her on the way out of the flames, hot metal digging into her thick skin, but doing no real damage. That is, until a line of orange, spewing from one of the chain guns, strikes her left eye. The orb absorbs hundreds of rounds before bursting liquid nasty all over the monster's face.

Drakon shrieks in pain and thrashes as she continues forward. When the dark lizard reaches the South Lawn Fountain, the top of her lowered snout slams into the thick stone wall. The head stops while the body moves forward. The giant head folds under the body as it lifts up and over. The angle is so extreme that I find myself hoping the thing's neck will be snapped.

The monster's tail thrashes wildly, trying to find some kind of equilibrium, but the body continues up and over, landing in the fountain with a splash. For a moment, it appears that we've managed a small victory, but then a grenade bursts—directly over one of the orange membranes on the creature's exposed underside—sending shards of metal downward and plumes of glowing fluid upward.

"Get down!" I shout, tackling Endo to the roof.

The resulting explosion knocks everyone down and knocks the air from my lungs, but we're spared from the searing heat and flames. The metal fragments created relatively small holes. Had it been a missile, the White House and everyone on this roof, would have been reduced to ash.

"Hold your fire!" I shout, and then remember that I've got access to Devine. Crouching behind the wall, I pull out my smart phone, activate the Devine network and broadcast to all emergency personnel listening, careful not to identify myself. "This is Agent Dunne of the Secret Service, do not, I repeat do *not* hit the target's membranes!" I don't need to explain why to the people atop the White House roof. They all just got a stark reminder. But with three more Kaiju incoming, each containing enough boom-juice to level D.C., I think a quick refresher is a good idea.

As confirmations start to come in from various military and emergency sources, I hang up the phone and hit the call button for Ranger.

He answers, out of breath. "What?"

"Ranger, I need an ETA."

"Two minutes for me," he says. His voice shakes as he runs. "One for...our special friend."

"Copy that," I say, and hang up, dialing Woodstock. The line connects, and I don't wait for a greeting. "Status?"

"In the air and hanging back," Woodstock replies. "But these guys are moving fast; seventy miles per hour, straight through the suburbs. They're getting shot to shit, but they're not even feeling it."

"ETA?"

"We're about twenty miles out. We'll be inside the city limits in ten minutes. To the White House in fifteen."

"Copy that," I say. "Be safe."

I hang up the phone and pocket it. My job here isn't to coordinate the response, it's to *respond*. Personally. As much as I hate it, that's the only way this mess is going to be resolved.

With a high pitched squeal I can feel in my teeth, Drakon rolls over. Seeing an opportunity, the first of the M1 Abrams tanks to react to the Kaiju's sudden appearance, launches a round at Drakon's side. The tank fires a supersonic 120mm kinetic round with a depleted uranium tip. It's capable of punching through just about anything on the planet. Including, it would seem, Kaiju flesh.

The round strikes Drakon's right forelimb, exploding with tremendous force and spraying chunks of brown meat and black skin across the lawn.

Drakon roars in pain and bounces on its feet, turning back and forth. It's almost comical, like the thing is saying, 'What hit me? What hit me?' It must figure out the answer because it leaps through the air and drops down on the tank, crushing it with the creature's weight. Adding insult to injury, Drakon takes hold of the tank's gun turret, lifts the crumpled tank off the ground and throws it across the lawn, toward a second tank still taking aim. The tanks collide in a tangle of very expensive metal, and the men buried somewhere within.

Drakon settles its one good eye back on the White House and charges. She's limping heavily, but doesn't seem to have been slowed, and certainly doesn't mind the pain.

Gunfire and grenades pepper the monster as it closes the distance, but the missiles hold back. The target is too close. Just as I hear the chop of approaching helicopters, Drakon arrives. The monster rises above us like a tidal wave, bathing us in orange light from its glowing membranes, forcing the men on the roof to hold their fire—not that a few bullets would change anything. The monster's jaws snap open, splitting both vertically and horizontally, revealing four sets of sharp teeth and giving the creature a bite radius that would make Mick Jagger jealous. But it doesn't roar or even bite. From within the ring of sharp, arm-sized teeth, a black sphere launches up and over the White House roof.

At first it looks like a glob of tar, but then it opens up, revealing thick limbs, hooked fingers and claws. *Gordon*. While his entrance is impressively flamboyant, the man's arrival—if he's still a man at all—makes me ill.

Before anyone even thinks to react, Gordon lands on the tallest point of the roof, denting the metal surface. He scans the frozen groups of soldiers, looking for someone. Looking for me, I realize.

"Open fire!" I shout, counting on the men to remember avoiding those explosive orange membranes that make such tempting targets. Gordon spots me just as the men on the roof send a barrage of bullets in his direction. He leaps down to the far side of the roof. I'm no longer able to see him, but I don't need to. The screams rising up are image enough.

Working in concert with Gordon, Drakon assaults the roof, slamming her giant hand down, crushing men and tearing through the top two floors of the White House. With a gleeful roar, the monster leans down and catches two men within her jaws, lifting them up and silencing their screams with a quick chomp, before tilting her head back and swallowing them whole.

Next, Drakon turns her attention to my side of the roof. She reaches out, but pauses, as though confused. With a shake of her head, the monster yanks her hand away like a child who touched a hot stove. Gordon wants me for himself.

"Down!" Endo shouts, returning the favor of tackling him, by shoving me down and jumping on top of me. A twisting mass of helicopter launched rockets scream overhead, striking Drakon with enough force to knock her sideways. As the monster falls from view and Endo pulls me to my feet, I say, "Didn't realize you cared."

"Our plan hinges on you not dying," he says.

Yeah, no pressure.

"Hudson!" The voice is deep, booming and hits me like an emotional missile. Gordon charges across the roof, covered in other men's blood. His eyes burn with fury. Froth slides from his clenched teeth with each step.

I lift my P90 and hold the trigger down, unleashing fifty rounds in seconds. His body shakes from the barrage, but he doesn't slow. While I reload, Endo takes aim with his more powerful assault rifle, punching round after round into Gordon's forehead. The engine-killing rounds just get stuck in the thick flesh. But it hurts. Gordon, unlike his Kaiju, still experiences pain like a human being. He reacts like one, too, raising his meaty hand, to defend his face.

With the P90 reloaded, I aim more carefully, but hold the trigger down again. I have to fight the recoil, but I manage to send most of the rounds into my target—Gordon's knee. The leg buckles as Gordon shouts in pain, but he lunges forward with his good leg, arms outstretched.

My brain tells me to move. To dive. To duck. But there's no avoiding this freight train. The best I can do is take it like a man, or in this case, like a ragdoll.

Gordon hits hard, but he doesn't slam me to the roof as expected. Instead, he lifts me up and over the sidewall, tackling me over the edge of the roof. On the inside, I'm rolling my eyes and thinking, "Shiiiit." On the outside, I'm screaming.

40

The world turns through Jell-O. Or at least that's what it feels like. I'm falling, wrapped in the tight embrace of my mortal enemy. But I'm also spinning. No, not spinning...flipping. I'm fli—

The impact sends a wave of pain through my body, numbing my toes and fingers. But I'm not dead! And I'm no longer held in place. Despite my body screaming to remain motionless, I sit up and stagger away.

Gordon lies atop the granite staircase of the White House's south portico. We fell two stories down, but rolled so that Gordon absorbed most of the impact. *A stroke of good luck.*

Gordon sits up, grinning.

Or...not.

He could have killed me if he wanted to. It's obvious now. He could have popped my head in his hand like a too-full water balloon. He could have *not* flipped over. But he wanted me alive for a little while longer. Although that suits me just fine, it confuses me.

Until I see the look in his eye. He's enjoying this. Like a cat, toying with a mouse, he's going to kill me slowly, savoring each injury. And then, he'll kill me. It's a strategic risk, but why would he doubt victory? He's virtually impervious to harm and has four Kaiju for back up. He has enough power to destroy entire nations. What would he have to fear from me?

I smile back at him, knowing the answer to the unasked question. I'm a sneaky son-of-a-bitch.

"I admire your confidence," Gordon says, getting to his feet. "But it's misguided."

I stagger away, clutching my side, acting a bit more injured than I am. Doesn't take much acting. I'm pretty messed up, but the pain is still so broad that I can't identify specific injuries. As Gordon stalks toward me, I glance over my shoulder, but all I can see is Drakon, rampaging around the East Wing of the White House. I try not to react to it. It's where I sent Beck. If they haven't made it to the PEOC yet, they might be in real trouble.

"There won't be any help coming," he says, glancing up. I follow his eyes. Not a soldier in sight. "You're on your own, Hudson." He smiles. "Time to see what you're made of."

"You probably mean that literally, right?" I say, buying time.

He makes a show of licking his lips, almost seductively. "I'll keep you alive long enough to tell you how you taste."

A shadow shifts on the portico behind Gordon.

I stop my retreat. "Do you even know how nasty you are?"

Gordon sneers. Prepares to throw himself at me. But he never gets the chance. The shadow from the portico leaps through the air without a sound and lands hard on Gordon's shoulders. I see claws, razor sharp, slip into his flesh, locking on tightly. Gordon shouts in surprise and pain, falling forward under the weight of his attacker, who falls first, using Gordon's own momentum to lift him up and over. Powerful black legs extend and the claws release.

Gordon sails through the air, slamming into a tree, thirty feet away.

I wince-smile at my rescuer. "Just in time, Lilly."

"He's bigger than you described," the cat-like Lilly says, crouching low to the ground, her tail twitching. And she's right, Gordon is growing. Far slower than the Kaiju, but if he kept growing, he might become a Kaiju himself in twenty years. We're not going to give him that chance.

Convincing Mark Hawkins, aka Ranger, to allow Lilly to take part in this fight wasn't easy. In years, she's just six, but like an animal, she has aged more quickly and is now a young woman. Maybe mid-twenties in human years. But to Hawkins, she's still a kid, and he's spent the last year protecting her. To make matters worse, she's a mother. With five baby cat-people, who are currently under the care of Grandpappy Goodtracks and Joliet. But when I told him what I could do for them—how I could keep Lilly and her children safe, he relinquished.

"Too big?" I ask her.

"He's not nearly as scary as Kaiju."

I'm confused for a moment. Of course he's not more frightening than a 300-foot-tall monster. But then I remember Hawkins's story of how he found Lilly, at a place he calls 'Island 731.' Her mother, a monstrous chimera composed of both human and predatory animal parts, had been named *Kaiju*. If Gordon is a walk in the park compared to dear old mom, I think I might need to reclassify my own childhood issues as mild. That Lilly isn't the monster she appears to be is a strong reflection on her character, and Hawkins's influence.

Gordon screams in anger as he climbs to his feet. He lashes out at the tree that broke his fall, slamming his fist into the solid wood. The tree shakes as splinters fly.

"Strong," Lilly says, sounding impressed.

"Can you handle this?" I ask.

She nods. "He can't hurt what he can't catch."

Lilly springs into action, charging toward Gordon on all fours. I nearly cheer when I see the look of confusion on Gordon's face. He has no idea who he's up against, where she came from or what she can do. But he's about to find out. Lilly leaps onto Gordon's chest, her claws sinking in deep. He closes his arms to crush her, but the limbs close only on air. Lilly is gone again. Ten feet above him, clinging to the tree trunk, upside down.

Gordon glances down at his chest. Streams of brown blood leak from his charcoal skin. He screams and punches the tree again, this time shattering the trunk. As the tree falls, Lilly leaps easily away. She turns back, muscles tense, waiting for the chase to begin.

But Gordon isn't all monster. Not yet anyway. He's a soldier with a mission. Gordon turns toward me. The look in his eyes reveals he's done playing. The second he catches me, I'm dead. He takes two steps, but doesn't make it any further. Lilly rushes by behind him, clawing at the back of his legs. Gordon winces with pain and swings, but Lilly is already gone. He takes one last look at me and then focuses all his attention on Lilly, knowing that his mission won't move forward until the cat-woman defending me is dead.

As I hobble up the portico stairs, my phone rings. I glance at the screen—it's Endo—and answer the call. "Beck is in trouble," he says.

"What? How do you—"

"Dunne," he says. "Focus on Beck."

It takes just a moment to slip out of my mind and into Beck's. It's unnervingly easy. Suddenly, I'm seeing through his eyes and feeling his emotions, which are still brave and more concerned about doing the right thing than preserving his own life. He's dragging a bloodied Dunne down an East Wing hallway while Drakon hacks away at the building, trying to reach them.

When I come back to myself a moment later, ready to charge into the White House, I pause. The ground is shaking, and not just from the battle waging around me. It's a familiar jarring rattle.

I turn west just as the Eisenhower Executive Office Building explodes outward, kicked by a mammoth, black-skinned, tan-clawed foot. My eyes turn upward, taking in the gigantic form of Nemesis. And perhaps for the first time since Nemesis emerged in Maine, I cheer at her appearance. This was the part of my master plan that I took on faith, believing that Nemesis wouldn't be far and that she would respond to me being in danger.

She roars loudly. So loudly it hurts. The sounds of battle pause for a moment, as all eyes turn in her direction. Drakon's head pulls out of the East Wing and peers around the White House's ruined south side. There's a flash of surprise in her one good eye, but then it squints, and she sneers. Drakon lets out a warbling roar, stepping out onto the South Lawn. Then she charges, moving very quickly, commencing an oversized version of Lilly's fight against the much larger Gordon. A real David and Goliath battle. Except this time, Goliath isn't a dude, and I'm rooting for him...her.

Before Drakon reaches Nemesis, my phone rings. Woodstock. I answer it. "What?"

"They're moving really fast now." It's Collins. "Jon, they're going to reach you in five minutes. When do you want us to—"

"Not yet," I say, rushing up the stairs. "I'm not ready yet. And neither is Maigo."

A shriek pulls my attention west again. Drakon has leapt in the air, its double jaws open wide, heading for Nemesis's neck. I'm sure the attack is instinctive and typically a killer blow in the animal kingdom. But this is Nemesis. Her neck is lined with orange membranes, all primed and ready to blow.

My shoulders sag.

"Oh damn."

41

I stand transfixed by the sight of my impending doom. Drakon rises through the air, eager teeth seeming to stretch out, ready to puncture the membranes on the sides of Nemesis's neck and erase the drama unfolding at the White House. Strategically, it's a smart move. Only Gordon would survive. But since Gordon wants, or maybe needs, to kill me himself, it's contrary to his wishes. He's just a little too busy to realize that Drakon's gone off-plan.

But all of my concerns are for naught. Nemesis is far from defenseless. And Drakon is half her size.

Leaning back, away from Drakon's biting jaws, Nemesis reaches up and catches her attacker around the waist. The lizard Kaiju thrashes wildly, raking Nemesis's arm with her claws. When that doesn't work, Drakon thrashes out with her massive tail, striking Nemesis on the side. But the flat flesh of the creature's tail is better for swimming than injuring a beast like Nemesis, who takes hold of the tail and pulls. At first, I think she's trying to rend Drakon in two, but she lets go of the monster's waist and swings all 200 feet around, slamming it into the EEOB, destroying what remained. And she's not done there.

Nemesis continues thrashing Drakon, slamming the monster back and forth, pummeling the life out of the smaller Kaiju, while decimating the city. I cringe, fully remembering why I shouldn't cheer for Nemesis. If there was anyone in those buildings... And

I brought her here. Like with Alexander Tilly, I offered the nation's capital up as a sacrifice, and like the blood sacrifices of old, I hope it will somehow atone for mankind's darkness with the higher power known as Nemesis.

Buildings crumble, one after another, filling the air with plumes of debris and smoke, partly concealing Nemesis and Drakon. The duo roar in tandem. Nemesis sounds angry and wrathful. But Drakon just sounds pitiful, like a giant wailing beast. And then I get to see why.

Nemesis steps forward, clear of the smoke, lifting Drakon high into the air, her claws piercing the smaller Kaiju's sides. With a victorious roar, Nemesis slams Drakon down onto the angel-topped First Division Monument, a spear-like statue. I'm sure the memorial will be crushed, but to my surprise, it emerges from Drakon's back with a geyser of brown flesh and blood, creating the world's first Kaiju-kabob.

Drakon's body writhes and thrashes, but the monster can't move. Nemesis has it pinned. With a shudder, the Kaiju falls still. Dead. Nemesis has now killed two of Gordon's five. I hear him scream, his voice distant, but full of anger and anguish. He's either witnessed Drakon's demise or felt it. Possibly both. If he reacts to their deaths the way I might Collins's or Woodstock's, he's going to be more dangerous than ever.

Pushing my concern for Lilly aside, I turn my attention back to Nemesis, wondering what she'll do now that Drakon is dead. Will she go for Gordon? While that would be a good thing, generally speaking, Nemesis isn't exactly worried about her surroundings. She might level the White House in her effort to reach him, killing me, Endo and Lilly, not to mention all the soldiers, Secret Service agents and the newly brave President.

But that's not what happens. Nemesis stands up tall with a huff, looking east. She's spotted something and lets out an earth-shaking roar. A moment later, a second roar, like a warbling fog horn, replies. I recognize the call.

Scylla. The hammerhead Kaiju. It's in the city!

Nemesis charges across the South Lawn, crushing monuments, felling trees and destroying an unfortunate tank, killing the crew. The men and armaments on the far side of the lawn have wisely begun to retreat, but Nemesis doesn't slow, and not all of them make it out in time. Nemesis's giant feet crush the stragglers, and she begins wading through the Commerce Building like it was a field of grass.

Scylla roars again, clearing the shock from my mind and reminding me of what I need to do. I charge inside the White House, now empty except for distant shouts and a gray smoke that hangs in the hall like a fog. I run through the oval-shaped entryway and slide to a stop on a royal-looking, red rug in the hallway. I turn back and forth, trying to remember the building's layout.

Motion through the haze catches my attention. I move toward it, hoping to find a Secret Service agent. Instead, I find President Beck, dragging a bloodied and unconscious Agent Dunne. Beck stops when he sees me. Blood covers his face, and the neural implant is missing.

"What happened?" I ask.

"That thing nearly got us," he says. "There's no way to reach the bunker that way."

Despite the connection between us being broken, Beck seems oblivious to my presence here being strange, and he's still acting brave. Perhaps the effects will be permanent? I almost feel bad about altering the man's mind, but seeing him in action and saving Dunne's life? It's inspiring.

"Is there another way down?" I ask.

He nods. "A tunnel in the West Wing, beneath the situation room."

"The West Wing isn't in any danger now, sir. Take him that way, and stay down there until I come and get you. I'll take care of the Kaiju."

He pauses, staring at me. *Is his old self returning?*

"I've always admired your resolve, Hudson," he says. "I'm sorry for ever doubting your ability to respond to this crisis. I can't explain why, but I don't think I could have ever said that before today."

I'm dumbfounded, mostly because I didn't put the words in his mouth. "Thank you, sir. You should get going."

He nods and starts dragging Dunne away.

"And when you get there, make sure everyone knows to not attack Nemesis."

He pauses again, looking unsure. "Not attack? Why the hell not?"

"Not enough time to explain," I say. "You're just going to have to trust me."

He looks like he might disagree, but then says, "Good enough," and continues on his way through the gray smog.

"Oh!" I shout, before losing sight of the man. "Where are the stairs up?"

Beck motions to the right side of the hall with his head. "Second door on the right."

I give him a casual salute, say, "Thanks," and make for the stairs, taking them two at a time, despite the pain continuing to wrack my body.

By the third floor, I'm above the smoke, and I know where I'm going. I find the dark hallway easily, following the trail of injured soldiers and Secret Service agents being treated by their less injured comrades. One of agents sees where I'm headed and snatches my wrist. "You can't go out there. It's too dangerous."

"Anyone else out there?" I ask.

"Just one guy," he says. "He's dressed as an agent, but I don't recognize him." He squints at me. "Or you. Who the hell are you?"

I answer honestly. "DHS Fusion Center-P."

He lets go of my arm. "Thank God."

I'm a little bit stunned by this reaction. I'm not sure I ever realized how much hope people put in my small division of the government. But since we're the only ones who really specialize in Kaiju, he must believe I'm as adept at my job as he is at his. Speaking of which... "President Beck is headed to the PEOC via the West Wing tunnel. He's got Agent Dunne. Best if you all get down there. There's a good chance things will get...explosive."

"Understood," he says with a nod. "God speed, sir."

I offer him a half smile and enter the red-lit tunnel leading to the roof. My legs feel heavy as I ascend the stairs at the end. Doing my best to ignore the pain and the scent of blood, I push through the now deformed door at the end. The roof is quiet, abandoned by the White House's defenders. The missile launchers and chain guns are in shambles. The most defended building in the world is now defenseless.

Well, almost.

I'm still here. But am I alone?

"Endo!"

No reply. I hobble northeast, around the destroyed south side and toward the sound of wanton destruction being dished out on the city. "Endo!"

"Over here!" I see Endo standing by a large air conditioning unit, which blocks my view of the city. He hurries over, grinning strangely.

"I thought you were dead," he says.

"Pssh," I say with a wave of my hand. "Getting tackled off the roof was all part of my plan."

He tugs me along, not acting at all like himself. He's almost jovial. "You have to see this."

He gets me jogging, which hurts, but starts to feel good as my stiffening limbs loosen. As we round the air conditioning unit, and reach the back wall, Endo thrusts his hands out at the view. The sight saps my energy. My legs go wobbly. And all I can think is, *I did this*.

Endo looks at me, a twinkle in his eyes. "Isn't it amazing?"

42

Mark Hawkins had seen some crazy things in his life. He'd fought and killed a grizzly bear with nothing but a knife. As a park ranger at Yellowstone National Park, he had worked on a number of search-and-rescue missions that ended with a corpse, which as an expert tracker, he was always the first to find. And just two years ago, he'd been shipwrecked on an island in the Pacific full of horrible, scientifically created chimeras. The monsters, which included a crocodile with tentacles, were perfectly good at one thing—killing people. The worst of them was Lilly's mother, *Kaiju*, a name he never thought he'd hear again, but which he had now heard in countless news reports since Nemesis emerged in Boston. After escaping the island and going underground with Lilly, Hawkins had believed the strangest, most dangerous days of his life were behind him.

He was wrong.

He was so wrong.

Sprinting down Pennsylvania Avenue, Hawkins ran against the flow of fleeing humanity, moving among the brave soldiers and tanks headed toward the sounds of battle, which for the most part were shrieking, roaring monsters.

"Look out!" Someone yelled.

Hawkins looked up as the corner of the Commerce Building disintegrated and debris exploded out in all directions. He dove to the sidewalk, taking cover as concrete sprayed past. A soldier with slower reflexes fell beside him, a slab of sharp marble embedded in his face.

Hawkins stared at the grim sight. He wanted to scream. He wanted to run away. But he'd seen worse than this soldier's deformed face. He'd seen friends turned into monsters, into incubators. And he'd survived that mess by acting, not lying down.

Nemesis roared as Hawkins stood, drawing his attention. The monstrous Kaiju was heading in the direction he'd come from, which was a good thing, but he wasn't there to deal with the full-sized monster; he was there for someone else. A man named Gordon. A traitor to his country, perhaps not all that dissimilar from the clandestine group at DARPA who had kept Island 731 operational since World War II.

Hawkins turned right onto Executive Avenue at a sprint, dodging past a burning tank and a group of soldiers tending to the wounded. He wanted to stop and help, but he wasn't responsible for those men. It was Lilly he was concerned about. Hudson had offered to create a preserve—fenced-in private land, where Lilly and her daughters could live in peace. But it came at a high price. He needed Lilly's muscles. He needed Lilly the monster, not Lilly the girl.

While Lilly, who had been separate from the world but desperate to experience it, was on board from the get go, Hawkins had had serious reservations. It wasn't until Hudson offered to look into the DARPA mess and find out who was responsible, that Hawkins had come around. If Lilly and her...litter, could be safe—truly safe for the rest of their lives—the risk could be worthwhile.

But Hawkins had never pictured anything like this. It was a warzone.

He slid to a stop in the mud of what once was the White House's front lawn. In the distance, past a stand of flattened trees, he could see the Kaiju known as Drakon, impaled atop a monument. Brown blood pooled around the scene.

This was *worse* than a warzone.

An aggravated shout turned his attention north, toward the White House. He didn't recognize the baritone voice, but he recognized the tone of it. That was Lilly's doing. She was kind and gentle, but she was a young woman and could be infuriating when she wanted to be.

Sticking to the trees, and feeling more at home, Hawkins moved through the shadows, well concealed thanks to the body armor Hudson had given him. He held his weapon of choice, a compound bow, at the ready. The bow shot arrows at 400-feet per second. It was quieter than a BB gun and highly accurate, thanks to its fiber optic sight. The weapon was powerful enough to take down nearly any living thing on land, short of an elephant, and the prey—or in this case, the enemy—wouldn't be tipped off to his location because of sound. Even better, Hudson's colleague, Endo, had supplied some specially modified arrow heads. If they performed as promised, he thought they would make a real difference.

His back-up weapon, supplied by Hudson, was slung over his back. The Benelli M4 semi-automatic shotgun could fire eight 12-gauge shells as fast as Hawkins could pull the trigger, each of which could remove a man's limb. He wasn't hunting a man, though. Hudson seemed to think the shotgun would only slow Gordon down. A weapon of last resort. "Aim for his face," had been Hudson's advice.

Watching Nemesis charge off through the city like it wasn't there, Hawkins would have preferred something closer to a giant-sized sci-fi laser cannon.

A second frustrated shout drew his attention north again. He crouched by the trunk of a tall maple tree and scanned the area. He spotted Lilly on the other side of the lawn, scrambling up a tree. A massive black hand reached around from the other side and dug its fingers into the bark, just missing Lilly.

If he caught her...

Hawkins nocked one of Endo's arrows, which he promised would pierce Gordon's thick skin. He looked down the sight, waiting for the right moment, trying to ignore the sounds of destruction and human suffering behind him. What mattered to him most was straight ahead, and in danger.

He drew the bowstring back, holding all that kinetic energy at bay. He breathed slowly. A practiced hunter. Ready to act, he pursed his lips and whistled a gentle bird call. He could barely hear the sound, but Lilly had exceptional ears, and she'd know what to do. When hunting as a team, she would rush out, forcing their prey to flee toward him. He would take care of the rest, not wanting Lilly to kill with her bare hands. While she was part cat and always would be, he wanted to make sure the feral instincts that kept her alive on Island 731 faded, so encounters like her first meeting with Hudson didn't happen again.

Lilly emerged from the trees, sailing through the air, fifteen feet up. He'd seen her jump from higher heights in the past, but it always made him flinch. He sucked in a quick breath, but she was soon on the ground and running toward him. An eight-foot-tall, thick-limbed goliath that looked vaguely human, thundered out behind her, backhanding the tree she'd been on.

"Up," Hawkins said, just loud enough for Lilly to hear. She sprang into the air, landing thirty feet above Hawkins in the tree, keeping Gordon's eyes fixed upwards.

Crouched down low, leaning against the tree trunk, Hawkins adjusted his aim. Hudson had warned against hitting the orange membrane on Gordon's chest. Hawkins had seen footage of what happened in Boston. He understood the danger and aimed high, for the head.

The arrow released silently, the gentle twang of the bowstring snapping forward drowned out by the chaos around them. The black arrow slipped through the night, invisible. Accurate. The projectile struck Gordon's thick forehead. Hawkins worried the arrow would snap or bounce off, but it didn't. As advertised, it slipped through the giant man's skin.

Then through his skull and the brain trapped beneath.

Gordon staggered to a stop, looking confused. He knew something fundamentally wrong had occurred to his body, but he didn't know what. Then he went cross-eyed and saw the arrow.

This is it, Hawkins thought, slipping back behind the tree. He carefully put the bow down and reached into his pocket. When he found what he was looking for, he peeked back at Gordon and felt his hope shrivel away like a Shrinky Dink in the oven.

Gordon yanked the arrow from his head, looked at it curiously and dropped it. He still looked a little stunned, but he was also scanning the trees. Hawkins slipped behind cover, waited a beat and peeked around the tree again.

Gordon was gone.

"Hello there," said the baritone voice, close enough to feel in his chest.

Hawkins whirled around to find the mammoth Gordon standing above him with a wicked sharp-toothed grin. Hawkins grabbed the bow and tried to scramble back, but he tripped over the tree's roots.

Gordon reached out.

Lilly descended with a shriek.

She landed on Gordon's arm and clung to it, her claws digging in deeply. Before the giant man-thing could react, she swiped her razor-sharp talons across his face twice and leapt away. Gordon roared and swung at her, but she was already up the tree, shouting for Hawkins to run.

But he didn't.

Instead, Hawkins got to his feet, unslung his shotgun and leveled it at Gordon's face. The Kaiju-man lowered his gaze back to Hawkins and sneered. "I'm going to eat you."

Hawkins knew that Hudson might say something like 'Eat this,' but he lacked the man's sense of humor. He just pulled the trigger, sending a cloud of 12 gauge into Gordon's face, filling the gaps between the criss-crossing lines left by Lilly's claws.

He then pulled the trigger seven more times, staggering Gordon back. Despite having eight shells of shot embedded in his face, the traitorous general remained on his feet.

When the shotgun's last report faded, Gordon took his hands away from his face and said, "I'm going to eat you *slowly*."

"Shit," Hawkins said, picking up the bow and preparing to run.

When Gordon took one mighty step forward, halving the distance between them, Hawkins knew he couldn't escape. After surviving the unthinkable, he'd finally met the monster that would kill him.

43

All of the chaos around me—the sirens, gunfire, klaxons, screaming and crumbling buildings—cease to exist in a moment of sickening clarity. I'm a dead man. Not because of any immediate physical threat, but because if the events of today are seen as anything other than a stellar victory, the blame for all this is going to chase me down like a laser-guided missile. I feel faint as the blood drains from my face.

Watching the U.S. Capitol Building be hacked apart by two Kaiju can have that effect. At least, it can when you're the guy who led them here.

Nemesis arrived at the north side of the Capitol just as Scylla reached the south. There was a brief roar-off, with both monsters hollering at each other like two angry inebriants on either side of a car. While the drunks might then run around the car to slap each other silly, the two Kaiju are going through the building. Nemesis makes short work of the Senate Chamber while Scylla flattens the House.

Unlike me, Endo seems to be taking great pleasure in the destruction, laughing lightly, an open mouthed smile frozen on his face. When the Kaiju reach the rotunda and lay into it with their giant claws, the dome exploding like a crushed egg, Endo turns to me. "It's like Godzilla versus King Kong."

A vague memory of a childhood movie returns. Godzilla on one side of a tall Japanese building. King Kong on the other. The monsters smashing through the building to get at each other. Endo is right. It's like the monsters are doing an homage.

Endo holds a small pair of binoculars out to me. "So you can see."

I'm not sure I want to see this any closer than I can right now, but I take the lenses and put them to my eyes just in time to witness the end of an iconic American building of untold historical and financial value.

With a swipe of Nemesis's mighty arm, the Capitol Building ceases to exist. In her fervor to reach Scylla, Nemesis has left herself open to attack. While Nemesis is overextended, the hammerhead monster lunges forward. Its lower jaw drops open, revealing those horrible teeth—the longest and sharpest on any of the Kaiju. The massive jaws wrap around Nemesis's forearm, and compress.

There is resistance for a moment, but the blade-like teeth slowly slip through the thick flesh. Nemesis doesn't react at first, and I think the Kaiju must not have pain sensors in their armor or skin. But once the teeth are a few feet in, Nemesis throws her head back and roars in pain.

She flinches back, lifting her arm and dragging Scylla through the Capitol Building's remains. Scylla holds on, latched in place, while Nemesis shakes her arm back and forth, reacting to the pain without thought.

The teeth sink deeper. Nemesis's roar becomes high-pitched. Something stirs within me. All of my fear and trepidation is forgotten. I stand and shake my fist at Nemesis. "Fight back!"

Endo glances at me. He doesn't say anything, but I can see he's pleased by my outburst.

I grip the side wall around the top of the White House roof as Scylla begins shaking its head, thrashing back and forth. Red blood flows from Nemesis's arm, dripping on the Capitol ruins.

Slowly, Nemesis lifts her arm, higher and higher until Scylla is lifted off the ground. The display of strength is impressive to say the least, but Scylla hardly notices. It just clings to the arm like a dog to a dangling rope, wiggling back and forth. I think it might even be growling. When Nemesis levels a brown-eyed stare at Scylla, the Kaiju finally stops moving.

There's a shift that takes place, and it has nothing to do with physical violence—yet. Scylla's body language changes slightly, like it knows it's severely fucked, but can't back out.

A distant roar, deep and powerful, announces the approach of Karkinos. Typhon isn't far behind. I can see them just over the horizon, rising up over the city, just a few miles off, but approaching quickly. There isn't a lot of time before this becomes a three-on-one fight, and while Scylla is still fifty feet shorter than Nemesis, the other two look to be her match.

A sneer forms on the sides of Nemesis's mouth, revealing sharp teeth. She's moving past the pain and into the mindset in which she feels most at home: rage.

Nemesis unleashes a roar the likes of which I've never heard out of her, drool spraying from her mouth. She lifts Scylla higher and then yanks her arm down. Scylla's body swings out and then drops. As the Kaiju's giant body swings back toward Nemesis, she kicks out with one of her massive feet. Scylla's body folds around the foot as it drives into the monster's gut and forces the air from its lungs in a gargling scream. The impact forces Scylla's jaws open. The teeth slip free with geysers of blood. And then Scylla is airborne, punted over the ruins of the Capitol.

The hammer-headed Kaiju lands across buildings, which absorb its fall like a memory foam cushion, except that when the giant stands and shakes off the attack, the buildings remain squashed.

Ignoring the approaching Kaiju, Nemesis leans forward and roars again, but she doesn't move. She's instigating her adversary. Scylla takes the bait, thundering toward Nemesis, mouth agape.

When Scylla reaches the point of no return, Nemesis spins around, dragging her tail through a line of cars that are sent spiraling through the air. When her back is to Scylla, she pulls the tail around behind her, whipping it up and out, catching Scylla beneath its outstretched arms. One of the nasty spikes on the end of Nemesis's tail stabs into the monster's side, and the force of the blow knocks Scylla up and over, flipping the Kaiju head-over-heels. It seems impossible, that something so large could spin through the air like that, but there it is; a big-ass Kaiju, cartwheeling like Mary Lou Retton.

Scylla slams through the Ulysses S. Grant Memorial, crushing both horse and rider, before landing in the Capitol Reflecting Pool with a mighty splash. The impact rolls beneath the White House like an earthquake. Scylla thrashes in the water, draining the large pool. Its groans are pitiful. The monster attempts to roll and sit up, but fails. Then it falls back with a grunt, brown blood flowing from its side. Scylla is down, but not out. Its eyes remain open, its chest heaving with each breath. Mostly it looks confused.

It's never felt pain before, I think.

And now that it has, it's stunned. Bewildered. But definitely not mortally wounded. Not if it's related to Nemesis. It won't be long before Scylla's back on its feet. And with the arrival of Karkinos and Typhon, that would be a bad thing.

Nemesis is going to need some help.

I lower the binoculars and take out my phone, dialing Woodstock.

"We're here." It's Alessi.

"Why didn't Woodstock answer?" I ask.

"He's flying," comes the curt answer.

"Why didn't Collins—"

"She was shot," Alessi says.

In the fraction of a second before she speaks again, I find myself feeling lightheaded. Panic races through my body, erasing the effects of the adrenaline that's been coursing through my veins for the past twenty minutes. I feel my legs grow weak. I feel short of breath. My chest hurts.

"Her armor stopped the bullet," Alessi says, "but she's pretty sore."

"I'm fine," Collins says in the background, her voice barely audible over the chopper's thrumming rotor blades.

"Where are you?" I ask.

"A mile out from the two bigger Kaiju," Alessi says. "To the east. We're within range."

I glance through the binoculars, looking past the twin titans that are Karkinos and Typhon. Even if I could see past their towering bodies, the smoke, fires and flashing lights of a city gripped by horror make it impossible for me to spot Betty's running lights in the night sky. "How many shots do we get at this?"

"Two," she says. "Which one should we target?"

I look at the two approaching Kaiju. Karkinos is a beefier version of Nemesis. It's a little shorter, but far thicker and more muscular, easily out-weighing Nemesis. It's also covered in boney spikes, and sports a carapace running down its back, no doubt hiding a pair of reflective wings. I used to think that Nemesis perfectly represented what I thought a monster-god of vengeance would look like, but Karkinos reveals that Nemesis is a more delicate version of what she could have been, probably thanks to Maigo's DNA.

Typhon is eerily human-like. Very masculine as well. Of all the new Kaiju, he's the only one I really feel comfortable assigning a sex to. This monster is a dude, hands down, even if he does lack any kind of discernable Kaiju junk. He carries himself with a confidence that is obnoxious. Like he's actually a god and we're all ants, barely worth his attention. While the other Kaiju are ruled by emotion, Typhon seems almost cold and calculating. But he's also far less defended. While he's got spikes and claws in strategic areas of his body—elbows, knees and forearms, most of him is covered in thick, ropey flesh. The perfect target.

"Typhon," I say. "Target Typhon."

"Are you sure?" Endo asks. He's only heard one side of the conversation, but he knows the plan. "Typhon looks..."

"Smart," I say. "Yeah, I know. But there's no way the neural implant is going to get past Karkinos's armor."

He thinks on it briefly and then nods, turning back to the impending rumble. I glance up, too, watching as Nemesis turns to fight the two newcomers. For a moment, I think she's made a mistake, turning her back on Scylla, but she raises that killer tail in the air and slams it down on Scylla's belly. It doesn't pierce the skin, but Scylla lurches up, howling in pain.

"Are you ready to go?" I ask into the phone.

"I already adjusted the frequency to match your headset and we're locked on," Alessi says.

I put my hand on top of my head, feeling the modified beanie cap. It's tight and in place, ready to connect my mind to another. If my bucket list included an entry for *Most Idiotic Thing Anyone Has Ever Done in the History of the World and Probably the Universe*, I could check it off after this. Connecting to Nemesis was one thing. She didn't resist. But one of these Kaiju? They're the very definition of hostile. My mental presence isn't going to be welcome. I could end up in a coma, like Endo, or I could end up lobotomized. "Go ahead. I'm ready."

44

I'm able to pinpoint Betty's position when they launch the neural implant. I can't hear the rocket propelling the device through the night sky, but I can see the plume of fire at its rear. As I watch the projectile's progress, I'm struck by a realization. Whatever defense force that was assaulting these Kaiju, has stopped or pulled back.

"Endo," I shout. "Find out where the military is!"

He looks at me, confused for a moment. I probably shouldn't be focused on such things right before a Kaiju mind-meld. But then I can see he understands the significance. If the military is heading for the hills, maybe I made Beck a little too brave, and he's willing to drop that nuke on his own head.

And ours.

And Collins's.

Endo gets on his phone while I continue watching the implant's progress. It slides through the air, a twinkling light.

Too bright, I think.

While Karkinos starts an emotion-fueled roaring match with Nemesis, the two long-tailed Kaiju squaring off, Typhon stands still, watching. His head is titled slightly, his eyes unwavering. I'm not sure Typhon feels much at all, beyond loathing. As the implant closes the distance toward the side of his head, he glances at it.

I breathe deeply, preparing myself for the connection. I'm not sure what to expect, aside from the agonizing pain Endo described.

Typhon slowly turns toward the implant, and the rocket adjusts its trajectory, remaining on course. But then the Kaiju proves his intelligence by raising one of his mighty hands and swatting the implant from the sky like it were simply an annoying bug. I don't think he knew exactly what it was—there's no way he's that smart—but he recognizes it as a threat. He's seen enough missiles to know they're not friendly.

Although part of me is relieved that I'm not currently engaged in a mental scuffle with Typhon, this is a horrible development. Karkinos is naturally defended from the implant and it seems that Typhon won't let anything strike his face. Even if the Air Force were bombarding the pair with missiles and the implant snuck through, it's likely it would be destroyed by an errant explosion.

That's when I realize we have an easier target. I turn my attention back to Scylla. The Kaiju looks like he's lounging in the little water that remains in the Reflecting Pool. His upper lip crinkles over and over, revealing his long teeth. He's still stunned, but for how long?

I'm about to dial Woodstock when my phone chirps. I accept the call without looking at the screen. "Scylla."

"What?" a female voice says.

The voice is familiar, but it's not Collins or Alessi. "Who is this?"

"Betty," says the woman.

I feel like I've been slapped. *"Girlfriend Betty?"*

"What other kind of Betty is there?"

"How did you get this number?" I ask.

"Some guy named Watson," she says. "But listen. With everything that's happened, I've seen you on TV. I started thinking. Maybe I was—"

I say the only thing I can think of, "Click," and then hang up, making a mental note to have a chat with Watson about security.

My phone rings again and I answer. "Betty, you better—"

"You can address me," Alessi says. "Not the helicopter."

Helicopter Betty. Thank God. "Target Scylla," I say.

"I hear you," she says. "I'm just not sure where to target her."

"Endo," I say, pulling him away from his conversation with whoever it is he called. "We're going to try the implant on Scylla. Where should we—"

"Back of the head," he says. "Behind the eye. Either side will do." Then he's back to his conversation.

I relay the information, and Alessi hands me over to Collins while she preps the second—and final—attempt.

"Hey," Collins says, almost casually. "I just wanted to let you know that if you become a vegetable after this, I'm not going to sit around feeding you pudding."

I can't help but smile. "But I love hospital pudding."

"It would make you fat, lying there all immobile," she says.

"This is true. What if I give you permission in advance to take advantage of my vegetative body? Have your way with me?"

She laughs, which further dispels some of my tension. "You sure know what to say to a woman."

"What?" I say. "Who wouldn't want to fool around with a pasty white, atrophying, unconscious man?"

I'm laughing now too, and I'm starting to second-guess this plan. We could just walk away now. Let nature take its course. Sure, we might spend the rest of our lives in hiding from Gordon and his Kaiju, but we'd be alive and together.

Unfortunately for me, I'm drawn toward doing the right thing like Nemesis is to vengeance. I can't walk away. No matter what the cost. Someone has to put an end to this madness, and I'm pretty much the only one who can.

"We're almost in position," Collins says, her voice sobering up.

I scan the night sky and find the running lights blinking red and white, much closer than before. They're a half mile from Scylla, holding steady at a hundred feet.

Before I can order them to fire, I hear a rough, organic scraping sound and turn back to Nemesis. Karkinos and Typhon have held their position, a safe distance from Nemesis. Perhaps sizing her up, looking for weaknesses. But Nemesis, who has more experience in the destruction category, not to mention the Kaiju-slaying category, isn't about to give them time.

Her chest heaves. Her mouth opens.

She's about to hock another explosive loogie. I've come up with a few different names for the attack. Meteoric Boom Wad was in the lead for a while. But when I thought about the act of spitting at someone and what it means, I came up with Scorching Contempt, an attack reserved for when she's just had enough of her attacker's shit. "Hold your fire," I shout into the phone. "Get down. Down! Down! Down!"

I have no idea if Collins heard me or if Woodstock took action. There isn't time. I take hold of Endo's arm, yanking him along. He's running behind me a moment later, sprinting across the White House roof. There's a wet pop behind us. I can't see it, but I know Nemesis has just fired off a bright orange wad. We have just seconds.

The door is open when we arrive, soldiers venturing outside again. "Back!" I wave my arms at them like a wounded bird. "Back inside!"

Happily, the men listen, ducking back while one of them holds the door open for Endo and me. We partly run, partly fall down the stairs. The soldier slams the door closed behind us. He looks down and shouts something at us, but his voice is drowned out by a thunderous boom that rattles the entire building. The shaking lasts for just five seconds, but the power goes out, plunging the already dark, red-lit hallway into absolute darkness.

For a moment, the men in the hallway are silent, perhaps all as surprised as I am to still be alive. I find the stairs in the dark and climb to the top, placing my hand against its steel surface. It's warm, but not hot. The explosion didn't reach the White House.

I yank the door open and stumble into the night. The air reeks of smoke, and not the campfire variety. This is the acrid smoke of civilization burning. Concrete, plastic, chemicals and people. It can't be healthy to breathe, but I hardly notice it as I run back to my rooftop perch. Putting the binoculars to my eyes, I look for Betty. The helicopter is nowhere in sight.

But are they dead?

I take my phone out, but notice my surroundings for the first time. Glowing orange timbers float through the air like a million fireflies. A massive circle, a mile around Nemesis in all directions, has been scorched. The White House is just a half mile beyond the destruction. Nemesis stands at the center of the destruction, unfazed. Her opponents appear equally uninjured by the explosion. They're the only things still standing.

Endo steps up to me, looking concerned. "The helicopter?"

Like me, he's selfishly more worried about the chopper than the fact that a large portion of Washington, D.C. just got erased. I shake my head and ask, "Who is she? Alessi?"

She's not a girlfriend or lover. I've never gotten that vibe. But they care for each other deeply.

"Half-sister," he says.

Geez. I dial the number. It rings through to voicemail, and I try again with the same results. I'm about to suggest we go find them when twin roars make me cringe. Karkinos is charging, head down, spikes up. Typhon is moving too, arcing around to flank Nemesis. The real fight is about to begin.

45

Ashley Collins awoke to the smell of smoke. She coughed twice, each flex of her lungs bringing a fresh stab of pain to her skull. She groaned and put her hand to the side of her head, the source of the pain. Her hair was tacky wet. Blood.

She blinked her eyes. With clearer vision, she looked around Betty's interior. *What...?* Unable to make sense of the sideways world, Collins closed her eyes again and took several long breaths, focusing her thoughts.

They had received a warning from Jon. She remembered a sudden, lurching dive behind a building. Then the helicopter tilted and they dropped.

We crashed, she realized, opening her eyes again.

The helicopter lay on its side. Collins was still strapped in place in the back seat. A spider-web fracture in the window beside her, now looking down at the pavement, revealed where she'd hit her head. Woodstock and Alessi were both missing. The view through the shattered cockpit window was fractured, but she could see a city street, lined with cars. Further ahead, at an intersection, black smoke rolled down the side street, lit by thousands of glowing, fairy-like embers.

One of the Kaiju immolated, Collins thought. *We're lucky to be alive.*

Bracing her left arm against the window, she unbuckled from the seat. Gravity yanked her down, slamming her against the window. Her body ached all over, and she felt a nearly overwhelming desire to sleep, but she fought against it, remembering what was at stake. *Who* was at stake.

Jon is depending on us.

She slid into the front seat and noticed two things at once: the chopper still had power and the passenger door was open. Careful not to break anything on the control panel, Collins climbed up and out of the open door. Outside the chopper, she could hear the distant roaring of angry Kaiju, unaffected by the blast, but the sounds of the city and the military had faded. Now other sounds filled the void.

"Sonuvabitch!"

Woodstock.

Collins slid herself over the chopper's side, moving toward the voice, and leaned over the edge. Woodstock and Alessi were both below her, working on the chopper, but they didn't look good. Woodstock had a visibly broken leg. Alessi yanked on a wrench with one arm while the other hung useless. Despite their injuries, they were trying to free the neural implant launcher mounted to the chopper's underside.

"I can't get it with one arm," Alessi complained.

"Well, I can't very well stand, now can I?" Woodstock said, "So you're going to have to—"

"I think I can get it," Collins said.

Alessi looked up, saw Collins and all but collapsed. "Thank God."

Collins slid over the side and dropped to the macadam. She landed gracefully, despite the protests of her body and her head. She was in serious pain, but compared to Woodstock and Alessi, she was healthy.

Alessi held up the wrench. "There's just one bolt left."

"You should have woken me up," Collins said, taking the wrench.

"Tried," Woodstock says. "Your arms and legs might be working fine, but you need to take it easy. A concussion is nothing to screw around with."

Collins went to work on the bolt with one arm while cradling the launcher in the other. "You're just saying that so you can tell Jon you said it."

Woodstock slid himself back against the tire of an abandoned car, wincing with the movement as his legs straightened. "Pretty much."

"This thing will still launch?" Collins asked.

"I can trigger it remotely," Alessi said. "But someone still needs to point it in the right direction."

Collins felt the bolt about to fall away. "How much does it weigh?"

Alessi shrugged. "Hundred pounds."

Collins tightened her hold on the launcher just as the bolt fell away. She dropped the wrench and got both hands beneath the cylinder. Felt like more than a hundred pounds, but she'd lifted—and carried—more than that in the past. Not with a concussion, but there was no time for whining.

"You sure you got that?" Woodstock asked.

Collins grunted, hefting the cylinder up and propping it against her shoulder. "My grandfather used to say 'It's not the size of the dog in the fight, it's the size of the fight in the dog.'"

"Spoken like a true woman of Maine," Woodstock said with a smile. "You're meltin' my heart."

"Your grandfather was quoting Mark Twain," Alessi said, leaning against the chopper's belly.

"Yeah, well, my grandfather was well read." Collins looked up at the building behind which they'd taken shelter and crashed. It looked mostly intact. "You're sure this will work?"

Alessi took a phone from her pocket and spoke the number twice. "Call me when you're in position. I'll take care of the rest."

Collins had her personal phone in her pocket. She gave a nod and headed for the building's open front doors, hoping the blast hadn't destroyed local cell towers. Broken glass crunched beneath her feet as she moved into the building's lobby. The reception desk looked more like a bunker. A metal detector led to the far side of the entryway where she could see a sign for the stairs. She didn't know what the building was used for, but she assumed it contained overflow offices for House and Senate personnel.

The interior of the building was lit by emergency lights, glowing against a few of the walls. She could see, but just barely. She moved by sliding her feet forward, afraid of tripping over some unseen obstacle. But the path was clear, and she soon reached a row of elevator doors followed by the doorway to the stairs.

A wave of dizziness swept through her body. Stars danced in her vision. She carefully set the metal cylinder down and took several deep breaths, focusing on remaining upright. If she went over, she didn't think she'd get back up for a while.

I'm never going to make it up the stairs, she thought, recalling the building's fifteen-story height.

She glanced at the elevator. Would they still be running? It was possible that emergency power in the government building would operate the elevators, at least for a short time, so VIPs didn't get stuck. Dragging the cylinder across the marble floor, she pushed the call button. The elevator dinged and the doors slid open.

Collins didn't think about religion much, but she had no doubt some higher power had just intervened on her behalf. "Thank you, baby Jesus." She stepped inside and hit the button for the highest floor. The doors slid shut. The elevator shuddered and rose. It felt like slow going for an elevator, and the overhead light flickered a few times, but it rose up steadily.

The doors jittered open, as though struggling to complete a final task. The hallway beyond was lit by dim emergency lights. Feeling a little more rested after leaning against the elevator wall, Collins put the cylinder against her shoulder again and moved into the hall. She quickly found the stair entry to her left and hobbled to the door. Inside the stairwell, she looked up. Two flights to go.

She took several, rapid, deep breaths, saturating her lungs with oxygen. The effort cleared the cobwebs some, but did nothing for the pain. She took the stairs quickly, taking deep breaths the whole way. By the time she reached the second landing, she was sweating and out of breath, but the effort got her blood flowing and fought against her desire to simply pass out.

A green metal door blocked her path to the roof. She tried the handle and found it locked, as expected. With a sigh, she placed the launcher down on the concrete landing and drew her .50 caliber handgun, happy that she'd reloaded the weapon after escaping the secret Zoomb laboratory.

This is going to hurt, she thought, wishing she could cover her ears. With just a moment's hesitation, she pulled the trigger once. The cacophonous report made her shout, and clutch her free hand to her ear, but the powerful round did its job, destroying the door's lock.

She took the now-loose handle, shook it about and pulled. The door ground open, unleashing a warm smoky haze. Collins coughed and felt her nausea return, but she pushed past it, picking up the launcher and heading into the battle-lit night.

She staggered onto the roof, heading toward the sound of battle. When she reached the charred edge, she looked out into hell. A massive swath of the city had been reduced to charcoal. Fires burned around the perimeter. Judging by the amount of smoke rising from below, she believed her building was burning, too.

Crouching near the building's edge, she placed the launcher on the stone-covered roof and dialed Alessi on her phone. "You're already there?" Alessi asked, sounding surprised.

"Elevator worked," Collins said. "Please tell me you're ready."

"Just point the launcher toward Scylla. I'll use the guidance system to target her and fire the rocket, but...it's going to get hot for you."

"I understand how rockets work," Collins said. "Let's just get this done."

She put the phone on speaker mode and dropped it in her pocket. Then she hoisted the launcher onto her shoulder and stepped closer to the edge. Nemesis stood a mile away, facing Collins. Karkinos and stoic Typhon stood in front of Collins, their backs to her, oblivious to her tiny presense. They appeared to be sizing each other up, slowly moving in broad destructive circles like wrestlers in a ring.

She found Scylla still lying in the reflecting pool, but starting to stir. They didn't have long. She pointed the launcher toward Scylla and shouted, "Good to go!"

"Hold on," came Alessi's muffled voice. "Once this thing launches, you can move, okay?"

"Just fire it!" Collins shouted. Her head was spinning, her arms shaking.

"Target locked," Alessi said. "Firing in three, two, one—"

The rocket inside the canister ignited, blowing the back off. She could feel the heat singe her shoulder, but she held the launcher in place. Then the rocket was free, kicking back a wave of heat. Collins shouted in pain, dropped the launcher and fell to the roof, where she remained, unmoving, as the rocket-propelled neural implant cut a path over the ruins of downtown Washington, D.C.

46

Mark Hawkins shouted with surprise as his feet left the ground. He was lifted up by an arm far stronger than the average human's. But this surprise was a happy one, because the fist wrapped around the back of his armor belonged to Lilly, not Gordon.

Seeing his prey escaping, Gordon lunged, but he was too late. Lilly's express elevator carried Hawkins thirty feet up, and then across, slipping through entwined branches, moving from tree to tree, faster than Gordon could run on the ground.

When Lilly finally stopped moving, she deposited him on a high branch and asked, "Okay?"

"Fine," he replied. "Thanks."

She gave a feline smile and disappeared in a blur of black fur.

After collecting himself, Hawkins nocked an arrow and searched for Gordon, feeling like Robin Hood as he looked over his bow's fiber-optic sight, standing on a branch thirty feet above the ground. He was concealed by the leaf-laden branches, but the foliage also hindered his view. He mumbled curses while he moved further out on the branch, which bent from his weight.

The view ahead cleared and he locked his legs around the branch to stay upright and took aim again. With the drawstring pulled taut, he whistled a bird call.

He could hear Gordon chasing Lilly below, and the giant monsters in the distance, but amid all that, the sound of a bird call reply came loud and clear. Lilly was on her way. She passed by below. A blur in the night. Superhuman.

Gordon moved quickly too, but despite his dark coloration, he stood out. It took just a half second for Hawkins to adjust his aim and let go of the bowstring. The arrow whistled through the air, heading downward, puncturing leaves and then finding its target. The projectile slipped through the thick flesh of Gordon's right shoulder, burying itself six inches deep.

With a roar of frustration, Gordon stopped. He looked at the arrow, snarled and snapped it off with a flick of his hand, leaving six inches inside his body. Then he looked up, straight through the leaves, following the arrow's trajectory in reverse, straight to Hawkins.

"You're going to need more than a children's toy," Gordon said.

The giant man took one step toward the tree while Hawkins nocked another arrow, but then he stopped and turned toward the east. Hawkins, never one to waste an easy shot, let the arrow fly. It struck Gordon behind his neck, but the man didn't even flinch. Instead, he crouched down on the ground and rolled his body into a ball.

What the...?

Hawkins looked east in time to see a bright orange glob gliding through the air. The giant known as Karkinos roared and swung one of its massive, dual clawed hands at the thing. Then, there was light as bright as the universe's creation.

Hawkins shouted in surprise, shielding his eyes, but he lost his grip on the tree in the process. He began to fall, but he clenched his legs tighter and stopped himself at an angle. He remained there, stuck at a sixty degree angle for all of a half second. Then the sound hit. And the pressure wave. And the heat.

Hawkins was torn from the branch and flung. His mind whirled as the explosion set his ears ringing. He spun through the air, growing dizzy as he fell toward his doom. But as his arc through the air turned downward, he felt cradled, held tightly.

Opening his eyes, he saw Lilly staring down at him. Her yellow eyes were alive and determined. "I have you."

When they reached the ground, Lilly absorbed the impact with her legs as though they'd fallen just a few feet. She then put Hawkins on his feet.

He worried about her safety so much, but here she was, saving him. Lilly, in just a few short years, had grown up. She was a mother. A skilled hunter. A warrior. And now his rescuer, returning the favor he'd granted her by taking her off that island.

Before he had a chance to thank Lilly, he looked over her shoulder. The far side of the South Lawn was on fire, but that only mildly concerned him. A mushroom cloud billowed into the air in the distance. For a moment, he worried about radiation, but then he remembered the glowing orange glob he'd seen. He, like everyone else in the world, knew what happened when those orange membranes on Nemesis's body ruptured. And Nemesis's new trick had been to launch smaller globs of the stuff from her mouth.

If she wasn't careful, Nemesis was going to kill the very people trying to help her. Or was it the other way around? Hudson's plan had been vague on that area. In the end, Hawkins took it as an 'enemy of my enemy' situation. But how could a creature like Nemesis understand who was on her side and who wasn't? He doubted the giant would even notice their presence, let alone act to keep them alive.

"Is this how people will see me?" Lilly asked, looking at the fresh destruction. "Am I a monster? A Kaiju?"

That question, from Lilly, was loaded. The word Kaiju to her was more personal. Her mother's name. But she understood it now, knowing that monsters, in general, were 'Kaiju' to the world. And her mother *was* a monster.

"Not even close," Hawkins said with a grin.

"I don't want to hide anymore," she said.

"It might not be that simple."

"Only monsters have to hide," Lilly said.

Hawkins understood the point, but wasn't convinced. Then he thought about the number of cameras likely recording the White House and the surrounding area. Her battle against Gordon would be...

Gordon!

A black shadow tore through the night.

"Look out!" Hawkins shouted.

Before he could react to his own warning, Hawkins was lifted and thrown straight up. He reached out with his arms and caught a low branch. Looking back, he saw Lilly duck just in time to avoid Gordon's swing. He followed up the roundhouse with a crushing blow. Lilly leapt to the side while Gordon's fist punched a crater into the ground.

Rather than running, Lilly sprang back at Gordon, catching him by surprise. She raked her claws against his chest twice, narrowly missing the orange membranes she'd been warned about, leaned away from his hugging arms and kicking him in the gut. When Gordon pitched forward, she kneed him in the chin, snapping his head back.

She moved with grace and speed, but Hawkins could see she was losing herself. Some primal part of her was taking over, urging her to attack. Against anyone else, the tactic would have been lethal and bloody, but Gordon's body absorbed the damage. Black flesh and brown blood flew away from his torso as she continued the barrage, but each strike seemed to have less effect.

Soon, Gordon was standing up straight, showing no signs of pain, despite the cat-woman burrowing a hole in his chest. Oblivious to her opponent's change, Lilly didn't notice him reach out for her. He caught her around the waist and lifted her away.

Lilly shrieked angrily, swiping at his wrist with her clawed fingers while kicking and scratching with her feet. She was caught and helpless.

Hawkins reached for where his bow normally hung. It was missing. As was the shotgun. He looked up to his previous perch and found the bow dangling from a branch. Moving with the practiced swiftness of someone who spent a lot of time in trees, he climbed upwards, leaping between branches, hoisting himself higher.

The climb took just five seconds, but in that time, Lilly's savagery had faded and been replaced by cries of pain. Hawkins snagged the bow, turned around and balanced himself. He nocked an arrow, drew the string back and let it fly. The poorly aimed shot struck the back of Gordon's leg, bouncing harmlessly away. But it got Gordon's attention.

The big man turned around. Lilly still struggled, but wasn't making any sound now. Gordon was crushing her body, making it impossible for her to draw a breath.

Hawkins took careful aim this time, but did so quickly, and let another arrow loose. This one found its target, striking Gordon's chest, just above his own explosive membrane. The shot should have hit the man's heart, but he seemed indifferent. With his free hand, he swiped at the arrow and broke it away.

The next two arrows had the same effect, and Lilly's body had gone limp. Feeling desperate, Hawkins began moving down the tree. "Let her go!"

He stopped, just out of reach from Gordon and nocked another arrow. He had just five left. But before he could fire it, Gordon shouted in surprise, grabbing his head. "No! No, no, no!"

Gordon fell to his knees and pounded the earth, just missing Lilly. While the general's back was turned, Hawkins buried two more arrows in him, both unnoticed.

With a roar of anger, Gordon stopped pounding the ground and snapped his head toward the White House. "Hudson... I'm going to kill you, you son-of-a-bitch!" He leapt to his feet and pounded in the direction of the ruined White House. Hawkins knew it was their job to keep Gordon busy while Hudson did his thing, but there wasn't much left he could do.

Or was there?

After glancing at Lilly and seeing her chest rising and falling, he fired his last three arrows into Gordon's back, positioning each around where he thought that glowing membrane was located. Gordon showed no sign of pain or discomfort. He just charged forward, heading for the White House and Hudson.

Hawkins reached into his pocket, hoping to end it right there and then, but the pocket was empty. He'd lost the transmitter Endo had given him.

Unable to do more, Hawkins fell to his knees beside Lilly. He lifted her head in his hands and petted her furry cheek. "Wake up, baby. C'mon, wake up."

47

Nemesis reacts to Karkinos's charge by rolling her head and torso downward, angling those huge spikes on her back at the approaching Kaiju. Karkinos, perhaps lost in emotion or too stupid to care, continues forward, reaching out for Nemesis and roaring the whole way. Karkinos hits hard, partially impaling itself on Nemesis's back. For a moment it appears the Kaiju's weight will be too much, but I see the muscles in Nemesis's legs flex. Her arms push off the scorched earth. And Karkinos, whose forward momentum never really stopped, is suddenly upside down.

The whole world shakes when the massive Kaiju lands. Ash plumes into the air, obscuring the battle, but not enough that I miss what comes next.

Typhon.

While Nemesis flipped Karkinos, he closed the distance from the side. Moving with human quickness and agility, he snuck in behind Nemesis while her back was still arched. Before she can react to his presence, the giant man-thing has his clawed hands under the sides of her chin, yanking her head back. She tries to push back, thrusting her spikes toward his abdomen, but he plants a foot against her back, pushing forward on her body while pulling hard on her chin.

It's a killer move, likely to break Maigo's neck.

Maigo...

A nearly uncontrollable anger grips me as I no longer see a Kaiju being attacked, but a little girl who already suffered a similar fate at the hands of a very human monster.

In the distance, beyond the sounds of battle, I hear the monotone roar of approaching jets. For a moment, I fear the worst, that a nuclear bomb is about to drop down on the city, but the chop of rotor blades joins the mix. The military hasn't fled, they got organized. Not that they'll do much damage, but maybe they'll—

"Argh!" I fall to my knees, hands clutching my head. *It's going to explode*, I think. *My head is going to explode!*

The pressure is unbearable, like a black hole just formed at the center of my cranium and is sucking me in, spaghettifying my brain. Ironically, a black spot appears in my vision. It grows larger, blocking my view. Is it real? Is this a physical thing I'm seeing? I fall back, cringing away from it, terrified by the darkness. I see Endo around the black spot's periphery, standing over me, shouting something, but I can't hear him. Then I can't see him.

Darkness is all that remains. It's cold and silent. Empty.

While I can't see, I sense something in the black. A force. An evil presence. Full of hate.

It knows I'm here.

It wants to kill me. Destroy me.

I try to run, but where can I go? I'm nowhere.

I'm... I hear music.

Not music. A TV. A laugh track. Someone is watching a sitcom.

I feel the rug beneath my fingers before I can see it, but the image soon resolves. It's a beige and gold design. Ugly as shit. But I know it.

I turn my head up. I'm in my childhood living room.

The scent of pine fills my nose. It's Christmas again. Not again...

I'm crouching by the tree, the familiar ornaments hanging on it create an ache in my chest. I know this moment. I know what I'll find. And despite a nearly overwhelming urge to run and hide, I step forward.

Standing on the far side of the room is my father. His work shirt is open, revealing his white T-shirt, freshly stained with duck sauce from supper. He's holding a gun. I'm not sure where he got it. I've never seen a real gun before.

I'm paralyzed with fear. Too afraid to say anything. And it gets so much worse when I see her. My mother lies on the linoleum floor—the rug is gone. She's dead. Shot.

"It was an accident," my father says, then raises the gun and shoots my mother again. "She did it to herself."

This isn't right.

This isn't what happened.

This is...Maigo.

"Open your present, Jon."

I turn toward the voice. Maigo, the beautiful little girl with the Hello Kitty backpack and a bloody hole in her chest, stares up at me from the floor, lying beside my mother. Or is it *her* mother?

"Your mother killed herself, Jon," my father says. But he's not my father anymore. His face is stretched out. Distorted. Like a hammerhead shark.

The broken puzzle of my psyche starts to reassemble.

I'm in Scylla's mind, but the monster is fighting back; pushing me out with the strength of its raw emotion.

"Your mother killed herself, but she killed you first!" The gun rises toward my chest and fires.

Pain flares like an explosion.

I fall to the floor, gasping for each breath.

Maigo watches me with large, black, dead eyes. "Open your present, Jon."

With the last of my strength, I roll to the Christmas tree. A small, ribbon-wrapped gift box sits under the tree. I reach for it.

Scylla-father screams in anger, no longer intelligible, and storms over to me. Somehow I know that if he reaches me and kills me, I'm screwed—and not just in this mental world, but in the real world.

With the last of my strength, I tug on the bow. It slips apart easily. The box tips toward me and opens, spilling its contents onto the floor. Dark red blood oozes out, rolling down the lines of grout like Maigo's mother's blood.

What kind of gift is blood? I think.

Then I remember who it's from and what it's for.

The blood isn't Maigo's or her mother's.

It's Nemesis's.

As my vision fades and Scylla-dad closes in, I slap my hand down in the viscous fluid. It's warm and tacky. A small measure of strength returns on contact with the blood, but it's not much. I need to ingest it, to allow Nemesis in. I lift my hand, bring it to my face and lick.

It tastes horrible. I want nothing more than to spit it out. But I don't. I hold it in my mouth, even as it begins to scorch my tongue. Then I swallow.

The burn moves through my body, tearing a scream from my mouth. But the burn isn't physical. I'm not on fire.

What I'm feeling is anger.

Rage.

White hot, burning fury. I've never felt any emotion as strongly. As clearly. The hate and the pain it brings is...

I would destroy the world if I could.

I would end the universe.

This was Maigo's gift—the raw, manic indignation that fuels Nemesis, unhindered by the girl's calming presence.

Scylla's psyche doesn't stand a chance. While the monster is a descendant of Nemesis-Prime, it didn't endure the tortures of the beings who left Prime on Earth to exact judgment on mankind. Scylla has never really experienced pain. Or loss. Or desperation. And it lacks any kind of self-direction, having been led by Gordon since its birth.

No longer a frightened child, I open my eyes and face the monster, which is now equal parts my father, Alexander Tilly and Scylla. The thing roars and charges, but it never reaches me. It lurches to a stop, surprise filling its wide-set eyes.

The two of us look down together. My arms...they're not human. Gray skin covers my biceps, growing thicker and darker near the ends of my arms, where my immense hands, and the claws at the ends of my fingers, are buried in my enemy's gut. I stare at the wound, which would normally horrify me, and smile. Then I pull my arms in toward each other, severing the monster's torso in two. As the two halves fall to the floor, the room disappears.

I'm outside again.

In the real world, lying on my back, staring at the sky.

But everything looks different. My vision is screwy, like I can see more of the world than ever before. I'm still in pain, but it's numb somehow. I open my mouth, which feels sore and loose, and try to speak Endo's name. All that comes out is a strange sounding, far too loud and deep grunt.

What is wrong with me?

My whole body feels strange. I lift my hand, wondering if I've been injured. But instead of my black-clad arm and human hand, I see a long mass of thick black skin covered in plates of armor. My hand is huge, like in the dream, ending at massive claws.

This is Scylla's body. I'm controlling the monster.

Holy fucking shit! I'm a Kaiju!

48

This is, hands down, the strangest experience of my life. Even stranger than the time in college when Ricky Mazoli snuck 'shrooms onto my pizza, and I hallucinated that I was being eaten by a giant pepperoni with udders that sprayed rainbow milk.

It's not my weird vision. I'm getting used to that, probably because it's still being processed by Scylla's brain. And it's not my new body. It feels different, but I've still got two arms, two legs and a head. It makes sense, especially because I understand that this isn't really me. I'm still on top of the White House, a mile and a half away.

It's the scale.

When I sit up, I'm overcome by a feeling of being too high, like I'm leaning over the side of a building and am going to fall. The sense of vertigo becomes so strong that my stomach—Scylla's stomach—heaves. I pitch to the side, open my massive mouth and Kaiju-vomit into the Reflecting Pool. Large chunks of whale meat, fish and—*oh god*—people spill out. I can taste the vile stew as it streams out a second time, this time propelled by disgust.

When there's nothing left inside the monster, I fight to control my revulsion and get moving. I lean to the side, groaning like a foghorn with laryngitis. Standing is easier than I thought, but once

I'm at my full 300-foot-tall height, looking at the world through these crazy eyes, I have to stop and focus.

Scylla must look hysterical to anyone watching. The Kaiju generally look and act like you'd expect giant monsters to. But now, Scylla is acting like Jon Hudson after spinning around in circles. I've got my big, nasty hands on my spiky knees. I'm pitched forward, catching my breath.

The city around me looks fake. Like a model. This must be what it felt like to be one of those Godzilla actors, all dressed up and surrounded by a model city, ready for destruction. *Pretend it's a model,* I tell myself. *You're still just six feet tall. None of this is real.*

This line of thinking helps, but it's the high-pitched roar that really distracts me from the vertigo. I turn my heavy head toward the sound. Typhon still has Nemesis by the head. She doesn't have long.

I try to shout out that I'm coming, but it's just an awkward roar. I charge out of the Reflecting Pool toward the previous location of the Capitol Building. In some ways, I feel like I'm moving slowly, but in others, I'm moving very fast. *It's the size,* I realize. When I swing my human arm, it feels very fast, but I'm only covering a few feet's distance. With Scylla, each step carries me a hundred feet at a time. I might not be pounding out a few strides per second, like a sprinting human, but I'm actually moving a hell of a lot faster.

Karkinos is on the ground between me and Typhon. The monster is thrashing about, fighting against its own bulk, trying to get back to its feet. I tuck that observation away for later and leap over its thrashing tail, which is tipped by a scythe-like blade.

Still feeling Nemesis's extreme brand of anger, I'm merciless when I reach Typhon. I slam my pointed fingers into the Kaiju's side, plunging them deeply into him. He lets go of Nemesis, but doesn't cry out or roar. Instead he turns his horrible, stoic head toward me. Toward Scylla. He's clearly confused by Scylla's attack, but his brows slowly furrow.

Scylla is now officially on Typhon's shit list.

He reaches for my head with both hands, no doubt intending to crush Scylla's vulnerable eyes, but this isn't Scylla he's fighting. I duck back, take hold of one of his arms, twist and throw. The larger

Typhon, a creature that weighs untold tons, rolls over my back and falls onto the blackened concrete.

I step back from the fallen Kaiju and glance at Nemesis. She rolls her head around, and then levels her brown eyes at me. *Oh, shit.* Does she know Scylla is helping? Will she attack me? I feel like I should do something to let her know I'm me, but I can't talk, I doubt Nemesis or Maigo know sign language, and I think doing something human, like the YMCA dance, might just confuse everyone.

With a huff, Nemesis turns away from me and glares at Typhon, who is getting back to his feet along with Karkinos.

As she watches the pair of Kaiju, her lips turn up in a sneer, showing off those sharp teeth. Her brow furrows deeply. A sinister glimmer enters her eyes.

I can feel myself smiling, and I wonder if Scylla is too. Seeing this side of Nemesis, used for good, is exhilarating. Then she barks at me, angry and annoyed. She can sense my mood. And I understand the problem. Controlling Scylla becomes difficult. I need to stay angry.

That shouldn't be hard. I think about Gordon, about Alexander Tilly and about my father. I remember Christmas morning. I focus on the blood covering the linoleum floor. I feel Maigo's betrayal as she watched her mother die and was then murdered by her own father.

Nemesis roars, and I join in, once again fueled by righteous anger.

Karkinos and Typhon are unfazed. They roar right back.

But they're not dealing with Nemesis alone now. And they're not nearly as angry. And they have one other problem. This isn't my body. I don't give a shit what happens to it.

I act first, charging Typhon. I swing hard, aiming to knock his head off, but he's quick and moves aside. My giant arm pulls me forward. I'm unprepared for its weight. But I'm caught. By Karkinos. The Kaiju's claws snap closed on my arms, while its jaws clamp down on my armored shoulder. I roar in pain, but fall silent when I see Typhon's claws stabbing at my throat.

Before Typhon's strike connects, Nemesis lunges in, biting down on his arm and tackling the giant to the side. Saved by Nemesis. That might be a first for mankind.

Despite the last-second rescue, I'm still trapped, and Karkinos is squeezing hard with those vice-like claws. If not for the toughness of the plating on Scylla's arms, I suspect they would have been severed.

Twisting my arms back, despite the pain, I flail Scylla's large hands and hooked claws backward, finding the meat of Karkinos's thick legs. The Kaiju lunges back, freeing my arms, but it bites down tightly and peels off a large armor plate from Scylla's shoulder.

As I stagger away, I see Nemesis struggling with Typhon. Despite Nemesis's agility and speed, Typhon is faster and appears to be out-thinking her. For each of her missed attacks, Typhon rakes her with his claws, peeling layers of skin away from her body, exposing the more fragile white flesh beneath.

He knows exactly what he's doing. Once Nemesis's thick skin has been removed, she'll be completely vulnerable.

Time to switch things up. I run away from Karkinos and catch both Nemesis and Typhon off guard. Nemesis steps back, but recovers quickly, probably because she's not the one I'm barreling toward. Typhon reaches out a hand to stiff arm me.

Bad move.

I dive forward, opening Scylla's mouth as widely as I can. Typhon's hand slams down my throat. The pain and discomfort is immense, but this was my plan. This isn't my body. I don't care what happens to it. And in a way, this is what Scylla was built for. I bite down hard. I feel a few of my teeth break away, but most slip nicely through Typhon's arm, severing flesh and sinews from either end.

Typhon pounds on the back of my flat head, the impacts traveling through my giant body like earthquakes. But I'm lost in a rage. I barely feel the blows. I'm in a bloodthirsty frenzy, and yet, I'm still able to remember enough Shark Week specials to know what I should do next.

I thrash. Back and forth. Violently. I can feel my long teeth snapping, but it doesn't matter. Typhon's flesh gets the worst of it. His hot blood fills my mouth. And then I'm free, stumbling back while still thrashing. I stop when I catch Typhon staring at his handless limb.

I cough his hand up and kick it to the side.

Karkinos suddenly falls to the ground beside Typhon. Its body is torn up, but still mostly hale. The giant is quicker to its feet this time, squaring off with Nemesis again, whose shredded flesh is leaking red blood. She might be taller than Karkinos, but the doppelganger Kaiju is more powerful. Nemesis, on the other hand, is a bit of a savage. She has the end of Karkinos's tail in her mouth. She spits it away.

We're a real pair, Maigo.

Typhon roars, and it's a sick sound, like a crocodile puking up a shrieking cat. Accentuating the horrible sound is Typhon's face. It splits vertically and opens, as four, long, bone-like mandibles lined with hooks spring out.

Even Nemesis reels back with a *wutdafuck* look on her face.

Round two is about to begin, and I have a strong feeling this will be the end of it.

But like any good tag-team smackdown, a newcomer suddenly appears. The Air Force is back. But they're not streaking past, firing random missiles. They're in a holding pattern, a mile out. A line of harrier jets and attack helicopters hover at the edge of the burnt city. I wish I could hear what they were planning and help direct them, but at the moment, I'm a 300-foot monstrosity. I don't think they'll listen.

Then it happens. All at once, the legion of helicopters and jets unleash a cloud of missiles. I look ahead, judging their course. My gaze falls upon Nemesis. To the military, all four Kaiju are the enemy, and Nemesis is the most feared. And right now, with her skin falling away, she's the most obvious target. The problem with that, aside from the fact that Nemesis is our only chance of stopping Gordon's Kaiju, is that they're going to hit several of her explosive membranes and that could level the rest of the city.

"No!" I shout, though it sounds more like, "Orgh!"

I step in front of Nemesis and turn my back. The missiles hit one by one, digging through Scylla's body, tearing away great hunks of flesh. I can feel each explosion, searing flesh. Blood flows down my great back. But Nemesis is protected, and what remains of the city is unharmed.

Nemesis meets my eyes for just a moment. I see surprise and appreciation in them. And then I'm blinded by pain. Real pain, from my gut. I turn my wide head down and see clawed fingers protruding through Scylla's stomach.

Not my stomach, I tell myself.

As the hand retracts, I feel the fingers wrap around Scylla's spine.

This is it. Scylla is a goner. Nemesis is on her own.

NEMESIS

49

Typhon's hand tightens around Scylla's spine, and I feel sharp pain, unlike anything I've felt before, lance up my back. I might not be inhabiting my own body, but it sure as hell feels like it. And if I don't pull out of Scylla's mind soon, I'm going to experience the Kaiju's death, which could possibly result in my own. No one has said as much, but if my consciousness is locked in a dead mind... Even if that's not the case, I don't think I want to know what it feels like to die. All I need to do is concentrate. Loosen my grip on the Kaiju's mind and return to my own. It's like backing out of a room, except the room and door don't exist.

But I can't. When the agony of Typhon's killer attack screams through Scylla's body, the gift of rage given to me by Maigo is ignited afresh, like one of those birthday candles you can't blow out. The fire burns hot and bright, drowning out the pain. With the last of Scylla's strength, I leap up.

I feel the giant spine break as I rise up and twist around. Vertebrae snap with the sound of a felled tree. The Kaiju's legs go limp, severed from the mind. But I don't care. The parts of Scylla I need are all still working.

Typhon's hand, slick with brown blood, can't stop me from spinning. When I face the giant, whose mandibles are flexed open in anger—or is it surprise?—I reach out and grasp them, oblivious to the spikes slipping into the flesh of Scylla's hands.

Then I pull, drawing Typhon's head closer.

The monster resists, seeing his fate.

With a Nemesis-like rage-fueled roar, I yank harder. One of the mandibles snaps free with a spray of brown blood. Typhon screeches and forgets himself for just a moment.

It's all I need.

With a final lunge, I open Scylla's mouth wide, wrapping the jaws and long sharp teeth over Typhon's head. What are likely the most powerful jaws on the planet snap shut. Long teeth slide through Typhon's neck. While the life drains out of Scylla, I command her to shake, to thrash and to never let go.

I can feel Typhon's head coming loose in my mouth, a gush of hot blood spraying down my throat. Both Kaiju begin falling to the ground.

Death, the only unstoppable enemy of life, is claiming them both.

I turn my focus away from Scylla's body. I free the monster's mind, allowing it to experience its own confusing death. I will my body to return to me. I try to feel my own lungs breathing. My fingers. My body.

A tingling sensation moves through me, and I think I've returned, but everything is wrong. I can't breathe. Everything feels tight. I'm dying.

I'm stuck in Scylla's body!

"How does it feel, Hudson?" I barely hear the voice, but I recognize it. *Gordon.* Is he speaking to me through Scylla's mind?

Suddenly, I snap back to full consciousness, inside my own body, which is wrapped in a tight embrace. Gordon is squeezing the life out of me.

My thoughts turn to Hawkins and Lilly for a moment.

If Gordon is here, are they...?

Gordon applies more pressure. My back isn't far from snapping. I know, from recent experience.

I look for help. For Endo.

He's lying on the roof, unconscious. Maybe dead.

"You killed my child," he says.

"Nem-es-sis," I manage to say.

He understands the argument I'm attempting to make. He shakes his head. "You, and that bitch, Maigo. *You're* guiding her now."

My vertebrae pop like I'm visiting an extreme chiropractor. If he stopped now, I might just feel the dull ache of a spinal alignment. He doesn't stop. He's going to squeeze until I burst; a ketchup packet in the hands of a 'roid-raging wrestler.

And then, with a suddenness that makes me wonder if my soul has fled my mortal form, I'm free. The soul theory disappears when I hit the roof and my body screams at me. My first thought is that I'm getting sick of hospitals. My second is, *but I do like pudding.* My third is more timely.

What the hell just happened?

From my sideways view on the roof, I watch Gordon stumble to the roof's edge. He's clutching his head, staggering like his legs have gone weak. "What have you done?"

I can't see what he's looking at, but I know the direction he's looking, and I know exactly what I did. I can still taste Typhon's blood in my mouth, even though it was never actually in *my* mouth.

I know a good action hero would say something antagonistic right now. And part of me really wants to pour salt on his fresh wound. But screw that. Not dying sounds better. While Gordon lets out a horrible sounding wail, I drag myself across the roof. I'm trying to get up, but I haven't regained full control of my body yet. I worry that he already broke my back, but I can move all my limbs, I'm just not very coordinated yet.

I've made it only ten feet when Gordon turns around to face me. Without saying a word, he crosses the distance between us with three long strides. I try to squirm away, but I don't make it far. He grips the armor over my back and lifts me off the ground. I feel like a scrawny kid in the hands of a bully. He drags me to the side of the roof, facing the Capitol ruins. He lifts me up, but doesn't throw me over the side, which would kill me right quick.

He wants me to watch.

Karkinos and Nemesis are squaring off, eyes locked on each other, despite the continuing barrage from the Air Force. Missiles pepper both Kaiju, but they barely react to the explosions. The real threat is each other. But Nemesis is taking a beating. Gouts of her thick, protective skin are being knocked away by the modern barrage. Karkinos fares much better as the behemoth's body is mostly covered by thick plates of armor. It's probably not even feeling the missiles.

"In the end," Gordon says, "I knew there could only be one."

"How *Highlander* of you," I quip.

Gordon shakes the funny out of me, sobering me up.

"Watch," he says. "The ancient Greeks got it right. The children of the gods always usurp their parents."

A missile streaks in, missing Karkinos and carrying on toward Nemesis. It strikes the side of her head and detonates, making her flinch away, either from the pain or the loud noise right next to her ear.

Karkinos takes advantage of the brief distraction and charges. Nemesis reels back, but it's too late. Karkinos swings her massive arms again and again, pounding Nemesis like a boxer on the ropes. Nemesis backs away, but the constant stream of missiles stumbles her up.

Still the faster of the two, Nemesis spins and swings her tail out. The trident-tipped tail is capable of sweeping through entire buildings, but Karkinos's armored legs take the blow without any damage. Nemesis turns around just in time to face the rushing Karkinos, but there is little she can do about the charging behemoth.

Karkinos reaches up with both of its giant pincer-like claws and catches Nemesis's arms.

Nemesis, the taller of the two, bites down on the back of Karkinos's neck, but the armor plating fends off what could have been a killer strike. While Nemesis tries to peel the armor away, those giant pincers compress her forearms until the pain becomes unbearable. Nemesis lets out a high pitched roar, turning her head to the sky. She pulls back, struggling to free herself from Karkinos's grasp before her arms are severed.

With a slick tear, Nemesis's black skin peels away. She falls back, the skin of her forearms removed like sleeves.

Karkinos puts one of the slabs of skin in her mouth and shakes it around before spitting it out.

Nemesis looks spent, while Karkinos seems almost euphoric.

But then, surprising me and Gordon, who flinches, Nemesis charges with a roar, reaching for Karkinos's head with her more vulnerable, but still powerful, hands.

Karkinos's defense is unconventional, but brutally effective. The Kaiju lowers its head, tilting forward, so the great, blade-like spikes at the top of its back come over and down like butcher blades. As Nemesis comes in close, the massive blades come down on her shoulders, cutting through her black flesh, severing what little skin held it all in place. Great sheets of black fall from Nemesis's body now, totally exposing her to injury from Karkinos and the military.

In Boston, this pure white form of hers served a purpose. She unfurled the reflective wings hidden beneath the carapace of her back and reflected the sun's light into a powerful, burning beam of retribution. But now, in the dark, with the scene lit by burning buildings and moonlight, I don't think that's an option for her. Her greatest weapon has become her weakness.

Nemesis falls to her knees, driven down by the blades in her shoulders. She doesn't move when Karkinos stands back up, pulling the blades free. Red blood flows over her white form, reminding anyone who is watching that she is not fully Kaiju, that flowing through the monster, is human blood.

Gordon begins to chuckle.

Karkinos turns around, winding up its tail for a strike. While the bladed end is missing, the appendage is still covered in bony plates and hooked spikes. The blow comes quick, kicking up a cyclone of ash as it sails over the ground and pounds Nemesis in the side.

Nemesis falls to her side, eyes closed, body limp. The ground shakes when she lands hard, her body still. Unmoving. I wait for some sign of life, but see nothing.

The Air Force's continuing missile barrage targets Karkinos now. The giant's back takes the damage while the monster turns toward the White House.

Gordon holds me up a little higher.

Karkinos roars and steps in our direction.

I've never really wondered what it would be like to be a sacrificial virgin, but it looks like I'm going to find out.

50

The White House roof quakes with each of Karkinos's footsteps, jolting more and more as the immensely heavy Kaiju nears. Its yellow eyes remain fixed on me, which seems impossible, because I'm so friggin small. It would be like me looking into the eyes of a cockroach before I squashed it.

"You've won," I say to Gordon. "You don't need to do this."

"Cowardice is a new tactic for you, Jon," Gordon says. I hate that he uses my first name, like we really know each other. Like we used to be pals. I've only ever known the man as a monster. "I thought you were stronger than that."

"I'm not talking about my life," I say, pausing as Karkinos takes another thunderous step forward. "I'm talking about the rest of the world. You have your own Nemesis now. No one can touch you. Just go live your life."

"I've seen what you can do," Gordon says, tapping his head with his free hand. "What Endo tried to do to me. Do you really believe the government, or fucking Zoomb for that matter, will let a 300-foot-tall monster live peacefully? Besides, this world needs to be judged. It sings for it."

"Nemesis has shown mercy," I point out. "You can't—"

"Nemesis has shown weakness," he says, placing a hand over his chest. "I don't blame her. I took her heart. The engine that should have driven her resides in me. The world's judgment has fallen to me."

"So Karkinos is to be the next Nemesis?" I ask.

"Karkinos..." Gordon tries out the name. He grins. "I like it. But Karkinos is not Nemesis. It's a tool." His grin becomes wicked. "*I am Nemesis. And I will judge the world and everyone in it. Starting with you.*"

With a final stomp that seems to shudder the whole planet, Karkinos stops its approach within the corner of the U.S. Treasury Building, a good 500 feet away. Even at this distance, it's huge, rising high up into the air. It feels strange, being small again, like Karkinos is cheating. I knew what it felt like to engage this monster as equals.

"Jon Hudson," Gordon says, "and the rest of this miserable city, I sentence you to death by fire."

Karkinos reaches its giant claws up toward the large glowing membranes on its chest.

It's going to self-immolate!

I'm about to ask Gordon if he's serious, but then I remember that he's built to withstand the scorching flame. When the fires die down and everything for several miles to the west is a wasteland, Gordon will be the only thing left standing.

The massive claws slip inside the membranes, and I swear I see a smile on the Kaiju's fanged mouth. It might just be reflecting Gordon's pleasure, but I take personal offense at the grin. I lift both fists, giving the giant a defiant double middle finger.

The Kaiju pulls its hands free with a slurp.

Twin rivers of orange fluid pour from Karkinos's chest like an explosive Niagara Falls.

The delay between puncture and ignition is just a few seconds.

My thoughts turn to Collins. If she's behind Karkinos, she should make it through this. I send her my love and close my eyes.

The rumble of my death begins, but it sounds different. Strange. In fact, I don't think the explosion will even register before I'm vaporized.

My eyes snap open.

Gordon is shouting in anger.

A wall of white blocks my view. Sparkling feathers hang from wings spanning 500 feet.

Nemesis!

Maigo...

In her white form she's—

KRAKOOM!

The explosive force knocks Gordon back. I fly from his hand and slide across the rooftop.

My eyes turn back to Nemesis.

Her massive wings shake violently, but they remain solid, blocking the inferno. Bright orange flames rush by, hundreds of feet overhead. I can feel the heat, but it's only like a hot summer day. Flames streak out to the sides as well, but Nemesis's proximity to Karkinos means that she is taking the brunt of this attack, saving what remains of the city.

Saving me.

Again.

Tears fill my eyes. I know she can't survive this.

The burst of fire fades.

The wings stop shaking and immediately, the large reflective panels people call feathers start to fall away, fluttering to the ground like diamonds, except that one side has been charred black.

Nemesis falls to one knee, trailing a column of smoke. The stench is revolting, not just because of the smell, but because I know what it's from. Nemesis has been cooked.

She falls in on herself slowly.

Still breathing.

But as she drops down, Karkinos is revealed, standing. Steam rises from its drained chest. Its face is frozen in anger.

Totally frozen.

That's when I notice the change in the Kaiju's body. A straight black line has been etched into its armor, head to toe.

Understanding what has happened, I hop to my feet and nearly cheer as Karkinos comes apart. Tons of flesh separate, as strands of viscous fluid stretch out between the halves and snap. Karkinos's body, cut clean through, falls down, and then apart. When the monster's cleaved body hits the ground with twin thunderous booms I can feel in my teeth, I let out that victory cry.

Nemesis didn't just save me, or Washington, she saved us all.

But I don't think Nemesis deserves the credit. Left to her own devices, that spirit of vengeance would have happily eradicated the human race. It was the human side of her, a little girl, who made the difference and was willing to give her life—again.

When Gordon screams, I flinch back, having forgotten all about him. He's staring out at Karkinos's split body. He starts punching himself. Hard. Then he remembers that there is someone else he can take his anger out on.

He reels around and charges toward me.

With his long stride, he'll reach me in seven steps. He makes it only four, though.

"Hey!"

The voice is young and feminine, but her appearance is anything but. Lilly leaps at Gordon from the side, and drives her legs into his arm. She's far smaller than him, but she is strong. Really strong. Gordon is slammed to the side, decimating an actual air conditioning unit.

While he pries himself free from the metal case now twisted around his body, lost in a frenzy, I expect Lilly to press the attack. Maybe go for something vital. His throat possibly. But she doesn't. She waits.

Hawkins steps up next to her. Like me, he's taken a beating, but he's alive.

"We weren't done with you," he says to Gordon, holding up a small device. I recognize it as the transmitter Endo gave him.

For the arrows.

My eyes widen when I see the collection of arrows jutting out of Gordon's body.

Holy...

Hawkins pushes the button.

Gordon's body bulges out from the inside, as the arrow heads explode. His thick skin contains the energy, which makes the damage that much more horrible. The arrows are forced out of their entry holes, followed by spraying flesh and blood. Then he falls still, his body twisted and distorted. Fluid leaks from the wounds and his nose, mouth and eyes. But the explosive membranes have been left intact. Hawkins had been warned about them and kept the arrow tips, and their explosive potential, far away from Gordon's core.

Helped to my feet by Lilly, I hobble over to Gordon. I can't very well check for a pulse, but I don't need to. He's not breathing, and well, he's basically a big black sack of nasty. Dead for sure.

"Thanks," I say to Lilly, and then I look at Hawkins. "To both of you."

The pair just nods, their duty done. Despite their physical differences, I can see a lot of Hawkins in Lilly's demeanor. They really are like father and daughter now, a feeling I understand only slightly, thanks to my connection with Maigo, which I now fear is completely severed.

Lilly helps me to the White House's rooftop wall, where Nemesis is still crouched down. Endo is gone. No real surprise there. We'd become something like friends over the past few weeks, but he was still a criminal and I was still the law. Like Batman and Catwoman, our bromance was doomed to fail. And honestly, right now I don't give a rat's ass. Let him go. I'm more concerned about the people who are still here.

"Maigo," I say, but I get no response. "Maigo!"

A quiver runs through the giant's skin, shaking free more of the glistening feathers. She rises up slowly and turns. Her face is blackened, cooked like chicken over a too-hot grill. I think I see bone. This creature and the girl bonded to her have suffered so much in their lives. Neither of them deserve this. And, in my mind, neither of them deserves death.

If there is any chance that they can survive, it needs to be now.

"Go!" I shout. "Get the hell out of here!"

She stares down at me for a moment and then stands on shaky legs. The blackened skin covering her body cracks, oozing red blood and eliciting a groan. But then she's up and moving.

She heads south, toward the Washington Monument, staggering over the South Lawn and the Ellipse. With each step, I can feel her energy draining.

C'mon...go!

She falters at the Washington Monument, clinging to its strong form for support.

And then, despite her proximity to one of the country's most beloved and recognizable treasures, the Air Force returns in force. Jets streak by, leaving strings of missiles in their wake. Nemesis is struck from behind. Her wings haven't fully closed and the carapace that protects them is still open. Blood sprays from her exposed back.

She roars in agony.

"Stop!" I scream. "*Stop!*"

The next cluster of missiles drops Nemesis. Her clawed fingers drag gouges through the Washington Monument as she clings to it.

On the ground, she drags herself to the water while helicopters move in and unleash a torrent of chain guns and rockets into her back. She groans in agony, pulling herself into the Tidal Basin.

But instead of swimming, she floats.

The Basin's water turns red.

Nemesis heaves twice, like she's coughing underwater, and then with a bubbly sigh, she lies still.

There are no more Kaiju in the world.

Maigo is dead.

As despair takes hold of my heart, my phone rings. Numb, I pluck the device from my pocket and glance at the screen out of habit. Collins's smiling face, a photo taken three months ago while looking for the Chupacabra, stares back at me. I smile and answer the phone. "Ash?"

"I'm sorry, babe," she says. "I know what she meant to you."

"Nothing compared to you," I say, sucking back my sadness and replacing it with relief. "Where are you?"

EPILOGUE

Two months after the destruction of Washington, D.C. and the demise of all the Kaiju, including Nemesis, the world feels quasi-normal again. And not all in a good way. Crime is back up. A couple of unfinished wars have flared back up. Free of the fear of judgment, the human race is showing its true colors again.

But there is more good than bad. The FC-P is operational, complete with our own hundred-acre training installation in the woods of Maine. The property is fenced off and heavily monitored. Hawkins, Joliet and Lilly have settled into a cabin, smack dab in the middle of the land. But they're not prisoners.

They're employees, though Hawkins is the only one receiving a paycheck, and that is under an alias to protect his identification from the rogue group within DARPA that they fear will come for Lilly, should she be discovered. We've just scratched the surface on that investigation, because we have to move quietly. Not only is DARPA out of our jurisdiction, but they have resources that make our brick house headquarters look silly. Though we do have a secret weapon in Lilly. She's been out on two field missions with Collins and me, quickly making us feel obsolete, using her heightened senses to rapidly dispel reports of strange creatures. She's a natural, but she's also killing my mojo.

Which is why Collins and me are out on our own this time around. Not that the site is anyplace glamorous. And the memories of this place sting. We're on Craney Island, a sliver of land in the middle of the Potomac River, twenty-five miles south of D.C., which is in ruins and will stay that way for a long time, though the President insists on running the country from the damaged White House. Having retained his bravery and new moral code, Beck has become an exemplary leader, bringing a panicked country back from the brink. Part of me wishes I could undo what I did to him.

But then he calls and asks my advice, and I can't help but smile. I told Endo that I'd implanted just two thoughts into Beck's mind: *be brave and do the right thing.* But that wasn't the truth. I pushed three new thoughts on him. *Be brave. Do the right thing.* And: *Trust Jon Hudson.*

And trust me he did. Not only has he restored the FC-P to its former status, retaining our budget and giving me the freedom to perform operations with a black budget—things that are required when building a reserve for a cat-woman and investigating DARPA— he also occasionally asks for my input on everything from foreign policy to his choice in tie color. I filter most of his calls through Cooper, whose baby bump is now in full view. Watson nearly quit, but when Cooper stayed, he couldn't leave. I suspect his main reason for leaving was to protect her, which is noble and right, but Cooper knows the FC-P needs her. Needs both of them. And with Gordon— and Nemesis—dead, our headquarters is secret-ish once again.

Craney Island is 200 feet long and mostly rock with a few large bushes. No one comes out here. There's no reason to. But we got some reports of something strange being wedged in between the rocks. Since Nemesis died upriver from here, we decided it was worth our attention. The military carted away all the Kaiju bodies long before anyone had a chance to complain. If we were able to find some part of Nemesis, we would be able to study her independently, just in case we face something like a Kaiju again, or if Nemesis-Prime's creators ever return to see how their instrument of justice is faring.

"See anything?" Collins asks, as I stumble over the rocks.

Our bodies have recovered from the beatings we took. Even Woodstock is up and about again, bitching about Betty's fate, but thoroughly enjoying Helicopter Betty 2.0, which is a Black Hawk, painted bright red.

I work my way along the shore, opposite Collins, who is on the far side of the island, a whopping twenty feet away. "I'm not sure that we—hold on."

A slick-looking, gray mass stands out among the brown stones. As I get closer, I see that it's quite large and looks like some kind of giant chrysalis. Definitely FC-P material, but it doesn't look like any part of Nemesis I've ever seen. "Here!"

Collins joins me by the gray mass, lips twisted to the side. "What the hell is it?"

I shake my head. "Looks organic, but..."

"It's too big for the boat," she points out. We crossed the river in a rented Boston Whaler. And if the boat weren't too small, this thing is too big for Collins and me to carry.

"We'll just have to see what's inside," I say, taking out my jackknife.

"I'm not sure that's a good idea," she says.

I wave her off. "I brought gloves." After stretching a pair of rubber gloves over my hands, I poke the blade into the fleshy surface. Pulling slowly, I cut a long slit. Nothing bad happens, so I push forward, slipping both hands inside the incision. I give Collins a half-hearted grin, suspecting this is going to be gross, and I pull.

The walls slip apart, tearing and falling away. I leap back as the insides liquefy and slide out into the river. *Gross.*

But my revulsion is quickly forgotten. There *is* something inside, like a seed at the center of a rotten peach.

I step closer. "Oh my god." I jump into the goo. "Ash! Help me!"

When she sees what I do, she pulls the engagement ring off her finger, sticks it in her pocket and jumps down beside me, tearing away layers of clear film with her bare hands. The sticky sheets are stiff, but they come away, one at a time. As we tear through the layers, what looked like a fuzzy human form resolves.

It's a girl. She has tan skin and shoulder-length, black hair.

I pause for a moment, realization gripping me, and then I'm back at it, ripping and pulling amid tears. When the body slips free, I catch the girl under her arms and lift her away to a patch of grass. It's cold out, near freezing, but the girl's body is hot and steaming, not to mention lifeless. I lay her down, prepared to start chest compressions.

Then she coughs.

I turn her sideways as she continues to cough, clearing slimy fluid from her lungs. When she's done, I roll her onto her back. Her eyes blink open. She looks at Collins and then at me. Her brown eyes are so familiar. I've seen them in a dream, in photos and in the face of a monster.

"Maigo," I say.

She smiles. A slight thing. With a delicate hand, she reaches up and touches my face. For just a flash, I'm standing in front of a Christmas tree again. But all the pain and fear of that moment, for both of us, is gone, the burden lifted.

Maigo's smile widens and she says, "She had gifts for us both."

A NOTE FROM THE AUTHOR

Dear Reader,

I wanted to take a moment to thank you for reading *Project Maigo*. Ten years ago, if you'd have told me I'd be writing Kaiju novels for a living, I would have never believed you. And yet, here were are, with not just one Kaiju thriller, but *two*! Even more if you count *Island 731* and all the other monster books I've written.

I hope that you enjoyed this monstrous installment of what I hope will become a long-running series of Kaiju novels...and movies, TV shows and comic books. Nemesis is already on her way to being featured in a video game, *Colossal Kaiju Combat: The Fall of Nemesis*. My dream for Nemesis is that she'll be America's first really iconic Kaiju to rival Godzilla. She's off to a good start, but not even her 350-foot-tall girth is going to reach such a lofty goal without help.

So show your support for Nemesis! Post reviews online, at retailers and on Goodreads. Tell your friends about the book. Post fan art. Spread the word however you can, and we can keep this series going and maybe get Nemesis on the big screen! Or the TV. Or action-figures! C'mon, you know you want to make 12-year-old Jeremy's dreams come true.

Thank you again for all your amazing support, and for reading *Project Maigo*!

—*Jeremy Robinson*

ART GALLERIES

These art galleries include the original creature concept designs by the amazing Matt Frank. Following Matt's designs is an incredible Nemesis poster designed by illustrator James Biggie. After the poster, you'll find a fan art gallery, including more than twenty-five pieces of art!

MATT FRANK CREATURE DESIGNS

This first gallery includes the original creature concept designs for Nemesis (Maigo), Scrion, Drakon, Scylla, Typhon and Karkinos, all by the amazing Matt Frank, whose work you might recognize from many Godzilla comic books. While they were based on descriptions straight out of the book, the concepts also influenced the story, as both took shape simultaneously.

Check him out at: www.mattfrankart.com.

SCYLLA

SCRION

DRAKON

TYPHON

KARKINOS

NEMESIS

JAMES BIGGIE POSTER

I commissioned this next piece, after purchasing three prints of James's fantastic Godzilla-related art.

You can look for him at society6.com/JamesBiggie.

WINGED TILTER OF SCALES AND LIVES

NEMESIS

ネメンス

FAN ART GALLERY

Soon after the release of *Project Nemesis*, I started receiving fan art inspired by the book. Other than two or three pieces over the years, my 40-ish books never generated a lot in the way of fan art. But *Project Nemesis* managed to stoke the imaginative fires for a large number of people. As an artist myself, I get a lot of pleasure out of fan art, and as I wrote *Project Maigo*, I decided that I would like to share some of that art with my readers, which is what you'll find on the following pages. There's a large range of ages and skill levels on display, but one thing comes across in every image: a love for the Kaiju known as Nemesis! And that is amazing and inspiring to me as a writer.

If you would like your fan art to be featured in any future Nemesis books, send it to me at info@jeremyrobinsononline.com, with a 300 dpi image quality. The only real rule is that the images have to feature Nemesis (or any of the characters and new Kaiju from *Project Maigo*) and cannot feature any trademarked or copyrighted Kaiju, such as Godzilla, Gamera, etc... Thank you very much to all the amazing artists who submitted their work for publication in *Project Maigo*, and I look forward to seeing more!

—JR

LIL' NEMESIS BY RODNEY RODGERS

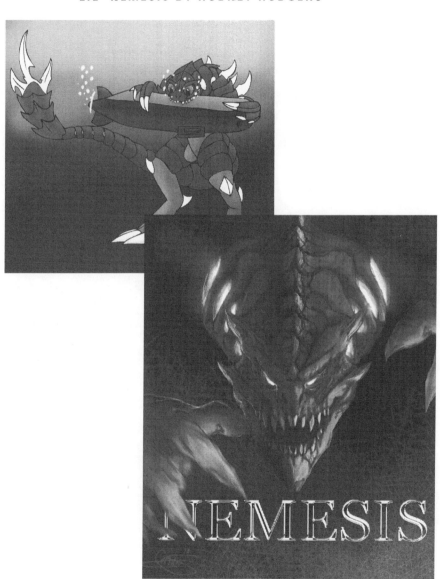

DARK NEMESIS BY CINDY SOUMERU
UCALIPTIC.DEVIANTART.COM

MOMENTOSIS NEMESIS BY VAMENG LI
MOMENTOSIS.DEVIANTART.COM

NEMESIS SURPRISE BY JOHN SCOTT

BUBBLE NEMESIS BY BAMBOO SHOOTS MOON-PANDA

NEMESIS SCRATCH
BY MIKE ROBERGE

Project: Nemesis

BY JEREMY ROBINSON

PROJECT NEMESIS BY DAVE JOHNSON

NEMESIS BATTLE BY ZACHARY RAMSEY
ROSENKRUEX.DEVIANTART.COM

NEMESIS VS.
HIMEL AUGEN
BY QUIN RUSSU

PROJECT NEMESIS BY STEVE THAO
WINTERGAIA.DEVIANTART.COM

NEMESIS & X-1 BY JENNY MILLER
EXUITIRTEISS.DEVIANTART.COM

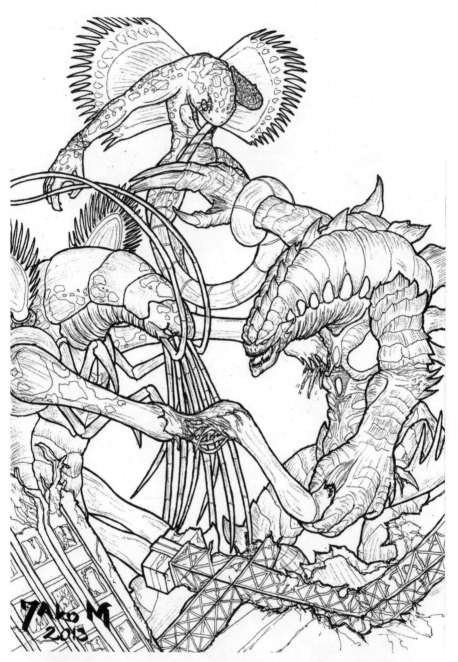

NEMESIS VS REKKER VS KUMAK BY JACEK MURAWSKI

JAKO-M.DEVIANTART.COM

MORE THAN A MONSTER
& NEMESIS GASPS
BY ZACH COLE

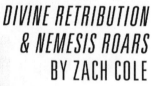

DIVINE RETRIBUTION
& NEMESIS ROARS
BY ZACH COLE

NEMESIS VS CRYSTAR
& NEMESIS REVELATION
BY DR STUDIOS
DR-STUDIOS.DEVIANTART.COM

THE FOLLOWING SIX PAGE COMIC WAS ADAPTED
FROM PROJECT NEMESIS BY DR STUDIOS

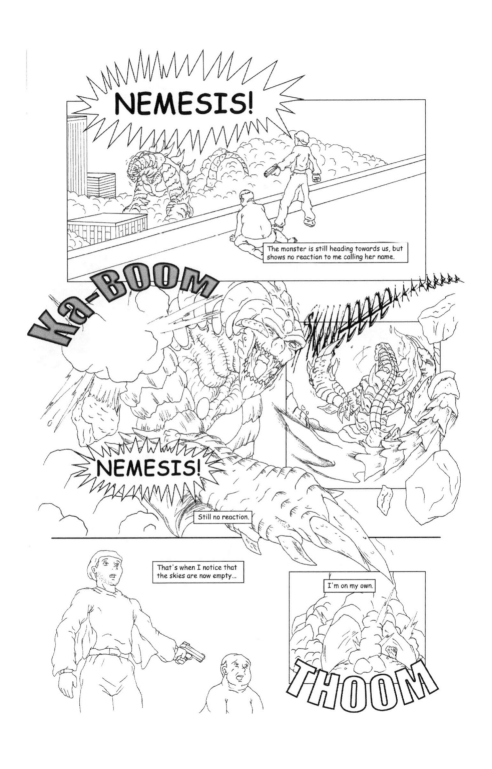

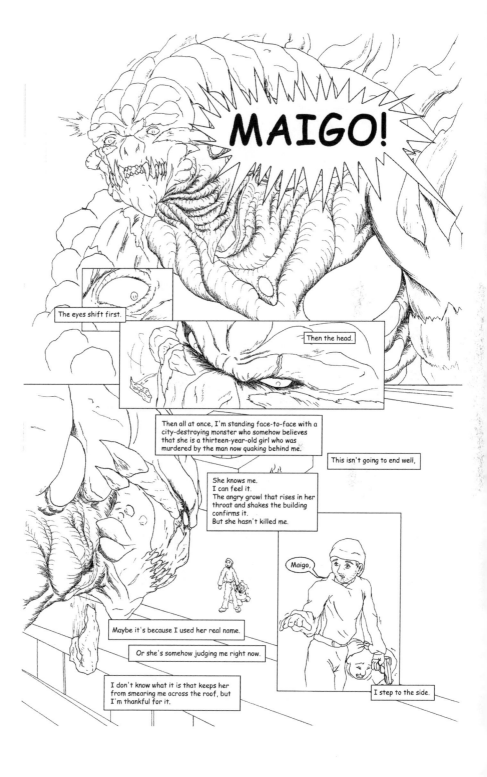

Then it splits.

ABOUT THE AUTHOR

JEREMY ROBINSON is the international bestselling author of fifty novels and novellas including *Uprising, Island 731, SecondWorld*, the Jack Sigler thriller series, and *Project Nemesis*, the highest selling original (non-licensed) kaiju novel of all time. He's known for mixing elements of science, history and mythology, which has earned him the #1 spot in Science Fiction and Action-Adventure, and secured him as the top creature feature author.

Robinson is also known as the bestselling horror writer, Jeremy Bishop, author of *The Sentinel* and the controversial novel, *Torment*. His novels have been translated into twelve languages. He lives in New Hampshire with his wife and three children.

Visit him online at: www.jeremyrobinsononline.com.

ABOUT THE ARTIST

MATT FRANK is a comic book illustrator and cover artist who has worked on well known titles such as *Transformers* and *Ray Harryhausen Presents*, but he is perhaps most well known for his contributions to multiple *Godzilla* comic books. He lives in Texas and enjoys pineapple juice.

Visit him online at: www.mattfrankart.com

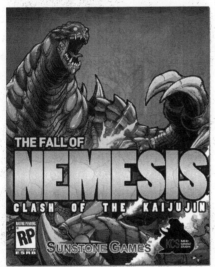

IN CASE YOU MISSED THEM...
MORE KAIJU NOVELS FROM JEREMY ROBINSON

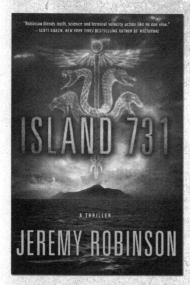

"Robinson puts his distinctive mark on Michael Crichton territory with this terrifying present day riff on The Island of Dr. Moreau. Action and scientific explanation are appropriately proportioned, making this one of the best Jurassic Park successors."
—*Publisher's Weekly* - Starred Review

Discover the origins of Mark Hawkins and Lilly, and the monster named Kaiju!

"Reading Jeremy Robinson novels is hazardous to your sleep patterns. He spins monster yarns so well you cannot stop turning pages. Giant monsters, creepy islands and writing that is both smart and furious in intensity and pace."
—*Famous Monsters of Filmland*

Read the Kaiju novel that started it all and brought giant monsters into the mainstream literary world.

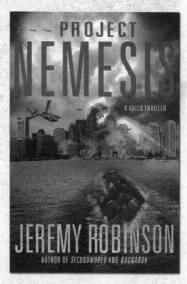

AVAILABLE NOW!

17928058R00192

Made in the USA
Middletown, DE
14 February 2015